The Adventures *of*
Jon Paul Chavalier

NICKLAUS LEE

ISBN: 978-1-4834-1796-7 (sc)
ISBN: 978-1-4834-1798-1 (hc)
ISBN: 978-1-4834-1797-4 (e)

Library of Congress Control Number: 2014916086

Because of the dynamic nature of the Internet, any web addresses or links contained
in this book may have changed since publication and may no longer be valid. The views
expressed in this work are solely those of the author and do not necessarily reflect the
views of the publisher, and the publisher hereby disclaims any responsibility for them.

Any people depicted in stock imagery provided by Thinkstock are models,
and such images are being used for illustrative purposes only.
Certain stock imagery © Thinkstock.

Lulu Publishing Services rev. date: 09/23/2014

To my son Lane, who never stopped believing in me;
And to my family—thank you.

Contents

"I was walking down by the museum, and as I was just looking around, I saw a very shiny object."

"What was it, Jon?"

"It was a coin."

"Did you pick it up?" asked Paul.

"Of course. There was no one else around, so I figured I could keep it. I thought that was strange, because there are always people around waiting to go on museum tours. Honestly, I was strangely drawn to this coin. It was as if it was calling me to it. It was like a magnet; I was unable to resist its pull."

At this point, Paul was suddenly a bit uneasy. He was beginning to feel something might be wrong deep in the pit of his stomach. "You should be careful, Jon; you never know where it came from. It might be cursed or even have bad luck attached to it."

But Jon was having none of that. He could already feel the power of the coin. It made him feel important; it made him feel stronger. He felt a sense of euphoria when he held it in his hands. "I think I'll show it to Michelle tonight," he said.

"You mean she hasn't seen it yet?" asked Paul.

"No."

"She will tell you the same as me—there is something very wrong about that coin. I just have a bad feeling about it," said Paul.

Jon was not listening—he was thinking about holding the golden and oh-so-very shiny coin in his hands. "Well, my friend, I should be heading back home," he told Paul.

"Okay, Jon, but please be careful with that coin," warned Paul. And with that, they shook hands and parted ways for home.

***

Jon was so excited to be showing the coin to Michelle. She would be so happy to see such a beautiful thing. As he walked the short distance home, though, he began to feel strange—like something was compelling him to hold the coin in his hands, to take it out of his pocket and make a wish or something. *How odd, and what a strange feeling*, he thought. Suddenly, he knew! He had a flash of genius—or maybe just intuition, something that never seemed to happen to him much—he would use the coin to make a wish, nothing too much, just to try it and see what happened.

He felt nervous and sweat started to drip down his brow. What if this really worked? *What if I do this and something really happens?* He thought. He wiped his brow with his shirtsleeve and, feeling excited, grabbed the coin from his pocket and thought out loud for a second

"What should I wish for?" Then it hit him. "I will wish for another coin." And as soon as he said it, *poof*! There in his hands was another shiny and new coin!

It worked! He thought. *But how and why?* He was feeling a bit shaky now. As he approached his apartment, he began to calm down and thought, *maybe I already had the other coin; maybe it was all just my imagination.* This briefly relieved his troubled mind. He climbed the stairs to his apartment and began to wonder how he would explain this to Michelle, how he would tell her—or even if he should tell her. His mind raced as he opened the door.

"Michelle, I'm home," called Jon Paul.

"I'm in the kitchen," she said. "How was your walk, honey?"

"It was fine." And he wondered all over again if he should tell her about the coin in his pocket.

"Your father called. He was asking if we were coming over Sunday for dinner."

Jon Paul looked at her and smiled. "I guess we can if you want to."

He was not very interested in visiting his parents' house. He had two shiny gold coins in his pocket—enticing him, drawing him into their world. As the afternoon wore on, Jon Paul became a bit more relaxed and became sure that showing the golden coins to Michelle would be the right thing to do, so with a deep breath and a bit of courage, he called to her, "Michelle, can you come in here, please?"

"Sure thing, honey, be right there," she said as she began walking over to him. Jon Paul watched her walk. He loved to watch her walk—she was so very beautiful to him. As she approached, he motioned for her to sit next to him on the couch.

"I want to show you something I found," he said.

"What is it?" Michelle asked.

"A golden coin."

"Where did you get it?"

"I found it when I was walking by the museum."

As Jon Paul showed her the coin, she gasped in awe. "It is so beautiful!"

"Yes, and I think it's magical," he said quietly.

"What do you mean, Jon Paul?"

"Well, as I was holding it, a thought came to me to make a wish. At first, I was thinking that would be crazy, but then I thought, okay, why not—what could happen?"

"And did you make a wish, Jon Paul?"

"I did. I wished for another coin—and then there it was in my hand."

Now, Michelle was no fool; she thought Jon Paul was playing a prank on her, as he sometimes liked to do, so she said, "Have you made any more wishes since then?"

"No," said Jon Paul.

"Well, then, let's see if it really works," said Michelle. Even though Michelle was now aware of the coin, she also began to have some doubts about it—maybe it was evil or even cursed.

"What should we wish for?" asked Jon Paul.

"I don't know," said Michelle.

"How about another coin, like I did before?" asked Jon Paul. Michelle thought that would be a good wish, so Jon Paul, agreeing with her, said, "I wish I had another gold coin." And as soon as he said it, *poof*! There in his hand was another golden coin.

Suddenly, Michelle began to feel uneasy about this golden coin, feeling it must be cursed or that it could bring bad luck—or maybe even death—to the owner. She wondered who had the coin before Jon Paul and why they lost it. Was it on purpose or maybe by accident to trap another person? Michelle was getting nervous.

"I don't think you should keep it, Jon Paul. It might be cursed or evil."

"Ah, c'mon, Michelle, what harm can it do?"

Little did Jon Paul know how wrong he was. This coin was centuries old; it had been in the possession of some of the world's most powerful and evil men in the history of the planet. A cursed coin for sure had found its way to Jon Paul—was it chance?

"So now we have three shiny new coins," said Jon Paul excitedly.

"I think I should go and finish my work in the kitchen," said Michelle, who was visibly upset and now beginning to fear this dreaded coin.

"Okay, Michelle, I am going to call my dad and see about Sunday dinner."

Being that it was Friday, and Jon Paul had the weekend to figure out more about this coin, he was glad he was alone with it. He could feel its power growing and the power growing in him too. As the afternoon wore on and night appeared, Jon Paul was restless. The thought of calling his dad was too much for him; he would call him tomorrow when he felt better. He was more restless than usual, so he decided to go to bed early and try to sleep. This magical coin was drawing him in deeper and deeper. Jon Paul did not sleep well; he tossed and turned and rolled and awoke and tossed some more. When he did sleep, it was only in brief intervals, and he would dream in those in-between times—full dreams, dreams about hate and wars and killing people. He had never dreamt about that before now. Jon Paul had found something that would change his life forever. He did not remember the tall man from years past who had told him about finding a shiny thing that would change his life.

The next morning was cold for this time of year. There was a crispness in the morning air that was bone-chilling to Jon Paul; he had always like the warmer weather.

"Morning, honey," said Michelle, yawning and stretching. "Rough night, Jon Paul?"

"Yes. I never could get to sleep very well, and I kept having these strange dreams about the coin and men killing and some kind of a war with dead bodies all around me."

"Wow, that is strange," said Michelle. "Do you want some breakfast?"

"Um, not very hungry this morning," he replied.

"Okay, well, I am going to make some toast and sausage. I will make extra, in case you get hungry later," said Michelle. She then got up, got dressed, and went downstairs to make breakfast. Jon Paul was not feeling so good. Last night's intermittent dreams had him upset and so tired that he had no desire to do anything. However, he decided to get up and try and make the day better. But then a strange thought occurred to him. *What if I use the coin to wish I felt better, like I had a full night's sleep? I wonder if that would work,* he thought.

Jon Paul grabbed the coin and said, "I wish I felt better, like I had a full night's sleep." And as soon as he said this, *poof*! He was his old self again, and he felt like he'd had a full night's sleep. *Wow,* he thought, *this coin is magical.*

He began to feel the power of the coin again, which was making him a bit queasy. He got up, got dressed, and went downstairs to where Michelle was making breakfast. It smelled wonderful, and Jon Paul was suddenly very hungry and feeling like he was a young kid again.

As he sat down at the table with its wobbly legs, Michelle noticed the difference in him and said, "Wow, you look great. What happened?"

Jon replied, "I wished for a full night's sleep and to feel refreshed, and the coin did this to me."

Michelle was shocked by this. She knew something was wrong. "Jon Paul, you need to get rid of that coin now!"

Jon Paul felt anger growing in him. *"Never! Maybe I will get rid of you!"* he screamed.

Michelle was shocked. Never in their three-year relationship had he ever spoken to her like this. She began to cry; tears fell down her cheeks. Jon Paul suddenly realized what he had done and calmly said, "Forgive me, my dear Michelle, I don't know what came over me." But Michelle knew the coin was cursed and that it was beginning to take over his life, taking him to a very dark place that neither of them wanted to go to.

"I think I will talk with Paul and get his opinion on what I should do with this coin."

"Okay, but please be careful, Jon Paul. I am worried about you," said Michelle.

As he got up to leave, he gave Michelle a nice, soft kiss and walked out the door. He was glad to be out of there. The dreams from the night before had left him shaking and confused, but the magic of the coin made him feel better. What was it that made this strange gold coin work, and what else could it do? As he walked, his mind raced with thoughts of the night before. Just who was this general he saw in his dream, and what was he doing with the same coin that he now possessed?

As he approached Paul Pierre's apartment, he was sure his old friend could help him figure this out. He rang the buzzer. "Yea, who is it?" asked a gruff voice.

"It is Jon Paul."

"Oh, hi. Come on up, Jon Paul." The door buzzed. He grabbed the old handle and pulled the door open, climbed the stairs to his good friend and confidante's apartment, and knocked.

"Good morning, my friend!" said Paul.

"Morning, Paul," said Jon, obviously in deep thought.

"How are you, Jon Paul?" Paul asked.

"I am feeling a bit strange."

"Stranger than usual?" said Paul, laughing.

"Yes. I want to talk some more about this coin I found."

Suddenly Paul became concerned. He too had felt the strange power of the coin and was worried it might be cursed or maybe evil. "So tell me Jon Paul, what is it that has you so upset today?"

"Remember when I told you yesterday that I was going to show it to Michelle? Well, I did, and then she started saying it was cursed or evil or something like that. As we were talking, I told her about the wish I had made. She didn't believe me, so I did it again. And now I have three gold coins."

"Did she believe you after she saw the coin appear?" said Paul.

"Yes, but then she began to get upset, saying it was wrong and maybe even cursed and I should just get rid of it. Then I yelled at her for no reason, telling her, 'maybe I should get rid of you!'"

"Wow. What happened after that?"

"Nothing. I was feeling pure rage. All I wanted to do was hurt her."

"What happened next?"

"I suddenly realized what I had said, and I apologized to her. I didn't even feel like I was myself at that moment—I was someone else."

"Like someone else, Jon Paul?"

"Yeah, like I was possessed or something. The coin made me feel powerful and strange."

Paul was now convinced that the coin was cursed, but how to convince Jon Paul to get rid of it? The coin had such a powerful hold on him that this was going to be a problem. Paul thought for a moment. "You know, Jon Paul, we should take the coin to someone at the museum to see if anyone can tell us more about it—like where it came from and what we should do with it."

Jon Paul was not sure about this. He liked having the coin; he liked the power he felt when he held it. "Well, maybe, Paul, but I think I will go back home and think about that for a few days."

Chapter Two

— • • • —

THE STRANGER

Paul was a little surprised at the sudden change in Jon Paul. "Okay, my friend, I will see you later, then."

"Okay, Paul, see you later." Jon Paul got up and walked out the door.

As it was mid-morning when Jon Paul went to see his friend Paul, he thought maybe he would take a short walk down to the sea docks—maybe ask a few fishermen if they had heard anything about a lost coin or even some stories about a gold coin. When you wanted to hear tall tales or stories, that is where you went. The fishing docks were not too far from his friend Paul's apartment and close to the museum where he had found the coin.

As he got closer to the docks, he began to smell the scent of fish. Sometimes it was very strong, but today it was not too bad. He noticed some men over by a boat talking, and as he approached them, one of the men noticed him and said, "Hello, stranger, how can we help you?"

Jon Paul came closer and said, "Hello. I was wondering if any of you have any tales about a lost coin or have heard of someone finding one?"

Several of the men looked at him curiously; however, one man in the back stood up and said, "I have heard a tale about a coin from the Middle East that was used in wars for good luck."

Jon Paul was intrigued. "Yeah? Please tell me more. I would love to hear about it."

"Well, as I remember it," the man said, "many years ago, there was a great battle between two nations in the Middle East. The people of one nation fought for their belief in God and thought they were holy and their way was the only way to live; people of the other nation also fought, sure that their way was right, thinking it was holy. This bloody battle had been going on for many years. I believe one nation was called the Ottoman Empire, and the other was called, The People of the Land of the Jackal.

Now, these two warring nations were very evenly matched, both sides unable to win or even get an advantage over the other. One day, though, a tall and strangely dressed man approached the camp of the Ottomans and asked to see the general. Of course, he was denied. The guard standing by was still trying to figure out how this man was able to just walk into their well-protected and guarded camp without even being seen or escorted to the general when another guard approached him and said, 'Who is this man, corporal?'

'Sir, I don't know. He just walked up to me and started demanding to see the general.'

'Well, then, let's take him to see the general. Did you search him?'

'No, sir, I haven't yet.'

'Corporal, search this man immediately!'

The corporal did just that and found no weapons on him, and after several moments had passed with this strange man still insisting on seeing the general, the first officer finally said, 'Okay, I will take you to see him.' So he was escorted to the general's tent and, needless to say, the general was not too happy with his first officer.

'Yes, lieutenant, what is it?' the general said.

'Sir, I have brought you a man who says he can help you win the war.'

The general, being a suspicious man by nature, laughed and looked at the stranger and said, 'How are you going to help me win this war?'

This man began to tell the general about how he had been to the Dark Continent of Africa and had been trained by a master in the Dark Arts. After he had completed his training and was out traveling the desert, he was approached by a rogue genie riding a white camel that traded him a golden coin for a small cache of shiny glass objects."

Jon Paul was listening intently as the man continued.

"The coin was a cursed coin, given by the genie to trap unknowing humans into slavery. As the years passed, the man learned to use the coin for good, but it is very powerful and other genies are desirous of the coin and continue to search for it to possess it themselves. The general sat back and was slightly amused as he listened to this man tell his tale. The stranger continued to try and convince the general he would be safe and his enemies would never be able to find out he had the coin as long as he kept it hidden and showed it to no one else. As the general's patience began to wane, this story he was listening to became more difficult to believe, and he seriously doubted the stranger's words. He was just about to have this madman thrown out of his tent when the stranger said, 'I can prove it is magical. Ask me for something, anything!'

The general sat there for a moment and finally said, 'Okay, but if this doesn't work, I will have your head!'

The stranger said to the general, 'Wish away.'

'I wish for the most beautiful Turkish woman in all the land to do my bidding.'

As soon as the general said this, *poof*! There she was standing before him, the fairest woman in all the Ottoman Empire. The general was shocked and nearly fell out of his chair. He then ordered the lieutenant to leave and never speak of this or he would have him executed on the spot. The general agreed to take the coin and keep it hidden and only to use it to help him win the war; however, he had other plans for the coin.

This is the story, as I heard it when I was a boy," said the fisherman, finishing his tale.

Jon Paul and several other men who had been listening to the story were completely spellbound by the man's words. Jon Paul was sure he was holding the same coin. He thanked the fisherman and the others for their time and walked away from the docks. He was convinced he had in his possession the same very old and very powerful coin. What should he do? His mind raced with the possibilities of the coin and what he could do with it.

As he walked home to Michelle, he wondered if it really was all that bad. *I mean, it is just a coin*, he thought. Well, yeah, but it could grant wishes, and it made him feel powerful, like he could do anything.

When he got back home, Michelle was waiting for him and asked, "How was your visit with Paul?"

"It was okay. He was just as curious as I am about this coin. After I left his apartment, I went to the fishing docks and talked with some fisherman, who told me a most fascinating story."

Jon Paul told Michelle the same story the fisherman had told him. As she listened, she was sure he must get rid of the damned coin as soon as possible, but how to convince Jon Paul of the danger of keeping the golden coin? Jon Paul was so very excited to tell her the tale of the coin; he went on for a few hours as she sat there and listened intently. He seemed to be in the grasp of the coin almost completely. There was no turning back for him now—he had to discover the power of the coin.

Jon Paul spent the rest of the day and most of the evening talking with Michelle. His thoughts would wander to the coin and he would think, *I wonder what else the coin can do for me. Can it bring me anything I want; can it make me rich and powerful, maybe make me live forever?* These and other thoughts occurred to him as they went upstairs to bed for the night.

Jon Paul did not sleep well again, and in the in-between times when Jon Paul actually got some sleep, he would dream of war and of killing people and of the general who owned the coin before him. When morning broke, Jon Paul felt a little better. He'd had some sleep, even though it was broken up by such strange dreams. He looked to see if Michelle had been awake like him, but she was still fast asleep. He gently got up, got dressed, and went downstairs, hoping he had not disturbed her.

He was hungry the next morning. As he cooked himself breakfast, he began to wonder, *Can the coin make me breakfast?* He grabbed the coin from his pocket and said, "I want a king's breakfast now." And then, *poof!* There, on his kitchen table, was a meal fit for a king. He was amazed, to say the least. Jon Paul felt like he was changing his life.

He could use this coin to make a better life for him and Michelle, and he was going to do it. Then, just as he had decided he would use the coin to better their lives, he saw Michelle standing in the doorway. He was a bit startled as he watched her smile fade into a frown. He knew she did not want him to have the coin. She thought it was cursed, and she was right. The golden coin had had many owners. Some were good men and some were bad, some killed men in wars and some killed other men just for spite, but a magical coin has its flip side. Not only can you use it to get what you want (it can also be used to help, not that it happens very often); the coin also has a way of turning even the most pious man evil.

As Michelle sat down at the table, she only had to look at Jon Paul and he knew she was very upset with him and his cursed coin. But he didn't care.

The coin was going to bring him a better life, whether he was with her or not. He had made up his mind to use the coin for their betterment, but if Michelle was not willing, he would use the coin for his own benefit.

"Michelle," said Jon Paul. "I know you don't like me having this coin, but think what it can do—it can bring us so many things."

Michelle looked at him and said, "I know you think that coin can do all that, but I don't need anything else. We were fine before you found that coin. Now I am afraid for us, afraid you will leave me and find yourself in wrong places and your life could be in danger."

"But, Michelle, it can do so much for us."

"I don't care. I wish you would get rid of that coin—or we are through."

Jon Paul had never heard Michelle talk like this; she was giving him an ultimatum, and he didn't like it. He didn't like to be pushed like that. He knew he had a coin that could possibly give him anything he wished. "Michelle, why don't you just see that this coin can be our friend; it can do anything we ask it to?"

"I don't care about that coin, Jon Paul. I just want things back the way they were."

"Well, that can never be, Michelle. I am going to take a walk. I will be back later."

As Jon Paul got up to leave, Michelle ran to him with tears in her eyes. "Please don't choose the coin over me. I love you, Jon Paul."

As he walked away, Michelle decided she would call Paul Pierre, his best friend for many years, and talk with him about Jon. As she dialed the phone, she thought about how bad her life would be without the man she loved so much, the man she had planned on spending her life with. She fought back the tears as Paul answered. "Hello?"

"Hello, Paul, this is Michelle."

"Oh, hi, Michelle. What's up?"

"Paul, I am worried about Jon Paul. He is beginning to act very strange, and he is becoming distant from me."

"Did something happen today, Michelle?"

"Yes, he used the coin to make a whole table full of food."

"A whole breakfast appeared on the table?"

"Yes. I didn't ask him, but I knew for sure that is what he did; we didn't have enough food for something like that. I gave him an ultimatum and told him I wanted him to get rid of the coin. He looked at me strangely and then just got up and said he was going for a walk."

"I see. I had feared something like this might happen; he is becoming possessed by the coin. The power of the coin is taking over his mind, body, and soul."

"What can we do, Paul?"

"I don't know, Michelle, though right now, we must act as nonchalant as we can. I wouldn't want to alarm him."

"So we just play it cool until one of us can get the coin from him and get rid of it?"

"Yes, that sounds like a good, safe plan for now, Michelle."

"Thanks, Paul. I don't know what I would do without you."

"No worries, Michelle. Call me if anything else happens."

"Okay, Paul; thanks again. Bye."

"Bye."

And with that, Paul and Michelle began their plan to rid themselves of the dreaded coin. Somehow and some way, they would take it from him and be free of its accursed magic.

Jon Paul, in the meantime, walked for quite a long time; even for him, he had so many things to think about.

Chapter Three

— • • • —

THE COIN

Jon Paul was feeling rather odd. He knew the coin was doing something to him but he just wasn't sure what. As he walked, he found himself back near the same pier he had visited yesterday. When he got to the dock, he noticed something strange—the fishermen were not there; they were not anywhere to be found.

At this time in the late morning, the men should be back from fishing with their morning catch. No one was there. Wait! There, at the very end of the pier, was a lone fishing boat. He would walk down there and talk with the captain and ask if he knew the other boat that was docked here yesterday.

"Hello, sir," said Jon Paul.

The captain looked up. "Hello. What can I do for you, young man?"

"Well, sir, I was here yesterday and I talked with this small crew of men, and I was wondering if you knew who they were and where they might be?"

"Hmmm, yesterday, you say? I don't remember any boat here or any crew of men. Where were they docked?"

"Right there at the beginning of the dock," said Jon Paul.

"Are you joking, son? I was here most of the day, and I never saw any boat or a crew of men."

"What? You mean you didn't see anybody or a boat with several men?" asked Jon Paul.

"No, sir, I didn't see anyone, as I said, and I was here all day tying lines for today's catch."

Jon Paul was disturbed by this; he didn't know what to make of it. "Thank you, Captain," he said and walked away. Maybe the captain was lying, but why would he lie? What if someone had seen him find the coin and pick it up? What if someone wanted it back? All these questions and more raced in his mind as he walked.

Jon Paul had been walking for some time when he decided to stop at his local bar; he sometimes felt better after he had a couple of beers. The bar he was going to was called The Goat's Head Bar. It was slow most of the time, not too many visitors. It had been around since the seventeenth century and was one of the oldest places in all of southern France. It had its reputation as being a bit of a rough place, though. Anyone looking for a fight was sure to find it there. Jon Paul, however, felt comfortable there. He had visited the place many times in the past, and he enjoyed the atmosphere of the tavern.

"Well, hello, stranger," said the barkeep. He had not seen Jon Paul in a few weeks. "How is your life this day?" he asked.

"It is not good, Jacques. I am having some troubles at home."

"Do tell, Jon Paul," he said, pouring him a fresh glass of ale.

"Michelle has given me an ultimatum. I am to choose her or ..." Jon Paul stopped cold in his speech; he'd almost blurted out about the coin. He didn't want anyone else to know about it. Someone might want to take it from him or try to cause him harm if they knew what it could do. "... ah, just, you know—choose her," he stammered.

Jacques was listening closely as Jon Paul said this. He had known Jon Paul for a few years now, and to hear of him having troubles at home was out of the ordinary.

"What did she say to you, Jon Paul? What happened exactly?" he asked.

"Well, she is upset with me for wanting a better life for us. She thinks I will leave her or something."

"Did you say you were leaving her?" Jacques asked.

"No."

"Well, then, drink up, my friend. You have nothing to worry about; she is just having some inner problems of her own. Reassure her of your love and make it right. You will be fine then."

"Thanks, Jacques," said Jon Paul. "Can I get another?"

"Sure thing, Jon Paul," Jacques answered.

And so Jon Paul began to drink. Time passed slowly in the bar, but that is exactly what Jon Paul needed—he needed to get away; he needed to clear his head and get some distance from the home problems that were beginning to grow around him. He didn't know what was coming or what to expect, but fate had something more in store for him. It was just a matter of time.

***

Paul Pierre was sitting at home when Michelle called him. "Hello," he answered.

"Hello, Paul, this is Michelle."

"Hi, Michelle, didn't recognize your voice at first—what's up?"

"Well, Paul, I haven't heard from Jon Paul in a few hours and he has been gone a long time. I am getting worried he might have done something with that coin. Have you heard anything from him?"

"No, not yet today. Maybe he just needed some time alone to think."

"I hope that is all it is. Do you think he will be home soon? I miss him so much and I am so very worried," said Michelle.

"Yeah, I am sure he will be there soon. Just give him a little time to relax."

"Okay, then. Thanks, Paul. I better go. Talk with you soon. Bye."

"Bye, Michelle."

As Michelle hung up the phone, she had a feeling something was wrong. It was not like Jon Paul to not call and tell her he was okay.

Jon Paul was enjoying his ale when he noticed it had been a few hours that he had been gone and he still had not called his father to confirm Sunday's dinner plans. The ultimatum from Michelle weighed heavy on his mind, too, and he was still in a state of confusion as he finished his drink. He got up, looked at the bartender, and said, "I will see you later, Jacques."

Jacques waved and said, "Take it easy, Jon Paul, and be careful."

Jon Paul hadn't heard those last words, as he was already out the door and walking down the street. There was a gentle breeze as he walked, and it seemed to him it was pushing him along the way. He thought it quite pleasant; in fact, it was even a bit relaxing. Maybe it was just the beer talking or something else was coming and he sensed it, somehow …

The long walk back from the bar was uneventful. Jon Paul just walked and didn't think about anything. He had always walked, ever since he was a young boy. It had a way of helping him release his anger and his emotions. It helped him free his mind from the troubles of the day. As he got closer to home, he thought, *what shall I tell Michelle? She has put this pressure and this ultimatum on me, and it is not right. How dare she do this to me!* He was getting upset as he thought this, and as he climbed the stairs to their apartment, he knew what he would say to her.

When he opened the door, she ran to him and embraced him tightly. "I missed you! Jon Paul, where were you?"

"I went for a walk. Then I ended up at the bar."

"Is everything all right?" Michelle asked.

"Yeah, everything is good, Michelle," he lied. He was playing it cool and keeping to himself. He knew he would have to do this until he could find a way to make this change for the better. "I better call my dad." Michelle nodded and handed him the phone, and he dialed the number.

"Hello?"

"Hi, Dad."

"Jon Paul?"

"Yes, Dad."

"How is your weekend going, Jon Paul?"

"It is all right. How's Mom?"

"She is good. I am supposed to ask you if you and Michelle are coming over and what time you will be here."

"Ah, I don't know, Dad, how about 5:00 p.m.?"

"5:00 p.m. That is fine, Jon Paul."

"Hey, Dad?"

"Yeah?"

"I need to talk with you when we get there, okay?"

"Sure, son, anything serious?"

"Maybe, Dad, it's just a personal matter and I want your opinion on it."

"No problem, son, see you later."

"Okay, Dad, see you later." They both said good-bye and hung up the phones. Jon Paul was feeling better after talking with his father, knowing that he would be able to help him. His father was a very smart man. He had graduated with a master's in psychology and had served his country in the military as well. Jon Paul wondered if he had missed the boat on intelligence when it came to his family. He had always struggled, yet he had fun in his young life.

***

He had told his father they would be there at 5:00 p.m. for dinner. This was a bi-weekly occurrence for Jon Paul and Michelle. They liked to visit his parents every other weekend or so to have dinner and socialize. Jon Paul's mother was a homemaker who enjoyed cooking for her son and daughters, whom Jon Paul didn't get to see very often. Jon Paul's sisters had all married and moved away to different areas in France. Jon Paul was the only one close enough to visit on a regular basis.

His three sisters lived quite different lives than Jon Paul. The oldest was Cleo Marie Johnson, who was a practicing dental hygienist. The next was Marie Antoinette O'Claire. She was a homemaker like their mom. The last sister and the youngest was Sara Michelle Pouisant, who was more like Jon Paul, and he was closest to her. They had always been closer than the others—maybe because they were closer in age than the rest. Sara had had her bad luck, too, like Jon Paul, yet their lives had always been exciting, to say the least. There was always something that kept them going, something that made their lives interesting.

Although Jon Paul and his sister Sara called each other often, he had not told her about the coin he had found. It was his coin, his power. Michelle had been in the kitchen working while Jon Paul was on the phone. When she came out, she asked him, "Jon Paul, what time are we going to your parents' house?"

"Around five," he said.

"Do we need to bring anything?" she asked.

"Umm, no, we don't need to. Mom has it covered." Jon Paul was thinking should he tell his dad about the coin and Michelle's ultimatum. He didn't know, but he was sure his dad would tell him something.

***

Paul Pierre had known Jon Paul for many years now, and he could tell that Jon Paul was in deep trouble with this mysterious coin he had found.

19

When Paul Pierre was young, he had a strange incident with a tall and oddly dressed man. He had always thought it rather strange that a person of that caliber would talk with a young man. Paul might have been about twelve years old at the time, maybe more. He couldn't remember exactly.

Paul Pierre had grown up in a successful, middle-class family. They were not rich, but very comfortable, and the children never had a need or want for anything. His father Jack worked in the oil industry, and his mother Angelique was a homemaker. Paul was a very easygoing child growing up. He didn't argue with his parents, or even with his other siblings. He was very intelligent compared to the rest of his peers. In school, he excelled where others fell behind.

Paul was a great student. He studied more than most, which is also why he didn't have much of a social life when he was young. When he went away to college at Notre Dame, he met Jon Paul for the first time. They became fast friends immediately. Paul liked the way their humor was similar; a lot of the times, they laughed at the same jokes. They had a natural chemistry, as best friends do; it was an easy friendship.

Sometimes they would go to the local bar in-between classes or after school and have a glass or two of beer, oftentimes playing a game of darts or pool. Jon Paul was always better at pool than Paul, but Paul was better at darts, so they would bet against each other in a friendly competition. Sometimes Jon Paul would win and sometimes Paul would win—it was an even give-and-take.

One time, when Paul was in class, he had fallen asleep after having been up all night studying. He had had a very strange dream in which he dreamt that he met a strangely dressed and very tall man from his childhood days—the same tall man that he had met and talked to as a youth. As it turned out, this very same tall man would also come into the life of one Jon Paul Chavalier.

As Paul remembered the dream, he was sure it had some kind of meaning. The tall man had told him the tale of a magical gold coin that had been used to win wars and that had also been used to take some men's lives. Generals had used the coin, as had other powerful men, to control their futures. Paul had always thought the dream peculiar, but he knew somehow, someday, it might have meaning.

Many years had passed since they were in college, and Paul had forgotten about the dream he had until he saw Jon Paul's coin. This had triggered the memory that had been buried for a long time. As Paul gazed at the coin for the first time and had listened to Jon Paul tell him about its magical powers, he knew it was the same coin the tall man from his youth had told him about. He knew it was cursed and he would have to get rid of it somehow. Jon Paul, however, loved the coin. He knew it was meant for him. Just like some people are destined for greatness, this was his time to shine. This coin was his golden ticket to the good life, his brass ring. He would not let it get away from him, ever.

Jon Paul and Michelle readied themselves for their visit to his parents' house. It was not too far, only about thirty miles—a short ride, not more than an hour on the high-speed train, depending on how many stops it made. As they walked to the train depot, neither said much. Michelle thought about how she could help Jon Paul's mom, and Jon Paul thought about what to say to his father and exactly how he would say it. Would he tell him about his new coin? Should he? Or how about the way it granted wishes instantly? These questions and more raced around in his wearied mind as they boarded the train, found seats, and started the journey to his parents' house.

Jon Paul had not slept much these last few days, what with the coin and Michelle's ultimatum. As the train approached the station, Jon Paul and Michelle got themselves ready to leave. They had brought some fruit for Jon Paul's parents, who loved fresh fruit, and the market near where Jon Paul lived had the best in all of southern France.

"Michelle," said Jon Paul.

"Yes?" she said.

"Did you grab the fruit we brought?"

"Yes, I got it," she said as they got off the train. They walked the short distance to the waiting area, where they saw Jon Paul's youngest sister, Sara.

"Sara!" cried Jon Paul.

"Hey, Jon Paul," said Sara.

"What are you doing here?" Jon Paul asked. "It is wonderful to see you, sis."

"Hi, Michelle," said Sara.

"Hi, Sara, how are you?" asked Michelle.

"Just great." And after they had hugged, Sara jokingly said, "Well, are we just going to stand here, or should we head out to Mom and Dad's?"

Jon Paul laughed. He had always loved the way Sara could say the funniest things. The drive to their parents' house was uneventful and quiet. It was only a short drive, ten minutes, but for Jon Paul, time seemed to last longer.

"Something on your mind, Jon Paul?" asked Sara.

"No, sis, just lost in thought."

"Okay, well, don't be so damn quiet. Tell me what have you been doing since we last spoke."

Jon Paul was not so sure he wanted to tell his sister about the coin, nor did he think it a good idea just yet. "I have been working on some things," he replied.

"What things, Jon Paul?"

"Just some work with a local handyman I know." Michelle shot a disapproving glance at Jon Paul. She knew he was lying to his sister.

"Does he pay you enough?" Sara asked.

"Well, you know, it could be better." Jon Paul hoped this little lie would do for now; he was a bit uncomfortable lying to his sister like this.

Jon Paul had always been close with his sister Sara. He knew he might have to tell her all that was going on in his life soon, or she would figure out something was wrong. Jon Paul's parents' house was a nice five-bedroom home with three floors and a garage for his father's old classic car collection. His father would work on them occasionally and maintain them tirelessly. Jon Paul had always been impressed with this, but he had never had the motivation to work like that. His father had a nice collection of cars; some were even from America, like his 1967 Pontiac Firebird, or his 1967 Ford Mustang. He also had in his collection some other cars just as old, like his 1970 Renault. His father was a very good mechanic, and he kept these cars in perfect working order, or at least as well as can be expected for such old cars.

As Jon Paul walked into his parents' house, memories flooded his mind. He remembered a lot of the good times he had as a young boy in this house. Jon Paul had many fond memories of sitting by the fire on Christmas day with his mom and dad and three sisters, sipping hot apple cider.

"Hi, Dad," said Jon Paul.

"Hi, Jon Paul, glad you could make it. Hi, Michelle, how are you?"

"I am fine; thanks, Dad." Michelle had begun to call Jon Paul's father *Dad* a year ago. She was sure Jon Paul would marry her sometime in the future, and Jon Paul's dad was okay with her calling him that.

"Sara, would you please put their coats away for them?" Frederick asked.

"Sure, Dad," she said.

"Let's go sit down in the living room."

"Okay, Dad," Jon Paul replied. Michelle went with him and sat down next to him on the sofa; his dad sat on the easy chair next to them.

"Does anyone need a drink?" asked Frederick.

"No thanks, Dad, I am good."

"Michelle?"

"Not right now, thanks for asking. Maybe after dinner."

"Well, kids, how is life in Toulon County?" Frederick asked.

"It is good, Dad. Not too much happens there, you know. I have been doing some work with a local contractor who lives close to me."

"Does he keep you busy enough with work, Jon?"

"Yeah, we get busy sometimes and it can be overwhelming, but we also have some downtime as well."

"You know what I say: a good day's hard work never hurt anybody." Jon Paul's dad liked to work hard. He prided himself on the fact that he could do almost anything he put his mind to. Several moments passed and just as the silence was becoming deafening to Jon Paul, in walked his mother.

"Hi, Jon Paul, Michelle!" she said excitedly. "Has your father been entertaining you?"

"Hi, Mom," said Jon Paul.

"Hi, Elysse," said Michelle. Michelle had not begun to call her *Mom* yet.

Jon Paul's mom smiled at both of them and said, "Well, I better get back to the kitchen before something burns." She turned and walked back to the kitchen.

"So how are you two this weekend?" asked Frederick. "I am so glad you came home today. We wanted to surprise you with your sister's visit—were you surprised?"

"Yeah, Dad, I was surprised. I didn't know she was coming too," Jon Paul replied.

Sara was back downstairs now after putting their coats away. She walked over to where her father was sitting and sat down beside him in the other easy chair. "So tell me, Jon Paul, what is new and exciting in your life?"

"Not much, sis."

He was getting that uncomfortable feeling again with this question. She was beginning to pry too much. He wondered if Michelle had told her about the coin, and if she did, what did she tell her? He would have to have a talk with Michelle and find out if she went behind his back and did this.

Jon Paul was trying to think of something to say that would change the subject and take the spotlight away from him. "How is work, Sara? Are you staying busy? And where is Claude? Did he have to work?" asked Jon.

"No, he decided to stay home with the baby; he wasn't feeling too well," said Sara.

"Sorry to hear that, sis, make sure you tell him I hope he feels better soon."

"Thanks, Jon Paul. I am sure he just needs some rest, he has been working some very long hours."

Jon Paul began to wonder what his mom was cooking; the smell was drawing him in. As he got up to walk into the kitchen, he got a whiff of what he thought was French-fried potatoes and maybe some kind of a stew. It was making him hungry; his appetite was returning. Jon Paul walked into the kitchen and began to remember the wonderful smells from his days as a young boy when he would sneak into the kitchen and sample his mom's cooking while she wasn't looking. This time was no different; he walked over to the stove where several different dishes were still cooking and found a spoon. *Ahhh*, he thought as he tasted the potatoes, *delicious*! Now what was cooking in the other pot? Just as he was about to taste the stew, in walked his mom.

"Jon Paul!" she yelled. "You never change."

Jon Paul laughed. "Well, Mom, if your cooking wasn't so good!"

She smiled and said, "Well, how is it?"

"It is always the best, Mom, can't wait to eat!"

"Just a few more minutes, Jon Paul."

"Okay, Mom."

Just then his sister walked in. "Hi, Mom. Can I help with anything?" asked Sara.

"Can you set the table please, dear?"

"Sure, Mom," said Sara. Sara set the table and helped her mom get ready for dinner.

Jon Paul had gone back to the living room to visit with his dad for a few minutes and to tell him dinner was almost ready. He was still sitting by the couch in the easy chair, talking with Michelle.

"What are you guys talking about?" asked Jon Paul.

"Nothing in particular, Jon Paul," said Michelle.

"Oh, well, I guess I didn't miss anything then?"

"Not at all, son," replied Frederick.

Now, since dinner was ready, Jon Paul's mother came out of the kitchen and said, "Okay, everyone, dinner is ready. Let's eat."

They all went into the dining room and had a great meal. As they ate dinner, Jon Paul wondered how he should tell his father about the coin and Michelle's ultimatum. He thought he'd wait until after dinner to ask his dad to talk with him. An hour passed as they sat at the table and enjoyed Sunday dinner. When they finally decided to get up and move around, they again went into the living room and sat. "So, Dad, how is retirement?" asked Jon Paul.

"It is okay, son, lots more to do now that I am not working."

"What do you mean, Dad?"

"There are so many projects that your mom has me doing. I am working more now than when I was working!" Everyone laughed. Sara got her humor from their dad. He was a funny man when he wanted to be.

"Dad, are you working on any new projects in the garage?" asked Jon Paul.

"Now that you ask, I have been working on a new design for the front end of my Ferrari."

"Really? How about we go take a look, Dad?"

Jon Paul and his dad Frederick went out to the garage to look at his newest design for his car. Sara and her mom stayed in the house with Michelle. They were not interested in cars or anything that had to do with cars; that was a man thing. When Jon Paul and his dad got to the garage, Jon Paul noticed his father had it very clean—so clean, in fact, that there was no dirt or even a spot of grease anywhere. It was completely flawless.

"Gee, Dad, did you clean the garage for me?" he asked jokingly.

"Oh, sure, Jon Paul, I cleaned *my garage* for your viewing pleasure," he said sarcastically.

Jon Paul laughed. "Well, it looks great, Dad. What have you been working on?" They talked for a half hour about Frederick's newest design for a new tie-rod front suspension system before Jon Paul's dad noticed that his son was fidgeting. Jon Paul had always done this when he was anxious or nervous and had something to say.

"Okay, son, what is it?"

"What do you mean, Dad?"

"Tell me what this is all about. What is troubling your mind?"

"Dad, a few days ago I was walking down by the museum, you know, and, well …" Jon Paul scratched his head, "… anyway, while I was walking, I saw something shiny on the ground in the distance."

"What was it?"

"Well, Dad, as I got closer, I could see it was a coin—a new, very shiny gold coin."

"What kind of gold coin, Jon Paul?"

"I don't know exactly, Dad, but what was strange is there was no one around at that time of the morning."

"What do you mean, Jon Paul?"

"I am saying I was totally alone. I didn't see anyone, anywhere."

"Well, that is a bit strange, but what has you so troubled?"

"I stopped, and after I picked it up, I decided to walk back home and tell Michelle about it. After I had walked for a while, I began to get a feeling, or maybe it was an urge, I don't know."

"What kind of feeling or urge, Jon Paul?"

"I felt like I should hold the coin and make a wish, like a very small voice in my ear was urging me to do this."

"A *wish*?" he asked, not believing.

"Yes, Dad, a wish, so while I was walking, a thought came to me: How about I wish for another coin?"

"And did you wish for it?"

"I did, and believe it or not, there in my hand was another gold coin, instantly."

"Are you serious, Jon Paul?"

"Totally, Dad, it is a wish-granting magical coin."

"Did you bring it with you tonight?" he asked.

"No, Dad, it is safe at home, hidden."

"Does Michelle know about it?"

"Yes, I told her, but she thinks it is cursed and has given me an ultimatum—choose her or the coin."

"I see now what has you so perplexed, my son, especially given that this gold coin is possibly cursed or hexed in some way. It has her feeling very nervous for you. Any sort of unordinary power would make her nervous; she is a simple woman, Jon, and this coin has her worried for you and for her and your future together."

"What should I do, Dad?"

"Take the coin to the museum and ask for—I believe his name is Dr. Martin. He should be able to help you or at least point you in the right direction."

"Thanks, Dad, I knew you could help."

"Oh, one more thing, Jon Paul. Be very careful with that coin—it could be dangerous."

Jon Paul talked with his dad more and they decided he should walk down to the museum possibly on Monday to find this Dr. Martin. "Thanks again, Dad, for all the great advice."

"Anytime, Jon Paul. I am always here for you, whatever you need." When they got back in the house, he saw his sister, his mom, and Michelle had been sitting in the living room talking, and being a curious man, he said, "So what have you women been talking about all this time?"

Right away, his mom sat up and said, "Oh, you know, Jon Paul, lots of girly stuff." His sister giggled.

"All right Mom, you win. Michelle, are you ready? We should probably get home."

"Sure thing, honey, whenever you are ready," she said.

As they got up and Jon Paul went to get their coats, Sara looked at Jon Paul's dad and said, "Is everything all right? You guys were out there for quite awhile."

"Everything is fine, Michelle. Jon Paul had a few things he wanted to discuss, but nothing for you to worry about, sweetie."

When Jon Paul got back downstairs, he walked over to Michelle and helped her with her coat and then gave his sister her coat and helped her put it on.

"Thanks, Jon Paul," said Sara.

"No problem, sis. Mom, thanks for dinner and for being such a great cook."

"You are welcome, honey," she said.

"Thanks for listening to me, Dad."

"You got it, son."

And with all that, they hugged and kissed each other on the cheek and went out the door to Sara's car and drove back to the train station. The drive went by quickly and nobody said much. Jon Paul was feeling better because he had told his father about Michelle's ultimatum and the gold coin that he had found. As they pulled into the station, it was mostly deserted at that time of the evening; there were not a lot of people traveling tonight.

"Hey, Jon Paul, did you have a good visit tonight?" his sister asked.

"Yeah, it was all right," he said.

"It was nice to see you, Sara," Michelle said.

"It was great to see you too, Michelle."

"Call me in a few days, Jon Paul."

"Okay, Sara, I will," Jon Paul replied.

Jon Paul and Michelle got on the train, found seats, and waved to his sister as the train pulled away from the station. They both thought about the visit and how each other had enjoyed it. "Did you have a good visit with your dad?"

"Yeah, we talked about a few things and he gave me some good advice, as he always does."

"Good, I am glad you are feeling better. You are feeling better, right?"

"Yeah, Michelle, I am good." They sat for a while in silence, but this time Jon Paul was not bothered by it. He was truly feeling a weight had been lifted from his shoulders.

"Michelle, we should do something when we get home."

Michelle's eyes brightened as she looked at Jon Paul. "Okay, sure, what do you have in mind?" she asked.

"Um, I don't know, just maybe something fun, together."

Michelle was very excited to hear this; she began thinking Jon Paul was choosing her over the coin and they could get back to their lives. Jon Paul had other ideas, though; he was thinking about his next wish. The train ride back had given him time to think, time to plan his next big wish. He knew it would separate Michelle from him, but Jon Paul was beginning to lose interest in Michelle.

When they arrived back at the station, it was getting late. The moon was high in the night sky and shining bright, and there was a cold chill in the air as they walked home to their apartment. As they settled in for the night, Michelle looked at Jon Paul and asked, "Well, Jon Paul, what do you want to do for fun?"

"You know, Michelle, I am getting tired. Do you mind if we just relax now?"

"Sure, honey, that is fine. We can do something fun tomorrow." Michelle smiled at Jon Paul, who smiled back at her as he sat down on the couch to watch TV.

Michelle decided to busy herself in the kitchen; maybe she would work on the dinner meal for tomorrow. Jon Paul began to wonder what he should wish for, maybe money or riches and power, but that would mean he was choosing the coin over Michelle. Was he ready to give up on three years of life with the woman he loved? Jon Paul didn't know, but the growing inner conflict would soon reveal the truth to him.

As he thought about his plans with the coin and his life with Michelle, he thought, *maybe I could wish for a painting; that would be harmless and innocent enough.* He decided that he would tell Michelle he was walking down the street, and if he saw it in one of the local stores and thought about her, this would surely solve the problem of her ultimatum. This could work, and it would. *Now I just have to wait till tomorrow morning,* he thought. Since he walked each and every day, he would simply bring the painting home with him and tell Michelle it was for her. Michelle was happy she had a nice visit with Jon Paul's family. She didn't get to visit her family very often, so this was a way for her to feel like she was home.

Her parents lived far away, and Jon Paul's family was becoming hers; the visits with them always made her feel good. Jon Paul watched TV and continued to think and plan his next wish to perfection. He knew it would be good. While he sat there, he also had thoughts about his friend Paul. He wondered how his day had been. Paul was always talking about his next woman. He was a bit of a womanizer. Jon Paul enjoyed the fact that Paul was a bit more of a ladies' man than he was. Even when they were in college, Paul was always the lucky one. Jon Paul found his own stability in his friend Paul's conquests, though. Jon Paul had always been quick on his feet, although not like some, his mental quickness came from pure instinct.

Chapter Four

— • • • —

THE LIE

Michelle had met Jon Paul at a bar many years ago. Both were enjoying a glass of their favorite draft when he had seen her across the room and walked over to her and sat down. They began to talk, and there was instant chemistry between them. Now, after a few years together, Jon Paul wondered if he had made the right choice. Of course they would argue on occasion, but that was normal for couples.

Michelle had grown up in the northern part of France with her two sisters: Kimmie, who was younger than her, and their older sister, Racine. All three sisters had graduated college, and two were still living in northern France close to their parents' house. Michelle didn't see her sisters or even her parents often. She had moved to the south of France to seek her love and fortune, and she had found both with Jon Paul. Living in Toulon was not so easy, though. It had a slow economy and an equally slow job market. When they had met at the bar that one fateful night, neither knew what their lives would soon become.

While Jon Paul sat and thought, he occasionally would glance around his small apartment and look at his belongings. This had a way of making him feel more secure. He had several fake but nice paintings by different artists; all were copies, though, of some famous artist like Monet or even one from Van Gogh, and a few from Renoir. These were paintings he loved to look at; they reminded him of his walks in the museum.

Suddenly, Jon Paul became very aware of his plan; an inner voice was telling him very subtly to execute it with perfection. He had not heard this inner voice before. He now just had to wait until the morning to complete his plan. Michelle had finished planning her meal for the following evening and had joined Jon Paul on the couch. As the evening got very late, both Jon Paul and Michelle began to get sleepy.

"Michelle, I am getting sleepy. I think I will go to bed, you coming?"

"Yes, sweetie, I am right behind you."

As they climbed the stairs to their bedroom, Jon Paul knew he had a good plan with the painting. Michelle knew nothing. The morning broke with them both waking at the same time, yawning and stretching. "Morning," said Jon Paul.

"Good morning to you," said Michelle.

"Would you like me to make you some breakfast, Michelle?"

"Sure, that would be great!" she said.

Jon Paul got up, got dressed, and went downstairs to the kitchen to make breakfast for the both of them. As he prepared a simple meal for them, he thought about his wish. He could finish breakfast, clean up, and take his walk. He would then find a place to make his wish when he was far enough away, and then he'd bring the painting back to give to Michelle. Michelle walked downstairs to the kitchen and said, "It smells good, Jon Paul."

"Thanks, honey. I am making your favorite, grilled toast with sausage and some fresh-squeezed orange juice."

"Mmm," said Michelle. She watched him cook. Michelle always loved it when Jon Paul cooked for her. When he finished cooking breakfast, they both sat down and enjoyed the meal; then Jon Paul looked at Michelle and said, "I am thinking of walking down by the old shops this morning."

"Really," said Michelle.

"Yeah, I am feeling a bit nostalgic today," said Jon Paul.

Michelle smiled and said, "Be careful, Jon, there can be some strange people there sometimes."

"Aww, honey, don't worry; I will be fine."

When they had finished eating, Jon Paul cleaned up the dishes and then got ready for his morning walk. It would be an interesting day if he could get a hold of the Dr. Martin his dad had told him about yesterday. He figured after he had his walk and wished for the painting, he would try to call this Dr. Martin when he got home and see what he could tell him.

As he put on his coat to leave, Michelle embraced him and said, "Be careful, Jon Paul. I love you."

"Thanks, sweetie, love you too," he said.

Jon Paul walked out the door and closed it behind him. He knew full well what he was going to do, and Michelle would either love the painting or not. He walked down the hall to the exit sign and out into the cool morning air, which had an uplifting feeling for him. Jon Paul felt more alive than he had in several days. He had a clear sense of direction, which had eluded him since he found the coin. Almost all of his thoughts were about the coin. Jon Paul walked and he walked; he was lost in thought.

***

Paul Pierre had suspected the coin was cursed; from the moment Jon Paul showed it to him, he knew. He knew it had been the same coin that the tall man had told him about. His memory of the coin had been a chilling reminder of what he had forgotten from his youth. As Paul sat wondering if he would see his friend this morning, he realized something—maybe Jon Paul had been involved with the coin before! In a past life, perhaps Jon Paul had possessed the coin as he did today. This was an intriguing thought.

Paul was an educated man and not given to fantasy. He knew that if he was to find out more about the coin, he must talk with someone who knew about ancient artifacts, but who, he wondered? He decided to try and find an expert as fast as he could. Paul was going to call and see if his friend Jon Paul was coming over for tea to make sure he had time to find an expert to help him.

"Hello," said Michelle.

"Hello, Michelle, this is Paul."

"Oh, hi, Paul, what's up?"

"I was wondering if Jon Paul is home."

"No, he left a little while ago. He said he was going to walk down by the old shops today."

"Oh, really, Michelle? I am going to try to find someone who can help us with that coin."

"Okay, who?"

"I don't know yet. I am looking for someone now."

"Well, Paul, will you let me know what you find out, please?"

"Of course, Michelle. Don't worry; we will get this taken care of."

"Thanks, Paul. Will you call me and let me know if Jon Paul shows up and make sure you call me when he leaves?"

"Sure, Michelle; remember to just act normal, okay?"

"Okay, Paul, I will try."

"Okay, bye, Michelle."

"Bye, Paul."

Paul was sure he would be able to find out more about the coin from someone, somewhere; he was just not sure where yet.

***

Jon Paul had been walking for some time, long enough for him to be sure that Michelle wouldn't be suspicious if he returned too soon. The Old Town Shops were just that: old. At least, that is what the locals called them. Most of the stores had that quaint look to them, with small windows to look in and old, pointed roofs that were reminiscent of days gone by. A lot of the shops had homemade wares in them, and the owners took pride in their particular handicrafts and talents to make some very unique and original French designs. One store in particular caught Jon Paul's attention. The name on the front of the shop said "Gasparis Old Town Paintings."

This would be the perfect shop for me to say I visited and saw the painting and just had to buy it for Michelle, he thought. *Should I really go in there and look, just in case she asks? No, I will just look through the window and get an idea of what they have.* Jon Paul walked over closer to the shop and looked in the window. *Not much to see,* he thought. But the few paintings that he could see gave him a clear idea of what he could wish for. Jon Paul walked away, thinking he needed to find a quiet place where he could make a wish for a painting.

As he walked, he looked around. A few people were walking here and there; some did look a bit suspicious, but this didn't worry Jon Paul. He had a magical coin! Finally, as he approached an alleyway that was a little dark and secluded, he knew that would be the perfect place. Jon Paul was a little nervous as he pulled the coin from his pocket and felt its power surge through him like electricity. He was alive more than ever! He thought, *how could Michelle not want to have the coin give her things?* Jon Paul readied himself. *Okay, here I go,* he thought, and then he said, "I wish for a beautiful Monet painting."

Poof! Suddenly, there in his hands was a beautiful Monet painting. *Wow,* he thought, *that was easy*—and it was for him, but he didn't realize that with each wish he made, the power of the coin would draw him in deeper and deeper.

***

Paul Pierre was deep in thought about what was happening to Jon Paul and whom he could contact to get some information on the coin. As he sat and looked through the local directory pages, he found a few different people that might be able to help him. One name in particular stood out as a local expert that might work: Dr. Dave Martin.

***

Jon Paul was standing there, fascinated with what this coin had just done for him; he thought, *if the coin can do this for me, there must be no end to its powers and what it can do.* Just then, a few curious men took notice of Jon Paul and his painting.

***

Paul Pierre had decided to call this man, Dr. Martin, and ask him if he could help, when suddenly, he felt something was horribly wrong!

***

Jon Paul had not noticed the men walking over to him at first, but as they got closer, he broke his stare away from the painting. "Hey, whatcha got there?" said one of the men.

"Nothing," said Jon Paul.

"Well, maybe we will have a look."

Jon Paul did not like where this was going. He knew there could be some rough men down here, and now he was in a direct confrontation with three of them. "If you will excuse me, gents, I must be going," said Jon Paul.

"Whoa there, friend. I think you need to give us that painting, *now!*"

Jon Paul, seeing that they were serious and they would probably kill him if he didn't give them the painting, tried to stall. "Ah, you don't want this old painting. It's not worth anything," he said.

"We think it is. Hand it over now."

Jon Paul was not about to give up his new painting, so just then he remembered the coin in his pocket! What if he made a wish for them to go away? He thought for a moment and finally said, "Wait, I have something better than this old painting."

The men looked on curiously as Jon Paul set the painting on the ground and reached into his pocket, and then produced the shiny gold coin for them to see. The men gasped in awe as it reflected the sun's rays in their eyes. "See, this is a magic coin; it can give you anything you wish." Then, when Jon Paul saw that he had them in his trap, he said, "I wish for all of you to be gone!"

Instantly, they vanished from his sight. Jon Paul had saved himself and his painting from a group of thugs that probably would have killed him for the painting. He was elated with power. Jon Paul was feeling so powerful that he didn't realize he had just sent three men to their graves with a simple wish from a very powerful and cursed coin. He walked home with a bounce in his step and a certain confidence in knowing he was invincible—as long as he had his coin.

***

Paul Pierre wrote down Dr. Martin's number and closed the book. He thought about getting himself a cup of tea to start with before he called Dr. Martin. While he still couldn't shake the feeling that something was wrong, he walked to the cupboard where he kept his tea and with each passing moment, the feeling that had gripped him earlier lessened. As he boiled water for his tea, he began to relax more, and the feeling of something being very wrong subsided. Moments passed, and as the water finally boiled, he was almost sure something strange had happened; he didn't know what just yet. Suddenly, the buzzer to his apartment rang.

"Yes, who is it?"

"It is Jon Paul."

Paul pushed the door security button to let him in. Jon Paul walked to his friend's apartment and knocked on the door.

"Hello, my friend," Paul said, smiling. "Come on in. What have you got there, a painting?"

"Yes, it is for Michelle."

"Where did you get it, Jon Paul?"

"I got it down by the Old Shops."

"The Old Shops—what store did you buy it at?"

"Actually, I didn't buy it. I was trying to find a way to answer Michelle's ultimatum, and I came up with the idea to get her a painting to show her my answer."

"What do you mean, you didn't buy it?" asked Paul.

"I wished for it."

"What?"

"Yeah, I was trying to find a way to give her something, and then I thought about just giving her a painting."

"It is very nice, Jon Paul. It looks real."

"No, I don't think it's real. I just wished for a beautiful Monet painting."

"Yeah, I think it is real, Jon Paul."

Jon Paul was amazed. Could the coin have actually given him a real painting? Paul was no expert on artwork, but he was positive that it was real.

"Hang on, Jon Paul. Let me get my eyepiece to look at it closer."

"Okay, Paul. Mind if I get myself a cup of tea?"

"Go ahead, Jon Paul. I just boiled some water. I thought you might be here soon."

When Paul returned from his study, he had his eyepiece and began to look at the brushstrokes on the painting. *Well, I'll be damned; yes, it is real!* He thought. *Surely Jon Paul would know this; should I tell him?* Paul chose not to inform his friend of his discovery. But he was sure, though, of one thing: he must find a way to get that cursed coin from Jon Paul before it corrupted him completely.

"You will never guess what happened to me while I was looking at the painting, Paul."

"What happened then, Jon?"

"I was standing there, you know, admiring the painting, and then the next thing, three men started walking toward me."

"What did you do?"

"Well, I was thinking they might be trouble, and sure enough, when they got close, they saw my painting and said they wanted it. Paul, I thought they were going to kill me for this simple painting. Anyway, while I was standing there, I started thinking, what if I showed them the coin and then wished them away?"

"And did you wish them away, Jon Paul?"

"Yes, I did. I waited for them to be looking at my coin and then as soon as they were, I wished for them to be gone, and they were—just like that." Jon Paul snapped his fingers to imitate the instant results of his wish.

"Wow, I am glad you were not hurt, Jon Paul. I had this funny feeling that something was wrong, and I guess it must have been you."

"Yeah, well, I am good—no, I am *great!*" he exclaimed with a sudden passion. Paul slowly sipped his tea. He talked with Jon Paul for another hour, when Jon Paul decided it was time to leave so he could give the painting to Michelle.

"Well, my friend, I better get going."

"Okay, Jon Paul, I have got some work to do myself today," said Paul Pierre.

"Good-bye, my friend," said Jon Paul.

"Good-bye, Jon Paul. Tell Michelle I said hi."

"Okay, see you later." He waved and walked out the door with his painting in his hands. He would give it to Michelle and she would see how the coin could give them a better life. Jon Paul loved having the coin. He felt it was his destiny to be a rich and powerful man.

As Jon Paul approached his apartment, he was sure he was doing the right thing. Michelle would love the painting, and their lives would be good again. Jon Paul unlocked the door and went inside. Michelle was sitting on the couch watching TV.

"Hi, sweetie. I brought you something."

"Jon Paul, what did you do?"

"I saw this painting and thought you would love it, so I bought it."

"I *do,* Jon Paul! It is beautiful! Where did you buy it?"

"I saw it at this little shop. It was just sitting there and I thought of you."

"Oh, Jon Paul, it is wonderful. Thank you." Michelle was completely overwhelmed with the painting; little did she realize it was real.

While Jon Paul looked for a place to hang it, Michelle busied herself with household chores. She was too excited to sit and watch TV anymore. She loved keeping their small but cozy apartment neat and clean; it was her pride and joy.

"Hey, Michelle, come take a look. I think I found the perfect place to hang your painting." Michelle walked into their living room and saw Jon Paul had hung it on the wall above their small but functional fireplace. It was perfect, she thought.

"You know, Jon Paul, we should have Paul take a look at it; it looks so perfect."

"Maybe you're right, Michelle, but not now. I want to enjoy it for a while first."

Michelle was not surprised at Jon Paul's response. He often liked to look at their artwork; he had told her it relaxed him and gave him something to focus on when he was stressed.

"Jon Paul, what was the name of the shop where you bought it?"

"I think it was called Gasparis Old Town Paintings."

"Oh, yeah, I have heard of that place. He does have some nice ones in there."

Jon Paul was getting a bit nervous at Michelle's line of questioning. If she was going to keep on asking him questions, he would have to lie more to keep her satisfied with his answers.

"You know, Michelle, let's not talk about it anymore. I just want you to enjoy the beauty of it, okay?" Just as Michelle was about to answer Jon Paul, the phone rang, and she walked back to the kitchen to answer it.

"Hello, Michelle?"

"Yes, hello, this is Michelle."

"Hi, Michelle, it is Paul."

"Oh, hi Paul!" said Michelle.

"Michelle, Jon Paul was here earlier and he has a painting for you."

"Yeah, he's home now."

"Oh, okay, then I will be brief. Michelle, I believe that painting is real."

"*What*? Jon Paul told me he bought it down at some shop today."

"Yes, that is what he told me too at first, but Michelle, he wished for it with that coin. Jon Paul could never afford a real original Monet painting."

"Paul, what should I do?" Tears began to stream down her face. Michelle's heart was breaking as she thought she was losing the man she loved.

"I think you should be as normal as you can. Don't alarm him or let on that you know it is real, or that you suspect anything."

"Okay, Paul. I will do my best."

"Take care, Michelle. I will talk with you later."

"Thanks Paul. Bye."

"Bye." Now, Michelle was not the strongest woman in the world. She did have a hard time not showing her feelings. She steadied herself, took a deep breath, and walked out to the living room to talk with Jon Paul and tell him Paul had just called.

Jon Paul was sitting on the couch when Michelle walked out to him. "That was Paul on the phone."

"Oh, yeah, what did he have to say?"

"He said he was fine and that you had stopped by his place earlier."

"Yeah, on my way back home, I stopped and had a cup of tea."

"Jon Paul, I have to ask you a question."

"Yes?"

"Did you really buy that painting?"

"Yeah, I saw it and thought of you, honey."

"Don't lie to me, Jon Paul."

"Really, you want the truth?"

"Yes, please, Jon Paul. I have to know."

"Okay, fine, so I wished for it, so what!"

"Oh, Jon Paul, you said you bought it." Tears were now flowing down Michelle's face. Her heart was breaking.

"So what if I did wish for it? Is that so bad?" he yelled at her.

"Oh, Jon Paul, you … you don't understand."

"Understand what?"

"That … that the coin is cursed," she sobbed.

"You know, Michelle, I thought you would understand, but I guess you don't. I'm outta here."

"Wait, Jon Paul!"

"Don't touch me! I'm leaving." Jon Paul slammed the door as he stormed out of their apartment and down to the street. He would walk, as he always did when he was upset.

***

Paul Pierre was dialing the phone when he heard the neighbors arguing. *Damn drunks*, he thought, *why don't they move somewhere else?* As he finished dialing the number, he heard the phone ring on the other end. He was thinking about the dreaded coin. Why had it appeared in their lives now, and why had it been found by Jon Paul?

"Hello, Dr. Martin's office. How can I help you?"

"Ah, hello, I was wondering if I could speak with Dr. Martin."

"Sorry, he is not in right now. Can I take a message?"

"No, I will call later. When might he be back in?"

"He is out of town on business right now. He won't be back for a couple of days," said the secretary.

"Oh, okay, I will try back later, then. Thanks." Paul Pierre would now have to wait a few days before he could get an answer to his questions about the coin.

***

Jon Paul walked and he walked. Never had he been so upset with Michelle and his friend Paul. He felt like they had conspired to steal the coin from him and make it their own. He knew they would never get his coin from him. He had found it, and he had used it; it was his. He walked, and soon his walk led him to his old favorite place, the bar. Jon Paul thought, *I need a drink. That will help me calm down and figure out what to do with those two traitors.*

As Jon Paul entered the smoky and darkly lit bar, he was seen by the lone waitress there, Lizzette Bourg. She was a fine woman, always dressed in her blue jeans and T-shirt; she had emerald-green eyes and honey-blonde hair, always combed perfectly as it hung straight down her shoulders and back. She had worked at the bar for several years now; it was her only source of

41

income, and it wasn't bad. There were a few customers she really liked; Jon Paul was one of them.

"Hi, Lizzette," said Jon Paul.

"Hi, Jon Paul. How is life? You look like you need a drink."

"Yes, Liz, I need a drink, please."

"Sure thing, honey, same as usual?"

"Yeah, Liz, same as usual."

Lizzette poured him a drink. Jon Paul felt upset that it was so apparent in his voice and his eyes that he needed a drink.

"So tell me, Jon Paul, what's up with you?"

"Nothing," he said.

"C'mon, I know that face, tell me what happened."

Jon Paul was not about to tell her he had a magic wish-granting coin. As he revealed to Liz what had happened, she sat there, amazed. He told her about how Michelle and he had an argument and how she didn't understand him, and how he was so upset that he had to storm out of there. Liz thought Jon Paul and Michelle would be together for life; in fact, many who knew them also thought the same. They were so happy together, or so it seemed. On occasion, Michelle would accompany Jon to the bar, but it was rare that she did, to say the least. Liz wondered if Jon Paul and Michelle would call it quits. She'd always had a thing for Jon Paul, and he knew it too.

"Liz, would you ever treat me so bad and question me on my decisions?"

"Jon Paul, you know I wouldn't!"

"Then how about another drink?" asked Jon Paul.

Liz smiled coyly. "Maybe I will join you this time, Jon Paul."

Chapter Five

$\bullet\bullet\bullet$

THE SIN

The two of them began to drink. Lizzette would help the few customers that wandered in and then go back to sit with Jon Paul. Time slipped away. They sat and enjoyed themselves. The bar had been slow the whole evening, so Liz suggested to Jon Paul that she close up early, and Jon Paul agreed it was a good idea.

"Jon Paul, why don't you join me at my place for a nightcap?"

"Liz, I don't know. I mean, just a nightcap?"

"Yeah, just a nightcap, Jon Paul. The change of scenery will do you some good. What do you say?"

"Okay, Liz, a nightcap it is. Do you need any help cleaning up?"

"Yeah, thanks, Jon Paul. If you could put the chairs and the stools on the tables, I can finish up and we can go."

"You got it, Liz." He helped her clean up so they could get out of there and over to her place.

"Okay, Jon Paul, I think that is about it. You ready to go?"

"Yep, let's go, Liz." Liz and Jon Paul walked out the door and Liz locked it behind her. She smiled at Jon Paul as she turned and said, "I don't live too far from here. It is just a short walk."

Jon Paul smiled at Liz and nodded in approval. As they walked, they talked, and it seemed that Lizzette and Jon Paul had quite a lot in common: both loved fine art, both liked to walk, and both loved tea. Indeed, they had much in common. When they got to her apartment, Jon Paul noticed it looked old and distinguished to him; he was impressed with her taste in old

French buildings. They walked to her front door and opened it, and as they walked into her place, Jon Paul thought it was very clean. It reminded him of his own home; she had many nice works of art and even some very nice statues. Jon Paul thought he could live there. As they settled in, Liz poured him a drink and then poured herself one too. She sat next to him on the sofa and said, "You know, Jon Paul, I have always thought you to be a very sexy and handsome man."

"Really, Liz? I have always thought you to be a very beautiful woman." Jon Paul and Liz sat and enjoyed their drinks, and soon, they had moved to her bedroom. Jon Paul was taking a step, whether consciously or unconsciously, to break from Michelle. He was moving on.

***

Michelle sat at home and cried. She wondered if she and Jon Paul were through. Michelle had always loved him so very much, but this might have been the last straw. She felt like she didn't know Jon Paul anymore; he had never got that mad at her—ever—in their three years together. He was becoming like a stranger to her. As she sat and cried some more, she began to get sleepy, and soon she had drifted off by crying herself to sleep.

She knew that she and Paul Pierre would have to figure out how to get the coin from Jon Paul if the two of them were to try and stay together. Michelle slept, and even though her dreams were sad and interrupted by her sobs, she had strange and terrifying dreams, dreams not unlike Jon Paul's, with mad men running around killing people and men in wars. This was new for her; she never had dreams of such violence and depravity. Little did she know that this was a harbinger of her past revealing itself to her in her very own dreams.

As the sun began to rise, Jon Paul also began to stir. He had always been an early riser, and today was no different. He looked at Liz and wondered why she had been so hesitant in showing him her true feelings. If she had these same feelings for him, why didn't she ever show him or tell him? Jon Paul sat up and looked for his clothes. He got dressed, and just before he could wake Liz, she sat up and said, "Good morning, lover!"

"Good morning, Liz."

"Mmm, I love the mornings. Don't you, Jon Paul?"

"Yeah, they can be really nice sometimes." Jon Paul was feeling a little awkward with Liz. He wasn't quite sure how to respond to her. He didn't know where this thing was going; was it just a one-night stand, or could there be more? Should there be more?

"Do you want to get some breakfast?" asked Jon Paul.

"Sure, where do you want to go?" replied Liz.

"Well, we could eat here if you have enough food, or we could go out somewhere."

"I have enough food for us both," said Liz. She dressed, and they both walked to her kitchen. She had a comfortable apartment; it was not too large but had enough space to move around in. It had two bedrooms and one bath, a large kitchen and a small living area. Liz grabbed some food from the fridge and started to make breakfast.

Jon Paul was enjoying every moment away from Michelle; he didn't even think of her once. Time was moving slowly for Liz and Jon Paul. They ate breakfast, and since Liz didn't work today, they decided to take a walk. The morning was clear and bright and the weather was very mild, a perfect day to take a walk. While they were out walking, they continued to talk, and sometimes they would say the silliest things. They both would laugh and smile at each other. They were falling in love.

The streets of Toulon were not crowded this time of the morning. There were a few people rushing off to work, but nothing too busy. Their walk eventually brought them to a local restaurant called Pepe's Pastries and Coffee. They went in to have a morning snack. As they were seated, a waitress came over to take their order. "Hi, I am Maggie, and I will be your waitress today. Can I get you some coffee or maybe some tea?"

Jon Paul said, "Yes I will have a cup of raspberry tea. Liz, do you want anything?"

"Yes, can I have the same and also a croissant, please?"

"Can you bring me a croissant too, please, with butter?" asked Jon Paul.

"Of course, sir, will there be anything else?"

"No, that will be good for now." The waitress smiled and walked away. She was good at her job. *Funny thing,* she thought, *I think that is Jon Paul, so where is Michelle?*

Jon Paul and Liz sat and talked and enjoyed their morning, both lost in each other's smiles. When Maggie brought out their order, she was looking closer at Jon Paul as she set the plates down on their table. "Will there be anything else, sir?" asked Maggie.

"Liz, do you want anything else?"

"No, thank you, I am good."

"Thanks for coming in, Jon Paul," said Maggie.

Jon Paul was surprised at what she had said. "Do I know you?" he asked.

"No, not really. I mean, we have never met properly. I went to school with Michelle; she has mentioned you quite a few times when I have talked with her on the phone. How is she, by the way?" asked Maggie.

"She is fine; thanks for asking."

"Good, will you tell her to call me?" asked Maggie.

"Sure, thanks, Maggie. C'mon, Liz, let's go."

Jon Paul and Liz left the small restaurant. Maggie had seen them and was now suspicious. She had thought Jon Paul and Michelle were still together, and now Jon Paul was having breakfast with this other woman. Who was she? Wondered Maggie, but maybe they were just friends. Was Jon Paul really cheating? They did seem rather friendly, and they also were smiling a lot. *Well*, thought Maggie, *I better call Michelle and see if she is okay*, but she decided to wait until she got home to call her friend.

Jon Paul and Liz walked back to her place. He didn't say much; he was thinking about how he would explain this to Michelle.

***

Michelle had spent the night crying again and drifting in and out of sleep, and when she decided to get up, she felt no better. The broken dreams and lack of good sleep had her feeling ill. She wondered where Jon Paul had been last night. She made herself a cup of tea, hoping it might help calm her nerves. She wondered, *Did Jon Paul stay somewhere safe last night?* Maybe he just went to a motel and spent the night there, hoping to cool down after their argument, Michelle thought as the morning grew.

***

Jon Paul and Liz got back to her apartment and went inside, and as they sat down to talk, Jon Paul was the first to speak. "Liz, I think I better go. I am going to have to talk with Michelle about us."

Liz looked at him and said, "Yes, you need to talk with her and tell her about us, Jon Paul."

"Then I guess I better go."

As he got up to leave, Liz grabbed him and gave him a very passionate kiss and then said, "Jon Paul, you will call me later."

Jon Paul nodded in agreement and turned the knob on the door and walked out. He was not sure what he would do. Michelle had been a part of his life for so long now, but the feelings he had for Liz were growing just as strong as the ones he had for Michelle. Just then, as he was about leave, he turned and ran back to Liz's and knocked.

"Yes?" she said.

"Liz, its Jon Paul. Open the door, please!" Liz opened the door. Jon Paul grabbed her and kissed her and said, "Liz, I want you to think for a moment. If you could have anything in the world and you had one wish to get it, what would you wish for?"

Liz was stunned. The passion of his kiss nearly knocked her off her feet, and as her head cleared, she looked deep into his eyes, thought for a moment, and finally said, "Jon Paul, I wish for you!"

Jon Paul had the coin in his hand as she said this, and now he would truly be hers, forever.

Seconds passed as they stared at each other. Finally, Liz broke the silence and said, "Jon Paul, go talk with Michelle. I will see you later." She smiled at him, and he smiled in return. Jon Paul had given her a wish that made her heart sing, a wish that would tie them together forever. Jon Paul walked back to talk with Michelle; he knew he must end it. There would be tears, but he was in full and total love with Liz—and that was that.

***

Michelle sat in silence as she felt her heart pounding. She didn't want to break up with Jon Paul, but depending on how he felt this morning, they just might. Jon Paul walked up the stairs to his apartment. He opened the door and saw Michelle sitting on the couch looking bad; she had obviously been crying.

"Hi, Michelle."

"Hi, Jon Paul."

As he looked at her, he knew he had broken her heart, but Jon Paul's heart belonged to another. He sat down beside her. "How are you feeling?" he asked.

"How am I feeling? How am I feeling? How do you think, Jon Paul?"

"I don't know—that is why I asked."

"Where were you last night, Jon Paul?"

"I stayed at a friend's house."

"Who, Jon Paul? What friend?"

"Never mind that now; I am here. Do you want to talk about yesterday?"

"Yes, I think we should talk about it some more, Jon Paul."

They sat and talked. Hours passed as they discussed their future and any plans they may have once had. When the dark of night approached, Jon Paul and Michelle had been talking for many hours. Michelle was thinking they still had a chance. Jon Paul, however, knew he would have to keep Michelle around for a little while longer until it was the right time for her to leave for good. They had sorted things out somewhat; at least, that is what Michelle thought.

"Jon Paul, I am tired. I am going to bed."

"Okay, Michelle, I will be there shortly."

Michelle went upstairs to get ready for bed. She was exhausted— mentally, physically, and emotionally—from yesterday's argument and today's talking. Jon Paul was thinking about Liz; he was wondering if he should call her now that Michelle had gone to bed. He decided to call and just say hello and that he would find a way to see her tomorrow at the bar. He dialed her number.

"Hello."

"Hello, Liz, it's Jon Paul."

"Hi, Jon Paul. I was wondering when you were going to call."

"Listen, Liz, I only have a minute to talk, but I wanted to call and say hi before you went to bed."

"Hi," she said.

"Hi," he said back.

"Liz, I am going to visit you at work tomorrow, okay?"

"Yes, that will be great, Jon Paul. What time?"

"How about noon?"

"Okay, Jon Paul. That is fine."

They had made plans to see each other tomorrow. Jon Paul would take his usual walk, but this time, he would have a specific destination. Jon Paul slept on their couch all night. He didn't have the strength to walk upstairs and get in bed with Michelle; besides, he really didn't want to. He had given his heart to Liz, and they would be together soon. The morning was bleak and rainy. *Perfect*, thought Jon Paul. *I have to walk in the rain.* Jon Paul preferred the warmer side of the weather.

Michelle began to stir. She heard Jon Paul in the kitchen, cooking breakfast. She wondered if he had made some for her. Michelle put on her robe and walked downstairs to the kitchen. "Got any for me?" she asked.

"Sure, Michelle, I made enough for us both." They sat down together and had a nice, quiet breakfast. Jon Paul was the first to speak. "Michelle, I am going to take a short walk this morning. All this rain has me feeling more restless than usual."

"Jon Paul, are you going to see Paul today?"

"Yeah, probably. I don't know, really. I just need to be alone for a little bit, okay?"

"Sure thing, honey, just be careful."

"I will, Michelle." He finished his breakfast and got ready, put on his raincoat and hat, and said good-bye to Michelle. He knew one day it would be permanent; he would walk out that door and never return. The steady drizzle had Jon Paul walking in it, feeling like he had done it a thousand times before, but it had never felt like it did to him today. It was as if the rain was washing him clean of his sin. *Funny*, he thought, *rain is really quite refreshing this time of the year.*

Michelle busied herself with some small chores around their apartment. She was feeling better about their relationship; maybe it could work, she thought. The argument they had was terrible, but they had talked, and for now, everything seemed okay. If Jon Paul was still upset, she hadn't noticed. She at least had gotten some sleep and was feeling somewhat better.

***

Jon Paul walked, and as he walked, he thought about his night with Liz.

She is wonderful, he thought, *why couldn't I have met her first?* As Jon Paul got closer to the bar, the drizzle slowed down, and now it was just cool and damp. He was nearing the door to the Goat's Head bar, and as he approached it, he suddenly had a thought of Liz. Wow!

He pulled the handle and went inside. There were a few customers already and he saw the bartender Jacques there as well.

"Hi, Jacques. How are you on this wet day?" he asked.

"I am great, Jon Paul. What'll you have today?"

"Ah, how about a shot of brandy?" he said.

"Sure thing, Jon Paul!"

"Has Liz got here yet, Jacques?"

"Yeah, she is in the back office. She will be out shortly, Jon Paul."

"Thanks." Jon Paul sat and sipped his brandy and waited for Liz. She had been in the storeroom counting stock and had almost finished her work in the back office when she decided to walk out to the bar. Upon seeing Jon Paul, she ran to him and hugged him tightly.

"Hi, Jon Paul," she said, smiling.

"Hey girl," said Jon Paul.

When Liz finally let him go, they stared at each other for a brief moment and smiled, and then Jon Paul sat back down. "How are you today, Liz?" he asked.

"I am good, Jon Paul, how about you?"

"Good, except for this rain."

"I better get back to work, Jon Paul. I wouldn't want to raise any suspicions, just yet," she said, smiling and winking at him. Jon Paul smiled and nodded in agreement. He was glad to see her.

***

Michelle was doing some cleaning around their apartment when the phone rang. "Hello."

"Hello, Michelle, this is Paul."

"Hi, Paul, what's up?"

"Well, I was wondering how Jon Paul is."

"Oh, Paul, we had such a horrible fight yesterday."

"What happened?" he asked.

"He lied to me about the painting, and when I asked for the truth, he got upset and stormed out of here."

"Really, he stormed out?"

"Yes, and he didn't even come home the night before, Paul. He said he stayed at a friend's house."

"Wow, I didn't know. He hasn't come by here, and he hasn't called me, either. Do you think he is upset with me too?"

"I don't know, Paul; he seemed fine this morning. He said he was going for a walk to be alone for a little bit."

"Okay, I see. Well, when he gets back, will you have him call me, please? And Michelle, remember to just do your best to try and stay calm. We need to get the coin from him somehow."

"Sure, Paul, I will. Take care. Miss you," she said.

Paul was a bit surprised at Michelle's response; it made him stutter for a second, and then he said, "Ah … umm, yeah, miss you too, Michelle." Paul hung up the phone and sat there a little confused. Why had Michelle said that? Did she have another meaning to her statement? He wondered.

For several months now, Michelle had begun to look at Paul a little differently—not in a bad way, just as more than a friend. She'd had certain thoughts about him, and now it seemed some of those thoughts and feelings were beginning to surface. Paul had never really thought about Michelle that way. Yes, she was beautiful; yes, she had long, light-brown hair and deep-blue eyes, exactly what he looked for in a woman, but she and Jon Paul were a couple. You never cross that line; that is an unwritten rule, one he has never broken. One he would never break. Paul continued to think about what Michelle had said and what it meant—to him.

***

Jon Paul sat in the bar for some time sipping his brandy. Each time Liz would catch him staring at her, they both would flirt just a little and smile at each other. Both were having a good day. Time slipped away for Liz and Jon Paul, and after awhile, he decided it was time for him to leave. "Hey, Liz, I better go," he said, getting up from his chair.

"You better call me tonight, Jon Paul," she said.

"I will, Liz, see you later." She winked at him and Jon Paul smiled coyly. *Hopefully no one else saw that*, he thought.

But Jon Paul was wrong. A few men there had seen them flirting, and some even wondered about the two of them. Jon Paul walked the long way home. He was still thinking about Liz and their night together; it had been so passionate and so wonderfully new. Jon Paul would try to call Liz tonight when Michelle went to sleep. He would just wait it out till she went to bed.

***

Michelle had kept herself busy for most of the day with small household chores. It was a way for her to keep from going crazy worrying about her and Jon Paul.

Michelle was just beginning to think about Paul, when she heard the door unlock and in walked Jon Paul.

"Hi, Michelle, I'm home."

"Hi, Jon Paul. I am here." They sat down and began to talk about their day. Both had certain things they wanted to say. Jon Paul wanted to talk more about their fight, and Michelle thought it better to talk about it later. Neither side got too much accomplished, at least as far as resolving their fight. The rest of the night was slow and uneventful. Jon Paul sat and watched TV, and Michelle sat beside him, occasionally getting up to refresh their drinks or grab a quick snack.

When it came time for them to go to bed, Jon Paul was hesitant and thought he might want a bedtime snack before he went to sleep, so Michelle went alone. Jon Paul would join her in a few minutes. While Michelle was getting ready for bed, Jon Paul saw his chance. He could call Liz now and talk for a quick minute. It would have to suffice for now. He picked up the phone and dialed.

"Hello," said Liz.

"Hello, lover," said Jon Paul. Liz laughed.

"Hello yourself," she replied.

"How are you tonight?" asked Jon.

"I am fine; been waiting for your call," said Liz.

"Sorry, baby. I called as soon as I could."

"Well, I am glad you did. I didn't want to go to bed without hearing your voice tonight."

"Yeah, me either. I miss you, Lizzy."

"I miss you, Jon Paul."

"Listen, Liz, I better cut this short. Maybe I can see you tomorrow."

"Yeah, but I am working the late shift tomorrow."

"If I can't make it in to see you, then I will call—okay?"

"Okay, Jon Paul, see you later."

"Night, Liz."

They hung up the phones; each had heard the other's voice, and they were content to wait till tomorrow to see each other. Jon Paul would try to find a way to see Liz without drawing attention to himself, and Liz would just have to do the same. Jon Paul walked up the stairs to his bedroom. Michelle was already in bed. He was dreading this night. After being with Liz, there was no way he wanted to be with anyone else, least of all Michelle. But he got himself ready for bed and crawled in. Michelle stirred and looked at him. "Jon Paul, are you okay?"

"Yeah, I just have a bit of a headache."

"Do you want me to get you some aspirin?" asked Michelle.

"No thanks, sweetie, I already took some."

Michelle fell asleep quickly; she was so tired from a lack of good sleep. Jon Paul, however, didn't sleep. His mind was on Liz. He so wanted to be with her and sleep in her warm bed; he was unable to unwind, so he laid there and stared at the ceiling. As the moments passed and Jon Paul wondered how long it had been, the minutes turned into hours. Soon it would be morning, and he would have to wake up next to Michelle. For Jon Paul, sleep had become a game he could never win, but eventually, he just gave in and drifted off to sleep. He finally found some peace of mind in his dreams, or so he was to believe … Jon Paul's dreams were again of a madman killing other men in some kind of war; he had no idea that these dreams were a glimpse of his past.

The next morning as they awoke, Jon Paul was feeling a little better. He had gotten some sleep and was sort of refreshed. Michelle had slept like a rock all night; she was feeling recharged, bright-eyed and bushy-tailed, cheerful as well. "Good morning, Jon Paul."

"Good morning," was all he said. He had other things on his mind, namely Liz. They both got up and got dressed and then went downstairs to the kitchen to find something to eat.

"Jon Paul, what do you want for breakfast?"

"Umm, whatever you want to cook is fine with me." Michelle cooked breakfast. She made eggs, toast, and those little breaded treats Jon Paul loved so much. As they sat and ate, neither said much; both were thinking about other things.

"Jon Paul, are you going anywhere specific today?"

"I hadn't thought about it yet, but maybe down to the docks."

"Do you mind if I come along with you this morning?"

Jon Paul was a bit surprised at her question and said, "How about tomorrow? I might stop by Paul's this morning too."

"Really, Jon Paul, I just want to be with you."

"I know, Michelle, but I still need time to myself—okay?"

"Okay, how about I make us a nice dinner tonight?"

"Yeah, sounds good, Michelle." Jon Paul and Michelle finished eating, and while Michelle was cleaning up the dishes, Jon Paul grabbed his coat and went out the door. He didn't kiss Michelle or even give her a hug. He was happy to be out of there for a while. Michelle hadn't noticed Jon Paul getting up and leaving, but when she did, she just thought he must need time alone, like he had said. She didn't think it peculiar at all, especially after what they had just been through. Michelle began to plan her meal for that night. She would cook a nice dinner for them both and it would be like old times before their fight, she thought.

***

Paul was sitting, having his morning tea, when the phone rang. "Hello."

"Hi, Paul, it's Michelle."

"Hi, Michelle, what's up?"

"Nothing, Paul, just wanted to tell you Jon Paul left a while ago. I was wondering, if he stops by there, could you call me when he leaves?"

"Sure thing, Michelle, is everything all right?"

"Yes, things are okay, but Jon Paul seems very distant from me."

"Did he say something?"

"No, he is just cold and far away from me and is a bit distracted, I think."

"Does he suspect anything is wrong, Michelle?"

"No, I don't think so."

"Well, then, take it easy and remember to try and stay calm; we will find a way to get that coin from him."

"Thanks, Paul, you are my best friend right now. I don't know what I would do without you."

"Anytime, Michelle, anytime. I am always here for you."

"See you later, Paul."

"See you later, Michelle, bye."

Paul and Michelle were becoming fast friends. They had a common bond together in Jon Paul, and this would bring them closer than ever before—something neither of them was looking for.

***

Jon Paul walked down to the docks. Although this took him some time to do, he wasn't far from Paul Pierre's apartment, and he thought he might stop by there to see if Paul had conspired with Michelle to steal the coin from him. The docks were nearly empty. Most of the fishing boats had already left for the morning's catch and hadn't returned yet, but there were a few still there. Jon Paul decided to talk with some of them.

As he approached a lone fisherman tying his hooks, the fisherman looked up and said, "Hey there, young man. What can I do for you?"

"Do you give rides on your boat?"

"Sure do, for a price."

"How much?" asked Jon Paul.

"For you, sonny boy, fifty euros per hour."

"Fifty euros per hour? Deal," said Jon Paul. He didn't know he was getting a good deal; he just wanted a ride on a boat for a couple of hours. They untied the ropes from the docks and got ready to take a ride. This would be the first boat ride Jon Paul had been on in a long time—in fact, since he was young. The boat's engine roared as they pulled out to sea. Jon Paul was excited to be on the ocean again; he felt a certain ease with it. He thought, *I wonder if the captain will let me do some fishing for a while? Yeah, probably for a price.*

But that didn't matter to Jon Paul. He was having a really good time and the salty smell of the sea brought back memories of when he was a youth sailing with his father in the south bay of France.

***

Paul Pierre had decided to try and call Dr. Martin again today while he was alone this morning. He dialed the phone.

"Good morning. Dr. Martin's office; how may I help you?"

"Is Dr. Martin in this morning?" asked Paul.

"No, I am sorry, he's not; he won't be back till tomorrow, sir. Do you wish to leave a message for him?"

"Ah, no, I will just call back tomorrow. What time will he be in?"

"He will be in at ten a.m., sir."

"Okay, thanks, I will try him then. Bye."

Paul would just have to wait to speak with Dr. Martin till tomorrow, and that was fine, he thought. Hopefully he would be able to get some background information on this coin of Jon's. Paul was sure the coin was very old; in fact, he was even sure it had been used for evil and selfish purposes. The history of the coin had him very curious, yet he knew so very little about it.

***

Jon Paul was sitting on the port side of the boat when the captain approached him. "Do you want to do some fishing, son?"

"Yeah, sure, that would be great!" said Jon Paul.

"Okay, if you want, but I am going to have to charge you a few more euros."

"Yeah, sure, captain, how much now?"

"How about twenty-five and we will call it even?"

Jon Paul was beginning to think this captain was trying to take him for his money, so he said to him, "Okay, twenty-five it is—but nothing more."

"Deal," said the captain. Jon Paul wasn't worried about the money. He knew he could make a wish when the captain wasn't looking and have plenty of money to pay for both his boat ride and fishing trip. They settled into a quiet morning as Jon Paul dropped his line over the side of the boat and let it sink for a while.

He would catch a fish today and bring it home for dinner, he thought. This would show Michelle that he had answered her ultimatum. Time passed for Jon Paul. He wasn't getting any bites or even nibbles. He was getting frustrated; this was supposed to be a relaxing boat ride. He began fidgeting in his pocket, and suddenly, he thought *the coin*! Yes, he could make a wish for a big fish; that would be great! When the captain wasn't looking and had walked over to the other side of the boat, Jon Paul held the coin tight and said, "I wish for a big fish to land on my hook right now." *Poof*! There it was.

As he yelled in delight, his line became tight and the pole began to bend with the weight of the fish. It was pulling the line strongly, and when the captain heard his yell, he ran over and said, "Whoa, you got a big one there! Take it slow now and let him tire himself out first; just reel him in a little at a time."

Jon Paul reeled him in slowly. He let the big fish tire himself out, and as he got near the boat, the captain had his net ready. "Slowly, get him closer to the boat, boy. Slowly," said the captain. Jon Paul did exactly as he was told, and as the fish got close to the boat, the captain was looking at it. "Wow, that is one of the biggest fish I have ever seen. Careful now, let's get him on board."

Jon Paul reeled him in, and the captain used his big net to help bring the great fish on deck. He was a giant; the captain hadn't seen a fish this big in years. He was sure this might be a record. The captain had heard tales of fish this big, especially this kind of fish, but he had never seen one this big in all of his fifty years of fishing.

"You must be some kind of lucky, my boy. I never seen one this big!"

Jon Paul laughed under his breath; he knew it was the magic of the coin. As they headed back to shore and the fishing docks, Jon Paul thought he would be able to call Liz later at his apartment when he would have Michelle go to the market for some fresh fruit and some vegetables to cook for their dinner tonight. When they arrived back at the docks, there were some other boats there too; many men had returned from their morning's catch and were getting ready to sell their fish at the local market. Jon Paul was not interested in selling his catch; he was going to eat the great fish.

When the captain wasn't looking, Jon Paul grabbed his magic coin and made his wish for money to pay the captain. Instantly in his hands was the money. He paid the captain, thanked him, and then he got off the boat with his catch and began the walk back to his apartment. His boat ride had made him forget about Paul Pierre for the moment. He walked with his head held high; this was a great day for him. As Jon Paul approached his apartment, he was beginning to feel the weight of the great fish. It was heavy, quite a burden. He sighed; he had carried the fish the whole way back and was now happy to finally be home. He put the key in the lock, turned the doorknob, and went in.

"Michelle, I am home."

"Hi, Jon Paul. What is that?" she exclaimed.

"That is my catch of the year, Michelle."

"That is a really big fish. Where did you get it?"

"Well, I did go to the docks, and I ended up taking a boat ride with this captain who let me fish while we were out to sea."

"So you caught it?" asked Michelle.

"Yes, Michelle, I caught it," he said, growing annoyed at her questioning. "Why are you doubting me?"

"I'm not doubting you, Jon Paul. I was just asking."

"Okay, then, I want to have some of this fish for our dinner tonight."

"Okay, I will cook some of this fish for us tonight for our dinner; do you want anything else, Jon Paul?"

"Umm, no, whatever else is fine—oh wait, Michelle."

"Yes, Jon Paul, what is it?"

"I need you to go to the market and get some fresh fruit and some vegetables for tonight too."

"You sure, Jon Paul? We have some vegetables here."

"Yes, I want fresh to celebrate my catch of the year."

Now Jon Paul had come up with a way to get Michelle out of his apartment, at least for a little while, so he could call his love Liz. The day passed in silence for Jon Paul and Michelle; neither said much. Michelle busied herself in the kitchen preparing the meal, and Jon Paul did some cleaning chores around their apartment. When it came time for Michelle to leave for the market, Jon Paul was elated to see her go. Now he could call his beloved Liz and hear her sweet voice.

"Jon Paul, I am ready to go to the market."

"Yeah, okay, Michelle. Can you grab a bottle of wine too?"

"Sure, honey, anything specific?"

"No, whatever will be fine, Michelle."

Michelle got herself ready to leave and Jon Paul walked her to the door. "I would go with you, honey, but I am a bit tired after today." He smiled at her.

The moment was not lost on her; she smiled back and said, "Thanks, Jon Paul. I know you needed a day like today. I will be fine." She closed the door behind her and walked down the street to the market. Michelle was feeling good about their relationship. Jon Paul was now sitting by the phone dialing the bar where Liz worked; he remembered she was working the late shift.

"Hello, the Goat's Head Bar."

"Hi. I was wondering if I might speak with Lizzette," asked Jon Paul.

"Sure, hang on, okay? Who is this?"

"Jon Paul."

"Hold on, Jon Paul," said Jacques.

"Hello, this is Liz."

"Hi, Lizzy, it's Jon Paul."

"Jon Paul, hi, how are you?" she said excitedly.

"I am fine, Liz. I miss you."

"I miss you too, Jon Paul. Are you coming to see me tonight?"

"I don't know if I can. I want to, but I don't think I can get out tonight."

"How about tomorrow? I will be home in the morning, so can we do something then?"

"Yes, Liz, I will find a way to see you tomorrow."

"You better, Jon Paul. I want to see you."

"Okay, Liz, we will see each other tomorrow. I promise."

Jon Paul and Liz would find a way to see each other tomorrow. Now Jon Paul was going to have to come up with another plan so he could see her, but that might not be easy.

Michelle had finished her shopping at the market and was walking back when she began to have a thought—was Jon Paul hiding something?

She had never seen a fish that big, and it was strange that Jon Paul caught it. He never went fishing or even on a boat ride, and where did he get the extra money for that? *What is going on here?* She thought. Michelle kept walking until she reached their apartment; she had quickened her pace and was back in no time. She wanted to see Jon Paul face-to-face and confront him about the fish, maybe ask him if anything strange happened. She was going to ask him in a way that hopefully didn't arouse any suspicions about her intentions with his coin. Any sort of arguments could ruin it for her and Paul to be able to get rid of the coin. She must be sly, she thought. As she opened the door and came in, Jon Paul walked over to her and helped her with the bags of food. They brought them into the kitchen and sat them on the counter where they could unpack them and use them for the meal.

"Wow, Michelle, it all looks great."

"Thanks, honey. I think I got everything you wanted."

"Yeah, looks like it. Do you need any help?" asked Jon Paul.

"No, no; you just go sit in the living room and relax, watch some TV. I will tell you when it is ready."

"Okay, Michelle. I will be out here if you need any help."

Jon Paul went into the living room to relax and wait for dinner. Michelle was a great cook, and he really did enjoy her cooking so very much. Jon Paul sat and as he sat and waited for dinner, he remembered something his father had told him a few days ago: to call the museum and ask for some doctor named Martin. He started to think, *do I really need to call this man? I know what the coin can do for me. I think I will just let it go and keep it to myself from now on; the less people that know about my coin, the less they will want to try and take it from me.*

While this made him feel better, he still was suspicious about his friend Paul and Michelle. Jon Paul decided to just watch TV and not worry too much about that now. Michelle prepared the fish, got the fruit ready, and started to steam the vegetables. This was going to be a meal to brag about, she thought. While everything was cooking, Michelle thought she would call Paul to see if Jon Paul had stopped by there today, even though he said he didn't. As Michelle dialed the phone, she kept watch on the dinner with a sharp eye.

"Hello," said Paul.

"Hello, Paul, it's Michelle," she said, almost whispering.

"Hi, Michelle. What's happening?"

"Nothing right now. Everything is fine. I am cooking a fish for dinner tonight."

"Fish sounds nice," said Paul.

"Yeah, but Paul, I think there is something strange with this fish."

"What do you mean, Michelle?"

"It is so big, Paul; I mean, I have never seen a fish this big. Jon Paul said he caught it today on some fishing boat."

"Well, it is strange that he went fishing. That, he never does; do you think he might have wished for it?"

"Maybe, Paul, I don't know. I think I better go for now. Do you think you could come over tomorrow so we could talk about it some more?"

"Sure, that would be great! What time?"

"Let me call you; we have to wait for Jon Paul to leave first."

"Sure thing, Michelle. I will see you tomorrow."

"Yes, see you tomorrow, Paul. Bye."

Jon Paul had been in the living room watching TV while all this had taken place. Because he had a question for Michelle about dinner, he had walked into the kitchen, and all he heard was, "See you tomorrow, Paul." Jon Paul had overheard Michelle talking to Paul; he began to think there might be something funny going on. Although he had no proof, he did know that the two of them were planning on seeing each other tomorrow. He walked back into the living room and sat down; anger began to fill his heart, hatred also. His mind wandered with all sorts of thoughts, like could he trust Michelle? Maybe she was cheating on him with his best friend! He didn't know for sure, but he felt determined to learn the truth about the two of them. One thing he did know for sure—they were jealous of his coin and wanted it for themselves. Jon Paul's paranoia had grown; he also failed to realize that Michelle was no longer his—she had found another.

As dinner cooked, Michelle watched it carefully. She didn't want to take a chance on ruining their night together. After all, this was like a first for them; after such a big fight, she wanted to make sure they were still a couple. Michelle was going to do all she could to make sure it worked out.

Jon Paul sat in his chair and thought. His paranoia grew, and he soon began to think there was something going on. While Michelle cooked dinner, Jon Paul was thinking of ways to trap her into admitting that she was messing around. He really had nothing to go on except what he had heard her say to Paul. Jon Paul thought, *Maybe I am wrong. Maybe I am just overreacting. Why would they want to see each other? What could the two of them have to talk about ... unless ... ah-ha! I know what it is: they want my coin! Oh, they will never get it. I will die before I give up this coin to those two.*

"Jon Paul, dinner's almost ready. Just a few more minutes, okay?" This shook Jon Paul to his core. He had been so deep in thought, he had not heard her till she had finished saying *minutes*, and then it all clicked and brought him back to reality.

"Yeah, be right in, Michelle."

Michelle had made a beautiful dinner for them, fresh-caught fish, fresh vegetables and fruit from the market. The table had two candlesticks lit with white candles and there was a nice, open bottle of red wine. The mood was nice and romantic, and she hoped this would have Jon Paul feeling like his old self again. It had been awhile since she went all out like this.

Jon Paul walked into the kitchen and was surprised. Michelle had done a wonderful job of making a romantic dinner for the both of them. He sat down at the table and could smell the great meal prepared by Michelle, who had been trained years ago by one of the best chefs in all of France.

Michelle served him a piece of fish with some fresh garlic bread, a plate of steamed veggies and some steamed rice. A dinner fit for a king for sure. She then served herself and sat down across from him. "How is everything, Jon Paul?" she asked in a loving way.

"It is very good, Michelle, you have outdone yourself with this one."

"Thank you, Jon Paul, that is sweet."

He smiled at her, and they both continued to eat. They sat and enjoyed the meal without saying a whole lot. They had been together for many years now, so the silence was not uncomfortable for them. Once in a while, one of them would say something, but nothing lengthy in conversation. This continued for an hour, each one enjoying the other's company with the occasional smile to let the other one know they were having a good time.

"Michelle, that was great!"

"Thanks, sweetie, glad you enjoyed it. Do you want anything else?"

"No, but we should do this again sometime."

"Whew, I don't know, Jon Paul. This was a lot of work; maybe if you helped me next time?"

"Yeah, sure, I can help you anytime, Michelle."

They finished eating and Jon Paul helped Michelle clean up the dishes and the rest of the kitchen. He was being a perfect boyfriend; at least, that was what Michelle thought.

"Michelle," said Jon Paul, "I think I will go sit down in the living room and watch some TV."

"Sure thing, honey, I will be there shortly," she replied. Soon, they were sitting on the couch together. It did not feel awkward for Jon Paul; they had done this a thousand times before. He was used to sitting next to Michelle. He did think about Liz, though.

***

Liz was cleaning up the bar when Jacques approached her. "Hey, Liz, I need to speak with you for a minute."

"Be right there, Jacques." She was wiping down the tables and putting the chairs on them so they could sweep the floor. When she had finished, she walked over to where Jacques was standing. "What's up, Jacques?" said Liz.

"Ah … mmm … I wanted to ask you about Jon Paul."

"What about him?"

"Well, it seems as of late, you are getting a bit friendly with him. Now, I have no problem with that, but he is still with Michelle."

"Yes, I know, it is just that they had a fight and we talked, and since then, we have gotten closer."

"How close?" asked Jacques.

"Just you don't worry about it—that it is between me and Jon Paul."

"Well, just be careful Liz; a lot of people in this bar don't approve of illicit love affairs."

"Thanks, Jacques, but I don't really care about what people in this bar think." Liz shot him a steady glance and Jacques knew he had said his piece and that was enough.

"Are we finished here?" Liz asked.

"Yeah, I can close up if you want to go home now."

"Umm, yeah, that will be good. I am a little tired tonight," Liz replied.

Liz walked home thinking about Jon Paul, wondering if he would call at this late hour. Probably not, but at least she would see him tomorrow, and that would have to be good for now.

***

63

Jon Paul and Michelle sat on the couch till it had become late. Michelle had fallen asleep and Jon Paul didn't want to wake her, so he had let her sleep. Soon, she opened her eyes and looked at him and said, "I think I am going to bed, you coming?"

"Yeah, you go ahead and get ready. I will be right there." Michelle got up and went upstairs to bed. Jon Paul sat there for a moment, wondering if he should call Liz.

Michelle was already in bed as Jon Paul walked into their bedroom. He had got himself ready for bed and joined her. "You know, Michelle, that was one great dinner!"

"Thanks, honey—glad you caught that fish so we could eat it!" replied Michelle.

"Yeah, that was a bit of luck," said Jon Paul, grinning.

"I think we have enough fish for the next three months, Jon Paul." Jon Paul laughed under his breath as he crawled into bed.

When morning broke, Jon Paul was feeling good. He had doubts about Paul and Michelle, so today he was going to try and find out more about the two of them. He awoke without disturbing Michelle, who was still lying peacefully beside him. He gently got up, got dressed, and went downstairs. He made himself a nice cup of hot tea and ate a sweet roll. He sat in the kitchen in silence. Oftentimes, he would think about visiting his friend Paul, but with this doubt about him and Michelle, he really didn't want to talk with him. While Jon Paul finished his roll and tea, he decided to take a walk early and then come home before Michelle awoke. He could think about how he wanted to approach this matter while he walked and hopefully found a solution to this problem.

Jon Paul walked out the door and into the cool morning air. It filled his lungs with a feeling of fullness and, breathing deeply, he walked briskly down the street. There were not a lot of people out this morning. Sometimes, though, there could be quite a few people walking to work or the local market, where he enjoyed shopping frequently. Today wasn't a holiday, he thought, maybe just a slow day, so he walked and walked.

Michelle was still fast asleep when Jon Paul got back to their apartment. He was very quiet as he moved about, so as not to disturb her sleep. Soon she had awoke and looked around their room.

"Jon Paul, are you here?"

"Yes, Michelle, I am here."

Michelle got up, got dressed, and walked downstairs to see Jon Paul. "Good morning, sweetie. How are you?" she asked.

"Good," replied Jon Paul.

"Did you go for a walk, Jon Paul?"

"Yeah, I went for a short one this morning. Michelle, I want to ask you a question."

"Yes, Jon Paul?"

"Who were you talking with on the phone last night?"

"Oh, that was Paul. He was wondering how you were; he said he hadn't talked with you for a while and was worried."

"Did he say anything else, Michelle?"

"Umm, no." Michelle was beginning to get worried.

"Are you sure, Michelle? That doesn't sound like Paul."

"It was nothing, Jon Paul. He was just asking about you, that's all."

"Okay, then, I won't worry about it." He was worried, though; he knew instinctively they were planning something that had to do with his coin. He would find out what it was; it was just a matter of time, he told himself.

Michelle smiled at Jon Paul and then walked into the kitchen to make herself some breakfast. She had not been there long when Jon Paul walked in. "What are you cooking?" he asked.

"Oh, just something simple, maybe some eggs and a croissant."

"That sounds good!" he said.

"Do you want me to make you some, Jon Paul?"

"No thanks, Michelle. I ate earlier before my walk. It does smell good, though."

As she made herself some breakfast, Jon Paul sat in the kitchen, watching her. He was looking to find some cracks in her weakened armor.

She poured them both a cup of tea and sat down at the table with its wobbly legs.

"You got any plans today, Jon Paul?" Michelle asked.

"Well, not really plans. I might take a walk down to the Old Town Shops."

She smiled. "You looking for anything in particular, Jon Paul?"

"No. Maybe. I don't know. I might find something I need. How about you, Michelle, you got any plans for today?"

"No, nothing much. I will probably work on dinner for tonight, anything you want in particular?"

"Let me think about it for a while, okay?" They sat and she ate and they drank their tea. All the while, Michelle was thinking about Paul, and Jon Paul was thinking about Liz. After an hour of sitting in the kitchen, Jon Paul was getting restless again. He was ready to take his walk down to the Old Town Shops. Although it was peculiar for him to walk twice in one morning, he was planning on it anyway. He was going to see Liz no matter what the cost. As he got up to get ready, Michelle looked at him and said, "You leaving, Jon Paul?"

"Yeah, I am about ready." He grabbed his coat and walked toward the door. Michelle walked behind him.

"Jon Paul, please be careful."

"Ah, yeah, thanks, Michelle. I will." She hugged him and he hugged her back, and for a brief moment, he forgot about Liz. Jon Paul walked out into the street and down the sidewalk. He was going to see his beloved Liz. As soon as Jon Paul had left the apartment, Michelle had picked up the phone and dialed Paul. She would have him come over so they could plan on how they could take the cursed coin from Jon Paul, no matter what.

"Hello," said Paul.

"Hi, Paul. It's Michelle."

"Hi, Michelle!" he said excitedly.

"Jon Paul just left. You wanna come over now?"

"Yeah. I can be there in about thirty minutes, okay?"

"Yeah, that will be good, Paul. Just hurry, okay? I don't know how long Jon Paul will be gone."

"Okay, Michelle. I will be there soon. Bye."

"Bye," she replied.

Paul got himself ready. He was going to see Michelle, and they would come up with a plan to take the coin from Jon Paul. Michelle was excited as well; she thought, *finally, we will be able to figure out a way to rid Jon Paul of that coin, and we can go back to the way it was before.* Michelle desperately wanted Jon Paul back the way he was before, but this would not be an easy task. The coin was possessing him, and there would be no turning back.

***

Jon Paul walked down the street toward Liz's apartment. He would surprise her by showing up unannounced and not really planned on, at least not at a set time. As he got closer to her apartment, he began to think, *Should I bring her something to show her how much I missed her, maybe some flowers or perhaps a necklace? Yes, a necklace would be nice. I will wish for a diamond necklace and then give it to her; all women love diamond necklaces.* So he grabbed the coin from his pocket. It felt warm, and it was pulsating in his hand. He felt flushed as he steadied himself and thought of what to say. He said, "I wish for a diamond necklace!" *Poof!* There it was, shiny and sparkling in his hand. He would give this to Liz to show her how much he loved her and missed her. He had just about gotten to Liz's apartment when he felt the coin again.

It seemed like it was talking to him; he thought he could hear strange voices. They were very far away from his mind, but he could just make out a few words now and then. It was like the coin was alive!

● ● ●

Chapter Six

THE MURDER

Paul Pierre had gotten himself ready and was now on his way to see Michelle. He had told her he would be there in about a half hour. He was right on time as he walked up to her building and pushed the button for her apartment.

"Yes," said Michelle.

"It is Paul."

"Come on in, Paul." The buzzer sounded, unlocking the door. He pulled on it and walked in. He hadn't been here in some time, but the building still looked nice. It was in great shape for being more than two hundred years old, he thought. He knocked on Michelle's door.

"Coming, Paul." When Michelle opened the door, Paul was astounded. Michelle looked so very beautiful the way the light shone off her hair and the way it accented her sapphire eyes. He had never seen her look this way before. For a moment, he forgot why he was there.

"Come in, Paul; you look great!"

"Thanks, Michelle; you look … ah, good too," he stammered. He felt his face turn beet-red as he said that. He hoped Michelle hadn't noticed.

"Do you want anything to drink, Paul?"

"No thanks, Michelle. We should talk about what we are going to do about Jon Paul."

"Paul, will you hold on? I am going to get a drink; be right back. You sit down on the couch if you want." Paul sat on the couch and waited for Michelle to return from the kitchen. Michelle had walked into the kitchen to get a drink. She brought it back out to the living room with her and sat down across from Paul. "So, Paul, what are we going to do about Jon Paul?"

"I don't really know, Michelle. I have been trying to call this Dr. Martin at the museum, but he won't be back till tomorrow, and he is the one man who can maybe tell us more about the coin."

"Is he an expert?"

"Yes, he specializes in antique coins from the Byzantine Empire time period."

"So how are we going to get that coin from Jon Paul, and just how do you know it is from the Byzantine Empire?"

"Now, Michelle, if you remember, my minor in college was ancient artifacts. I recognized the style of the coin as roughly that time period. Most, if not all, of the coins that were stamped at that time had the face of a certain general or a leader that the people followed. When Jon Paul first showed me the coin, I was almost certain of its time period. I went to the library yesterday and I found a similar one that was from the same, or at least close to the same, time period. I am sure I am right."

"Are you positive, Paul?"

"Yes, Michelle, but you know me, I am hardly ever wrong!"

"Oh, okay, Mr. Ego!" They both laughed at this, but Paul was right; even without a professional opinion, he had guessed the time period accurately.

***

Jon Paul walked up to the door and knocked. Liz opened it and said, "Jon Paul!"

He smiled and said, "Hi."

"Come in, come in," she said excitedly. They walked over to the couch, and before he could sit down, Liz grabbed him and planted a long, passionate kiss on him. Jon Paul responded the same to her.

"What a surprise you are, Jon Paul, I thought you were going to call first."

"I was, but then I thought, why not just come over and surprise you!"

"Well, you definitely did that!"

"Ah, Liz, I … ah, um, I bought something for you."

"Really, Jon Paul, you didn't have to."

"Yeah, I know, but I still did. So anyway, close your eyes first."

Liz did exactly as Jon Paul asked her. She was smiling from ear to ear with excitement. Jon Paul moved her hair away from her neck so he could put the necklace on her. As he fastened it, she heard a clicking sound as it clasped, and then he said, "Okay, you can look now."

As Liz looked at the diamond necklace, her jaw dropped; she was not expecting such a nice and obviously expensive gift. "Jon Paul, it is the most beautiful thing I have ever seen. Are you sure you want me to have it?"

"Of course, my love, it is only for you."

Liz began to cry. Tears of joy streamed down her face; Jon Paul gently wiped them away. "You know, Liz, I have never felt like this about anyone."

"Me either, Jon Paul." They embraced, feeling a closeness neither had ever felt before with anyone else. The love they had found for each other was beyond measure, it was like soul mates reunited and becoming one again. Jon Paul and Liz talked for several hours before he realized it was time for him to go.

"Liz, I better go. Time is moving, and I gotta get back."

"Can't you stay for just a little while longer, pleeeaaassssseee?"

"Well, only a little while, okay? I need time to figure this all out with Michelle."

Jon Paul had kept his promise to Liz. He had seen her, just like he said, and he had given her a beautiful necklace to wear, but now he needed to go. He didn't want to draw attention to himself just yet. He must be able to make a clean break with Michelle or things could be very risky for him, especially if she was conspiring with Paul to take his coin. Liz walked arm in arm with Jon Paul as he got up to leave her apartment, and as they got to the door, she gave him a very soft kiss and told him how much he meant to her.

Jon Paul nodded in agreement with her and said, "Liz, I just want you to know how much you mean to me."

"I know, baby; I know, and I feel the same. Call me tonight, okay?"

"You got it, as soon as I can," he said. Jon Paul walked out the door and down the street. His mind began to wander as he walked. He thought about Paul, and he also thought about Michelle; he wondered what they could be up to. Were they planning on trying to take the coin from him for their own selfish needs? *Of course they are,* he thought, *but they will never get it from me. It is mine forever! I will never let it go,* he vowed to himself.

***

Paul and Michelle were still talking when Paul noticed the time and said, "Michelle, I probably better go."

"Yeah, I guess Jon Paul could be back any minute now."

"You know, Michelle, you can call me anytime," he said and winked at her.

"Why, Paul, are you flirting with me?" she asked coyly.

"Maybe—what if I am?" he said, smiling.

"I don't know, Paul, you could be asking for trouble," she said, smiling.

"Well, I think I could handle that."

As Paul got up to leave, Michelle followed him to the door, and as he opened it, she embraced him tightly and said, "Paul, I don't know what I would do without you." He looked at her longingly, and they shared a soft kiss.

Paul walked out the door and Michelle walked back into the kitchen. She had crossed the line with Paul, but strangely enough, it didn't feel wrong, what with Jon Paul pulling away from her and becoming more and more distant. She had kissed Paul and although she didn't realize it, a smile had planted itself on her face. As Michelle kept herself busy in the kitchen, she had no idea how things were about to change, and not for the better.

The phone rang, and Michelle went to answer it. "Hello," she said.

"Hi, Michelle?"

"Yes, this is Michelle."

"Hi, Michelle, this is Maggie."

"Oh, hi, Maggie, how are you?"

"Fine, thanks. Michelle, how are you?"

"I am good, Maggie, seems like ages since we last spoke."

"Yes, it has been awhile," Maggie replied.

"So what have you been doing?"

"Oh, you know, just working at the restaurant, and I still do a little painting now and then."

"How nice."

"Um, Michelle, I don't mean to cut this short, but I wanted to ask you a question."

"What is it, Maggie?"

"Umm, well the other day, I was working, you know, and it was early in the morning, but anyway, this couple comes in and sits down—at least, they looked like a couple."

"Yes, go on."

"I didn't recognize them at first—at least, the woman I didn't know—but they sat down and I took their order."

Michelle took a deep breath and said, "Okay, you took their order, and then what?"

"Like I said, I didn't recognize them at first, but when I brought them their order, I remembered the man."

"So who was he, Maggie?"

"I am so sorry, Michelle; please forgive me, but it was Jon Paul."

Michelle was shocked. She didn't know whether to believe her or not, but then she remembered the other night when Jon Paul didn't come home till the next day. He had said he stayed at a friend's house.

"Michelle, are you going to be all right?"

"No, Maggie, I am not, but thanks for calling to tell me."

"Michelle, I am sorry I had to be the one to tell you about this."

"It is okay, Maggie. I will be fine. I gotta go. Bye."

"Bye."

The two women hung up the phone, and Michelle was still shocked about the news of Jon Paul. She was so upset that she was shaking.

Jon Paul was nearing his home. As he walked, he wondered if Paul had been busy trying to think of ways to get his coin from him. He walked up the stairs to his home, turned the key in the lock, and walked in. Michelle was sitting in the kitchen, her face wet with tears. As he walked closer to her, he knew.

"Jon Paul, how could you?" she cried.

"How could I what?"

"You know, you son of a bitch!"

"What?"

"You, you … I hate you, Jon Paul!"

"Yeah, well, so what? I told you I would use the coin for our benefit, and you wanted nothing to do with it."

"Oh, Jon Paul, you have changed. You are not the same man I fell in love with."

"Everybody changes, Michelle."

Michelle sobbed and ran upstairs. She could not bear the thought of Jon Paul with another woman, yet she had just kissed Paul Pierre earlier—this fact had escaped her troubled mind.

Jon Paul sat in the kitchen, wondering how Michelle had found out about him and Liz. Maybe she had heard it somewhere, but she never went anywhere, so who could have told her? He sat and pondered this thought. No answers came to him. He was at a loss as to who had told her or how she could have found out.

***

Maggie had done what she thought best; she had revealed the truth to her friend Michelle, and the pieces had fallen where they were. Michelle's heart lay broken on the floor. Maggie could only hope that Michelle would be all right soon and be back on her feet in no time.

***

As Jon Paul contemplated in his kitchen for what seemed like an eternity to him, he tried to go over every possible scenario in his head, trying to figure out what had happened. Then, as he sat and gazed out the window, a thought occurred to him: Liz, the restaurant. Right then, he knew what had happened. Maggie, the waitress at the restaurant where he had breakfast the other day with Liz, had seen them together—she must have called Michelle and told her. It was funny how this hadn't occurred to him earlier. No wonder he was always the last one to get it, he thought. He walked upstairs to where Michelle was. She was sitting on the bed, crying. He said to her, "Michelle, I don't know what happened."

She looked at him, her cheeks streaked from tears smudging her eye shadow.

"Jon Paul, I don't even know what to say to you."

"There is nothing to say, Michelle."

"Don't you even care anymore, Jon Paul?"

"Of course I care, but you have gone too far, Michelle."

"*I* have gone too far?" she screamed.

"Yeah, you have pushed me beyond my limits, so—"

"So what now, Jon Paul?"

"I don't know, Michelle."

"Maybe you should leave, Jon Paul."

"Me leave?" he said, not believing her.

"Yes, you should go."

"I am not leaving. You leave, Michelle!"

"Maybe I will, Jon Paul!"

"Then go—what are you waiting for?"

"I will, then!" yelled Michelle. She then stood up, walked to the closet, and took out a suitcase. She threw it on the bed, opened up the dresser where she had some clothes, and began packing the suitcase.

"Oh, this is rich; you going somewhere?" Jon Paul said sarcastically.

"Yes, Jon Paul; if you won't leave, then I will. I can't be here with you anymore."

"Sure, you're leaving. I don't believe you." But Michelle was serious; she was packing and she was leaving him.

"Okay, Michelle, so just where do you think you are going?" She didn't answer him; she only continued to pack her things. "Michelle, you go then; I will be fine without you." Michelle finished packing some of her clothes, at least as much as she could get in a suitcase, and she walked to the door.

"I am leaving you, Jon Paul, and don't try to find me, either."

"Find you—*ha*! I would rather find a bad case of herpes."

"Good-bye, Jon Paul." She walked out the door with her suitcase behind her.

"See ya!" he said, smiling.

The door slammed, and Michelle left Jon Paul, just like she said. He was not sorry and he was not worried. He had Liz to be with, his true love.

***

Michelle walked down the street, and as she walked, she would cry briefly at the huge fight that she just had with Jon Paul. She looked for the closest inn she could find—strangely, though, they all seemed to be full. She finally found one that had a vacancy sign after walking for quite some time. Oddly enough, it was close to Paul Pierre's place.

Jon Paul sat down in his living room on the sofa. He sat and wondered what the hell had just happened. His love of three years was now gone, and he was not sure what to do now. She had been a part of his life for so long that it seemed strange to see her walk out the door. But her leaving had a profound effect on Jon Paul. As he sat there thinking, his mind began to race with thoughts of riches, of a long life, of power beyond his wildest dreams. All this could be achieved with the coin now that Michelle was gone. Now, if he could just clear his head from all these thoughts, he could relax. Jon Paul thought, *Maybe I could use a cup of tea.* He walked into the kitchen, found his favorite cup and tea, put some water on the stove to boil, and sat down to wait.

***

Michelle checked into a small inn called Le Grand Inn, just a few blocks from Paul's place. She thought about him and then remembered the kiss they had shared. It was nice, soft and tender, not rough and aggressive like Jon Paul's. She wondered what Paul was doing right now. She sat down in the chair close to the bed.

***

Jon Paul sat in his kitchen, sipping his favorite tea. He wondered if Michelle's walking out really had happened. It was like a dream to him. But she really did leave, and now he was alone in his apartment. He looked around the kitchen; it was quiet. *This is not bad,* he thought, *maybe I could repaint the walls and do some other work around here. I could have this place looking brand-new in no time.* Jon Paul decided he would do some work around his apartment to freshen up the place a little. Michelle's leaving was fading from his mind with each passing moment.

***

Michelle sat in her rented room and picked up the phone to call Paul. She dialed and sobbed at the same time.

"Hello, this is Paul."

"Paul," said Michelle, sobbing, "I left Jon Paul, and we are through."

"What has happened, Michelle?"

"We got in another fight. I found out he had an affair with some woman."

"I am so sorry, Michelle. What can I do?"

"Paul, I really need you to come and see me. I am at the little inn by your place—the one called Le Grand."

"I know the place, Michelle. I just need a few minutes to get ready and then I can be there, okay?"

"Thanks, Paul. I am in room six."

"Room six, got it. See you soon, Michelle. Oh, and Michelle, don't worry. Everything will be all right."

"Thanks, Paul. Bye."

Paul was going to see Michelle and he would make it all right. She needed a shoulder to cry on, and he was just the right one.

***

Jon Paul dialed the phone in his kitchen.

"Hello."

"Hello, Liz?"

"Yes."

"It is Jon Paul."

"Oh, hi, Jon Paul. I thought that was you."

"Liz, Michelle and I broke up."

"Really? What happened, Jon Paul?"

"She found out about us and then we argued and she left."

"Are you okay?"

"I will be. Do you work tonight, Liz?"

"No, I have the night off."

"Good, you want to come over here tonight?"

"Sure, Jon Paul. What time?"

"Well, how about six?"

"Okay, sweetie. I will be there at six p.m."

"Good, I will see you then."

"Jon Paul?"

"Yes, Liz."

"I miss you."

He hung up the phone and felt better. He would see Liz tonight and she could help him deal with the breakup. Liz kept herself busy with her daily chores of cleaning her apartment; she was going to see Jon Paul tonight, and hopefully she could comfort him by being there for him with whatever he needed. If he wanted her to cook him something, she would; if he just wanted to talk, then she would listen; she would do anything for Jon Paul.

Jon Paul sat and listened to the birds chirping outside his window and wondered how they could be so carefree and cheerful all the time. He was not feeling bad, just like he was dreaming, and this made him reflective. For a few hours, he sat in the kitchen, just listening. Finally, he decided to get up and go to the living room to watch some TV. He watched TV for the rest of the day without any thoughts of Michelle. He did think about Liz, though. Around five p.m., he roused himself from a quick nap and walked upstairs to freshen up. As he was standing in the bathroom, he began to get angry, and that anger grew.

He had thoughts of violence against Michelle and against Maggie the waitress. He knew this was wrong, but it somehow was making him feel better, like the thoughts were releasing him from his anger. He began to hear a small voice again in his head, very faint and faraway, but there. "You should kill her," said the small voice. "You should murder her," it said. "You should have ravenous dogs eat her." Jon Paul was not sure if that is what the voice had really said; was it all just in his head, or did he really hear those words? He listened more intently as the voice continued, "Take her body to the river and throw it in; cut her in pieces," he heard. Jon Paul was trying to listen very closely, when all of a sudden, the doorbell rang. It shocked him out of his daydream. He ran downstairs and pushed the buzzer. Liz opened the door and walked upstairs, where Jon Paul was waiting for her. She knocked. As he opened the door, she was standing there looking so beautiful, it took his breath away for a moment.

"Well, are you going to invite me in?" she asked.

"Of course I am, Liz, sorry about that."

She walked in the door and hugged him and gave him a small kiss on the lips. "How are you, Jon Paul?"

"Umm, okay, I guess—better now that you are here. Let's go sit down."

They went into the living room and sat. Liz sat next to Jon Paul and held him tightly. She hoped this would help him feel better, and it did. He drew strength from her and her embrace. His heart was mending and his soul was healing. As they sat and some time passed, they both became hungry.

Liz said, "I am hungry; do you want me to make you something?"

"Ah, yeah, now that you mention it, I am a bit hungry. Let's go see what I have in the fridge to eat." They went into the kitchen to find something to eat.

***

Paul Pierre was only a few blocks from where Michelle was, so it didn't take him long to get there. As he walked up to her door, he thought, *what should I say—that what Jon Paul did was unforgivable? How do I say this to her without causing her more grief?* He decided to just go with what felt right to him as he knocked on her door.

"Paul, is that you?" asked Michelle.

"Yeah, it's me, Michelle." She opened the door and let him in, her face wet from tears.

"Michelle, I am so sorry about this."

"Paul, what am I going to do?"

"Here, let's sit down first." So they sat and began to talk. Paul listened and would only say brief sentences. He let Michelle talk so that hopefully she could get it all out. He knew that a woman needed to talk to get to feeling better, at least in the short run. Paul and Michelle sat and talked for hours, as did Liz and Jon Paul. Both couples were on the mend. It would just take some time for them.

As time passed for Paul and Michelle, they began to get hungry. Neither had eaten in hours, so Paul was the first to speak up.

"Michelle, I know you might not be feeling up for this, but are you hungry?"

"No, not really, Paul, but you can eat something if you want."

"How about I bring you back something, and when you are ready, you can eat then."

"I don't know, Paul."

"Well, I will get extra and then if you want to, there will be some for you."

"Where are you going, Paul?"

"I think I will head over to that little bistro just down the street."

"Hurry back, Paul."

"Okay, Michelle, I will be right back. Are you going to be all right?"

"Just hurry, Paul."

"Okay, be right back, Michelle." He smiled as he closed the door behind him. He drove the short distance to the bistro and found a place to park, then went in and ordered some food and waited for it.

***

Jon Paul and Liz had been in the kitchen cooking up food when suddenly Jon Paul began to feel ill. "Liz, I need to sit down; something is wrong."

She looked at him nervously. "Sit here, Jon Paul." She helped him sit down at the table and said, "What is it, Jon Paul, what happened?"

"I don't know, suddenly I felt like I was going to pass out."

"Just sit here for a while and don't move. I will make you a cup of tea to calm your nerves."

He sat there while she made him a nice cup of tea. He was feeling better, but his head had been swimming with all sorts of thoughts. Maybe that is what had him feeling faint and ill. Liz brought him the tea and sat down beside him and held his hand. "Are you feeling better?"

"Yeah, a little, I think."

"You just sit here until you feel better, Jon Paul."

"Okay, Liz." He smiled at her and she, in turn, did the same. He was feeling better after awhile, but it was not the tea; it was the fact that he was hearing voices in his head and they were compelling him to do bad things.

"You know, Liz, I think I want to go sit in the living room." She helped him up and they walked into his living room to sit and watch TV. Time passed for Jon Paul and Liz, and soon it was very late. Liz had fallen asleep while holding Jon Paul, and he felt very relaxed.

"Hey, Liz," he said softly, "let's go to bed." She opened her eyes, smiled at him, and nodded in agreement. They walked up the stairs to his bedroom and went to bed.

***

Paul had been waiting for his food when he noticed a crowd had gathered behind him. They had come to the restaurant for dinner too, he thought. When the cashier called his number, he responded quickly. He was very hungry, "That will be twelve ninety-five, sir." He gave her fifteen euros, got his change back, and walked away. He could smell the wonderful cooking of this place as he walked back to his car. He thought, *I hope Michelle likes Bresse chicken.* He drove the short distance back to the motel. He couldn't wait to eat, the smell was so inviting. He knocked on the door. "Michelle, it is Paul."

She opened the door and let him in. He sat down at the small table and motioned for her to join him.

"It smells great, Paul. What did you get?"

"I got a Bresse chicken with gravy, fresh greens, and a sweet roll for desert."

"Mmm, it does sound good. I think I am getting hungry, Paul."

They sat and ate. They enjoyed each other's company, and there were no awkward silences. It was very natural for them to just look at each other and smile. After they had their fill of food, they moved over to the bed. Michelle was the first one to speak.

"Paul, would you stay with me here tonight?"

"You know I will, Michelle. I would do anything for you."

Michelle felt her heart grow, and her eyes filled with soft tears of joy; she had found Paul. Paul and Michelle had found each other, and after so much heartache with Jon Paul, it was only right that she would find him.

***

When Jon Paul awoke, he could see Liz sleeping ever-so-comfortably beside him. He had the best night's sleep he'd had in a long time. As he watched her sleep, he noticed a smile had found its way to his face. He was happy again. Jon Paul got dressed and walked downstairs to the kitchen. He was going to make breakfast for Liz and himself. He began cooking some poached eggs. He squeezed fresh oranges for juice and had her favorite croissant with jelly on a plate. He was also making a fresh cup of tea.

Liz awoke to find herself alone, although the sweet smell of breakfast was finding its way upstairs. She decided to call to Jon Paul, "Jon Paul, are you down there?"

"Yes, sweetie. I am cooking us some breakfast; get dressed and come down here."

Liz did just that; she put on her clothes and walked downstairs to Jon Paul.

"Wow! You look great in the mornings."

"Only in the mornings?" said Liz, smiling coyly.

Jon Paul chuckled and replied, "No, baby, all the time, you look great." She smiled and sat down at the table. When he had finished cooking their breakfast, he served it up on two plates.

Chapter Seven

•●•

THE PLAN

They sat across from each other so they could look into each other's eyes. Jon Paul and Liz were very happy they had found each other, and love was in the air. They ate breakfast and every once in awhile, they would look at each other and smile. Not many words were said, but then, who needs words when you are in love and a smile can say a million words? Liz got up to get herself another cup of tea when Jon Paul saw her and said, "Where are you going? Just you sit there; I will get whatever you need."

"Jon Paul, you are such a gentleman," said Liz.

He got up and poured her another cup of tea. "Liz, do you have any plans today? I mean, do you have to work?"

"Yes, I have to go open up today."

"Oh, okay, well, why don't you stay here until you need to go?"

"Well, I do need to get back to my place to get some clothes for work."

"Then I am coming with you," replied Jon Paul.

"Really, Jon Paul, you are such a gentleman." She smiled at him and flirted with him using her eyes. He noticed and smiled back, adding a wink. After they had finished eating, they cleaned up the kitchen and got ready to leave.

They were walking back to Liz's place so she could get ready for work. As they walked out the door, Jon Paul thought he heard a small, familiar voice in his mind again.

***

Paul and Michelle spent the night together. As they both awoke in the morning, neither was ashamed of what they had done. Michelle was single now, and although her breakup with Jon Paul was still fresh, she was moving on with her life. Paul looked at Michelle with new eyes; he had not seen her this way before and wondered why not. She was beautiful, young and vibrant, the kind he would go for. As he sat up, he looked at her and said, "Good morning, Michelle."

She looked at him and replied, "Good morning, Paul." Both smiled at each other again.

"Are you hungry?" asked Michelle.

"Yeah, I am a bit hungry."

"Let's go get some breakfast somewhere," Michelle said.

"Where do you want to go, Michelle?"

"I don't know; this is your side of town, so you tell me."

"Umm, I know we can go to the little bistro a few miles away."

"Sounds good, Paul; let's go."

They got up, got themselves dressed, and went to the little bistro Paul loved so well.

***

Jon Paul and Liz walked to her place, and the voice in his head got louder as they walked. He heard it say, *"Kill her; kill her; murder her; murder her—revenge."* This time, he was sure he had heard it right, but it didn't sound like his voice. It was coming from someplace very far away and very dark. Jon Paul wondered where this was coming from—could it be he was hearing something from the past, something that had to do with the coin? He began to think about it—could he actually get away with it? Could he get revenge on Michelle by using the coin to murder her? Make her disappear, like the thugs in the alley? He wondered if Liz would approve of it or whether she would admonish him for such an evil act. Maybe she would approve and there would be no evidence of it; the coin would make sure of that. So he thought and walked with Liz. He didn't tell her of the evil plan beginning to take form.

When they arrived at Liz's place, they went upstairs to her living room. Jon Paul sat on her couch while Liz got herself ready for work. He was thinking about the coin and how he could use it against Michelle.

The more he sat and thought, the more he grew to hate her. His mind twirled with evil thoughts on just how he could dismember her or maybe melt her skin with fire. Jon Paul was almost completely under the power of the coin. It spoke to him, and he heard it. He was turning evil.

Liz had finished dressing for work and came back downstairs to see Jon Paul. The first thing she noticed was some kind of dark aura that seemed to be enveloping Jon Paul. It didn't look like he knew it, but Liz was sure he was feeling it. He was still sitting on the couch, deep in thought. Liz looked at him and his dark aura. Jon Paul hadn't even noticed Liz sitting next to him.

"Jon Paul! Jon Paul!"

When she said this, he finally broke out of his trance and said, "Yes, what?"

"Where were you? I called to you and you were just staring off into space; you didn't even hear me."

"Sorry, Liz, I was just thinking about something."

"What were you thinking about so hard?"

"Nothing, Lizzy, just had a deep moment." Jon Paul wasn't going to tell her his evil plan.

"Well, how do I look?" she asked.

"You look absolutely beautiful, my dear." He smiled at her and winked. She was pleased with his response, and she smiled back.

"Jon Paul, what are you going to do tonight?"

"I think after we walk you to work, I will just go back home and try to get some of Michelle's things packed for her."

"Then you won't be coming by later to see me?"

"No, but I will be calling you later."

"Good, you better, mister." Liz smiled at Jon Paul and he smiled back. They were almost ready to leave to walk her to work.

Jon Paul had heard the coin and its thoughts were becoming his.

He had decided not to tell Liz his plans—at least not yet; maybe in the near future he would.

Liz and Jon Paul were ready to leave. He was going to walk her to work at the Goat's Head Bar and then he was going home to try and pack some of Michelle's possessions to give back to her whenever she came by to get them.

***

Paul and Michelle went to the little bistro down the street to have breakfast. They had truly enjoyed each other's company and now were starting a new life together. As they approached the bistro, there were a few early-morning customers gathering around to get breakfast, just as they were. They went inside to sit down to enjoy a nice meal and to talk more about what they both wanted from each other.

"So tell me, Michelle, what do you want in this life that you don't have now?"

"Right now, at this moment?"

"Yes."

"Well, for starters, how about a nice man to love me and treat me right?"

"Yes, what else?"

"For now, I have all I need with you, Paul."

He smiled at her and she smiled back. They had found each other and it was obvious to anyone in the restaurant.

***

While Jon Paul and Liz walked to the bar, neither said much. It was not uncommon for Jon Paul to keep silent for a while. Liz, however, was curious and asked, "Jon Paul, is there something on your mind?"

"No, not really, Liz, why do you ask?"

"Well, you are being so quiet. I thought maybe something was wrong."

"No, Liz, I just like to walk and enjoy my thoughts."

"Okay, then, just don't ignore me!" She smiled as she said this. Jon Paul smiled back to let her know he was sorry for ignoring her.

When he was deep in his thoughts, most of them were of how he could kill Michelle and get away with it. He had heard the coin and was now contemplating murder.

Soon, their walk to the bar had brought them close to her work. Liz was glad Jon Paul had accompanied her to her job; he was *her* man now, and that was that! Jon Paul loved her and felt that she was his true soul mate. Liz, of course, felt the same.

"Jon Paul, do you want to come in for a quick drink?"

"No, not for a drink, Liz, but I'll come in just for a few minutes, okay?"

"Sure thing, honey."

They went in and Jon Paul sat down at the bar. Liz checked in and started to get her day of work going. Jon Paul sat there for several minutes till Liz came out from the back of the storeroom, and then he said, "Liz, I better get going. You going to be all right?"

"Thanks, Jon Paul, I will be fine. What time are you going to call me tonight?"

"Umm, how about late, like about eleven p.m.?"

"Yeah, that will be good. I should be home by then."

Jon Paul gently grabbed Liz and gave her a nice kiss, and she responded the same. No one was around to see them, so it was okay for them to show their affection for each other. Jon Paul looked deeply into Liz's eyes and said, "Call you tonight, sweetie."

She looked back and said, "Can't wait!"

She winked at him and Jon Paul walked out of the bar and down the street to his home. But he had the mind of a killer now, and he was planning on getting rid of Michelle in the worst way possible—murder.

***

Paul and Michelle were enjoying their breakfast when Paul looked down at his watch and noticed the time. "Oh, crap, Michelle, I have to get home to call Dr. Martin."

"Who is Dr. Martin?"

"Remember? He is the expert at the museum who is going to help us with the coin."

She nodded in agreement. "I remember you mentioned something about him."

"Yes, he is a local expert on antiquities. I think he can help us to identify the coin's origin and maybe some of its history."

"I am done if you want to go," said Michelle.

"Yeah, I am ready too." They paid their bill and walked out of the restaurant and to his car, where they got in and drove back to his house so he could call Dr. Martin. As they arrived back at Paul's place, Michelle began to feel funny, as if something was wrong. She wondered if maybe it was just the early-morning food from the bistro—or was it something else?

"Are you okay, Michelle?"

"I don't know, Paul. I feel funny."

"What do you mean *funny*, Michelle—your stomach or your head?"

"I feel like something is very wrong with me."

Paul studied her face. He could tell she was scared, and she obviously felt something or could maybe sense something was not quite right with her.

"Let's go upstairs so you can lie down and rest."

"Okay, Paul."

Paul helped Michelle upstairs to his room and helped her lie down on his bed. He brought her an extra blanket for comfort and went to the kitchen to get her a small cup of tea. Michelle was shivering and shaking.

"Michelle, do you want me to get you anything else?" Paul asked her.

"No, thanks, Paul. You are very sweet for asking, though." Michelle managed a smile for Paul, and he smiled back.

***

Jon Paul was back at his home now, and had been holding the coin in his hands while thinking about Michelle. He was sure he was going to do this; he just wanted to have a plan first, something that would be foolproof. He sat and thought for a moment. The coin was heating up in his hand, and it made his hands begin to get sweaty. He could feel the power of the coin and it made him feel good. Suddenly, he had it—the perfect plan. He could wish for Michelle to get sick and die. That way, she could feel the pain that he had to endure while he was with her. It was a perfect plan. Now he just had to say the wish.

Jon Paul held the coin tight in his hand. He focused his mind on Michelle and said, "I wish for her to get sick and *die*! *Die*! *Die*!" Jon Paul had done it;

he had carried out his evil plan to perfection, and now Michelle would be the recipient of that hatred.

***

As Paul sat with Michelle and tried to comfort her, he noticed she seemed to be getting worse. Her color was fading from her cheeks and she did not look well. He began to worry. She was lying on the bed when suddenly, she began to twitch and shake violently. She vomited up the breakfast she and Paul had enjoyed so much earlier. She complained that she was seeing double and her head felt like it was going to explode. Paul was sure now he must get her to a hospital. She was having a serious episode and was very sick. As he picked her up to carry her to his car, she looked at him and said, "Paul, if I don't make it, I want you to know how much you mean to me now."

Paul looked at her and said, "I know, Michelle, just try to relax. We are going to the hospital right now. Hold on, okay?"

She looked at him with tears in her eyes; she knew these were her last moments on earth. Paul rushed her to the hospital as fast as he could. When he got there, he told the nurse it was an emergency and they needed to help her as fast as they could. "She is dying!" he said.

The nurses saw how bad Michelle's health had become, and they rushed her into the ER and began treatment. Michelle was fading fast. The doctors came in and applied CPR, then shock treatment, and then finally, adrenaline to her, but nothing was working. Michelle was dying. Michelle's heart gave out at just a few minutes past midnight. She lay dead on the table. Paul waited outside for the doctors to tell him how she was doing. As the doctors tried to save her, one of the nurses noticed a strange woman standing beside her. Where did she come from?

This woman was not allowed in the ER. She was not a nurse, nor should she be in there right now. Who was she? As the nurse watched, the woman made a wavering motion with her hands over Michelle's body, and suddenly, Michelle was stirring. Her heartbeat had returned and the doctors steadied it. The nurse watched the strange woman for what seemed to her to be an eternity. When she turned to ask the doctors if they saw her too, the woman had disappeared. Just as quickly as she had appeared, she was gone. The nurse was puzzled.

The nurse, being a devoted Catholic, was beginning to think maybe she had seen this poor girl's guardian angel; what else could explain the appearance of the strange woman that apparently no one else saw?

The doctors had finished with their work on Michelle and were having the nurses' finish up the rest. One nurse in particular—the one who had seen the strange woman—did not believe that the doctors had saved Michelle.

When one of the doctors walked out of the ER, the nurse caught up with him and said, "Excuse me, doctor, did you see the woman standing next to me?"

"No, I didn't, nurse—what woman?"

"There was a strange woman standing next to the patient when you were working on saving her life."

"What did this woman do, nurse?"

"I don't know, really, she just seemed to be helping her somehow."

"Where is this woman now?"

"She disappeared right after the young woman came back to life."

"What do you mean, she disappeared?"

"I don't know, doctor, I looked at you to ask you if you saw her, and when I turned around again, she was gone."

"Well, maybe she wasn't really there. Stress can cause some people to see unusual things in critical moments. Maybe you need to go take a break and sit down for a while. There was no one else there except for us."

"Yes, doctor, I will." The nurse decided to take a break for a while—after all, maybe she really didn't see anything. She would talk with this young woman after a while, when she was more stable, she thought.

The doctor walked down the hall to look for Paul, who had brought Michelle into the emergency room. He found him sitting impatiently in the waiting area. "Is there someone here who brought in the young woman named Michelle Duvalier?"

"Yes, doctor, I did. How is she?"

"She is going to be fine."

"What happened, doctor?"

"She had some sort of strange stomach infection that caused her heart to palpitate and then actually stop, but we revived her. She is on some medication to calm her and steady her heart for now."

"I see. So will she be here overnight, doctor?"

"Most definitely. We will continue to monitor her heart to make sure it is back to normal for a young woman of her age before we release her."

"Thanks, doc, I am glad I got her here in time."

"Yes, you did get her here in time. Now, if you will excuse me, I have other things to attend to. You can ask the nurse at the station when you may go in to see her."

Paul nodded to the doctor as he walked away. He had done the right thing by bringing Michelle to the hospital. He had saved her life, but he did not know it was Jon Paul who had wished for her death. As time passed at the hospital, the nurse that was keeping an eye on Michelle had decided it was time to go talk with her, so she opened the door to her room and said, "How are you feeling, dear?"

"I am still feeling a little weak. What happened to me?"

"You suffered a massive heart attack caused by some stomach virus, thus causing your heart to stop for a second."

"My ... my ... heart stopped?"

"Yes, but I have a question for you—did you see a woman standing next to you who was not wearing a nurse's outfit?"

"The woman, was she wearing a blue dress?" asked Michelle.

"Yes, I believe she was wearing a blue dress."

"Is she someone special, nurse?" asked Michelle.

"I don't know. She was not supposed to be there, and then when I was going to ask her who she was, she was gone."

"What do you mean, she was gone?"

"She disappeared, and now no one knows where she went or who she is."

Michelle looked warily at the nurse, not knowing whether to believe her or not.

"Listen, miss, I don't think the doctors saved you. I believe she was your guardian angel. You were dead and she brought you back, not the doctors. Are you a religious woman?"

"Not really—I mean, I haven't been to church in many years. Why would she save me?"

"I don't know, dear, you must be special."

Michelle began to cry. The tears streamed down her face, and the nurse calmly wiped them away. She smiled and said, "Don't worry, dear, you are going to be fine. I would suggest that as soon as you are released from here, you go to a church and say a prayer of thanks for her saving your life."

"Thank you. I will."

Michelle wept softly as the nurse got up and walked away; she was in a mild state of shock. Paul had been sitting until enough time had passed that he thought he might be able to see Michelle, so he got up and walked to the nurse's station to ask if he could go in to see her. One of the nurses told him he should wait for just a little while longer, and that she would come find him whenever he would be able to see her. Paul went back to the waiting area and sat down. The nurse who had seen the strange woman returned to her station, but when she saw Paul, she motioned for him to come over to her. As he walked over to her, he noticed the nice smile on her face and said, "Hi. How is Miss Duvalier?"

"Are you with her?" asked the nurse.

"Yes, I brought her in here."

"She will be fine. She has been through a lot in the last few hours. You need to give her some time before you go in to see her."

"How much time, nurse? I have just been waiting here for so long."

"Don't worry; like I said, she will be fine. Just give her a little more time."

"Okay, I will, but can someone please come tell me when I can go talk with her?"

"One more thing, sir: Can you take her to a church when she gets released from here?"

"Yeah, sure, but why?"

"I believe she was very lucky today. Just promise me you will do this."

"I promise I will take her to the nearest church as soon as she is released from here."

The nurse smiled at Paul and went back to her work. Paul walked back to the waiting area to kill more time. He desperately wanted to see Michelle and to talk with her.

***

Jon Paul had been sitting in his living room when he wished for Michelle's death, and he was feeling very powerful. He had the sensation he could do anything; it was overwhelming him. He wondered if he should try to find out if Michelle was really dead, but how? Where would he start? He didn't even know where she was staying. He thought maybe something had happened and someone would know about it. Who could he call? Eventually, he thought of calling the hospital. If there had been an accident, surely the hospital would know if they had just admitted a patient named Michelle Duvalier.

Jon Paul decided to look up the name of the hospital, and he found the number and dialed.

"Hello, St. Peter's Hospital. How may I direct your call?"

"I am trying to find out about a patient named Michelle Duvalier."

"Hold on, sir. When was she admitted?"

"I don't know the exact time, but maybe a few hours ago."

"Hold on, sir; yes, here she is. Are you a family member?"

"Yes, I am her fiancé."

"Okay, sir. She was admitted this morning at 10:37."

"Was she with anyone?"

"That I don't know, sir, but I can tell you her condition was gravely serious. Her heart actually gave out on her, but Dr. Koline was able to revive her."

"What do you mean, her heart gave out on her—it stopped?"

"Yes, sir, but she is fine now and recovering in the ER."

"Can I see her?"

"Yes, she is able to have visitors. Is there anything else I can help you with?"

"No thanks. I will be there shortly to see her, but don't tell her I am coming—I wish to surprise her."

"Okay, sir. Good-bye."

"Bye."

Jon Paul was furious. He had made his wish and it had worked, but the doctors were able to revive her? What the hell had happened? She should've been dead. Maybe the coin had its limits. Jon Paul got up and stomped around his apartment. He wanted her dead; obviously, something had gone wrong. Could he have done something wrong? Maybe he had said his wish wrong. *No matter*, he thought. *I will find the truth and I will fix it, no matter the cost.*

***

Paul got up to go see Michelle. The nurse had waved him over and given him the okay to see her now that she was stable. As Paul walked to her room, he had a brief thought about Jon Paul, and he wondered what he was doing. Maybe he should call him. Paul opened the door slowly and went in. Michelle was lying there looking rather comfortable. He thought she looked like an angel. When she heard him come in, her eyes lit up. She smiled a big smile and opened her arms for him to hug her. He sat down on the bed next to her and did just that. Tears began to form in her eyes. Paul gently wiped them away and said, "Michelle, you gave me quite a scare. How are you feeling?"

"I am feeling much better now," she said and smiled at Paul.

"Paul, did the nurse tell you about the strange woman in blue that was in my room?"

"A woman in blue? No, she didn't."

"The nurse thinks it was my guardian angel that saved me, not the doctors."

"What?"

"I saw her, too, for a second. But no one else did, except for the nurse."

"Really? Did she say anything to you?"

"No, I don't remember much. I saw her for only a second."

"That is weird. What did the nurse say about it?"

"She said I died and that the doctors did not bring me back, the woman did."

"Well, whatever, Michelle, I am just so happy you are still here with me!"

"Me too, Paul, me too."

They hugged again. Paul actually thought he might believe her for a second, but then he remembered that when people are in stressful situations, they sometimes think they see something special or someone that really isn't there, like a guardian angel.

He was not a believer in the supernatural, but he had learned about human behavior from school and knew it to be just that. Paul smiled at Michelle. As he got up, he was planning on calling this Dr. Martin from the museum as soon as he could. He wasn't going to do it at the hospital, though. He would wait till he got home.

"Michelle, I think I will go home for a while—like a couple hours—to eat some food and to try and call Dr. Martin. Then I will be back. Will you be all right if I go for a while?"

"Yes, Paul, I will be fine, but hurry back, okay? I miss you already." She smiled at him. Paul gave her a hug and a small kiss and then left. He was going home to call Dr. Martin to see if he could help him learn more about this dreaded coin of Jon Paul's.

***

Jon Paul sat in his house, infuriated at what had happened. Jon Paul was unsure of his thoughts now; he had made the wish, but she was still alive. How could this be? Maybe there were other things he didn't understand, like death or life, and the coin only started these things, but the rest was left up to fate. Jon Paul had to figure out what, if anything, went wrong and fix it if he could.

The afternoon went by slowly for Jon Paul. He did some light chores around his apartment and as he worked, he thought about his next move. He wanted to do something for Liz that would take her breath away. The necklace he gave her was nice, but he wanted to show her how much he loved her and that he wanted to spend his life with her. Jon Paul began to think about a ring. How about it, he thought. A ring would be great and it would represent his love forever. Jon Paul reached for the coin. He could feel it heating up in his hand as he held it tight. He thought for a moment and then said, "I wish for the perfect diamond ring." *Poof!* There it was—a beautiful diamond ring. It was perfect! He would give it to Liz when he saw her next.

Jon Paul was feeling better. The hatred had subsided and he was calming down now, especially since he was thinking about Liz and how she would love the diamond ring. He had just decided to sit down to watch some TV for a while to relax when the phone rang. "Hello."

"Hello, Jon Paul. It is Paul."

"Why are you calling me now, you son of a bitch?"

"Take it easy, Jon Paul. Why all the hostilities?"

"I know about you and Michelle!"

"What do you mean, Jon Paul?"

"Come on, Paul. I know how you snaked her out from under me."

"Jon Paul, I never did that. She came to me after your fight with her and explained everything to me. I never did anything wrong."

"*Yes, you did*! I thought we were friends, but now you have thrown that all away!" Jon Paul cried.

"Jon Paul, really, I didn't."

"No, I mean it. I don't ever want to speak with your lying ass again!"

"Wait, Jon Paul. Michelle is in the hospital."

"Yes, I know. I called there."

"You called there? But how could you have known she was there? Unless … you, you, Jon Paul, *you* did this to her, didn't you?"

"Did what, Paul?"

"You cursed her with that coin!"

"I never did, Paul."

Paul knew that his friend had done a very bad thing. He became more determined than ever to get the coin from him now. "Jon Paul, I know you are under the power of that damned coin, but know this—we will get it from you, no matter what it takes. I will take it from you and destroy it somehow, someway!"

"Really, Paul? You know where I live. Come on over anytime."

Jon Paul hung up the phone and sat back down on the couch. The argument with Paul had him rattled and feeling angry again. Maybe he could use some tea, he thought. He went into the kitchen to fix himself a cup of tea to calm his nerves.

***

Paul Pierre was just as upset. He had found out that his former best friend of many years had wished for Michelle to get sick and die. He sat shaking from the anger he now felt. He and Michelle would take that coin from him and save him from himself, even if he didn't want them to. Paul decided to call Dr. Martin as soon as he calmed down a little. He walked around his apartment for a few minutes till he was calm. When he was calmer, he thought he was ready to call the doctor, so he picked up the phone and dialed his number.

"Hello, Dr. Martin's office. How can I help you?"

"Yes, hello, can I speak with Dr. Martin?"

"Yes, just a minute. Who can I say is calling?"

"It is Paul Pierre."

"Just a minute, sir."

"Hello, this is Dr. Martin."

"Hello, Dr. Martin. My name is Paul, and I need your help. I have a question for you."

"Yes, Paul. What is your question?"

"Well, a while ago, my friend found a gold coin that appears to be very old. I was wondering if you could help me to identify it better and maybe find out some history about it, as well."

"Of course, I can help you. Bring it in and we can take a closer look at it."

"That might be a problem, doc. I don't have it and I am no longer on speaking terms with the owner right now."

"I see. Well, if you can describe it to me, I might be able to help."

"Okay, how about if I come down there to see you personally, doctor?"

"That sounds fine. We can look over some books that I have that might be able to help you identify it. I will have you talk with my secretary to schedule an appointment and then we will speak further."

"Okay, thanks, doc. See you soon."

Paul was transferred back to the secretary to make an appointment. He would see him the following day and then, hopefully, he would learn more about this coin. Paul had a good memory, so he was sure he could describe the coin in detail to the doctor and they would be able to find a picture or at least some kind of information on it, like: Where did it come from? Who owned it last? Was it lost on purpose?

Paul continued to sit there and then he thought, *maybe I should call Michelle, just to check on her.* But then he thought, *No, I will just go back to the hospital soon and see her in person. That is better.* He walked into his kitchen and found something to eat. All the stress of his day had made him hungry. He had forgotten to eat earlier, so it was about time he fueled up and felt better. He chewed his food slowly as he sat there. His mind had many thoughts of Jon Paul and what this so-called best friend had become—how could he sink so low? Was there nothing Jon Paul would not do? This coin had possessed him, and Jon Paul was not the same man he once knew. Paul would have to get rid of the coin in order to save Jon Paul, despite himself.

***

Jon Paul was enjoying his tea. He sat in his favorite chair and had a relaxing late afternoon staring out the window and listening to the birds. Every now and then, he would get up to look at the birds flying about, not having a care in the world. He wondered what it would be like to live life like that. On occasion, he would look at the shiny, new diamond ring he was going to give Liz.

***

Paul Pierre was on his way back to the hospital when he remembered something his old college professor had said in his human behavior class: *"The human mind is unable to conceive of something so vast as a thing to be called God. God is a concept that is to be used to relate to something so infinitely superior to us that this is the only way we can see or even think of God."*

Paul wondered why this particular memory had come to him now after so many years of being out of school. He parked his car and went into the hospital to see Michelle. As he neared the nurse's station, he noticed there were not as many nurses there as before; perhaps some had finished their shifts and had gone home for the day.

"Hi. I am looking for Michelle Duvalier's room."

"Are you a family member?"

"Yes, she is my fiancée."

"Hi. Yes, she has been moved out of intensive care and to room 308. It is just down the hall to the left. Follow the blue stripe on the floor; it will lead you to her room."

Paul nodded as he understood what the nurse had told him. *Funny thing,* he thought, *I am following a blue stripe!* He walked past other rooms with people in them; some were older and some were younger. He wondered what they were all in there for. He approached Michelle's room and saw the number 308. He went in, and there on the bed was his angel! She was so very beautiful, glowing, he thought. He wondered what he had done to deserve such a fine woman.

When Michelle saw him, her eyes lit up and she smiled from ear to ear. She held out her arms for him to give her a hug, and that is exactly what he did. He could feel his heart next to hers, and then they beat as one. He felt a smile on his face too.

"Hey, you, how are you feeling?"

"I am so much better now that you are here, Paul!"

"Thanks, Michelle." Paul almost felt embarrassed by her show of love.

"Did you talk with the doctor from the museum?"

"Actually, I did. I made an appointment to see him tomorrow."

"What did he say?"

"Nothing specific. He needs to see the coin first before he can tell me more." Paul got quiet as he sat for a moment.

"What is it, Paul?"

"I also talked with someone else."

"Who did you talk with, Paul?"

"I called Jon Paul to tell him about you." Michelle looked at him in wonderment. She could tell something was wrong, or maybe something had happened when they talked.

"I called him to find out if he knew what had happened to you."

"What did he say, Paul?"

"Michelle, I don't want to tell you this, but—"

"Please, Paul, what did he say?"

"Michelle, I am afraid he was the one who wished you sick."

Michelle began to cry; tears streamed down her pretty face. "Why, Paul? Why would he do such a thing?" Michelle hugged Paul tight, and he could feel her pain.

"I don't know, Michelle. I think the coin has corrupted him completely." Paul held her tight and tried to ease her discomfort. He knew he would be the one to take the cursed coin from Jon Paul and destroy it—somehow.

***

As the evening approached for Jon Paul, he dozed off on the couch. He awoke to see the diamond ring sitting there on the table in front of him, and he smiled. He was feeling hungry, so he got up to go into the kitchen to find something to eat. Although he was a good cook, he didn't feel like cooking this night, so he reached in his pocket for the coin, and as he held it, he began to feel its power. It felt like hot fire in the center of his hand. He thought and then he said, "I wish for a full table of food with a servant to help me clean it up after I am done." *Poof!*

There in his kitchen was a full table, and standing next to the table was a manservant holding a serving tray of goodies for Jon Paul to eat.

"Good evening, sir. How may I serve you?"

"Well, let's start with you bringing me a full plate of food."

"Yes, sir; very good, sir."

Jon Paul ate and ate. He ate so much that he thought his stomach might explode. Finally, he got to the point where he was finished and he said, "Thanks for dinner; now I think I am done."

"Very good, sir. Will there be anything else, perhaps an after-dinner mint?"

"Umm, no. I am stuffed. I can't eat any more. Wrap this all up and put it in the fridge, will you please?"

"Yes, sir, will do."

Jon Paul sat there and watched his manservant clean up all the food and the dishes. He thought he did a very good job. Jon Paul thought, *I could get used to living like this.*

Jon Paul got up and went into the living room to watch TV for a while. After a short time, the manservant came out of the kitchen and said, "I am finished, sir. Is there anything else you wish me to do?"

"No, that will be all. Oh yeah, by the way, what is your name?"

"It is Falid, sir. Rashid Alalaham Falid."

"Okay, Mr. Falid—is it okay if I call you that?"

"Yes, sir, that is fine. All my other masters have called me by that name."

"How many masters have you had, Mr. Falid?"

"Oh, sir, too many to count, but I served them tirelessly, as I will you."

"Thanks for telling me that, Mr. Falid."

"You are welcome, sir. Now if you don't mind and there is nothing else, I must leave you for the night."

"Leave? Where will you go?"

"I must return back to whence I came, but I shall be here whenever you call. You no longer need to use the coin to call me. I am bound to you for this life."

Jon Paul was stunned. He sat there for a moment. Then he waved at his new manservant, and he vanished in a cloud of smoke. Of course, this cloud of smoke was only visible to the one who had the coin. Jon Paul liked having a servant to help him, and he wondered why he had not thought of this earlier. If he had, maybe things would have been a little different for him. He had failed to realize that the coin was bringing him his heart's desire, but it was also bringing him fate's desire. Jon Paul was now walking down a path that such powerful men had known, powerful men who had ruled the earth in their day. This was to be Jon Paul's fate too.

***

Paul stayed with Michelle and held her hand most of the time. He and Michelle talked and tried to figure out why Jon Paul would do such an evil thing. The only reason they could come up with was that it was the coin. It had taken over his life and was only becoming worse. Jon Paul had actually wished for Michelle to become sick, and there was no telling what else he would do. Time moved quickly for Paul and Michelle, mostly because they sat and talked so much.

They were both sure it would be a battle to wrestle the coin from Jon Paul and that it would be best if it were Paul who did it. Paul and Michelle agreed that when Paul did finally get the coin from Jon Paul, he must destroy it, if possible. Paul made a solemn vow to Michelle that he would do it. "Michelle, I am giving you my word as a man. I vow that I will get that coin from Jon Paul, and I will destroy it somehow."

"Thanks, Paul. I know you can do it. We must get it from Jon Paul before he does something worse, so how are we going to do it?"

"I don't know, Michelle. Maybe you could call him and say you need to come get some of your things, and then when you get there, we could go in and somehow take it from him."

"Sounds risky, Paul. Maybe I could just ask him for a wish or something."

"Wait! That might do it. What if you were to ask him for a last wish before you left him, and then when he takes it out, I will grab it."

"Paul, that sounds very dangerous. What if you don't get it and he wishes you gone?"

"I know that it is a big chance, but what else can we do? We have to get him to take the coin out of his pocket so we can see it; then maybe I can grab it first, before he is ready."

"Paul, if I lose you, I don't know what I will do."

Chapter Eight

• ● •

BACKFIRE

Michelle's eyes began to tear up. She didn't want Paul to take such a risk, but his plan seemed like the only one that might actually work. Jon Paul never took the coin out of his pocket; it was always with him, like it was attached to him.

"Don't worry, Michelle. I will be careful, I promise." Now Paul and Michelle had a way to get rid of the coin by taking it from Jon Paul. Although it was a risk, it seemed their best plan. After Michelle got released from the hospital, they would put their plan into action.

***

Jon Paul sat on his couch and laughed silently to himself; he was enjoying his coin immensely. He smiled as he thought about what he could do with it. He hadn't noticed the time, but it was close to 11:00 p.m., almost time for him to call Liz. At exactly 11:00, he picked up the phone to call her.

She answered. "Hello."

"Hello, beautiful. How are you tonight?"

"Jon Paul, are you flirting with me?"

"Of course, Liz. How was work?"

"Work was okay. You know, the same old thing—not much changes at The Goats Head Bar."

"I know. So, I have some good news for you, my dear."

"What is it, Jon Paul?" she asked excitedly.

101

"I have a gift for you!"

"A gift. Jon Paul, what is it?"

"Now, you just have to wait. I don't want to ruin the surprise."

"Oh, Jon Paul, you shouldn't have."

"I know, but I wanted to give you something to show you how much you mean to me. I am coming over to see you tomorrow. What hours do you work?"

"I am off tomorrow, so any time will be great. I can't wait to see you, Jon Paul."

"Me too, Liz. I will come over in the morning, okay?"

"Yes, but will you call me first? I want to be ready before you see me."

"Okay, sure thing, Liz." Jon Paul and Liz would see each other the next day, and he would give her the ring. She would be overwhelmed, of course.

***

Paul and Michelle sat together on her bed. Since it was getting late, he decided he would go home for the night and be back in the morning to take her home—not to the motel, but to his place. He would have her live with him if she would have him.

"Michelle, I think I will go home now."

"Really, Paul? I was hoping you might stay for just a couple minutes longer."

"Of course I will stay, Michelle. Anything for you, my dear."

He sat with her for a little while longer, and then he went home. As he drove, he thought about how he would grab the coin from Jon Paul. He would have to make it on the first attempt; he could not miss. If he did, the results could be disastrous for him. Jon Paul could simply say, "I wish him gone," and that would be it for him. He drove and played the scene out in his head many times. Paul was quick. He had studied boxing as a young man, so he knew how to use his hands. It wouldn't be easy, but it probably would be his only way to get the coin from Jon Paul.

***

Michelle slept the night away after Paul left. She was still recuperating, and she needed all her strength if she was to battle Jon Paul.

***

After Jon Paul talked with Liz for a while, he had thoughts of his former best friend, Paul. He thought Paul might try to take the coin from him somehow, and he must not succeed. *Never will they take my coin*, he thought. He fell asleep on the couch and did not move till the next morning.

Morning broke, and Jon Paul had not moved one inch since the night before; He had slept exactly where he had fallen asleep, and his neck was sore from sleeping in an upright position. He began to remember his dreams; most were disjointed and only fragments of a whole, but a few things stood out as peculiar. In one, he remembered someone telling him to beware of a close friend, and in another, that the name of that friend was Paul. He sat up and wondered at the meaning of that dream. He didn't remember much else, but he knew there was something about that particular part.

When Jon Paul got up, he began to feel hungry, especially after such a big meal the night before. He walked to the kitchen he called out to his manservant, Mr. Falid. "Hello, Mr. Falid. Are you here?" No sooner had he said this than Mr. Falid appeared out of thin air.

"Good morning, sir. I am here; how can I serve you today?"

"Good morning, Mr. Falid. What would you suggest?"

"Ah, sir, if I may, perhaps I can surprise you with one of my favorites?"

"Yes, that would be nice, Mr. Falid."

"Please relax, sir. I will bring you a cup of your favorite tea, and if you can give me a few moments, I can fix something I am sure you will love."

"Sounds good. I will wait in the living room."

"Very good, sir," replied Mr. Falid. Jon Paul went back into his living room to wait for his breakfast. He felt important and awake. While he waited, Mr. Falid brought him a fresh cup of his favorite tea and the morning newspaper to read. He was enjoying himself immensely. Jon Paul sipped his tea and read the newspaper and sat relaxed until Mr. Falid called him and said, "Sir, your breakfast is ready."

"Thanks. Be right there, Mr. Falid." Jon Paul got up and walked into the kitchen. When he saw what his servant had done, he nearly fell over from shock. On his table was a setting for a king. There were two candles set in the middle with a fresh vase of purple flowers in between. The table had several dishes that smelled so good that Jon Paul thought he would faint from the smell. He sat down and Mr. Falid served him.

"Here, sir, is fresh-squeezed orange juice from the south of Italy. Next is fresh coffee from the hills of southern France, and next to you is the finest pork sausage money can buy. To your right are waffles with pure strawberry syrup, and on your left is escargot caught this morning for your eating pleasure. I have also added a small batch of eggs whipped with butter from Holland, and finally, from the German town of Dusseldorf, a fresh-made coffee cake with almonds and walnuts. Will there be anything else, sir?"

"Ah, no, I think you got it covered. I mean, wow! You go all out, don't you, Mr. Falid?"

"Yes, sir, only the best for you."

"Thanks, Mr. Falid. Would you mind if we talked for a few minutes before you leave?"

"Yes, sir. What would you like to talk about?"

"So tell me, Mr. Falid, where do you come from, and how did you know I have the coin?"

"I come from a small town in Pakistan. It is a small village, so I am sure you have never heard of it. I was born there in the year 620 AD."

"620 AD?" asked Jon Paul.

"Yes, sir. I have been alive for many years now. This was my curse—to live as a manservant for so many years till my crime was considered served."

"What crime, and who would consider it served?"

"You see, sir, I was a man like you in my early days. Once, I was walking in the desert at night, and I was approached by a strange man riding on a white camel. Well, in all my life, I had never seen a white camel or even heard of one. This man was tall and he had very nice purple satin robes and he wore rubies on his ring fingers with gold rings on the others. He had gold necklaces that reflected in the moonlight like shiny diamonds. It was very strange.

I asked him his name. He said, 'I am Sultan Hali Dan.' He also said he was from a land very far away. I don't remember anymore, as that place has faded into the mists of time. But he started telling me about the *Jinn*—or genie, as you know them—and how magic was their nature, and then he offered me what he said was a magic coin. He said it could bring me my heart's desire, but there was a catch—never was I to tell anyone about it or show it to anyone, or I would have a very heavy price to pay."

"And did you take the coin, Mr. Falid?"

"I did, sir! I took it from his hands and he vanished! Well, I was amazed, to say the least. After several years had passed and I had risen in my fame, my wealth, and my power, I became a general in the war and we never lost any battles. When I began to get older and more time had passed and the years were showing on me, I started to lose the lust for shiny things. The gold lost its luster and the jewels lost their sparkle, and soon I found myself alone. I began to think about women. I found myself loving many different women in my day. But there was one in particular that I could not resist. Her dark beauty and exotic nature compelled me to give her anything she wanted. Soon, we were married, and I could not help myself; I showed her the coin."

"What happened then, Mr. Falid?" asked Jon Paul as he sat and ate and enjoyed his manservant's tale.

"The sky began to rumble, the clouds closed in and it started to rain; a very heavy and violent storm began to pour down. My wife ran away to another room to keep safe, and in the midst of all that, a small cloud of smoke began to form on the floor in front of me. It changed colors as it slowly began to take form.

As a figure started to rise, I began to be very afraid. The figure grew and grew; he was much taller and much bigger than me. He took solid form and stood there staring at me with bright-blue, glowing eyes. He had flowing robes of satin with brilliant whites hanging around him. I stared back at him. I was unable to blink; his nature was so impressive that I wanted to run, but my legs were fixed to the ground. He looked at me and said, 'You have broken our agreement! Now you must pay for your sin!' The words were like thunder in my ears; each one was so loud, I thought I would be deaf soon. He continued: 'As it was in the past, so now it is begun again. We brought you a gift, and you humans have failed to listen or even worship us, so now your crime must have a punishment!' The words seemed to bounce off the walls, and I wondered if anyone else could hear them. I looked at the genie and said, 'How have I sinned against you? I have kept my part of the bargain.'

'Liar! You showed the coin to another, and now you shall be punished. You will never see another child of your own. You shall walk this Earth till I have decided to ease your punishment. You shall serve men as I have, without anything to say!'"

Jon Paul sat spellbound as Mr. Falid continued. "I was afraid for my life at that point."

"What did you do?"

"What could I do, sir? The genie had given me my sentence, and I am cursed to carry it out till the end."

"So what am I to do with this coin? I never saw any genie. I found it on the ground."

"Use the coin, sir; use it to bring you your heart's desire, whatever that might be—money or power or the enjoyment of many different women—anything you want, but beware, sir, the coin is cursed, and one day, I fear, the Jinn will want it back from you."

"Thanks, Mr. Falid. That is a fascinating story. Now, after I am finished, can you please clean up? I have something to do later."

"Yes, sir. It will be done as you wish, and may I add, sir—it is not a story, it is real, so please be careful with the coin."

Jon Paul looked at his manservant, and he could tell he was serious. "Thank you again, Mr. Falid. I will be careful." Jon Paul then finished up his king's breakfast and got ready to go see Liz.

***

When Paul Pierre awoke the next morning, he felt better, as if a weight had been lifted from his shoulders. Today was the day to go see Dr. Martin. He would drive down to the museum soon and describe the ancient coin to Dr. Martin, and maybe he could tell him more about it. Paul got ready to eat some breakfast. He wasn't particularly hungry, so he ate light, just a small bagel with some cream cheese and a small cup of tea to get him through the morning.

***

Jon Paul was sitting, fully satisfied with himself and his appetite, when Mr. Falid came out from the kitchen and said, "Sir, I have finished my work. Do you need me for anything else?"

"No thanks, Mr. Falid. I really enjoyed your story this morning, but you may leave me now."

"As you wish, sir." Mr. Falid vanished from his sight, presumably back to wherever he lived.

Jon Paul had the ring for Liz and he was ready to give it to her today, but first he wanted to find out if his old friend Paul was planning something against him. He could feel the coin heating up as he held it in his hand. He focused very hard and finally said, "Will Paul and Michelle try to take the coin from me?"

He sat for a moment, and slowly, a small voice began to be heard, "They are planning to see you; they are planning to take the coin from you; they are planning on this soon." The voice seemed to speak, as if burning ashes had a voice, but Jon Paul understood each and every word perfectly.

So, he thought, *they are planning on taking my coin! Well, good luck. They will never get it from me. I will hold it till the day I die!* He thought about how they might try to get it from him; he was pretty sure they would try something like saying Michelle wanted to see him or something. He would go along with it until he could thwart their plan, whatever it might be.

As Jon Paul got ready to go see Liz, he thought about how he wanted to make sure she would love the ring and him too, but he knew she already did. He wanted to give her the best of everything. He had a plan to see her, give her the ring and anything else she wanted, but it must be done in the right order. He couldn't just wish for everything all at once. It needed to be planned out to perfection, or so he thought. Jon Paul was almost ready to see Liz when the phone rang.

"Hello."

"Yes, hello, Jon Paul. This is Sara. How is everything?"

"Hi, Sara. I have bad news to tell you."

"What is it, Jon Paul?"

"I broke up with Michelle a few days ago."

"Are you serious?"

"Yes. She just kept pushing me and it got to be too much for me, and we fought and then she left."

"She left. Is she coming back?"

"No, we are done. It is finished."

"What will you do now, Jon Paul?"

"I don't know, but I have met an old friend and we have been hanging out together."

"Is it serious?"

"Yes. I know it is a bit sudden, but it feels right. It is different than when I was with Michelle; it is like we are soul mates."

"Well, Jon Paul, I am sorry it didn't work out with Michelle. I had this funny feeling something was wrong."

"Don't worry, Sara. I am fine, but I better go now. I will call you later."

"Okay, Jon Paul, call me later then."

"Sure thing, sis, take care, okay? Bye."

"Bye." Now that Sara knew the news, she would inform Jon Paul's family, and he would eventually have to explain this to them. They wouldn't understand.

Jon Paul walked out of his apartment and down the street to Liz's place. He was going to give her the ring, and she would be so very happy.

***

Paul finished his breakfast and got ready to leave. He was going to see the expert Dr. Martin at the museum and find out all he could about the coin. As he got into his car, he also thought about Michelle and how he would ask her to move in with him at his place, even if only to save her from Jon Paul.

***

As Jon Paul walked to Liz's house, he realized he had forgotten to call her first, and he was feeling a bit guilty about this. So he wondered if he should do anything else to show her he was sorry. He decided to just bring her the ring and see her reaction first. If she was mad, he would do something special for her.

As he got nearer to her apartment, he noticed the people walking the street were few and far between. He remembered that before he got the coin, he would often see lots of people walking to and from their particular destinations. Now, since he had the coin, he did not encounter many people at all. It was as if the coin was protecting him from—or perhaps, keeping him from—people.

***

Paul drove to the museum and parked his car. As he got out, he saw quite a lot of people walking around. He always saw many people. He climbed the marble stairs to the heavy front door and pulled it open. Once inside, he walked over to a security guard and asked him for directions to Dr. Martin's office. The security guard pointed him to a plaque on the wall that listed all the offices and the tenants. He looked and found that the doctor's office number was 516, so he turned, found the elevators, and walked over to them, then pushed the button and waited.

***

Jon Paul got closer to Liz's place, and as he walked up to the doors to her apartment, a strange feeling came over him. It was like he was being probed; he almost felt like he was about to be examined.

***

Paul rode the elevator to the fifth floor, and as the doors opened, he stepped out and looked at the numbers on the doors. The hall was brightly lit with nice paintings on the walls and what looked like new carpet on the floor. He walked past 510, then 515, and then finally came to 516. He turned the knob on the door and went in. Sitting behind a nice high desk was a smart-looking lady—obviously the secretary, he thought.

"Hi, my name is Paul Dubois. I called the other day."

"Please have a seat, Mr. Dubois. Dr. Martin will be with you shortly."

He sat down on a very comfortable couch that had the appearance and feel of genuine leather. Paul was used to nice things. After a few moments, a bright-looking man opened a door and walked out. He had a thin angular face, like a doctor, with bright-blue eyes, and Paul thought he looked intelligent.

"Mr. Dubois, I am Dr. Martin."

Paul stood up and shook his outstretched hand. He had a firm handshake. "Hello, Dr. Martin. How are you today?"

"I am very good, Mr. Dubois, very good."

They walked into his office and both sat down in leather high-backed chairs beside the desk. "So, tell me, Mr. Dubois, about this coin of yours."

"I can only tell you what I know so far, which is that a friend of mine was walking down by this museum and he said he saw this shiny thing on the ground. It even seemed to pull him to it, like a magnet."

"I see; go on, please."

"As he got closer, he saw it was a gold coin. He reached for it and, looking around, he saw that he was totally alone, which is strange for the museum in the late morning, don't you think?"

"Yes, that is strange."

"Anyway, he said he could feel the coin, like it had power."

"And did he say anything else about it?"

"Yes, after a while, he said he thought he had a funny feeling, as if he should make some kind of a wish with it."

"And did he make a wish?"

"Yes, he did. He wished for another coin."

"What happened after that?"

"He said he got another, just like that first one, in his hands, instantly."

"Let me get this straight. You are telling me this is a magic coin?"

"Yes."

"Okay, what did it look like—was it old, and did it have any specific markings or engravings on it of any kind?"

"Yes, it was about the size of a euro quarter."

"A euro quarter. Well, any special markings?"

"Yes, it had what looked like engraved letters on it that were very old, maybe Middle Eastern. It also had a kind of serpent across the middle of it."

"A serpent and old Middle East writings. Hmmm, I think I know your coin. Let's have a look at this book." Dr. Martin pulled out a very old book from his bookshelf; the book was more of a reference bible than an actual book. He flipped through some pages and stopped on a particular one. He scanned the page and stopped at the very last picture of an old coin from ancient Persia.

"Is this your coin?"

"It is very similar, for sure, but not exact."

"Well, then, I am going to need a few days to research some other books. Can you leave me your number and I will call you in a few days when I find it?"

"Yeah, sure. Do you need me to do anything else in the meantime?"

"No, Mr. Dubois, I will take care of it. I believe I know your coin, but it will take me some time to locate it. Just go about your normal routine."

"Thanks, doctor. I will wait to hear from you in a couple days."

"Yes, oh, and by the way, you can leave your number with my secretary."

Paul nodded as they shook hands, and he walked out the door to the secretary's desk. The woman took his number and filed it away. Paul walked out the door back to the elevator. He was happy this Dr. Martin would be able to help him. He was now going to see his new love, Michelle. As he walked to the parking lot, he thought about Michelle and how he should ask her to move in with him, but thought maybe he should wait awhile. *She has just been through a very serious ordeal, and maybe asking her now would be too soon. She needs to heal and regain her strength first,* he thought.

Paul would wait until Michelle was stronger and then he would ask her to move in with him. For now, he would just focus on getting the coin from Jon Paul and find a way to destroy it if he possibly could.

***

Jon Paul knocked on Liz's door, and when she opened it, she looked a little upset with him for not calling her first. He had told her he would, but with all the commotion from the morning, he had forgotten. She smiled at him and said, "Why didn't you call me first?"

"Sorry, Liz, I got in a rush, and things were very hectic this morning." He smiled at her.

"Well, it is okay. Come in and sit down. I was just about to take a shower. Give me a few minutes and I will be back down."

"Take your time, Liz. I will make myself a cup of tea, if that is okay."

"Of course, Jon Paul, you silly man—anything you want."

He smiled at her and Liz smiled back. She then walked upstairs to her shower to get ready for their day together. Jon Paul went into the kitchen and found the tea. He got some water boiling and waited for it, and then he sat in her kitchen and drank his tea. He could occasionally hear her moving around upstairs and wondered if he should go talk with her.

Liz got herself ready and dressed very nice for Jon Paul. She was glad he was here, even if he had forgotten to call first. That was okay, she thought. She wondered what they were going to do today. Jon Paul walked back into the living room to wait for Liz. He sat down on the couch, turned on her TV, and sat back to relax. As he watched the news, it seemed to him that it was always the same—riots here or some kind of other unrest in the West, and the Middle East with its problems. *Things never change,* he thought. He changed the channel until he found a show about antiques.

Watching the show about antiques had reminded him of that strange feeling he had earlier. It had passed, and he wondered what it had been.

When Liz walked down the stairs to Jon Paul, he thought she looked very beautiful. She was wearing a skin-tight pair of Levi's and a blue shirt that was lined with leather fringes on the sleeves and the collar. She also had a gold necklace that matched her earrings, which were also gold and shined brightly in the light.

"Wow, you look *great*!"

"Why, thank you, sir," she said, smiling.

Jon Paul stared at her until he thought his eyes were drying out. Then Liz said, "What are we going to do today?"

Her question snapped him from his daydream and he said, "I don't know. How about we take a walk to the Old Town Shops?"

"Hmmm, the Old Town Shops sound good."

"Why don't we go in about an hour? I want to sit down with you and talk first for a while."

"Oh, okay, what are you wanting to talk about? You are making me very nervous, Jon Paul."

"Nothing serious, sweetie. I just want to spend time with you before we go out in public."

She smiled at him and Jon Paul smiled back. He had the ring and he was waiting to give it to her at just the right moment.

***

Paul drove to the hospital and thought about Michelle. He would see her very soon, and that didn't seem soon enough for him. He parked his car at the hospital and he walked up the stairs and to the elevator that would lead him to her floor. Michelle was sitting up in her bed when he walked into her room. He thought she looked so beautiful in her white gown and fuzzy slippers.

"Paul!"

He bent down to her and gave her a hug. She looked very healthy this morning, and he wondered if she was ready to go back to her motel. "How are you feeling, Michelle?"

"I am wonderful, Paul. I am so glad you are here!"

"Me, too. I did have a bit of an adventure at the doctor's office earlier."

"Tell me, please."

"Well, I went to see this Dr. Martin. We talked for a while and he finally showed me some pictures of old Persian coins, but none seemed to look the same."

"So, nothing exact?"

"No. He asked me to give him a couple more days to do some more research and then he will call me when he has more for me to look at."

"So what kind of coin did he think it is?"

"He didn't say. He did seem very interested in doing the research, though."

She nodded in agreement at him. "Paul, I am a little worried about … you-know-who."

"Who, Jon Paul?"

"Yes, if he finds out what we are planning."

"He won't, Michelle. How can he?"

"I don't know. I just have a bad feeling about this."

"Try not to worry, Michelle. Everything will be all right. I promise." He gave her a hug and looked at her with a strong confidence that she could see, and this made her feel better. As they sat and held each other, Paul soon realized he wanted to ask Michelle a question.

"Michelle, are you ready to check out of here today?"

"Yes. The nurses told me that I can be released as soon as they get my paperwork done, but I might need someone to watch me for a few days." She smiled at him, and he knew exactly what she meant. Paul would be happy to stay with Michelle at her motel.

***

Jon Paul was sipping his tea when Liz noticed something in his hand. "What is that, Jon Paul?"

"What is what?" he said coyly.

"In your hand, silly."

"Oh, you mean this. It is nothing, just a little something I wanted to give you today."

He handed her the box with the ring in it. As she opened it, her eyes opened wide, a smile curved her face, and Jon Paul knew he had done the right thing. She stared at the ring as if she were hypnotized by its brilliant beauty. She put the ring on her finger, a perfect fit. She was so overjoyed that she began to cry tears of joy. Jon Paul knew at that moment that he and Liz would be together for this life, no matter what.

***

Paul got up and walked over to the nurse's station to ask if Michelle could be released. One of the nurses, whom he recognized from before, looked at him and said, "Hi, how can I help you?"

"Is Michelle Duvalier ready to be released today?"

"Hold on, sir, let me check and see if the doctor has given the release time." Paul waited, and after a few moments, the nurse said, "Yes, she can sign her papers anytime now. I sent the other nurse to tell her, but if you want, you can go wait with her in her room."

"Yes, thank you, that would be great." Paul walked back to Michelle's room and sat down beside her. She smiled at him he smiled back. "The nurse said as soon as you are ready, they can let you go home."

"I am ready to go now, Paul."

"Hang on, now, Michelle, just be careful. You have just gone through a major ordeal. I don't want you to get too excited yet."

"Very funny, Paul. I am fine. Can you help me with my clothes?"

"Sure, Michelle." Paul helped Michelle get her clothes, and then Michelle was ready to move on with her life—without Jon Paul. They had had some great years, but now she had found Paul. What would she tell her mom, or her sisters? She wondered.

They walked out to the nurse's station and asked for her release papers. The nurse on duty got them and handed them to her. She signed and said to the nurse, "Thank you for taking care of me, and could you tell the doctors who saved me thanks, too?"

The nurse smiled and said, "Sure thing; you take care of yourself, young lady."

"Okay, I will try." Michelle and Paul walked down the hall to the elevators, pushed the button, got in, and went down to the lobby to exit the hospital.

Paul had saved her life, but just barely in time, or at least, that is what everyone at the hospital thought—except for the one nurse. No one except Michelle and the one nurse had seen the woman dressed in blue. They walked to Paul's car and got in, and as he started the engine, he looked at Michelle and said, "So, my princess, where shall I take you?"

Laughing, Michelle said, "Take me home, you know—the motel." Paul nodded in agreement and drove down the road. The drive was quiet. Neither said a lot, but they did make eye contact. When Paul pulled into the motel parking lot, he found the spot closest to her room and parked the car. They got out, he opened the door for her, and they went inside.

"Are you happy to be home in this place?"

"Paul, I have no other place right now, so yeah, I am glad to be home."

"I was just kidding, Michelle."

"I know, Paul, and I am happy you are here with me. I really am."

"Thanks, Michelle. I am glad to be here with you, too." They hugged, and each felt the other's heartbeat.

***

Liz had the ring of her dreams on her finger and the man of her dreams next to her. She was very happy as they sat and talked, and she wondered what Jon Paul's plans were, so she decided to ask him. "Jon Paul, will you tell me—what are your plans for us?"

"Oh, that is a big secret, my dear," he said, smiling.

"Really a secret, Jon Paul?"

"Yes. I can't tell you everything, now, can I?"

"Yes, you can, mister!" she said teasingly.

"Oh, well, let me see, I think I could tell you this—we are in good company now. Everything is just going to get better and better."

"What does that mean?"

"Um, I will tell you later, okay?"

"I will remember, Jon Paul, and you better."

Jon Paul smiled and Liz smiled back. They both loved the way they could communicate just with their eyes, without using words. They enjoyed the time together at her house and then Jon Paul said, "Well, shall we go to the old shops for a while?"

Liz looked at him and said, "Did you just want to give me the ring first before we went to the Old Town Shops?"

"Yes, that was the plan."

"Well then, yeah, I am ready to go now, Jon Paul." Liz smiled at Jon Paul and they grabbed their coats and walked out the door. Liz and Jon Paul were walking there and would spend most of the day just looking and browsing— just being together in each other's company made them both very happy.

***

Paul and Michelle were sitting in her motel room when Michelle said, "Paul, I am so glad you are here with me. Ever since I left Jon Paul, you have become my light, my rock. If it wasn't for you, I might not even be here."

"Thanks, Michelle, but you must know how much you have come to mean to me."

"Yes, Paul, I think I do, and you mean that much to me, too."

They both smiled at each other and Paul, feeling good about his new relationship, said, "Michelle, I have something to tell you."

"Yes, Paul, what is it?"

"Ever since you kissed me at the apartment, I haven't thought about another woman, and as you know, I have had my share. But this is different; *you* are different."

"What do you mean, Paul?"

"You have opened my heart and helped me to love again." Michelle smiled at Paul and gave him a big hug. She knew he was falling in love with her and she in love with him.

"Paul, it is okay; now we have each other, and nothing can break us apart, not even Jon Paul with his coin." Paul looked at Michelle with curious eyes. He wanted to believe her, but he knew about the coin and what it could do.

"Michelle, you are right. I should be happy for us, and I am."

"Then don't you worry about anything. We will be fine. We have a plan to rid Jon Paul of the coin, and even though I feel it's risky for us, I think it can work if we time it just right."

"Yes, you are right, but I must time it perfectly, or it could be disastrous for us."

"Paul, I am getting kind of tired. I think I will lie down for a while, okay?"

"Of course, Michelle, you must rest and regain your strength. We have a lot of work to do."

Michelle lay down and rested. She and Paul had a good plan, but if they were going to succeed, they must have their wits about them, and if that meant Michelle needed to rest for a couple of days, then that is exactly what they would do.

***

Jon Paul and Liz walked to the Old Town Shops, as they were known. Most were locally owned by families. There was even one owned by a man who made jewelry, and he and his wife did most of the work there. There was one shop with a man who made and painted his own ceramics; he was a real craftsman. Some of his wares were very exquisite and expensive. Jon Paul had an eye for some of this man's finer things. He and Liz walked toward his shop, and as they got closer to the door, Jon Paul noticed that there was a woman in the shop looking around. She seemed familiar to him. Jon Paul slowly walked around with Liz following him. Occasionally, Liz would stop and look and even touch an object, and then stare in disbelief at the prices.

Jon Paul noticed this and said to her, "See anything you like?"

Smiling, she looked at him and said, "Yes, this piece here, but it is so expensive!"

Jon Paul looked at the price, smiled, and said, "Do you want it?"

Liz looked at him in shock and said, "Jon Paul, don't you go and buy this. I already have the most beautiful ring a girl could ever want."

"Are you sure you don't want me to buy it?"

"Yes, I am sure, Jon Paul. It is too expensive."

Liz had picked out a beautiful vase with such swirly lines that it looked like it was in motion; the blue and white and gold colors blended together so well, it looked as if they were interchangeable. As Liz admired the vase,

Jon Paul began to smile as the coin heated up in his hand. When he saw that Liz was not looking at him, he said, "I wish I had the money to buy this vase right now." Instantly, he had the money in his hands. He put the coin back in his pocket, walked up to the front of the store where the cash register was, and said to the owner of the shop, "I would like to purchase that vase she is holding."

"Yes, sir," said the man. "Will there be anything else?"

"No, thank you, that will be just fine for today."

"Thank you, sir. Please come again."

Jon Paul bought the vase for Liz, and she was amazed at his generosity. They had the man wrap it up in a nice covering, and then they walked out the door and down the street.

"Liz, I am getting hungry. Are you?"

"Now that you mention it, I am a little hungry."

"How about we find us something to eat for lunch?"

"Sounds good, Jon Paul, got anything in mind?"

"Um, yeah, there is a place not too far from here that has really good beef stew."

"Okay, let's go then." They began to walk to the little restaurant where they could get lunch.

The walk was nice for Jon Paul and Liz. She had her beautiful new diamond ring and now Jon Paul had just bought her a very expensive vase. Liz was having a great day. They walked around the small town shopping center, or as it was known to the locals, "The Old Town Shops." The restaurant to which they were walking was just behind the shops, so they didn't have far to go to get some lunch. As they got nearer the restaurant, a few business people had arrived for their lunches too. There were even a few seniors enjoying lunch, as well. They opened the door and went in to find a place to sit in the back, in a booth. They were looking for a little privacy, naturally. After a few moments, a waiter approached them and said, "Hello. I am your waiter, Remi. I will be serving you today. Is there anything I can start you off with, like a drink?"

Jon Paul looked at the waiter and said, "No thanks. How about you, Liz?"

"Can you just bring me a soft drink?"

"Yes, ma'am; we have Pepsi products or Coke products."

"Can you bring me a Pepsi, please?" asked Liz.

"And you, sir?"

"Yeah, just bring me the same."

"Very good, then. I will be right back with your drinks."

Jon Paul nodded at the waiter as he smiled and walked away. He began to look at the menu. After several minutes, the waiter appeared and set their drinks down on the table. He asked if they were ready to order; both said that they were. Jon Paul and Liz gave their order for some beef stew, and then after the waiter left, they began to talk.

"You know, Liz, I am having a really great day!"

"I am too, Jon Paul."

"You know, Liz, that woman at the shop looked familiar to me, and she kept staring at me."

"Do you think you know her from somewhere?"

"That is what I was thinking, but where?"

"I don't know."

As they sat and waited for their lunch and made conversation, Jon Paul kept thinking about the strange woman. After several moments, the waiter arrived with their beef stew, set it on the table, and asked if they needed anything else; both said they were good for now. As Jon Paul sat and ate, he remembered something about a woman that was friends with Michelle, or at least, Michelle had mentioned a woman that worked down by the Old Town Shops—maybe that was how he knew her. He decided to just forget her and enjoy his lunch and move on with Liz.

They did enjoy their lunch. They ate in what was a medium-sized restaurant and talked and laughed, enjoying each other's company. Time slipped away for Liz and Jon Paul, and soon they noticed the time and decided to leave. They'd had a wonderful lunch, but now it was time to get Liz back home to put away her vase and get ready for the evening. They walked back to Liz's place, and when they got settled more, they began to look for a place to put the vase.

"How about here, next to the mantle?" asked Jon Paul.

"No, how about over here by the end table? It matches better with the color of the table."

"You are right, Liz, it does look better there."

She smiled at him and he knew she was right; she had a better way of decorating then he did, and it showed. Jon Paul was enjoying himself quite a lot with Liz. He knew he had found the right woman, and he would do anything to keep her.

***

Paul and Michelle were in her motel room. Paul was keeping Michelle safe and taking care of her; this is what the doctors had told him he must do. The one particular nurse had told him to get her to a church to pray and say thanks. This thought, he was not so comfortable with; he wasn't the most religious of men, and the idea that a guardian angel had saved Michelle's life seemed a bit farfetched. He let her sleep as she needed. Michelle had just been through a very traumatic experience; she had actually died and been saved by the doctors. Paul was not so sure about the guardian angel that she said she saw.

As it was nearing lunch, Paul decided to go and get some food for Michelle. She was asleep on the bed, so he grabbed his coat and quietly left. He would find something light and easy for her to eat. As he drove around, he saw an old favorite of his where, when he was with Jon Paul, they would occasionally stop in and grab a bite. It was the tiny bistro that he had been to so many times before, and he would again visit it this day. He went in and looked over the menu. He settled on pastrami on rye for him and for Michelle, a minestrone soup with a lightly breaded chicken sandwich.

Although this might be too much for her right now, he could always save it for later if she got hungry. He paid for the food, got back in his car, and drove to the motel. He was getting hungry, as the smell of the pastrami was very fresh to him. He parked and went inside. She was still asleep, so he set the food on the table and took off his coat; then he grabbed his sandwich and began to eat.

Paul ate slowly and deliberately. He didn't want to wake Michelle, and he was really enjoying the taste of his food. After several minutes, Michelle began to stir. She opened her eyes, looked at Paul, and said, "Hi! Did you bring me anything?"

"Of course! I got you a minestrone soup and a chicken sandwich."

"Mmm, smells good, but I think I will just eat the soup for now. Can you save the sandwich for later?"

"Sure, Michelle; anything you like, my dear." He smiled at her and brought her the soup.

She sat up to eat it. "Wow, this is really good, Paul!"

"Yeah, I went to that little bistro down the street a few miles from here." Michelle smiled as she ate her soup. She knew it was good cooking when she tasted it, being a chef herself.

"Do you really like it?" he asked.

"Are you kidding me? It is one of the best soups I have ever tasted."

They sat and ate their lunch, and both Paul and Michelle enjoyed each other's company. Suddenly, the phone rang. Michelle looked at Paul, and he looked back at her with a puzzled look on his face. No one knew they were here, so who could be calling them?

"Hello."

"Hello, this is the front desk. We are checking to see if you need anything. The maid was not able to get into your room earlier, and if you require anything, please let me know. I can have it brought to you right away."

"No, thanks; we are good for now, but if we need anything, we will let you know."

"Very good, sir, thank you for your time. Please enjoy your stay here."

Paul hung up the phone and looked at Michelle. "That was the front desk. They were asking if we needed anything, and I told them no, but if we do, we will let them know."

"Okay, yeah, that is fine. We don't really need anything right now anyway," said Michelle.

Paul and Michelle finished their lunch, and Paul noticed that Michelle seemed to be getting tired. "Are you getting sleepy?"

"Yeah, I am, actually. Do you mind if I close my eyes for a little bit?"

"Michelle, you sleep as much as you need; I am here for you, no matter what."

He smiled at her and she smiled back. Michelle was becoming very comfortable with Paul. For the rest of the afternoon, Michelle slept. On occasion, she would wake and see Paul, smile at him, and fall back asleep. Paul would notice this and smile back. He was enjoying taking care of Michelle. In fact, he was almost sure he could do this for the rest of his life.

While the afternoon moved along, Paul watched TV. Sometimes, he fell asleep too, if only for brief moments at a time. He thought about Jon Paul and how he could get Michelle over to his place to put their plan into action. Every time, though, he would come up with the same idea. He would have Michelle call Jon Paul and ask if she could come by to pick up her things. This would be the most real thing she could say so as not to arouse suspicion in Jon Paul.

***

Jon Paul and Liz enjoyed their afternoon together. Often sipping their tea, they would sit and talk about their future. Liz had very definite plans, while Jon Paul really didn't. But he was sure of one thing: the coin would help him make a financially secure and successful life for himself and Liz.

"You know, Jon Paul, you should think about getting a different place."

"What do you mean?"

"With you and Michelle breaking up, I would think you might want a different place to live, a place where it is just you and me."

"You're right. I hadn't thought of that. Maybe I should—any ideas?"

"You could look for a nicer apartment, like a bigger and better one, or how about a mansion?" replied Liz.

"What, a mansion, seriously? I really could, but wait, slow down a little. We are getting ahead of ourselves. I need to think this through and get it right first."

"You're right, Jon Paul. Let's figure this out first."

Jon Paul and Liz talked about what they could do, and after a long conversation, they had come up with a plan for money and an estate with land and financial security. Both seemed pleased with their choice of a life plan. Jon Paul would use the coin for their future. Now, Jon Paul had not told Liz about the coin. As they sat talking, he thought, *maybe I should tell Liz about my coin.* After a few minutes of him going over the idea in his head, he decided he would tell her all about the golden, wish-granting coin. He waited for her to take a break in her conversation, and then he found the right words and said to her, "Liz, I want to tell you something."

"Yes, Jon Paul."

"Liz, do you ever wonder why I am able to buy you such expensive gifts?"

"Yes, I was wondering that, Jon Paul. I figured you had made some money and put it into a savings account."

"Not exactly, Liz. A few weeks ago, I was walking down by the museum, and I saw a shiny gold coin on the ground." Liz looked at him and nodded in agreement as he continued. "Well, I looked around and there was no one there, so I picked it up and put it in my pocket."

"Then what happened, Jon Paul?"

"Well, after I continued to walk for some time, I had this feeling—or maybe it was inspiration—to take the coin out of my pocket and make a wish with it!"

"Are you serious, Jon Paul?"

"Yes, I am totally serious." He reached in his pocket and took out the coin for her to see; she gasped in awe at the brilliance of the coin.

"Wow, I have never seen such a thing. Where do you think it comes from, Jon Paul?"

"I don't know, but it is like the longer I have the coin, the more it becomes a part of me."

"What do you mean, Jon Paul?"

"I hear voices when I hold it, and they tell me things."

"What things—bad things?"

"No, more like information on how to use it to make wishes."

Liz sat and stared at the coin; she wondered if it was all real.

"Jon Paul, can we make a wish right now?"

"I don't know. What would you wish for?"

"Well, how about some new diamond earrings to match my ring?"

"Okay, sure, that would be good." Jon Paul took the coin in his hand, closed his eyes, and began to concentrate. After a few seconds, he said, "I wish for diamond earrings to match the diamond ring on Liz's finger." *Poof!* There, in his hands, were diamond earrings, just as beautiful as the ring she was wearing. Liz was amazed; she looked at him with wide eyes. She couldn't believe it was so easy.

She wondered, *Where does the coin come from, and how does it do wishes?* Jon Paul smiled at Liz and handed her the earrings, and she immediately took out the ones she had in and put the new ones in her ears. They sparkled like the sun. She grinned from ear to ear. Liz looked spectacular. "Jon Paul, thank you for such a wonderful gift!"

"You don't feel weird about getting them from the coin?"

"Oh, no, Jon Paul, not at all. I think we are going to have a very bright future!" Liz was very happy with what had happened. Jon Paul, seeing her happiness, knew he had made the right choice. He and Liz would spend their lives in luxury and financial security.

"Jon Paul, do we have a good plan for our future, and are you sure about it?"

"Um, yes, I think we do. Can you just give me a little time to set things right? Our future will be so great, neither of us will know what to do!"

"Okay, Jon Paul. What should we do first?"

Jon Paul went on to explain to Liz how they must first clear up his past with Michelle before they began making their wishes. This would probably make them known to many people in their small town of Toulon. Toulon was a small city and some of the people knew each other by name, so it was not uncommon for them to say hello to each other. It was not so small that *everyone* knew each other, but it was still small enough to have a friendly atmosphere.

As evening began to approach, Jon Paul and Liz had been working on their plans for the future for several hours, so both were getting hungry.

"Liz, are you hungry?"

"I am a bit hungry," she said.

"You want to find something to eat?"

"Yeah, we could. What are you hungry for, Jon Paul?"

Jon Paul suddenly grabbed Liz and said, "You, baby!"

Liz smiled and said, "Jon Paul, you are too much."

"I know, baby; that is why you love me!"

"You know it."

"But seriously, Jon Paul, what do you want to eat?"

"I don't know, honey, you tell me, and I will get it for you."

Liz thought for a moment and finally said, "How about we go out for a nice romantic dinner at La Tortue?"

"La Tortue sounds good; let's go, then."

Jon Paul and Liz found their coats and walked out the door and down the street to the restaurant to have their romantic dinner. While they walked, they again talked about their future and what exactly they would do.

Liz was very excited to be having dinner with her man. She wore the jewelry he gave her proudly—and it showed.

***

Paul sat and watched Michelle sleep until finally she awoke. She sat up, looked at him, and said, "Are you watching me?"

"Why, yes, princess, I was." He smiled.

"I thought so. See anything you like?" Michelle smiled seductively at him. Paul smiled back and shook his head. Michelle had won that battle.

"Paul, what time is it?"

"It's a little past five, sweetie."

"Oh, okay, I was just wondering. I think I am a little hungry. Do we still have that chicken sandwich?"

"Yes, hold on. I will get it for you." Paul got up, grabbed the sandwich from the small fridge, and handed it to Michelle.

"Thanks, Paul," she said, smiling.

"Anytime—do you want something to drink too?"

"Um, yeah, what do we have?"

"I brought back a can of soda. Do you want that?"

"Yeah, that will be good. What about you, aren't you hungry?" asked Michelle.

"Not really; I mean, not right now, but soon I will be."

Paul watched Michelle eat her sandwich and drink her soda. He enjoyed waiting on her. It made him feel needed. His days of chasing different women were over. He had found a real woman, and his feelings for her had grown very deep.

Michelle ate and felt her strength returning; she would soon be ready to face Jon Paul. This would be a test of her courage. She was afraid of Jon Paul and what he would and could do with that coin. He was nearly unstoppable.

***

Jon Paul and Liz approached the restaurant and walked inside. A small crowd had gathered for an early dinner. Jon Paul noticed that a few even looked at him and then at Liz. Some were whispering under their breath, and although Jon Paul couldn't hear what they were saying, he was sure they were talking about the jewelry Liz was wearing.

As they were seated at a nice table, a couple next to them smiled and then looked away, obviously involved in their own conversation. The waiter looked at Jon Paul and asked him, "Sir, is there any drink you would like before ordering your dinner?"

"Yes, there is. Bring us a bottle of your finest wine; we are celebrating tonight!"

"Very good, sir, I shall be right out with your wine."

"Why, Jon Paul, you are so very romantic tonight."

Jon Paul smiled at Liz and said, "You know it, Lizzy—all for you!"

They sat there for a minute and then the waiter returned with their bottle of very expensive wine. "Sir, I took the liberty of bringing you a bottle of our very best champagne, a 1973 Lafite Rothschild."

"Thank you." The waiter opened the bottle and poured Jon Paul a small sample. He swished it around in his mouth for a second before swallowing it and said, "Yes, that is wonderful. It will do just fine, thank you."

"Very good, sir. Here are your menus. I will be back in a few moments to take you order." Jon Paul nodded in agreement as he handed a menu to Liz and kept one for himself.

"Liz, you order anything you want tonight. It is all about us, so don't worry about the price or anything. I have it covered."

She smiled at Jon Paul, winked at him, and said, "Okay, Jon Paul. I am so very happy you took me out tonight. I am having such a wonderful time."

"Me too, honey, me too."

Jon Paul and Liz sat there, drank their champagne, and enjoyed being with each other. After a few moments, the waiter approached and said, "Sir, are you ready to order?"

"Liz, are you ready?"

"I think so. Can I have the sirloin, medium done, with potatoes au gratin and steamed rice?"

"Very good, ma'am; and for you, sir?"

"I think I will have the same, except instead of the steamed rice, can I get steamed veggies?"

"Of course, sir. Will there be anything else?"

"No, I think that will be good for now, thank you."

The waiter smiled, took the menus, and walked away. Jon Paul and Liz looked at each other and smiled. "You know, Jon Paul, what we were talking about earlier—I think if we make a plan about a bigger place for you and

I, we should do it. I mean, what would happen if you … *lose the coin*?" She whispered the last part.

"Liz, don't worry; the coin is attached to me like it is a part of me. Even now, I can hear it talking to me in the back of my mind."

"What does it say to you, Jon Paul?"

"Mostly it talks about things I can do with it. It is like another voice is compelling me, and I am helpless to stop it. Sometimes I am only able to hear very little."

Liz was a little worried when she heard those words. She didn't realize how much the coin was a part of Jon Paul. Nevertheless, she was with him for life and would stand by him no matter what happened, she thought.

"Liz, by that, I mean that it is a strong voice that tells me things—things like how to wish for this or that, when to wish for it, and sometimes, it is just giving me words of wisdom."

Liz was puzzled by Jon Paul's statement; she wondered just what he meant by that. "What do you mean, Jon Paul?"

"Let's not worry about that right now, okay? You look very beautiful tonight."

Liz smiled and Jon Paul smiled back. As the waiter approached, they could smell their food and it smelled good. The waiter set the plates down on the table and asked, "Will there be anything else, sir?"

Jon Paul looked at Liz. She shook her head no, and he said, "No, thanks; we are good for now."

The waiter nodded in agreement and walked away, leaving them in peace to eat their meal. Jon Paul and Liz had a wonderful time. They laughed and ate and drank champagne. They were enjoying the finer things in life. After struggling for many years, Jon Paul was living the good life.

***

Paul and Michelle sat, and while Michelle ate her chicken sandwich, Paul began to get hungry. He wondered if he should go get something or just find something at the motel. Usually, this motel had a small dinner menu for its guests, and he was ready to eat something. "Michelle, where is the menu for this place?"

"Right here, honey."

"Thanks. I am getting hungry watching you eat. I think I will order something from the menu."

Michelle looked at Paul and said, "Sure, anything you want. I am positive it will be good."

As Paul looked over the small menu, his eyes settled on the beef soup with onions and a side of fries. He thought this sounded good, so he picked up the phone to order. "Hi, I would like to order some food."

"Hold on, sir. I can take your order; I just need to grab my pen. Okay, sir, what do you want?"

Paul told the staff person what he wanted. She took his order and told him it would be a few moments until it was ready, and then she asked what room he was in. Paul responded and said it would be fine and he would pay when he received his food rather than in the morning. The lady said that was fine and she would see him shortly with his dinner. Paul hung up the phone, looked at Michelle, and said, "Do you think you are ready to see Jon Paul tomorrow?"

"I don't know yet. Can we talk about this later, Paul, like tomorrow?"

"Sure thing. I just wanted to ask to see how you are feeling. You are really looking good and strong, too."

Michelle looked at Paul and said, "Thanks, Paul. I am feeling good. I don't know if I am ready to see Jon Paul, though."

"No problem, Michelle. I am not trying to rush you. We can talk about it tomorrow if you like."

Michelle smiled at him and nodded in agreement; this would be fine. They could carry out their plan tomorrow or the next day if she was feeling ready. Several moments passed, and then there was a knock at the door of Michelle's room. Paul responded by saying, "Yes, who is it?"

"I have an order of food for room six."

Paul opened the door and took the food from the woman; he handed her the money and a tip, said thank you, and closed the door. He sat down next to Michelle at the small table, opened the food tray, and began to eat. Paul and Michelle were enjoying their meal when suddenly, the phone rang.

"Hello," said Paul.

"Hello, sir. This is the front office just following up on your order. Was it delivered in a professional manner, and are you satisfied with our service?"

"Yes, the service was very good, and I am very happy with the meal. Thank you."

"Very good, sir. Enjoy the rest of your evening, and if there is anything you need, don't hesitate to call."

"Thanks, I will. Bye."

Paul was indeed satisfied with the service of this motel. He couldn't remember being treated so well at a motel in a very long time; it was quite refreshing, he thought. It was not often one could find a motel with top-quality service. He would remember this particular motel.

***

Jon Paul Liz enjoyed their dinner and were both beginning to feel full. They had eaten all they could and were now ready to leave the restaurant. When Jon Paul saw the waiter, he motioned for him to come over. As the waiter took notice of him, he walked over and said, "Yes, sir, is there anything else you would like this evening?"

"No, thanks, we are finished. Can you bring the check, please?"

"Yes, sir, I have it right here." He placed the check down on the table next to Jon Paul, who looked at it and then said, "Will you give us a few minutes, please?"

"Of course, sir. I shall be right back."

Jon Paul waited for the waiter to walk away; then, when he was sure the waiter could not see him, he reached in his pocket, felt the heat of the coin, grabbed it, and said, "I wish for the money to pay this bill." *Poof!* Instantly, he had money in his hands, more than enough to pay the bill. He again saw the waiter and motioned for him to come over to their table. He handed him the money and a big tip and said, "Here you are. Hope that tip is good, as well."

The waiter, knowing how much the bill was and how much Jon Paul had tipped him, said excitedly, "Thank you, sir; you are very generous!"

"No problem. The service was outstanding, and so was the food."

"Thank you, sir. Please come back anytime. We will always be ready to provide *you* with the finest service."

Jon Paul did not fail to notice the man's plea. He would indeed be back sometime soon. He and Liz put on their coats and walked out of the restaurant. They had a wonderful meal and now were deciding where to go next. "What do you want to do now, Liz? Do you just want to go back to my place?"

"Honey, after that meal, I am ready to go sit down for a few hours, and your place is as good as mine. Maybe we can talk more about our future."

Jon Paul smiled at her. He knew what she wanted talk about, and it wasn't their future. Liz wanted to talk about money and finding a house to buy. She was relentless about it, and Jon Paul loved her for it. In a small way, it really was about their future. But Jon Paul had much bigger plans than just a new house.

Liz and Jon Paul walked briskly back to his place. The evening had gotten a little cold and they were not without their coats, but walking did sometimes have its drawbacks. The walk was not long. They talked in short conversations and did not really say too much till they were almost at his place. Then Liz said, "Jon Paul, can we just relax and not do anything for a while tonight?"

"Sure thing, Liz. Is there anything wrong?"

"No, I am just feeling a little tired after our walk. I need to rest for a while."

"Anything you want, my dear. We will just sit on the couch and watch some TV."

"That sounds perfect, Jon Paul." They were fast approaching his apartment when Jon Paul realized he had forgotten his keys. They walked up to the mailboxes, found the manager's number, and rang his buzzer.

"Yes, who is it?"

"It is Jon Paul. I forgot my keys. Can you let us in?"

"Oh, sure, Jon Paul, be right there." The manager walked down the hall to the front door, opened it, and said, "What happened, Jon Paul?"

"I don't know. I must have left my keys in the apartment somewhere."

The manager laughed. Every once in awhile, Jon Paul would forget his keys and he would have to let him in. "Jon Paul, where is Michelle tonight?"

"We broke up and she moved out. This is Liz."

"Hi, Liz. I am Sammy; very nice to meet you. I try to get to know all my tenants, hope I am not being too nosy." Liz shook his hand and smiled. He seemed like a nice guy.

"No, not at all. Jon Paul and I have had a great evening, and I am happy you could help us out." They walked up to his apartment and opened the door. Jon Paul then said, "Thanks, Sammy. I owe you one."

Sammy smiled, looked at Jon Paul, and said, "Yes, you do, Jon Paul; yes, you do."

Jon Paul and Liz sat down on the couch. He turned on the TV and surfed through the channels until he found something he thought they would both enjoy. Soon, Liz had fallen asleep in Jon Paul's arms. He was very comfortable with her and with having her stay with him. He continued to sit on the couch till he became thirsty.

Jon Paul didn't want to disturb Liz, so he carefully slipped his arm out from under her shoulder, stood up gently, and walked into the kitchen to find a drink. Jon Paul looked in the fridge, and his eyes came upon a cold malt beverage that his manservant had put there a few days ago. Jon Paul hadn't yet taken the time to drink it or eat the meal that was also there. He was thirsty, though, so he took it out of the fridge, poured it into a glass, walked back to the living room, sat down gently, and began to drink his malt beer.

As time moved on, Jon Paul fell asleep next to Liz, and he had such dreams—dreams that were wild and vivid. He would be running really fast, or he would see himself as a big cat, like a leopard, running and hunting, chasing down prey. One dream even had him at war giving orders to kill someone. Jon Paul would not remember many of these dreams so well, but they were still trying to give him a message—a message that was lost on Jon Paul at the moment.

Liz watched him sleep. She felt happy and comfortable with Jon Paul. She did begin to wonder just what he was dreaming about that had him talking and thrashing around, waking her from her sleep. She was happier than she had ever been, at least that she could remember in a long time. Why hadn't she met Jon Paul years ago? Why didn't they get together that time, so long ago? Liz wondered why, and she found no answers. Jon Paul awoke suddenly to find her staring at him. He was not disturbed by this; he felt strangely comfortable, like she was watching out for him, keeping him safe from any and all danger. "Liz, why don't we go to bed and get some sleep. It has been a long day, and I am tired myself."

"Sure thing, baby, lead the way."

Jon Paul and Liz did go to bed. They'd had a long day and both were tired from all the day's excitement. They got ready for bed, and soon they were both were fast asleep—sleep so deep that there were only dreams, dreams of a most awful nature for Jon Paul …

"My general, the enemy is approaching fast; what shall we do?"

"Rally the troops, Lieutenant. Call for Captain Abad; he needs to be sent to me immediately."

The lieutenant left the general's tent to find Captain Abad. After searching through several different tents, he found him. "Captain Abad, the general wants to see you, now!"

"Yes, sir. I am on my way." The lieutenant walked back to the general's tent with Captain Abad. As they entered his tent, the general was briefing some other men. "Captain Abad, you must take control of the south side of the border. Leave nothing alive. Do you understand me, Captain? Leave nothing alive—no women, no children, no man or boy."

"Sir, I understand. I will leave immediately."

"Leave me, then," said the general.

This was one dream of Jon Paul's, but a dream he wouldn't remember. It was a dream that once involved him, in a past life, many years gone now.

***

Paul and Michelle spent the evening watching TV and relaxing. They had eaten their dinner and now just wanted to be with each other, even if that meant just sitting on the couch in a loving embrace. "You know, Paul, I think we can call Jon Paul tomorrow and go over there. Are you ready to try to get the coin from him?"

"Wow, you must be feeling good. I didn't think you would be ready for a couple days, but if you want to try tomorrow, we can."

"Yes, right now, I am almost sure we can, but if I am not up for it in the morning, we can try it later, like in couple days."

"Okay, let's see how you are feeling in the morning and then make our plan." He smiled at Michelle and she smiled back and nodded in agreement. Paul and Michelle had a plan, but it would not work till they could get to see Jon Paul and put it into action. The night wore on for them, and they both found themselves getting sleepy and tired. After a long day of recuperating, Paul and Michelle went to sleep. They would maybe try their plan the following day, depending on Michelle and her strength. Although it was a bit risky, it was still a good plan and the only one they could come up with that might actually work.

As she slept, Michelle dreamed of a life with Paul, but those happy dreams would be interrupted by dreams of a most sinister nature—dreams of Jon Paul and his evil coin.

In the morning, Paul awoke without disturbing Michelle; he sat up and wondered if today would be the day they tried to get Jon Paul's coin. He got up and decided to take a quick shower; hopefully, he wouldn't wake Michelle. Michelle awoke with the sound of the shower running. As she lay in bed, she thought she was hungry. Maybe she and Paul could find breakfast somewhere close. Nothing fancy, just a nice, sit-down breakfast. She got up, walked into the bathroom, and joined Paul in the shower.

When Paul and Michelle had finished showering, they began to talk.

"Michelle, I am hungry. Do you want to go somewhere and get some breakfast?"

"You know, Paul, that is what I was thinking too."

"What do you feel hungry for?"

"I don't know, something quick and easy, nothing fancy."

"That is *exactly* what I was thinking!"

"Well, let's try to find a place just close enough so we can get back here soon."

"Okay, Paul, you know this area better than me. Where shall we go?"

"I am thinking of that little bistro we passed by yesterday."

"Oh, yeah, that did look like a good place. Let's go there, Paul."

Paul and Michelle got dressed and ready to go find breakfast. As they walked out to his car, they both noticed what a beautiful morning it was; it was going to be a lovely day for them. They drove down the street and after a few moments, they arrived at the little bistro. Le Grand Café was the name, and it looked very inviting. There were small tables with umbrellas on them, and just off the sidewalk, a man was playing a saxophone. They walked inside and up to the counter. There was a very nice-looking young lady there; she smiled as she looked at Paul and Michelle, and then she said, "Good morning, can I take your order?"

Michelle was the first to speak. "Yes, can I get an espresso with a cinnamon roll, please?"

"Um, I will have a cafe mocha with a mint shot and the same roll," Paul said.

"Sure thing, folks, is that it for you?"

"Yeah, that is it," said Paul. The woman rang up their order and said, "That will be $12.45, sir." Paul took out the money and paid her. She took the money and then asked, "Are you sitting inside or will you be sitting outside today?"

Paul looked at Michelle and said, "I think we will sit outside and enjoy the beautiful morning today." Michelle nodded in agreement; the cashier nodded too. Paul and Michelle walked out to a small table and sat down next to another gentleman who was enjoying his coffee and reading the newspaper. They both looked around at the small but intimate little bistro. Neither had been to this specific place before, but they were really enjoying its French flair.

"Michelle, I am happy we decided to go out and get some breakfast. You need to get out of that motel and back into circulation."

"I know Paul, and you are right, I do feel good today."

"I am so happy to hear that Michelle. You do look good, too." He smiled at her and winked. Michelle smiled back and reached over and touched his arm.

"Thanks, Paul. You have helped me more than I could ever ask. I don't know what I would do without you." Paul smiled and they sat there for a few minutes more just enjoying the morning. The waitress came out and brought them their food. She set it down in front of them and said, "Can I get you anything else?"

"Michelle, do you want anything else?" asked Paul.

"No, not right now, thanks." The waitress smiled and walked away. Paul and Michelle ate breakfast and drank their coffees.

"Michelle, what do you think about going to see Jon Paul today?"

"Do you mind if we finish our breakfast first, and then can you give me some time to decide if I am ready?"

"Anything you want, Michelle." They finished their food. Time was slipping away; Paul noticed first and said, "I think we should get going. Are you ready?"

"Yeah, I am ready. Let's go." Paul and Michelle got up and walked back to his car. As he began to drive back to the motel, he thought about how he wanted to ask Michelle to move in with him. That way, he could be sure to help her in her recovery, or so he thought.

"Michelle, I was thinking—"

"Yes, Paul."

"I was thinking, why don't you come and stay with me for a few weeks? You know, just until you get back on your feet."

"I don't know, Paul. I would feel funny."

"No, no just that way. I can help you, and you can get back on your feet sooner."

"Well, are you sure, Paul?"

"Yes, I have plenty of room, and it will be no burden to me."

"If you are sure. Maybe I can help with the household chores too."

"Yeah, whatever. It will be better than staying at the motel."

"I still need to get my things from the motel, though."

"Okay, let's go get them now and check out. Then we can go back to my place and you can get settled in."

Michelle smiled, looked at Paul, and said, "Thanks, Paul. You are so very kind to me."

Paul smiled at Michelle. He would do anything for her, and this was just the start of it. But he and Michelle had a very dangerous road ahead of them, and it involved Jon Paul.

***

Jon Paul was sleeping when Liz first awoke. She gently got up and out of bed and then went downstairs into the kitchen to find something to eat. She rummaged through the fridge and saw the food from the other day. She found fresh juice and sat down at the table to eat.

Jon Paul awoke suddenly from a dream that had him giving orders to kill some woman and child in some strange place in a strange land. He was sweating and he sat up in bed, panting. The dreams were so real that he could see the fear in the woman's eyes and he could sense the fear in the crying child. He shot and killed them both, and then he awoke. As he got his senses back, he realized where he was, in bed in his own house. This helped him to calm down; it was only a dream—or was it?

Jon Paul stood up, got dressed, and walked downstairs to the kitchen where Liz was eating. He smiled at her as he sat down beside her and said, "Good morning, love, how did you sleep?"

"I slept great, Jon Paul, how about you?"

"Um, yeah—till this morning."

"What do you mean?"

"Nothing, I just had a bad dream."

"Are you hungry, Jon Paul? I could make you something."

"No, you just sit there. I will get a cup of tea; that will help me more than anything else."

Jon Paul boiled himself some water and got out his favorite tea. That always helped him feel better when he had a bad dream.

"Liz, I was thinking about what you said yesterday, and I think we can try it, but I want to make sure we do it right."

"What's that, Jon Paul?"

"You know, getting a bigger place."

"Oh, yeah, that, Jon Paul. I am happy wherever we live; it doesn't matter to me, just as long as we are together."

"Yes, I know that, Liz, but I want you to have only the best things in life."

"Thanks, Jon Paul, but I have everything I need right here." She smiled at Jon Paul and he smiled in return. Liz was his true love, and they would spend their lives together—something he was sure would happen with Michelle, but he was wrong. Jon Paul and Liz enjoyed their time that morning until the phone rang.

"Hello."

"Hello, Jon Paul?"

"Yes, this is Jon Paul."

"Jon Paul, this is Racine."

"Oh, hi, Racine, what's up?"

"Nothing, Jon Paul. Is Michelle there?"

"Ah, no. I don't know how to tell you this, but we broke up. She is not living here anymore."

"Are you serious? What happened?"

"We had a few arguments and she moved out."

"What did you argue about, if you don't mind me asking?"

"Nothing, just that she accused me of cheating and even gave me an ultimatum, but I know she is the one who cheated first."

"Really, Jon Paul? I am so sorry to hear that. Do you think she is okay?"

"I don't know, Racine, but if I hear from her, I will tell her to call you, okay?"

"Thanks, Jon Paul. I really thought you would be with her for life."

"Yeah, me too, guess I was wrong."

"Take care, Jon Paul."

"Thanks, you too. See you later."

"Bye."

"Bye." Jon Paul looked at Liz and smiled. "That was Michelle's older sister; she wanted to speak with her."

"I heard; is everything all right?"

"Yeah, it is fine; guess Michelle didn't call her yet to tell her the news."

Liz smiled at Jon Paul and gently grabbed his hand, placing it in hers. She knew he was a little saddened by the phone call. "Jon Paul, is there anything I can do to make you feel better?"

"No, not right now. It will take a little time for all this to blow over." Liz hugged Jon Paul and she could feel his heartbeat. She tried to comfort him, and she offered to help him any way she could. Liz would die for Jon Paul if he asked her to.

***

Paul and Michelle got back to the motel and packed her things, and although she didn't have a lot, it did take some time. As Michelle finished packing, Paul walked up to the front desk and paid for her time there. When he got back to her room, she was ready. She had all her bags and all her things packed up. They walked out to his car and he opened the trunk and put her suitcase in. Michelle looked at Paul and as she got in the car, she said, "Are you sure about this, Paul?"

"Yes; now, no more questions. We are doing this, and that is final."

He smiled at her and she smiled back. Michelle liked a man who took charge; she was not so comfortable making all the decisions. Paul drove to his apartment and they talked briefly about Jon Paul and the coin. Both agreed that their plan was a good one, even though it was risky. Paul parked his car as they arrived back at his place, and as he and Michelle got out, they both grabbed a different piece of her belongings. Paul got the suitcase and Michelle got the rest, and they went inside.

Michelle instantly felt comfortable in Paul's apartment. She set down her things, looked at Paul, and said, "Paul, where should I put this?" Paul turned to look and said, "Hang on, Michelle, I will show you." He took her by the hand and they walked over to a closet by his room.

"You can put anything you want in here."

"Thanks, Paul, for letting me stay here. It might take me some time to get back on my feet."

Michelle smiled at him and he smiled back.

"I know, and don't you worry about anything. You take as much time as you need."

Michelle put her luggage in the closet. Paul was smiling as he thought about Michelle. As many women as Paul had been with, Michelle was the only one he had ever felt this way about. Michelle sat down on the couch and took a deep breath. She was a little tired from all the morning's activities. Paul noticed this and said, "Michelle, are you okay?"

"Yes, thank you, Paul, just a little tired."

"Just take it easy for a while, okay?"

Michelle lay back on the couch and began to rest; her strength had not yet returned all the way.

Paul was just about to join her on the couch when, suddenly, the phone rang. "Hello."

"Hello, Mr. Dubois?"

"Yes, this is Paul Dubois."

"Mr. Dubois, this is Dr. Martin, from the museum."

"Yes, hello, Dr. Martin. How are you?"

"I am well, thank you. I have some news for you about your coin."

"News—please tell me."

"I have found out that your coin has had quite a colorful past. It seems it has been around for many, many years."

"Really? What did you find out about it, doctor?"

"It is surrounded by not only facts but also some superstition and myth."
Paul sat there mesmerized, listening to the doctor's story. He had no idea

the coin was so interesting. The doctor continued, "As I was saying, this particular coin was once owned by one of the most powerful generals in all of the history of wars. He was a ruthless man but also very successful. It seems the coin can be used to influence other people, and according to some myths and legends, it can be used to grant wishes."

"Tell me, Dr. Martin, where is it from exactly, and just how did it come into being? I mean, what makes this coin so powerful?"

"That is where some of the legends and myths of the coin come into play. Back when this coin was being used in the past, there is a story that says it was around when there were Jinn—or if you prefer, genies—roaming the lands of what we now call the Middle East, more precisely Iran, Iraq, and some parts of Egypt. These lands were a hotbed of stories, and the peoples there were very superstitious, and so tales of a golden coin that granted wishes were passed around campfires."

"Do the tales tell of the origin of the coin, Dr. Martin?"

"Oh, yes, indeed! This coin, according to the legends, was fashioned many millennia ago by a select few of the Jinn who hated mankind so much that they would use it to influence man and bring about his ultimate destruction. This golden coin would be used to bring about the total annihilation of all of mankind. The Jinn would use its influence to cause man to fall. Many of the Jinn were jealous of man and what he could do and accomplish. Man was chosen by God and this made the Jinn very jealous—so jealous, in fact, that they would work tirelessly to cause our deaths."

"Dr. Martin, this is fascinating. Is there more?"

"Yes, there is. Now, the Jinn had to find a few particular men who would be easy to influence, men that they could give the coin to. They would use it to curse the man and therefore make him a puppet to carry out their evil plans. Throughout history, there have been recorded stories of powerful men who had used this coin for their own benefit, men like Caligula, Caesar, Napoleon, and even more recently, Hitler. Well, as you are quite aware, these men were considered not only generals, but also madmen who wanted to rule the entire world. Eventually, through their own greed and God-like complexes, they were brought down and to ruin by other men, men who were 'good,' for a lack of a better term. The people that these men hurt and killed number in the thousands, perhaps even millions. The Jinn who chose these men had a particular plan in their evil minds, and although they didn't succeed as well as they hoped, they did cause the ruin and death of many. The usual result of these men and their possession of the coin had a flip side, if you will. Most of them were either killed themselves or were brought to ruin by the curse of the coin, and that is its bad side."

"Are you saying it has a good side, Dr. Martin?"

"Well, that depends on your particular point of view and your particular beliefs. Each of us sees things a little differently, and those men were no different than you or me; they were simply blinded by their greed and their thirst for power.

The last one to own the coin was a general by the name of Gi Do Chang. He was a general in the south of Korea. He committed many atrocities against his people, and he only lived a short time on this Earth before the people finally rose against him, took power from him, and had him killed by hanging. His bones were broken and reset at odd angles, and he most probably went through many other tortures not recorded in history books.

The story gets a little vague as some of the facts are blurred now. What I found out was that this General Chang used to walk around his palace holding a gold coin; it never left him, and when he wasn't torturing his people, he was using it to make strange things happen. Many people in his kingdom were frightened of him. There are other, smaller tales, but I won't bore you with those unless you want to hear them."

"Ah, thanks, doc, but your work is hardly boring. In fact, it is very fascinating. Is there any legend about how to destroy the coin? I mean, can we melt it or maybe give it to a museum or something?"

"There is a story (or if you prefer, a legend) that says that the coin can't be destroyed by man since it was the Jinn who created it from fire and gave it magic powers. It can only be destroyed by the Jinn who created it all those years ago. I had also read another smaller tale that said one day, the Jinn would try to get it back. It seems that once it is in the hands of a man they have chosen, the Jinn must wait for him to die or to give it back to them. They are unable to take it from him. One of the drawbacks of a cursed coin—even the Jinn can't control its magic."

"I see. Thank you for taking the time to call me, Dr. Martin. That information is very useful to me."

"If your friend has this coin, then I would say you are in for a great battle and you must be very careful. This is a very powerful and very dangerous coin, if it is real."

"Thanks, doc. I will be careful."

"Remember, Paul, if you ever need my help, just call."

"Thanks. Bye."

Paul hung up the phone and sat down, shocked. He had paced the floor the whole time he was listening to the tale of this cursed coin, and now he sat there in disbelief next to Michelle.

"Who was that, Paul?"

"Dr. Martin."

"Is everything all right, Paul?"

"No, Michelle, it is not. This coin of Jon Paul's is indeed very powerful and we need to be very careful with it, or it could corrupt us as well."

"What do you mean, Paul?"

"I mean we are in for a real battle with that coin. Once we get it from Jon Paul, I am going to have to put it somewhere safe or its influence could be too much for even me to resist."

Michelle sat there; she was a bit frightened. Paul told her the awful news, and she knew this might be their only chance to take the coin from Jon Paul.

***

Jon Paul and Liz enjoyed the morning. It was bright and sunny, and the birds were singing loudly. They both loved the sounds of nature.

"Liz, is there anything you want to do today?"

"Well, nothing in particular. Maybe we can just have a day without too much more stress."

"Stress, *ha*! I have no stress, Lizzy."

"You know what I mean, mister, with Michelle and all that."

"I know; I was just joking around. I really do appreciate the thought, but I am okay for now."

"Are you sure, Jon Paul?"

"Yes, I am fine, thanks, sweetie." Liz smiled at Jon Paul, and he knew she really cared about him. Liz was his true love and he knew it. As he sat there, he thought about her idea of a bigger house; the whole thing was very appealing to him. But he needed to make sure he and Michelle were through and that she would be unable to get any of his new money. He decided to wait for a few days before he would make another big wish.

"Liz, do you mind if we go sit in the living room? I love sitting here, but I need some TV to distract me."

"Sure, whatever you want, Jon Paul. Lead the way."

They got up, walked into the living room, and then sat back down and started to watch TV. Jon Paul was thinking about Michelle's sister and how he had had to tell her the news of the breakup first. As he sat there, he began to feel the coin heating up in his pocket. It always got hot when something was about to happen to him. He heard the small voice in his head; it said to him, *"Beware! They are coming!"* He wondered what this meant. He thought, *who, who is coming?* Then it hit him, like a flash of brilliance: Paul and Michelle. They were coming for his coin.

He would never let them take it; even if it meant their death or his, he would never surrender his coin. "Liz, will you excuse me for a moment? I need to go to the bathroom."

"Sure thing, honey," said Liz. Jon Paul got up and walked upstairs to the bathroom. *I will use the coin to find out what those two traitors are planning on doing,* he thought. He could feel the white-hot heat of the coin burning his pocket. As he took it out of his pocket, he knew it was time for his next wish. "I wish I knew what they were planning." And then, *poof!* Instantly, the knowledge of what Paul and Michelle were planning on doing was made aware to him. He knew they were going to try to take the coin from him by force and that it would happen soon. He put the coin back in his pocket and walked back downstairs to see Liz. She was sitting there very content on his couch, so he sat down next to her and said, "I am back."

She smiled at him and said, "Yes, silly, I know." He smiled at her, and just as he was about to tell her something, the phone rang.

"Hello."

"Hello, Jon Paul. This is Michelle."

"What do you want?"

"I was wondering if I could come over and pick up the rest of my clothes."

"When were you thinking, like what time?"

"Well, how about in a couple of hours?"

"Sure, that sounds good. I will be here all day, so anytime will be fine."

"Okay, we will see you soon. Bye."

"Bye." Jon Paul hung up the phone and wondered, *we?* Then he realized she meant herself and Paul, the cheat and the traitor. He knew their plan, and now it was about to take place. Was he ready for them, or would he falter? The lack of confidence he was feeling had Jon Paul doubting himself, but he knew he must succeed. He would protect his coin no matter what. Liz looked at him and said, "Who was that?"

"That was Michelle. She and Paul are coming over in a couple hours to pick up her things."

"Jon Paul, I think I better go then. I don't want to be here when they get here."

"You know you don't have to leave, Liz. This is my place, and you can stay here as long as you want."

"I know, but it will just be very uncomfortable for me to be here."

"If that is what you want, then fine, but I still want you to know you mean more to me than anything."

"I know, Jon Paul, and I feel the same. Please understand this."

"I do, and it is okay. I will come by and see you later."

"Will you call me first this time so I can get ready?"

"You know I will." Liz smiled at Jon Paul. She would walk home and wait for him; this was better for her than staying here with Jon Paul and waiting for Michelle to show up and so he could confront her.

***

Paul hung up the phone for Michelle. She looked nervously at him and said, "Are we sure, Paul?"

"I know it might seem like we are rushing this, but I believe after my talk with Dr. Martin that we need to act now, before things get worse and we can't get the coin from him."

"Okay, Paul, if you think we are ready, then I trust you. I am really scared, though."

"I know, Michelle, but you will be fine. Just stick to our plan and when you see me reach for the coin, stay clear."

"I will do my best, Paul; just don't drop it when you get it."

"Yeah, that is what worries me." Paul smiled at Michelle, hoping to instill her with confidence. She would do her best to distract Jon Paul so he could grab the coin.

***

Jon Paul walked Liz to the door. She put on her coat, hugged Jon Paul, and said, "Jon Paul, will you call me later, after they have left?"

"You know I will, Liz. I promise." Liz smiled and kissed him good-bye. Jon Paul smiled as she walked away, and he closed the door behind her. He was very happy with Liz. He had never felt this way with Michelle, at least not so completely. They had a different relationship; he did love her, just not the same as Liz. Jon Paul sat back down on the couch. He was thinking about what he had heard the coin say to him in his mind: *"Beware! They are coming!"*

He repeated it over and over in his head, till it was like a broken record. He sat there on the couch for what seemed like hours, but in reality, it was only a few minutes.

Chapter Nine

— • • • —

REVENGE TAKES HOLD

Jon Paul was deep in thought when his phone rang. It was his mother.

"Hello."

"Hello, Jon Paul."

"Mom?"

"Yes."

"How are you, Jon Paul?"

"I am okay, Mom. How is Dad?"

"He is fine, Jon Paul. I got a call from Michelle's sister."

"Michelle's sister—did she tell you?"

"Yes, she did; what happened?"

"It was a lot of things, Mom; she just kept putting these pressures on me. Then she said I was cheating. But I know it was her who cheated first."

"Oh, Jon Paul, I am sorry. Are you sure?"

"It is okay, Mom. We broke up and she has moved out, and I am with Liz now."

"Who is Liz?"

"She is my friend from the bar. I have known her for a few years now."

"The bar—does she work there?"

"Yes, she is a waitress."

"This is very sudden. Jon Paul, are you serious?"

"Yes, Mom, it is."

"Well, then, we are going to have to meet her soon."

"Okay, Mom, but can we wait a few weeks, though, so she can get used to all of us?"

"That will be fine, honey. You take care, and I will tell your father you are okay. I am sure he will be concerned with how you are."

"Thanks, Mom. I will call you in a couple of days."

"Okay, Jon Paul. Bye."

"Bye." Talking with his mom had been a good distraction for Jon Paul. It took his mind off the coin, if only for a few moments.

***

Paul sat there and thought for a moment. He had just told Michelle that Dr. Martin had called and that the news of the coin was not good. How would he tell her of its past, a past colored with tales of good and evil? "Michelle, we are indeed in a battle. That coin of Jon Paul's is very powerful and I believe if we don't get it soon, we may never be able to take it from him."

"Are you serious?"

"Deadly serious, Michelle. That coin has been owned by some of the worlds most powerful and evil men, men who killed for fun and men who killed for power."

"Do you think it will corrupt Jon Paul like that?"

"I truly don't know, but it might."

"Then we must not fail. We cannot fail, Paul." Michelle was right; they must get the coin from Jon Paul at all costs.

"We won't, Michelle. We won't." Paul stared at her hard. He was serious. He knew they must not fail. This would be a test of not only his courage but his manhood. Could he really succeed? Time would tell.

Paul and Michelle sat in quiet contemplation. Occasionally, they would look at each other and smile. Paul thought about the coin, and Michelle worried about how they might fail.

"Michelle, are you ready to go see Jon Paul?"

"I guess I am. I am really scared, though. What if you don't grab the coin soon enough?"

"Remember, Michelle, you must distract him with your words so I can grab it."

"I will try, Paul. Just don't miss." Michelle looked nervously at Paul and he smiled in return. He would grab the coin when Jon Paul was distracted and then they would leave, hopefully without much of a fight from Jon Paul.

***

Jon Paul sat on the couch, and memories flooded his worried mind. He remembered how Michelle used to make him such wonderful meals. He also remembered how she was always there for him. He remembered how they had fought bitterly and how Liz had come into his life right after that. Liz had mended his broken heart and given him reason to live again. He thought, *I must do something for Liz; what can I do to show her my love?* As he thought about the question in his mind, he could hear the birds chirping from his kitchen window.

***

"Michelle, are you ready?"

"Yes, Paul, but you better keep me safe. I don't trust Jon Paul anymore."

"Don't worry; if anything happens, just run as fast as you can away from there."

"Okay, I will." Paul and Michelle put on their coats and walked out of his place and to his car. As he started the engine, Michelle could feel the power of the motor respond, and that gave her some courage. It sounded powerful to her. Paul pulled out of the parking lot and into the street. Paul drove to his old friend's place and parked. He looked at Michelle and said, "Well, you ready?"

Michelle looked at Paul and said, "Okay, I am ready. Let's go save Jon Paul."

They both took a deep breath, got out of the car, and walked up to the door of Jon Paul's apartment building. They rang the door buzzer. Jon Paul pushed the button to let them in. The walk up the stairs seemed particularly long to them both, like they were walking the last mile of a condemned man. Michelle stopped at the door and, looking nervously at Paul, knocked. Jon Paul opened the door and, seeing them both, gave an evil scowl at them and said, "Come in."

Paul and Michelle walked in. Jon Paul motioned for them to sit down on the couch. "Can I get you anything to drink?" Jon Paul was watching them cautiously as he offered them a drink.

"Nothing for me, Jon Paul. I am fine," said Michelle.

"What about you, Paul?"

"No thanks, Jon Paul." Paul and Michelle were cautious as they looked at Jon Paul.

"Okay, so how do you want to do this, Michelle?"

"Um, I was thinking maybe I could go and pack my things, and then I could come back for whatever is left sometime later."

"That sounds fine. Go ahead and do that; I will stay here with my old friend," he said with an evil grin. Michelle walked upstairs and into her old room; she looked around for her last piece of luggage, found it, and set it on the bed. She then began to look through the closet to find the rest of her things. She packed her few remaining shirts and coats. She even had some new shoes that were still in the closet. She then moved to the dresser and, finding more stuff there, she packed what she could. She would have to come back later, as she still had more things that wouldn't fit in the suitcase.

Jon Paul had been sitting with Paul in the living room when he suddenly got up and said, "Be right back. I am going to check on Michelle." For some reason, Jon Paul had the feeling Michelle was snooping in his things, and he was right; she had been. She had been looking for the coin, hoping he might have left it on the dresser or maybe the nightstand. As he walked into their old room, he took her by surprise and Michelle jumped. "Jon Paul, I didn't see you there."

"Do you see me now?"

"Ha ha, Jon Paul, that is very funny." She laughed nervously. Jon Paul was like a stranger to her; he had changed so much, she didn't even know him.

"Do you need any help?"

"No, I got as much as I can carry today. I am going to have to come back later to get the rest."

"Later? I thought you could get it all this time."

"Please, Jon Paul, let's not argue. Can I just get the rest next time?"

"Okay, Michelle, but make sure you get it all on the next visit." Jon Paul stared coldly at her and she could feel the hate and evil in him; it burned her soul and made her very uncomfortable. She walked downstairs with the one piece of luggage and set it by the door. Paul got up to help her but she waived at him, signaling she was fine. Jon Paul was close to them as they stood by the door, he was anxious for them to leave. Paul looked at his old friend and said, "Thanks for letting us come by to get Michelle's things."

"Yeah, sure thing, Paul, no problem."

"Jon Paul, I was wondering if I might have one last look at that coin of yours. I was contacted by a Dr. Martin the other day, and he was asking if I knew its exact design. He wanted me to tell him so he could authenticate it for historical purposes, maybe even have it on display at the museum."

"I would like to see it, Jon Paul, at least one more time before I go. You at least owe me that," said Michelle.

Jon Paul looked at them. He was suspicious, and they could see it in his eyes.

"C'mon, Jon Paul, just for old time's sake?" said Paul.

"Please, Jon Paul, after all our years together, can't you leave me this one thing?"

"Okay, sure, you two, one last time." Jon Paul reached in his pocket and grabbed the coin. He brought it out into the light for them to see. It shined like a bright star. For a moment, they were all hypnotized by its brilliance. Then Michelle, seeing her opportunity, said, "Jon Paul, it is so beautiful, I don't remember it being so—"

Suddenly, Paul reached for the coin with lightning speed; he moved so fast, Jon Paul was unaware of it. As he got closer to Jon Paul's open hand with his own, Jon Paul closed his just as fast. He glared at them and Paul shouted at Michelle to run. Paul and Jon Paul began to struggle. They fought feverishly over the coin; Paul had a firm grasp on Jon Paul's hand and wouldn't let go. Jon Paul struggled against his grip. Suddenly, as quickly as it all had begun, they broke their grip on each other and Paul shouted, "Run, Michelle! Run!" Paul and Michelle ran down the hall away from Jon Paul. They left her luggage and got into his car as fast as they could. He started it and drove away, both of them panting in nervous exhaustion.

"Run, you traitors, run! Your lives are mine now!" Jon Paul shouted. He looked at the coin in his hand and, cursing them, said, "I wish them bad luck all the days of their lives! Never will they be happy anywhere; let them suffer, as I have suffered!"

The curse echoed off the walls as he said it. It was a powerful curse, and its effect would be almost immediate.

Paul and Michelle drove down the street in a panic. Their plan had backfired on them, and now Jon Paul knew they might try to take his coin again. There had for sure been some doubt at first, but now Jon Paul knew.

"Michelle, are you all right?"

"Yes, I am fine, just a little shaken. That was scary."

"I am glad he didn't have time to curse us."

"Do you think he will try, Paul?"

"What, curse us? No, we are no threat to him now; if anything, he will figure we have tried and given up."

"Are you sure, Paul?"

"Trust me, as long as we both have known him, don't you think I am right?"

"Yes, you are probably right, but I am still worried."

"I know, Michelle, but listen—we have tried to take his coin. Now, Jon Paul knows me well enough to know that I will not attempt anything like that again."

"Paul, can we stop by a church before we go home?"

"Sure thing, Michelle. There is one by my place; we can stop in there."

"Thanks, Paul. I just feel the need to get some divine help for us."

"I understand, Michelle. It is fine with me. We could use all the help we can get!"

Paul and Michelle stopped at the church. They would go in and pray for guidance and strength.

***

Jon Paul sat back down in his living room. He was so angered at the attempt of such fools. He thought, *How dare they try to take my coin; are they just stupid? Don't they know what I can do with it? I will not make that mistake again. From now on, I will ask my coin what those two fools are planning, and I will never let them get a second chance.* Jon Paul's anger slowly began to wane as time slipped away. He felt thirsty as he got up, and he walked into the kitchen; he opened the fridge and found himself a drink. He sat down at his wobbly table, looked out the window, and decided to call his manservant. "Mr. Falid, are you here?" he asked.

"Yes, sir. I am here." And in an instant, in a cloud of blue smoke, he was standing there. "How can I help you, sir?"

"Mr. Falid, I need some advice, if you will."

"Yes, sir. I will give my best."

"A few moments ago, these two idiots tried to take my coin from me. What should I do?"

"Sir, in my day, there was a man who tried to take it from me, too."

"So what did you do?"

"I cursed him with the disease of his bones; they turned to jelly and he was unable to walk. Then I cursed him to live a life in sorrow and pitiful ways. He lived a life in constant pain and humiliation."

"That sounds good to me, Mr. Falid."

"No, wait, sir; first, you must find a secure place to stay. Your enemies know where you live, and they can get to you."

"What do you suggest, Mr. Falid?"

"Sir, use the coin to get yourself a castle so they cannot get to you. Wish yourself rich, so you have the money to live a protected, safe, and secure life."

"Are you sure, Mr. Falid?"

"Yes, sir. They tried once and failed. They will try again; it is the way of the coin. It is the magic that makes it happen and all who own the coin get what they wish for. I myself lived a very opulent and luxurious life, protected from my enemies and from those who wished me harm and wanted to take my coin. All you must do is to simply say, 'I wish for a big, beautiful, safe, secure mansion or castle.'"

"Thanks, Mr. Falid, for your words of wisdom. I will do just that. Now, if you will leave me, I need time to myself to think."

"Thank you, sir. As you wish." Jon Paul would sit there in his kitchen for quite a long time.

***

Paul and Michelle left the church after praying and asking for divine guidance. They arrived back at Paul's place and sat down to talk about what had happened.

"Michelle, I think we just barely escaped with our lives this morning."

"That is what I was thinking, too."

"Do you think he cursed us, Paul?"

"I don't know. I don't feel any different, and we are still alive."

"Yeah, me neither, but I do believe he is evil enough to do something like that."

"Michelle, why don't we eat something? I mean, after all that, I need to replenish my strength."

"Yeah, me too, Paul."

They walked into the kitchen to find something to eat. Paul found some leftovers that he could heat up, and Michelle set the table for them. They ate in silence for the most part; on occasion, they would glance at each other and smile, but no words were spoken. Paul and Michelle had almost lost their lives with their clumsy attempt at taking the coin from Jon Paul.

Now that Jon Paul had cursed them, their lives were about to change. For some odd reason, Paul and Michelle's lives had not changed that much; although Jon Paul had cursed them, praying at a church seemed to have stopped the curse, at least temporarily.

***

"Damn those two; why did they have to try and take my coin?" Jon Paul thought out loud. He had spat a curse out on them and now was wondering if it was taking effect. Of course, they were in hiding now, but Jon Paul figured they had gone to Paul's house, so he could find them if he really wanted. Having sat on his couch for a couple hours thinking, he decided to call Liz and tell her what had happened.

"Hello."

"Hello, Liz. It's Jon Paul."

"Hi, Jon Paul. How are you? Did they pick up Michelle's things?"

"Funny you should ask."

"What has happened, Jon Paul?"

"They got here and I invited them in, and we sat on the couch. I even offered them drinks but neither one wanted anything. Then Michelle asked if she could go upstairs to pack the rest of her things. I said sure, that would be fine."

"What happened then, Jon Paul?"

"She went upstairs and I guess she was packing, but it was taking a long time. I started to get a funny feeling like she was up to something, so I went upstairs to see."

"Was she snooping around?"

"Yes, she was, so I said, 'Are you finished?' She jumped and said, 'I am going to have to come back to get the rest.' I said, 'Are you sure?' She said yes and then picked up the luggage she had packed and walked downstairs."

"Did they leave then, Jon Paul?"

"No, Paul asked to see my coin one last time for some doctor he talked with that can identify it."

"You didn't show them, did you?"

"Yes, I did, but I knew they were up to something. I just didn't think they would be so brave about it and try to take it right from my hand."

"Really, they tried to take it from you?"

"Yeah. Paul made a grab for it, but I closed my hand just in time. Then he wouldn't let go, and we fought for it."

"Are you hurt, Jon Paul?"

"No, I am okay. I did yell out a curse at them as they ran away. I wonder if it is affecting them."

"You cursed them?"

"Of course. I can't have my enemies trying to hurt me or you."

"Jon Paul, I think you should find another place to live. I mean, if they did this, who knows what they will try next time—maybe something even worse."

"I know, Liz, and I have been thinking maybe I should move, you know, to a bigger and better place, a place more secure and safer than this apartment."

"Jon Paul, that is a great idea. Do you need me to help you in any way?"

"Not yet, my dear Liz. I am still figuring this one out, but soon, okay?"

"Okay, sweetie, will you call me later, or even better, come by work so I can see you?"

"Lizzy, I will definitely call you first. Give me some time to figure this all out."

"I love you, Jon Paul."

"I know, baby, I love you too." Jon Paul hung up the phone and sat back in his chair.

Jon Paul had been thinking that if he were to wish for a bigger and better place, why not make it a big one, a really big one, like a mansion or a French chateau, with some land to go with it? That would be nice, and even his manservant had told him he needed to find a better place to live. If people were to find out he had a magic coin, he might run into trouble.

Paul and Michelle were eating in the kitchen when, suddenly, Paul started to feel sick.

"Michelle, I don't feel so good."

"I am starting to feel sick too, Paul. Do you think Jon Paul cursed us?"

"I don't know, Michelle, maybe."

"What should we do?"

"I don't know, but something is wrong. I—"

Suddenly, Paul was on the floor, clutching his stomach in pain. "Michelle, my stomach." He groaned.

"Me ... too ... Paul. Ahhh ..." Both Paul and Michelle had begun to feel the effects of the curse; it was taking hold of them.

"Michelle, we ... need ... to get to the ... hospital."

"I ... I ... can't drive, Paul, I—"

"Michelle, take my hand. We have to try and make it." Paul and Michelle struggled to get off the floor. They got to their feet and staggered to the car. Paul helped Michelle in as best he could and then got in himself.

"Michelle, are you okay?"

"No, Paul, I feel like my stomach ... I think I am dying!"

"I *know* it is the curse. Jon Paul must have cursed us. Just try and relax; I am going to hurry as fast as I can!"

"Okay."

He drove as fast as he could to the hospital. When the nurse at the station saw them obviously in pain, she immediately called for them to go to the emergency room.

"What has happened to you? What is wrong?" she asked.

"It is our stomachs—feels like they are on fire!" The nurse began to help Paul and Michelle into different beds. She began an IV drip, and soon after that, the doctor came rushing in.

Seeing the two of them, he started on Michelle, who seemed to be worse than Paul.

"Does this hurt?"

"Yes, Doctor, it is my stomach, ahhh ..."

"I see. Did you eat anything bad, like spoiled food or bad fish?"

"Yes, something like that, we were eating ... leftovers, and then we both just started having these sharp, um ... pains, like a knife was stabbed in my stomach and left there."

It was apparent to the doctor that they had eaten something bad.

"Nurse, take them both to X-ray. I want to see what is going on in there."

"Yes, doctor." The nurse took Michelle to X-ray first, and then brought her back to the room; she took Paul next. After a few minutes had passed, they had the X-rays and the doctor was looking at them. The X-ray showed nothing. Paul and Michelle were suffering from a curse, and this was just the beginning.

***

Jon Paul had been sitting in his chair when he decided that it was the time for him to make his greatest wish so far, a wish that would make him and Liz happy and safe for the rest of their lives: a wish for a big mansion.

***

As the doctor walked into the room where Paul and Michelle were, Paul saw him and said, "What is wrong with us, doc?"

"Nothing in the X-rays. I suspect you got some bad food. I will have the nurse give you something for the pain and some antibiotics for your stomachs."

"Thanks, doc, so nothing serious?"

"Oh, it's serious. You seem to have a type of food poisoning that can be deadly if not treated correctly and immediately. Try to relax, and the nurse will be here shortly."

But Paul couldn't relax; he knew instinctively that he had been cursed by Jon Paul. He felt like his insides were melting. Michelle lay there in the bed next to him. She, too, was feeling the effects of the curse; Michelle wondered

155

if she was dying. The quick stop at the church earlier must have had some sort of protection for Paul and Michelle. It had given them a few hours of peace before the curse had begun. The power of the coin was overwhelming, and it was just a matter of time before its effects were felt completely.

***

Jon Paul felt the coin heating up in his hand. It always did this as he was about to make a wish, but this time, it seemed to be pulsing in his hand. He thought for a moment that it might even burn him. As he began to concentrate very deeply, small beads of sweat began to form on his forehead. He thought slowly and completely for this particular wish; it was big, and he knew it. Jon Paul concentrated and finally said, "I wish for a big mansion with land that is safe and secure away from the city, protected from strangers."

At first, nothing happened, and Jon Paul wondered if he had used the coin too much; maybe it had maxed itself out. But then, as he stood there wondering, the room slowly seemed to start spinning. The walls became blurry, and the floor seemed to be moving under his feet. Jon Paul thought, *I am going to fall!* Then, as everything moved at light speed for what seemed like minutes to Jon Paul, it all began to slow down. It slowed and slowed until everything was still; the room had stopped spinning, and the walls were clear and the floor was steady. Jon Paul felt better, and he looked around. Jon Paul was confused. What had just happened? He was no longer in his little apartment, no. He was standing in a huge room with beautiful, and what appeared to be new, furniture. There was a hardwood floor that looked like it was oak, and there were glass coffee tables in between pieces of luxurious leather furniture. There were tall plants placed perfectly between couches, open windows that reached from the floor to the very high ceilings. He had done it! He was standing in a huge, beautiful mansion with all the furnishings one could dream of. It was magnificent, he thought.

Then, just as suddenly, he wondered, *where am I?* If he was now standing in his new house, where was it located? Was it still in France? Was it still in the city? Would he be able to get to Liz to show it to her? Jon Paul decided to look for the front door, maybe search around a little. As Jon Paul began to walk around his new mansion, he thought he heard something in another room, what appeared to be the kitchen.

"Hello, is someone there?" he asked.

"Yes, sir. It is Mr. Falid."

"Mr. Falid, what are you doing here?"

"Hello, sir. I am here at your command. You wished for this house, and I am bound to appear here as soon as the wish is granted."

"I see, and do you know this place, Mr. Falid?"

"I do, sir. May I show you around or get you something to drink?"

"How about we take a tour first before I get something to drink."

"Very good, sir, follow me. I will show you your new house."

"Mr. Falid, how do you know this house?"

"A good question, sir. As you wished for it through the magic of the coin, it was revealed to me and binds me to you and this house till your death."

"That is very interesting, Mr. Falid; so, are you released when I die?"

"I don't know exactly, sir, the Jinn who cursed me will tell me when I am free."

"Well, then, Mr. Falid, let's see this house, shall we?"

Jon Paul and his manservant walked his house. They looked at the library with its exquisite maple walls. They looked at the den with wall-to-wall carpet. They walked into the family room with a fireplace so big it could burn six-foot logs. There were beautiful paintings from some of France's most famous artists: Claude Monet, Renoir, and even William Bouguereau. Jon Paul was impressed as he toured his new home. He thought, *Liz is going to love this place. I can't wait to get her here.*

Mr. Falid and Jon Paul spent an hour going through the new house. They looked at each and every room. Jon Paul especially loved the billiard room, with a full-size billiard table and connecting bar just adjacent to it. It had an inlaid hardwood floor with perfect stars interspersed throughout it. Needless to say, it was beautiful. Soon after Jon Paul and Mr. Falid had toured his new house, Jon Paul decided he wanted to see the grounds as well.

"Mr. Falid, thank you for showing me the house, but I think I want to go outside and see the grounds now."

"Very good, sir. I will be here if you need anything."

"What do you mean, Mr. Falid? Are you here permanently now?"

"Yes, sir. I can't leave until your time is through here on this earth."

"I see. Well, thanks again, Mr. Falid. Now, if we can find the front door, I can be on my way outside."

"Follow me, sir. I will show you." Jon Paul followed his manservant to the front door and walked out; he was looking to see his land and just what exactly the coin had done for him. As he walked out of his new home, he stopped for a second, and his eyes grew wide in wonderment. Before him was a vast estate with many acres of land. In some ways, he was nervous. He knew nothing of living such a rich and luxuriant lifestyle, but he would learn.

As he stepped out and onto the front lawn, he noticed a dirt driveway that led to what appeared to be a big garage. He thought, *I will follow this and see where it goes.* It led him to a garage with six doors. He walked up to one of them and pulled it open; to his surprise, it opened quite easily. What he saw almost made Jon Paul freeze in his tracks. There, sitting as beautiful as can be, was a brand-new car. Jon Paul wondered if the keys were in it; maybe he could take it for a drive. He walked closer to the car when, suddenly, out of the shadows came a man. He was six feet tall with a scraggly beard. He had sharp blue eyes that seemed to pierce Jon Paul's soul. "Hello, sir. How can I help you?"

"Ah … I was wondering if I might take this car for a drive?"

"Of course, sir; all these cars are yours!"

"What?"

"I am your caretaker and groundskeeper. I also look after the cars and keep them in perfect working order for you."

"Cars? What cars? I don't see any cars."

"All of the cars in this garage, sir. There is a different one in each garage, for whenever you want to drive something different."

"Are you serious? What is your name?"

"I am called Franklin, sir. Franklin Bestion. You can call me anything you wish, sir."

Jon Paul was taken back a little by the man's appearance and his straightforward speech, and he said, "Very good, I will call you Mr. Bestion. Now, how about those keys?"

"They are already in the car, sir, waiting for you."

"Thank you, Mr. Bestion. I shall return shortly."

"Drive safe, sir. See you soon."

Jon Paul got in the car, started it up, and drove out of the garage and down his new driveway to the gate. Even though all these things were like new for Jon Paul, he was very comfortable with them. Jon Paul was feeling happy and so very secure. He had wished for this and it was so much more than just a wish; it was more than he could ever have dreamed of.

As he drove onto the street, he noticed the street was lined with trees, as was his long driveway that got him there. He drove further and as the trees moved back from the one-lane road, he began to see rolling hills. Green pastures told him he was still in France; at least, he hoped he was. Jon Paul drove past many farms and such beautiful countryside that he wondered why he had never moved to the country before.

The car he was driving was perfect for Jon Paul; it was like a part of him. With each subtle movement of his hands, the car would respond instantly. He was having such a great day!

As he drove and got closer to town, he began to notice some familiar things: a sign here or there, even a sign showing the way to the city docks. Then he knew exactly where he was! He was still in Toulon. His wish for a safe and secure house had him in the countryside at the very end of Toulon. That is where the rolling hills and the farmers and winemakers were. As he drove on, he looked around his car and saw he had a phone. Why didn't he notice this earlier? It must have been the excitement of the new house and the servant and the car, he thought. He picked up the phone and dialed Liz.

"Hello, Liz?"

"Hello. Is that you, Jon Paul?"

"Yes, and you will never guess where I am right now!"

"Where, Jon Paul? Tell me."

"I am in my new car driving on my way to see you!"

"You lie; you don't have a car."

"I do now!"

"What are you talking about, Jon Paul? If you are joking around—"

"I am not joking, Liz. I made a wish, and now I have a car too."

"A car *too*—what are you saying?"

"Well, my beautiful Liz, I did as you said. I wished for a house with land and that is exactly what I got, but it also came with a garage and a servant."

"A servant, a garage, and land—what did you say, Jon Paul?"

"Yes, all that and more. The servant comes with the house. You should see it, Liz; it is beautiful. The grass is so green and it is by rolling hills and farms."

"Is it in the country, Jon Paul?"

"Yes, that is a good guess, Liz."

"Really, Jon Paul? That sounds wonderful. When are you going to be here?"

"In about half an hour, is that all right?"

"Yes, that is fine. I have to work tonight, but we can spend the day together if you want."

"Of course I want, silly girl. I came here only for you."

"Jon Paul, that is sweet. What kind of car is it?"

"Well, you might not believe this—it is a Maserati. Red with a sunroof and the most comfortable leather seats you could ever imagine!"

"Jon Paul, are you serious?"

"I am totally serious, Liz. You will see; I am almost there."

"Wow that really sounds nice. I can't wait to see you!"

"Me either. I will be there soon, honey." Jon Paul hung up the phone and continued his drive to see Liz.

***

Paul and Michelle were still in the emergency room when the nurse came in and said, "How are you feeling now?"

Paul was the first to respond. "My stomach still feels like it is on fire. Can't you give us something stronger?" The nurse had given Paul and Michelle exactly what the doctor had prescribed for food poisoning; however, it was not working. As Michelle lay there listening to the nurse and Paul, she suddenly began to vomit blood. It was a very violent convulsion. She seemed to be getting worse.

The nurse looked at Michelle, walked over to her, and quickly checked her for signs of something worse. "Tell me, miss, does this hurt?" The nurse pushed gently on Michelle's abdomen.

"Oh, God, yes! It is killing me!" The nurse was sure something more was wrong than just food poisoning; she looked at Paul, who was now vomiting up blood as well. "Listen to me, you two, just try to relax. I am getting the doctor now!" The nurse got up and left the room; she was going to find the doctor that had examined them in the first place.

Paul and Michelle were feeling the effects of the curse Jon Paul had spat out at them. It was reaching its full potential when, suddenly, Michelle saw a bright light above her, and it was coming down. At first, she thought she was seeing things, and then the pain got worse. Michelle began to think she was seeing the light to the other side, to heaven. She thought, *I must be dying.*

"Paul, I am dying. Please don't let me die!"

"Michelle, don't die! I love you!"

"Paul, I love you too!" The light filled the room; it was not any ordinary light, though—this was the light of a guardian angel. Paul and Michelle's guardian angel had come to save them.

"Paul and Michelle, I am Seraphiel. Do not worry; I am here to heal you and save your lives." The angel seemed to talk in a way that sounded to Paul and Michelle like a choir singing the same words all at once. It was a strong voice, and it made them comfortable.

"You came here to save us? Why Paul and me? I mean, we are not special."

"Oh, but you are my child. Don't you remember me?"

"How would I remember you? Wait, I do remember you. You appeared to me a few weeks ago. I thought I was dreaming when I saw you." Michelle had searched her mind and found the answer. This was the same angel that had saved her before, when Jon Paul had cursed her to the grave.

"Yes, I saved you before. You have a path to carry out, and heaven has a plan for you."

"Heaven has a plan for me? What about Paul?"

"He is in that plan too. You are a part of each other."

Paul and Michelle smiled. They were in love, and the angel, feeling that love, glowed even brighter. "The path that you two are on will lead you to a great battle. A battle so great you might not survive it."

"What do you mean 'a great battle,' and how will we know with whom?"

"You already know with whom, my child. The battle will involve you and the coin of Jon Paul Chavalier."

"Jon Paul? How can we battle him? He is too strong for us."

"Do not worry. I will protect you from any more curses he might have in store for you. You will be immune to the effects of the coin."

"Will Paul be immune too?"

"Yes, you both shall be immune to the coin of the Jinn."

"What do we need to do?"

"First, I must cure you of the curse, and then we will continue." Then, the angel, glowing brightly, spread her wings and said some sort of prayer in a tongue unknown to Paul and Michelle. Instantly, they were cured and feeling perfect.

"Now, I will continue." The angel told them of their plan to rid Jon Paul of the evil coin created by the Jinn thousands of years ago—a coin so evil, it could corrupt even the most pious man. History could prove it, as so many men who had found the coin or had it brought to them by some evil being had proved its wickedness. The angel continued for some time. Paul began to wonder why the nurse and doctor had not come to see them by now.

"Um, Seraphiel, I don't mean to interrupt you, but why hasn't the doctor come in here by now?"

"It is simple, my child; they will not be here until I am finished and gone." Paul sat back and realized that he and Michelle were special; they were going to battle for the coin, and that was their destiny and fate. What would happen to Jon Paul was not clear. Would he die? Maybe he would just be put away somewhere for his evil actions.

"The fate of Jon Paul is uncertain. He has the coin, and you must take it from him. I will be there to help you, but I will remain unseen." The angel knew what Paul was thinking before he even said it.

"What should we do right now, Seraphiel?"

"Nothing. I will tell you soon and you must listen; time grows short and I must leave you for now. But know I am always close. The evil of the coin must be stopped now."

Paul and Michelle looked at the angel, who was glowing.

"Be at peace for now, my children. I shall return when it is time for us to battle the power of the coin." The angel arose in a most gentle and heavenly way, ascended up through the ceiling, and was instantly gone. She did leave behind a very pleasant odor for them to remember her by. Paul and Michelle were healed. They also were now immune to the effects of the coin. They had a destiny and fate that neither had known about.

The coin had brought them together in love and desperation, and now they were agents of heaven on this earth. The angel had told them that they would battle Jon Paul for the coin that and that there was a chance that neither might survive, for it would be an epic struggle against overwhelming odds. But with the help of their angel, they could overcome and survive this battle with Jon Paul.

Chapter Ten

— •●• —

WEALTH

Jon Paul pulled into the apartment building where Liz lived. He was thinking about how much she would love his new house.

Paul and Michelle had just been cured by the angel Seraphiel and had been given immunity from the effects of the coin; they both wondered just what the great battle would entail, as they would have heavenly assistance from above.

"Michelle, do you think we should tell anyone about what just happened?"

"No, Paul; the angel is going to help us, and I think we should leave it at that."

"Okay, Michelle, that sounds—"

Suddenly, the doctor and the nurse came rushing into their room, fearing the worst, only to find Paul and Michelle sitting up in bed, talking. "Nurse, are you seeing what I am seeing? I thought you said they were in extreme pain."

"Yes, doctor, I did. I can't explain what I am seeing." The doctor walked up to Paul and reached out for his wrist. He took it and began to check his blood pressure.

"How are you feeling, Mr. Dubois?"

"I am fine, Doctor, no pain at all. It must have passed."

The doctor looked at him and said, "How does your stomach feel, any indigestion or cramps?"

"No, doctor. I am fine."

"Nurse, will you examine the young lady, please?"

"Yes, Dr. Koline." The nurse did examine Michelle, and much to her surprise, she was feeling perfect too. The doctor, puzzled, looked at the two of them and finally said, "I don't know what has happened, but you seem to be fine. I find no evidence of any food poisoning or any stomach ailments at all. I would like to run some additional tests just to be sure. It shouldn't take more than a few hours."

The doctor gave them a knowing look and asked the nurse to draw some blood from both Paul and Michelle; he would order any tests he felt necessary to be sure they were fine. As the nurse began to draw blood from Michelle, she noticed a pleasant odor in the room. She didn't much think about it, but it seemed to be lingering there.

"Do you smell something sweet?" the nurse asked Michelle.

"No, it just smells like a hospital to me."

Michelle shot a look at Paul, who just smiled knowingly at her. The nurse finished her blood draw and left to bring the samples to the doctor, who would then run some additional tests to determine whether they were really fine.

***

Jon Paul walked up to Liz's door and knocked. She answered immediately.

"Come in, Jon Paul!"

"Hello, Liz. Thanks."

Jon Paul walked in and gave Liz a big hug and then a big kiss. "You know, Liz, I want to talk about something."

"Anything, Jon Paul, what's up?"

"Liz, on my drive in to see you, I was thinking, why don't you quit your job and come live with me?"

"Jon Paul, I don't know. That is a big step; I mean, I have worked at the Goat's Head for a few years now. What would I do?"

"Anything you want. I have unlimited funds and we can travel the world if you want, or we can sightsee all around France, visit family, or anything you want."

"Jon Paul, are you serious? I mean, I don't know. I am kind of scared."

"Scared of what? You have me, and I will do anything for you."

"I know, it's just that I have always worked, and—"

"Well, now you don't have to. Liz, look at me. I hold the world in the palm of my hands, and there is nothing we cannot do."

Liz stared at Jon Paul for a moment, and then a smile crossed her lips and she jumped in to his arms and said, "Okay, Jon Paul, let's do this!"

Jon Paul held her tight and lifted her up in the air, smiling.

"This is going to be the best time of our lives, Liz."

***

The doctor had been given the blood samples by the nurse and was almost finished running any tests he could think of to make sure his patients were okay. The nurse came into his lab and said, "Doctor, do you think it is strange that they are okay now? I mean, they were in so much pain that I thought they were dying."

"Yes, it is a little strange, but in all my years at this hospital, I have seen some odd things."

"Odd things, Doctor, like what?"

"Over the years, I have been witness to what some would call miracles at this hospital. There seems to be a recurring occurrence of this kind of phenomena here."

"Do you think that this is one of those times, Dr. Koline?"

"Maybe, nurse, maybe. I am just about finished here, so check on those two one last time, and if everything checks out, we can release them."

"Right away, Doctor. Can I tell them they are fine?"

"No, I will be there in a moment to do that after I finish up the paperwork on them."

The nurse left the doctor's lab and went to check on Paul and Michelle one last time.

***

Jon Paul and Liz were so much in love that anyone meeting them on the street would have no doubt how they felt about each other; it was that obvious.

Liz and Jon Paul walked upstairs to her room to begin packing some of her things—not that they could fit a whole lot in his new sports car, but they could get a few small things in until they could come back to get the rest in a bigger vehicle.

165

"Oh, Jon Paul, I can't believe we are doing this."

"Believe it, my dear. It is real, and we are going to have such great lives together!" Jon Paul smiled at her, and she knew he was telling the truth. Their lives would be exciting and rich and secure—no more worrying about the next check or if she had enough money for rent. Liz packed a small suitcase with just a few essentials that she would need, at least until they could get back to get the rest of her things.

"Oh, my God, Jon Paul, I need to call work and tell them I am quitting!"

"Yeah, too bad for Jacques. I hope he will find someone soon."

"Me too, I feel guilty just leaving him like this, Jon Paul."

"Don't worry, Liz, he has owned the bar for years now. He will find someone and he will be just fine."

"Okay, my love, I trust you and believe you. I am so excited to see our new house!"

Liz was truly excited to see her new house with Jon Paul. Neither Jon Paul nor Liz had had money in their lives before, and the new lifestyle of being rich and wanting for nothing was very appealing to them both. Jon Paul had settled into it faster than Liz, but then, he had the coin.

"Hey, Liz, you know what?"

"What, Jon Paul?"

"I was just thinking, you know, when I made my wish for a bigger house. Well, I never stopped to think what has happened to my old apartment!"

"What do you mean, Jon Paul?"

"When I made my wish, everything changed; the room was spinning and the walls were spinning, and then I was standing in the new house."

"Are you serious? We should go see if it is still there, Jon Paul."

"Yeah, I think you are right. Let's go see if it is still there." Liz picked up her small suitcase and left her apartment. They were going to Jon Paul's old apartment to see if his things were still there, including the apartment! As they got outside and closer to his new car, Liz smiled a grin as big as a Cheshire cat; she loved sports cars.

"Wow, Jon Paul, I have never seen a Maserati up close! It is so amazing!"

"Get in, babe—it is all ours!" Liz got in and slid into the special and oh-so-comfortable leather seat. Jon Paul started the engine. The sound of it made Liz shake with excitement.

"Jon Paul, I am so excited!"

"Me too, Liz, you ready?"

"Oh, yeah!" Jon Paul put the car in gear and sped off, tires squealing and engine roaring. He and Liz were grinning from ear to ear.

Jon Paul drove to his apartment fast. He was enjoying his new car. They arrived at his apartment in no time and parked close to the door. Everything looked the same.

"Liz, I think it all looks the same. Maybe nothing changed here."

"I don't know, Jon Paul. It does look the same; let's go see if your stuff is all still here."

Jon Paul and Liz walked up to the door and opened it. They walked to his apartment and stopped at the door, and Jon Paul looked at Liz with a little hesitancy in his eyes. He was unsure of what they would find when they went in. He turned the key in the lock and opened the door.

As they walked in, Jon Paul noticed nothing strange or even out of order; it all looked the same. They walked around his small apartment looking things over. It all was the same as he had left it. Jon Paul looked at Liz and said, "Everything still looks the same. I guess when I made my wish, the only thing that changed was me."

"Maybe what changed was not just you, Jon Paul; maybe it was created by the coin and you were placed in the mansion as a result."

"You know, that makes sense. It created a new, safe place for me, and somehow, I was transported to the new house."

"Yeah, that sounds right, Jon Paul." Jon Paul was right, the coin had created a new place for him and had transported him to it as it was created. He had guessed correctly; this was something the coin could do automatically. It protected its owner in some strange way.

"Liz, I know we don't have any more room in the car, so why don't we wait to pick up my things later."

"Sure thing, Jon Paul, we can come back later."

"Okay, let's go then." Jon Paul and Liz left his apartment as it was, and he brought nothing with him. They got in the car and began the long drive to the country, where his new home was waiting for them.

***

Paul and Michelle were sitting on the beds when the nurse came in to check on them.

"How are you two feeling?"

"I am just fine," said Paul.

"Yeah, I feel good too," replied Michelle.

"Then you have no pain or any discomfort at all?" asked the nurse.

"No, not me, how about you, Michelle?"

"No, me neither."

"Well, then, the doctor should be here in a minute. Try to relax for now, and he will be able to answer any questions you might have." The nurse smiled and then turned and walked out the door. Paul and Michelle were in perfect health, and the doctor would confirm this.

Paul was looking at Michelle when the doctor walked in, smiling, and said, "Well, you two, I have run every test I can think of, and I find no evidence of any infection or poisoning. You are cleared to go home. I have some papers for you to sign at the nurse's station before you leave. Do you have any questions for me?"

"I do, doc— what you think happened to us?" asked Paul.

"I really don't know. I suspect it was a type of food poisoning, but I have never seen it disappear so fast. Maybe you two are blessed—at least, I would feel that way if I had gone through what you went through." Paul smiled at Michelle. They both knew what had happened, and they weren't telling the doctor.

"If that is all, I will leave you two to your good health."

"Thanks, doc, you saved us." The doctor smiled at them and then walked away, closing the door behind him. Paul and Michelle got dressed in their street clothes and walked to the nurse's station to sign their release papers.

***

Jon Paul and Liz were driving to their new house in the country, and as they drove out of the city limits, they began to drive by open fields of green grass where farmers had their livestock. They saw sprawling wine fields where the local wine brewers had their fields of grapes. It was absolutely breathtaking—so much beauty and rolling hills, anyone seeing it could not help but think it was God's country. They drove for some time until Jon Paul saw that they were getting close and said, "Liz, we are almost home. Isn't it just beautiful here?"

"Jon Paul, I have never dreamed that I could be living in such a perfect place, with the man I love with all my heart." Liz smiled and reached out to hold Jon Paul's hand. Jon Paul held her hand tight. He could feel her heartbeat in his hand, and he knew that his heart beat in the same time as hers.

***

"Nurse, are we done here?"

"Yes, I think that will be all. You two take care—hope we don't see you again!" Paul and Michelle laughed, and the nurse smiled and laughed a bit too.

"I don't think you will be seeing us anytime soon," said Paul. Michelle and Paul then walked out of the hospital and to his car. They were glad to be alive. After Jon Paul had cursed them, Paul and Michelle were feeling better than they ever had, thanks to the angel Seraphiel. They got in his car and decided to drive back to Paul's apartment; after all, Michelle had some of her things there. In their scramble to get away from Jon Paul, they had had to leave her suitcase full of most of the rest of her things there.

"Hey, Michelle, when we get back, do you want to eat something? I am kind of hungry."

"You know, Paul, me too. I need to get my strength back."

"Okay, I think I have something for us to eat; if not, I can make us something."

"What have you got in mind, Paul?"

"How about I make us a beef stew with some veggies?"

"Mmm, yeah, that sounds good to me!"

Paul smiled at Michelle and nodded. He would make them something to eat as soon as they got to his place.

***

Jon Paul and Liz approached their new estate; the driveway was long and lined with trees. It was a most beautiful home. "Jon Paul, is this it? No way!"

"Yes way, baby, this is it—our new home. How do you like it?"

"Jon Paul, I … I …" Liz had no words to express her love and amazement at what see was seeing. Jon Paul looked at her and smiled. "I know, Liz, I know." Tears began to stream down her soft face, but these were tears of joy. Never in her life had Liz known such love.

Jon Paul drove up the driveway to the garage, where his caretaker Mr. Bestion was standing and waiting. He stopped the car just outside the garage door. He got out and helped Liz out, and then he looked at Mr. Bestion and said, "Hello, Mr. Bestion. How is your afternoon?"

"It is very good, sir. I have been working in the lawn around the house, and the grounds are in a most pristine state."

"Yes, they do look most wonderful. Thank you, Mr. Bestion."

"How was your drive, sir?"

"Very good. I want you to meet the future Mrs. Chavalier."

"Hello, ma'am, I am Franklin Bestion."

"Hello, Mr. Bestion—is that what I should call you?"

"Yes, ma'am, but you may call me anything you wish."

"I will just call you by your name, Mr. Bestion."

"Very good, ma'am."

"Mr. Bestion, how are the other cars? Are they clean and ready to drive?" Jon Paul asked.

"They are, sir. Do you need me to get a special one ready for you?"

"Not right now, but we will need one with more room for all of Miss Bourg's things soon, maybe tomorrow."

"I will have one ready for you, sir."

"Thank you, Mr. Bestion. I think we will go into the house now."

Mr. Bestion smiled and nodded at Jon Paul and Liz; they then began the walk up to the front door. Liz was in awe at the beauty of her new home. She kept looking at Jon Paul, thinking she was dreaming. She wondered what she had done to deserve such a wonderful man. The front door was big; it was solid oak surrounded by red mahogany pillars. It had small windows on each side of it that let some light in to the entryway. As Jon Paul and Liz walked into the entryway, the smell of something good hit them. Jon Paul set her one small piece of luggage on the marble floor and took Liz by the hand and led her into the kitchen, where Mr. Falid was cooking something that smelled great.

They walked through halls with very high ceilings painted with scenes from old-time biblical art, and pictures of a religious nature adorned the walls. Beautiful furniture set and spaced perfectly between glass tables gave an inviting look. They walked into the sprawling kitchen with its double ovens and marble countertops and, seeing Mr. Falid, Jon Paul said, "Hello, my friend, how are you this afternoon?"

Mr. Falid turned, smiled, and said, "Hello, sir. I am fine. How was your drive?"

"It was great! I love my new Maserati! This is the future Mrs. Chavalier, Liz Bourg."

"It is a pleasure to meet you, ma'am. If you ever need anything, just ask me."

Liz shook his hand and smiled. She was overwhelmed with all this newfound freedom. Never again would she worry about her future or her next paycheck. "Oh, Jon Paul, I forgot to call the bar!"

"No problem, my dear, use the phone in my office."

"Um, okay, where is your office?"

Jon Paul smiled at Liz and said, "Follow me, my dear. I will show you, and then when you are ready, you can set up your own office if you want. We have plenty of room for that." He took her by the hand and showed her his office. It was amazing. There were double doors that led to an open room with fifteen-foot-high ceilings. Bookshelves that stretched from the floor to ten feet tall were loaded with books of all kinds. Encyclopedias of different branches and different publishers were there too. He showed her the phone at the desk and let her sit down to call her work.

"Do you want me to stay here with you?"

"No, Jon Paul, I will be all right, but can you come back in a few moments to show me around the place? I need to know where I am going, and where's our room?"

"Of course, my dear Liz, I will go back to the kitchen and talk with Mr. Falid and then return and show you where everything is."

"Thanks, Jon Paul." She smiled at him, and Jon Paul, feeling her love, grabbed her and planted a very passionate kiss on her.

"Wow, Jon Paul, I … wow!" Jon Paul smiled and then turned and walked back to his kitchen. He truly loved Liz and she him.

Jon Paul walked back to the kitchen, and seeing Mr. Falid, asked him, "Mr. Falid, what are you cooking? It smells absolutely wonderful."

"Thank you, sir. I thought you might be hungry when you got back, so I put together a small lunch, or a late lunch, if you prefer." Jon Paul smiled at his manservant; he was pleased with him.

"I have prepared a small duck basted with a hollandaise sauce, potatoes in a white wine, and fresh vegetables with a vinaigrette dressing. For your beverage, I have set out a bottle of 1945 red wine from the valley of Toulon."

"Sounds great, Mr. Falid, how long till it is ready?"

"I need another fifteen minutes for the sauce to finish cooking, sir; if you wish, I can come find you when it is ready."

"Yes, that will be fine. I think I will take Miss Bourg to the game room to show her the billiard table."

"Very good, sir, I will find you in a few moments." Jon Paul walked away, leaving his manservant to finish cooking their lunch. Jon Paul was walking to his office when he began to feel the coin in his pocket; it was calling to him.

***

Paul and Michelle were close to his place. As Paul pulled up to the building and found a parking place, he glanced over at Michelle. "Michelle, do you want to do anything special tonight?"

"No, not really, I am just glad to be home with you so we can move forward with our lives." She smiled at Paul. "I think we should take a few days to get settled in before we start planning our next move, you know, with Jon Paul and the coin."

"Yeah, that is a good idea. We need to get a plan before we do anything else. Maybe the angel Seraphiel will be there to help us with that." They walked up to his apartment, and as they went in, Paul saw that Michelle was a bit confused. She seemed to be looking for something.

"Michelle, what is it?"

"What, Paul? Oh, I am looking for my Bible."

"I see. I was wondering what you were doing."

"Have you seen it?"

"Did you try my room, where you had it last?"

"No, I had forgotten I put it there." Michelle went to Paul's room and began to look for her Bible. She looked on the nightstand, but it wasn't there. She looked in the bathroom, but it wasn't there either. Where did she put that old book? Then, like a shiny beacon calling attention to her eyes, she saw it sitting there, glowing in the sunlight by the chair. It seemed to her it was gleaming. Michelle walked over to the chair and picked it up, and she felt a shock of energy as she held the ancient book in her hands; immediately, she bowed her head and said a silent prayer.

***

Liz had just finished her phone call when Jon Paul called to her. "Hey, Liz, are you still in here?"

"Yeah, Jon Paul. I just finished up."

"Oh, good, how did it go? Did Jacques understand?"

"No, he was really upset with me that I didn't even give him two weeks' notice. He asked what I was doing and how was I going to live."

"What did you tell him?"

"I didn't, I just left him hanging. I did say I will be just fine and I will call him in a few weeks to let him know I am okay."

"Well, that is okay. He is a good businessman; he will be fine."

"Yeah, so what are we going to do now? Does Mr. Falid have our lunch ready?"

"Not just yet. He will find us when it is ready, but for now, we are going to the game room so I can show you my new pool table!"

"Really, Jon Paul, a new pool table?"

"Yes, let's go." Jon Paul took her hand and led her down the long hallway to the stairs, which led to the lower level. As they descended the wide steps, Liz noticed a statue on the table by the wall. "Jon Paul, what is that statue?"

"Which one?"

"That one, on the table, right there."

"Oh, that one—that is by the great French painter Paul Cezanne. It is rare, as he only did a few of these precious works of art. He, of course, was only known for his paintings."

Liz stared at it in wonderment. She was beginning to learn their estate and all its priceless works of art. They continued their walk through the basement floor to the new billiard table. Jon Paul loved playing, and he looked at Liz and said, "How about a game, my dear?"

Liz looked at Jon Paul and said, "You know, Jon Paul, after working at the bar for all these years, I am pretty good!"

"Bring it on, baby!"

Liz smiled at Jon Paul, and he was grinning back at her. Jon Paul set the table up, grabbed a cue for him and one for Liz, and said, "You wanna break?"

"Oh, yeah, stand back." Liz hit the cue ball perfectly and balls went everywhere; some dropped in the pockets, and as Jon Paul watched, he knew he was in trouble.

***

Michelle walked back down to the living room. She had her Bible, and Paul was waiting for her on the couch. "I see you found it."

"Yes, and believe it or not, it was glowing, and it gave me a shock when I touched it."

"I believe you, Michelle, especially after today." Paul looked at Michelle and she knew what he was thinking; he was referring to their encounter with the angel Seraphiel.

"Paul, do you think the angel will come to us if I call her?"

"I don't know, Michelle, but it seems like a waste to call her for nothing right now. Let's wait for a few days before we do anything. I want you to get settled in here first, okay?"

"Are you sure, Paul? I mean, I just want to do something."

"I know, Michelle, but right now, revenge is the last thing we need to worry about. I know we are immune to the coin, but take it easy, okay?"

"Okay, Paul. I will wait for a while. Maybe you are right. I need to get settled first before we make any plans to fight with Jon Paul."

Paul smiled at Michelle and gave her a knowing nod; they would wait and get settled first before making any plans to rid Jon Paul of the coin. For Paul and Michelle, the next few weeks would be a settling period, with Michelle getting used to Paul and all of his quirky ways, and Paul getting used to Michelle and all of her particular ways. Neither had the stomach for a fight, and Jon Paul and his cursed coin would wait till they were ready. If that meant they would wait for months, then they would wait. The angel

Seraphiel would help them when the time was right, and they could be assured of their victory against Jon Paul.

***

Jon Paul and Liz were enjoying their game of billiards when Mr. Falid came walking into the game room. "Sir, your lunch is ready."

Jon Paul looked at his manservant and said, "Thank you, Mr. Falid, we will be there in a minute."

Mr. Falid nodded in agreement and went back up the stairs to the kitchen. Jon Paul smiled at Liz and said, "Okay, if I make this shot, we go eat lunch!"

Liz smiled at Jon Paul and said, "If you make this shot, I quit!"

Jon Paul smiled and took the shot. The cue ball hit the seven ball and went in the pocket. "Did you see that? Well, let's go eat lunch. We can come back down later and finish up our game, unless you're scared."

Liz stared at Jon Paul with a menacing look. "Am I scared? Does it look like I am scared, mister?" Liz smiled at Jon Paul, and he knew she was just kidding around. They had a chemistry that few people ever find; it was what made them so close. Jon Paul and Liz walked upstairs to the kitchen, where Mr. Falid had their lunch ready. "Mr. Falid, I think we will sit in the breakfast nook and have our lunch."

"Very good, sir. I was hoping you might say that. It is a beautiful day and I thought you might want to look out the windows as you eat your lunch."

"Mr. Falid, you have outdone yourself with this lunch. It looks great!"

Jon Paul and Liz walked out to the breakfast nook and sat down in the plush chairs, Jon Paul at the head of the walnut table and Liz at the other end. Mr. Falid brought out their lunch and Jon Paul was smiling; he and Liz were having their first meal in their new home.

"You know what, Liz? This is our first meal here."

"It is, Jon Paul. I love it here, and I love you."

"I love you too, Liz." Jon Paul and Liz smiled the smile of soul mates in complete love with each other. It was amazing to see two people so in love. As they ate their lunch, Jon Paul was feeling the coin again in his pocket. It was heating up.

"Jon Paul, what should we do this afternoon?" said Liz.

"I don't know, I was thinking about taking a walk around the grounds to see how everything is doing, and to check out security."

"That sound like fun, mind if I come with you?"

"You can always come with me, my dear. You need to learn about this too, you know, I might not be here forever." Jon Paul didn't know how right he was—and how prophetic.

Jon Paul and Liz finished eating and went out to check the grounds; they would also check the gardens to see the beautiful flowers that were growing so perfectly. They walked around for quite some time. Occasionally, they would stop and smell the lilacs that were in bloom, or the roses that were so tall you barely needed to bend over to smell them. Liz and Jon Paul were living the good life. "Liz, I was thinking, what should we do now that we are secure and have no worries?"

"Well, have you ever thought about running for office?"

"Running for office? Are you serious, Liz?"

"Yes, Jon Paul. I mean, why not, we have enough money now, and you would make a great politician."

"Liz, I can't believe you said that. I have never even thought about it, but now that you said it, I am thinking you might be right. Maybe I could run for office." Jon Paul and Liz were making a plan for their future, even if they didn't know it. Jon Paul had enough property and things he had acquired with the help of the coin, but he had never really made a wish to have lots of money in the bank. If he were to run for public office, he would need a large amount to keep his campaign running till he was elected. Jon Paul thought for a moment, and then he said, "Liz, I think we should get back. I have something I need to do at the house."

Liz looked at him strangely and finally said, "Is everything all right, Jon Paul?"

"Yes, my dear. I just need to check some things back at the house."

Jon Paul and Liz found their way back to their house. They had walked the grounds and had a wonderful time. Jon Paul, however, wanted to get back to the house so he could use his coin to become rich. He didn't know exactly how, but he was planning on using the coin as soon as he was alone; he didn't want Liz to see him using it for his wish.

"Jon Paul, I am going upstairs to our room. Are you leaving the house?"

"No, Liz, just going to my office to do some paperwork. I will join you in an hour or two."

"Okay, Jon Paul, I will be waiting." She smiled at Jon Paul and walked up the stairs to their bedroom. Jon Paul watched her walk up the stairs and out of sight; he could now go to his office to make his wish for money. As he entered his office, he made sure he closed the doors behind him. This was only for his eyes; no one else should see him making his wish.

Jon Paul reached for the coin in his pocket. He could feel it heating up in his hand as he thought about what he wanted to say. He remembered the name of the top bank in all of France, "Bank One of France," he smirked as he said out loud. "I wish to have millions and millions of dollars in my new bank account at Bank One of France." *Poof!* Instantly, Jon Paul was a millionaire; he had more money than he could ever spend in a lifetime. Jon Paul smiled as he wondered if his wish had come true; he sat at his desk and thought, *I better look up the number for the bank and call them to confirm if my money is there.* He found the phone book and the number for the bank and dialed the number.

"Hello, Bank One, how may I direct your call?"

"Ah, hello, I want to check my balance."

"Yes, sir, what is your account number?"

"I don't know. Can you find it from my name?"

"Of course, sir, what is your name?"

"Jon Paul Chavalier."

"Hold on one minute, sir, while I look that up."

"Okay." The bank clerk looked up Jon Paul's name and account number. She found it and saw the amount in it, and then she returned to the phone and said, "Yes, sir, I have found your account number. How can I help you today?"

"Well, I was wondering, can you tell me my account balance?"

"Yes, sir, with your high balance, we here at the bank want to extend any and all private services to you. Anything you need, just ask; we are here to provide the best service for accounts and very special customers like you."

"I see. Can you just tell me the balance as of right now?" The clerk told Jon Paul his balance and again offered him special services that were not available to normal customers. Jon Paul almost dropped the phone when he heard what she said. "Ah, yeah, that is what I have."

"Will there be anything else, Mr. Chavalier?"

"No, I think that will do for today. Thank you for your time. Oh, yeah, I almost forgot: What is my account number again?" The woman told Jon Paul his account number and he made sure to write it down. He would need this in the future when and if he was going to run for office.

Jon Paul hung up the phone in a mild state of shock. He had never heard of anyone having so much money in their bank account, and now he was one of the wealthiest men in all of France; the coin had come through for him, and he was impressed. He thought, *I wonder if I should tell Liz how much we have in the bank.* He decided that he would wait to tell her. She was not the nosy type, so it would be okay to wait. Jon Paul sat at his desk and looked around his office. Never had he had so much. He began to cry.

Liz had been in their bedroom putting on makeup when she began to notice she was running low on clothes. She would need to go shopping, or better yet, pick up her stuff from her apartment. She wondered if Jon Paul had thought of this.

Jon Paul opened the doors to his office and walked to the kitchen. He was going to get something to drink first before going upstairs.

"Mr. Falid, I need something to drink."

"Sir, what can I get you, maybe a scotch?"

"Um, no, how about some smooth brandy? I have had a bit of a stressful last few hours, and I need something to calm my nerves."

"A brandy it is, then." Mr. Falid smiled at Jon Paul and walked over to the counter to pour him a brandy. Jon Paul watched him and was amazed at the way he could move for a man of such age. He walked with grace and a certain flair that was captivating, to say the least. "Here you are, sir, can I get you anything else?"

"No, thank you, Mr. Falid, this will be fine for now." Jon Paul sat down at his counter and sipped his brandy. Mr. Falid saw the puzzled look on Jon Paul's face and asked him, "Sir, is something wrong? Can I help you?"

"No, nothing is wrong. I am just feeling a little overwhelmed with everything. Let me ask you something, Mr. Falid. Did you ever hold public office, I mean not like before, but political?"

"No, sir, not in that particular sense of the word, but I was a general in charge of a great army of men who conquered anyone in our path or our way."

"Yes, I remember; you once told me about your past history. Well, I am thinking about something Miss Bourg said to me earlier."

"And what was that, sir?"

"She jokingly suggested I run for office."

"Yes, sir, you would be a great president of France."

"Oh, no, nothing so high, Mr. Falid. Perhaps just a particular party, where I can make a difference."

"The coin can do anything you wish it to, sir. If you want to be president, then wish it; if you want something else, wish that instead. It has no limits."

"Yes, I know that, and that is what is worrying me—too many possibilities."

"Sir, maybe you should just focus on one thing, and try not to worry about the other stuff. I will always be here to offer you my support if you wish it."

"Yes, I know that, my friend, and I appreciate that. I will be all right in time. I just need to calm down and get my head straight."

"Anything I can do to help, sir?"

"Thanks for listening and for the advice. I will think about it, and, Mr. Falid, you are the best."

"Thank you, sir!" Jon Paul truly was a friend with his manservant; he trusted him and believed his advice. After all, he was very old and had had the coin before Jon Paul did. Jon Paul got up and walked upstairs to see Liz. She was in their dressing room looking at the empty clothes spaces and thinking she needed to pick up the rest of her stuff from her apartment, and then maybe go shopping to get more clothes. "Jon Paul, hi!"

"Hey, Liz, how are you?"

"I am great, Jon Paul. I was thinking, why don't we take a trip back to the city to my apartment to get the rest of my things. I mean, I am almost out of clothes."

"What! You don't need any clothes!" Jon Paul grabbed Liz around her waist, smiled at her, and said, "You could just be naked."

"Jon Paul, you are too much!" Liz smiled at Jon Paul, held him and kissed him fully on the lips, and then said, "Seriously, Jon Paul. I need more clothes. Can we go get the rest of my things, please?"

"Of course we can, my love, anytime you want."

She smiled at him and said, "Thanks, Jon Paul. Can we go tomorrow?"

"Sure, tomorrow is perfect. I will inform Mr. Bestion to have a car ready for us in the morning."

Liz smiled at Jon Paul and sat back down in her chair. She began to toss her hair around and Jon Paul watched her, amazed at her beauty.

***

As Paul and Michelle settled into their lives together as a couple, they began to learn about one another; Paul loved his morning tea, and Michelle preferred coffee. When she was with Jon Paul, she had always had tea, because that was his favorite. But now that she was with Paul, she decided she would rather have her coffee. Of course, Paul was okay with that. He was easy to get along with; nothing really ever bothered him. His education and comfortable upbringing had taught him to appreciate the small things in life, as they have the most meaning. Paul and Michelle were sitting in his apartment when Michelle spoke up. "Paul, when can we go eat at that little bistro again? I love it there."

"Um, how about tomorrow we go and have lunch there?"

"Tomorrow sounds good to me. Paul, I think we should try to enjoy our lives for now. We can do nothing till the angel Seraphiel tells us."

"Yeah, you are right; we should enjoy our life for now. The time will come when the angel will appear and tell us when we can try to get the coin from Jon Paul."

"Paul, do you think we will both survive this coming battle?"

"I don't know, Michelle, but I think we are in for a very dangerous fight." Michelle looked at Paul with a very concerned and apprehensive stare, and she suddenly got chills.

"Michelle, are you all right?"

"Yes, Paul, I just got the chills when you said that."

"Try not to worry, Michelle; we have your angel watching over us, and we will be fine. I promise."

Michelle smiled at Paul and felt his confidence; she drew strength from him, and he knew it. Paul and Michelle were close and becoming closer with each passing day.

***

Jon Paul and Liz were upstairs in their room when Jon Paul suddenly said, "Liz! You know what we should do right now?" Liz jumped as he said this. He had been sitting quietly beside her when he suddenly spoke.

"What, Jon Paul?"

"Why don't we call your mom and tell her about us!"

"Right now? I mean, we could, but I was thinking of waiting until we were a bit more settled."

"Settled, what more do you want to settle? We are here and this is our home, so let's call her."

"Okay, Jon Paul, we can call her. Have you told your parents about us?"

"Yeah, I told Mom and I am sure she has told the rest of my family. I should call her to tell her what's been happening."

"Yes, you should, Jon Paul. That is your mother, you know!"

"You are right, my dear, I need to call her; how about we call yours first and then mine?"

"That would be a good idea. Let me finish up here and then we can call, okay?"

"Okay, Lizzy, you make the first call, and then I will." Liz smiled at Jon Paul and finished putting her makeup in its case. She had been rearranging it for the last few minutes as they were talking.

"Jon Paul, what do you think I should tell her?"

"Why don't you just tell her the truth: you found me, quit the bar, and now are living a rich and luxurious life!"

"Jon Paul! You are crazy! I can't tell her that. She would be very upset with me."

"What do you mean? Just tell her the truth, and it will be fine."

"Jon Paul, how do you know it will be fine? Can you see the future?"

"Well, as a matter of fact, I can!"

"Jon Paul, stop it. You are just too much."

"Okay, seriously, just tell her we met and have fallen in love and you moved in with me."

Liz looked at Jon Paul. She thought that what he had said would be okay to tell her mom, and she said, "Okay, crazy man. I am going to tell her what you said and hope for the best."

"That's my girl; you know it will be fine." Liz and Jon Paul walked down to their kitchen to make the calls. They had decided that it would be more comfortable to sit there and talk than somewhere else. Liz was the first to dial her mom; she was going to tell her about Jon Paul and their new life and hope it would be fine.

"Hello, Mom?"

"Yes, hello, Liz?

"Yeah, Mom, it's me. I have news to tell you."

Liz didn't call her mom, Cheri Bourg, often; she lived a long way away from Liz. However, they never had a difficult time with each other, as some children do with their parents. Liz and her mom got on very well, so it was a small surprise when Liz called to tell her the news.

"Liz, I hope it is good news!"

"How are you doing, Mom?"

"I am well. The weather has been awful here, though; you probably don't get the news where you are."

"Mom, is everything else all right?"

"Yes, everything is fine; now, how about your news."

"Um, well, I guess I will come out and say it: I have met a wonderful man. We are in love and have moved in together."

"Really, Lizzette? I am so happy for you; tell me all about him." So Liz did just that. She told her mom how she had known Jon Paul for several years, and now they had found each other and were living together. Liz's mom was overjoyed; she thought her tomboyish daughter would never get married and might always be single, giving her no grandchildren.

Jon Paul listened as Liz talked to her mom for some time, and then she looked at him and said, "Do you want to say hi?"

Jon Paul looked surprised and nodded his head yes.

"Hey, Mom, Jon Paul wants to say hi, okay?"

"Yes, please put him on."

Liz handed him the phone and he said, "Hello, Mrs. Bourg, how are you?"

"I am fine, Jon Paul, thanks for asking. Now tell me about you two." Jon Paul related to her how he had known Liz for a few years, and now they had found each other. He told her that they had connected in a way neither thought possible, that they were soul mates and there was no denying it.

"Jon Paul, when are you coming to visit so we can meet in person?"

"I don't know right now. I will talk with Liz and we can make a plan to visit you soon."

"That sounds fine, Jon Paul. Can I talk with Liz again?"

"Of course, Mrs. Bourg, hold on." Jon Paul handed the phone back to Liz.

"Mom, I heard Jon Paul saying we will visit you soon. I will call you first to make sure it is okay to come."

"Okay, Liz, let me know a few days in advance so I can get things ready for your visit."

"Sure thing, Mom, I'd better go now."

"Okay, Lizzy, talk with you later, love you."

"Okay, Mom, love you too, bye."

"Bye." Liz hung up the phone. She was very happy; she hadn't seen her mom in a long time, and now she was going to bring the love of her life home to meet her.

"Jon Paul, when do you think we are going to be able to go see my mom?"

"Well, I don't know right now; we can figure that out later. For now, though, we should think about getting the rest of your things from your old apartment."

"Yes, I really do need to get my things." Liz and Jon Paul made a plan to go get her things as soon as possible. Jon Paul would need to go talk with his servant, Mr. Bestion, and make sure he had a car ready for them when they were ready to leave. Jon Paul walked out of his front door and down to his garage to see Mr. Bestion and tell him that they would be leaving in a few hours. Liz had gone back upstairs to her room to get a suitcase so she could bring some more of her clothes. She didn't have a lot of things, but what she had was definitely on the high end of fashion.

"Thanks, Mr. Bestion, for getting the car ready; we will be back in a little while. I have to do a few things before we leave."

"Thank you, sir, for letting me help you. I am sure you will love the Range Rover; it drives like a dream and has plenty of space for your things."

Jon Paul smiled at him and walked back up to his house; he would grab a few things and check his calendar to see what was on his schedule before he left, and he also wanted to call his mom and tell her the news. As he walked up the path to his front door, he wondered how he had ever lived before without so many things to help him, such as the conveniences of having a car—in his case, many very expensive and beautiful cars, all the best ones in the world, or at least, the best money could buy. He wondered why he had never imagined himself this way. Jon Paul was living the good life, and he was happy. The memory of what had happened with his former best friend and his ex-girlfriend was fading fast. Jon Paul walked up the stairs to his room, looking for Liz.

"Liz, are you in here?"

"Yes, Jon Paul. I am in the dressing room." Jon Paul walked through his bedroom, through the double doors that led into a sitting room, and then to the dressing room. Liz was sitting at her styling table looking at her hair and her clothes; she looked most beautiful, Jon Paul thought.

"Jon Paul, do you like this dress?"

"Yes, it is beautiful. You look *great*!"

"Jon Paul, are you teasing me?"

"No, honey, I think you look very beautiful."

"Thank you."

"Anytime, Liz. I am going to call my mom now. Do you want to say hi to her too?"

"Yes, Jon Paul, I am almost ready."

"Okay, Liz, I am going back to the kitchen to call her. I will wait for you."

Liz smiled at Jon Paul. He smiled back and then turned to head back to the kitchen; as he walked, he thought about what he was going to talk to his mom about. He wondered if he should tell her he had moved—maybe he shouldn't tell her how big of a house he was in now. He also thought, *Should I call my sister to tell her the good news?* Surely she would be happy for him. Jon Paul finally decided just to talk about whatever and see where the conversation went, and that would be the best way to handle it for now. He got to the bottom of the staircase when he noticed Mr. Falid walking toward him.

"Hello, sir. I have put together some food for your drive into the city, in case you get hungry."

"Really, Mr. Falid, thank you; you are the best!"

"Anytime, sir. I know it is a bit of a drive, and you will need your strength to keep driving, and on the return trip as well. Is there anything else you require of me?"

"Well, I think for now, you have it covered; we will be back late, I am sure, but keep the light on for us, okay?"

"Of course, sir, please be safe and careful."

"We will, Mr. Falid. Now I better call my mom and talk with her." Mr. Falid smiled and then walked back to his quarters. He had finished his work and was going to sit down for a while before he had to begin his next job.

Jon Paul sat down at the marble counter to wait for his love to come in there so they could talk with his mom together. He didn't have to wait long before he heard Liz coming in; the sound of her heels made a clicking noise as she walked across the marble floor toward him. She looked beyond beautiful to Jon Paul. She had on a black, lacy shirt with a short, dark-blue skirt, and it showed her legs off very well. Her hair was long and straight and hung down in a gentle way past her shoulders, and the black heels just finished her outfit perfectly. Jon Paul stared at her.

"I am ready. Let's call your mom." Jon Paul, still amazed at her beauty, didn't move. He was transfixed by her.

"Jon Paul!"

"Huh, oh … I … um, *damn*, Liz!" She smiled at Jon Paul and broke the spell. She sat down next to him and reached for the phone; she handed it to him, smiled, and said, "Are you ready to tell your mom about us?"

"Yeah, I am, Liz." Jon Paul dialed the number and waited.

"Hello."

"Hello, Mom, it's Jon Paul."

"Oh, hi, Jon Paul, how are you?"

"I am great, Mom. I have some news to tell you about Liz."

"Is something wrong, Jon Paul?"

"No, Mom, we have moved in together to a house I bought here in the country."

"Jon Paul, when did you buy a house, and why didn't you tell your father and me you were moving?"

"It was kinda sudden, and I wanted to get settled at least a bit before I called you guys."

"Okay, so where is this house located, Jon Paul?"

"We are out of the city of Toulon by about forty miles to the northeast, in the country, with wine fields and pastures all around us. It is beautiful and very isolated."

"It sounds wonderful, Jon Paul. How is Liz, by the way?"

"She is great, too; in fact, she is right here with me and wants to say hi."

"Put her on the phone, Jon Paul." Jon Paul handed the phone to Liz and smiled.

"Hello, Mrs. Chavalier, how are you?"

"I am doing well. How are you and my son getting along?"

"We are so very happy. Jon Paul does everything for me."

"Yes, he is a very special young man. I hope you are taking good care of him."

"I am doing my best, Mrs. Chavalier."

"Okay then, it was nice to talk with you. Can you put Jon Paul back on, please?" Liz handed the phone back to Jon Paul and he said, "So, Mom, what do you think?"

"She sounds wonderful, Jon Paul. I think you are moving a bit fast, but it is your life; be careful, okay?"

"I will, Mom, thanks and say hi to Dad, will you?"

"I will. Bye, Jon Paul."

"Bye." Jon Paul hung up his phone and looked at Liz, who was smiling at him.

"My mom thinks you are very nice, and she can't wait to meet you."

"Did she say that?"

"No, not exactly, but I know how she thinks. She and my dad are going to want to come visit us soon, and she is anxious to see our new place."

"When do you want to have them here?"

"Um, soon, but I am going to call her back to set a better time. You and I still need to get some things done here first; I mean, I still need to get my things from my apartment too."

"I totally forgot about your stuff at your old place. Do you think we can get it all in one trip?"

"I don't know. I mean, it is probably going to take a few hours."

"It doesn't matter how long it takes, Jon Paul. We have all the time in the world." Liz smiled at him and gave him a quick kiss on the lips, and he responded in kind. They stood up together and walked out their front door and down to the garage, where Mr. Bestion had the Range Rover ready and gassed up for them to take to the city. As they approached the garage, Jon Paul saw him first, and as they got to the big door, he said, "Mr. Bestion, is the car ready?"

"Sir, it is all ready for your drive into the city."

"Thank you so much. We will be back sometime later today."

"Be careful, sir. I will be here; if you need anything, just call."

"I will, Mr. Bestion." Jon Paul smiled as he opened the door for Liz and she got in, and then he walked around to the driver's side and got in himself. He started the engine, and he felt very comfortable in his new car, although it had a different feel than his Maserati. Jon Paul pulled out of his garage, waved at his servant, pulled out and into his dirt driveway, and drove down the long path to the street.

***

Paul and Michelle had been together for only a short time, but they were beginning to get used to each other's particular needs. Michelle liked to have dinner prepared before it was time to eat, and Paul was more likely to just make something at the last minute. This was their way, and it was something they both could eventually get used to. Paul usually spent the days working from home as a computer programmer and consultant, and Michelle got calls from local catering companies asking her for help in preparing dinners or lunches for clients. Michelle was paid very well for her services. Paul made a decent living too, so this allowed them both to work from home. Even though sometimes they would bump elbows, they were still happy with each other. One particular late morning, Paul was taking a coffee break when he noticed Michelle walking to the kitchen, and he said to her, "Hey, Michelle, why don't we go out for dinner tonight?"

"Tonight? I think that would be a wonderful idea, Paul!"

"Where do you want to go?"

"I don't know. Why don't you surprise me?" Michelle winked at Paul seductively.

"Okay, I will set up something for tonight, and you will be surprised!"

Michelle smiled at Paul and knew it would be fun. Paul was spontaneous, to say the least, unlike Jon Paul, who was predictable and never spontaneous. Michelle thought back to when she and Jon Paul were living together. She remembered that it was nice for so long, and she had even thought she would marry him and have his children, but then that all changed when he brought home the cursed golden coin. Now she had Paul. Michelle wondered how different her life would have been if she had met him first.

***

At The Goat's Head Bar, things had been the same. Time stopped when you were in there, and although it was dark, it was a refuge for a lot of lost souls. Since Liz had quit and left, Jacques Molay, the owner of the bar, had been putting in longer hours and was still looking for a replacement for Liz. One day, in walked a small waif of a woman, no more than five feet tall, with jet-black hair, tight blue jeans, and a nice cardigan sweater. She walked up to him and said, "Hello, are you still looking for a waitress?"

Jacques looked her up and down and finally said, "Yes, I am. Do you have experience?"

"Yes, I do. My name is Maggie Martin. I was a waitress at Pepe's Pastries and Coffee for three years. I recently quit, as I have relocated to a new apartment, and I am looking for a job."

"Okay, Miss Martin, let's see what you can do." Jacques took her to the back of the bar and started asking her about mixed drinks and how to prepare them, and she passed all his tests with flying colors; she would be Liz's replacement.

"Well, I think I have seen enough. You are very qualified to work here. When can you start?"

"I can start anytime. How about tomorrow?"

"Very good, be here tomorrow at twelve p.m., and we will get you going."

"Thanks, see you tomorrow!" She walked out of the place with her head held high; she had a job! Maggie Martin had been the one to see Jon Paul and Liz together. She also was the one who told Michelle about it, which ultimately caused the breakup of Jon Paul and Michelle. Little did she know that she was now in Jon Paul's favorite bar.

Chapter Eleven

— • • • —

POWER

Jon Paul and Liz drove through the countryside on their way back in to Toulon. The drive was not so long, but the view of the grape vineyards and the open, deep-green pastures made it all seem to fly by. Jon Paul couldn't help but think about Liz's suggestion that he run for political office. The idea was intriguing to him and was beginning to draw him in. The lure of power was very appealing to Jon Paul.

"You know, Liz, I've been thinking. Maybe I can run for office; how about the UMP[1]?"

"The UMP. How would you do it, Jon Paul? I mean, do you know anybody you can ask for help?"

"I haven't gotten that far yet, but if you think I can run and win, maybe I should seriously consider it."

"Yes, you can, Jon Paul, with the help of the coin."

"You're right, Liz. I had forgotten about that." It seemed that the one who controlled the coin was its master, and the more wishes one made, the less the coin cursed them—although some might think it a curse to have wealth and financial freedom. Jon Paul looked at Liz, smiled, and said, "Let's think this through some more before we make a final decision. If I do this, I want to make sure we do it right." Jon Paul was correct; he needed to do it right, or he might not win, but having the coin should ensure him a win. However, who knew what the tradeoff could be? He could lose Liz, or worse, his own life, from the curse of the coin.

---

[1]   The Union for a Popular Movement, France's controlling government party

"Liz, have I mentioned that the dreams I was having that were so violent and brutal have almost gone now?"

"Really, Jon Paul, they are subsiding?"

"Yeah, I don't know why, but the more that time seems to pass, the more I am able to sleep with normal dreams." Jon Paul had been having such dramatic and violent dreams about war and of killing men, or sometimes even women and children. He was relieved to tell Liz that they were not plaguing him so much anymore.

"That is good, Jon Paul; at least now you will be able to sleep better."

"Yes, hopefully now." Liz and Jon Paul continued their drive into the city, and they sat in silence the rest of the way as they continued to get closer to Liz's old apartment.

***

Paul was looking through the local phone book for the names of nice restaurants he might take Michelle to for her surprise dinner. He thumbed through several until his eyes fell upon a particular one where he had been a few times before; although it was a little expensive, it had very nice service, and the food was top-rated in all of the south of France. La Patouille was a five-star restaurant. Paul decided that would be perfect for his dinner with Michelle, so he picked up the phone and dialed.

"Hello, La Patouille. How can I help you?"

"Hello, do you have any tables open for tonight?"

"Yes, sir, we do. Would you like to make a reservation?"

"Yes, I would."

"How many in your party, sir?"

"There will be two; my name is Paul Dubois."

"Thank you, Mr. Dubois, what time shall I put you down for?"

"Let's make it at seven-thirty."

"Seven-thirty it is. See you then, Mr. Dubois."

"See you then. Bye." Paul hung up the phone and smiled. He was going to surprise Michelle with a nice dinner at a very nice restaurant.

***

Jon Paul and Liz were getting closer to her apartment when Jon Paul suddenly noticed something strange. "Liz, do you see that woman standing over there?"

"Where, Jon Paul?"

"Right there, by the stop sign."

"Yes, what about her?"

"I swear I know her from somewhere."

"But where, Jon Paul?"

"Um, I don't know, but she seems so familiar to me. Wait! I know. She is the one who served us that morning after our first night together."

"You are right, Jon Paul, that is her. I wonder what she is doing down here." Jon was right, it was Maggie Martin from the restaurant he had visited before, but what he didn't know was that she had recently moved there and was now working at his favorite bar.

Jon Paul continued to drive to Liz's old apartment. It didn't take long to get there, as Liz's apartment was fairly close to the bar. "Liz, I am just going to park as close to the door as I can. Do you think we can get all your stuff in one trip?"

"Maybe, Jon Paul, if I pack it tight, but what about my furniture? Should we just give it to someone?"

"Yeah, we can, that is a good idea. Just bring the things that you want the most, like your clothes and jewelry, and anything else of value, we will give the rest to anyone who wants it."

Liz nodded in agreement with Jon Paul. She would just bring what she thought was the most valuable to her and give the rest away. Her landlord would probably know someone who would want her old furniture. As they drove up and parked the car, Jon Paul noticed some odd things about her apartment, things he hadn't noticed before, such as the gargoyle on the roof that seemed to be staring straight at him. It made him a little uncomfortable, and he wondered why he hadn't seen it before. Opposite the gargoyle was a tall statue of one of the angels; it appeared to be Raphael, as it had a horn it was ready to blow. Jon Paul, for some reason, had failed to notice these two very menacing statues; they both made him uncomfortable.

They walked up the stairs to her place and opened the door. Her tiny apartment was so small compared to her now-luxurious estate with many acres and the best of everything. Liz wondered how she had ever lived there in the first place.

"Liz, how do you want to do this? Should we just pack all your clothes, and then you can get whatever else you need while I load them into the car?"

"Yes, Jon Paul, that sounds good. Let's do it that way, and then on our way out, I better stop and tell the landlord I am moving."

"Okay, Liz, that is the plan then." Jon Paul and Liz went to her room and started packing her things, mostly clothes, but she also had some other works of art that they would just give away. Liz really didn't need anything from her old apartment, but she was a sentimental girl and wanted her clothes and a few things.

After a few hours of packing, Jon Paul and Liz had most of her things ready to go. Jon Paul had been carrying them to the car in her suitcases and in bundles that he placed in the backseat. Liz had carried a few things from her kitchen, like her favorite glass and her favorite cooking pan. She had some other things that were of sentimental value to her, so she grabbed those too.

"Hey, Jon Paul, I am going to tell the landlord I am leaving and that anything I have left, he can have or give away." Jon Paul had been in the kitchen getting a drink, and as soon as he heard Liz talking to him, he immediately walked out to where she was. "Okay, do you want me to grab anything else while you are talking with him?"

"Anything you think I might need will be fine, Jon Paul. It won't take me too long, I hope." Liz smiled at Jon Paul; he was smiling back as she walked out the door to find her apartment's landlord.

***

Paul and Michelle had been keeping busy for most of the afternoon—especially Michelle, who had a few orders for her expertise in putting together lunch menus and dinner orders for some wedding party she was also invited to. Although Michelle didn't know the people getting married, she did think and even wonder if a wedding was in her future as well.

***

Jon Paul was continuing to pack some small things for Liz when he found something very odd. It appeared to be some sort of ancient artifact, perhaps a statue of some kind. As he studied it, strange thoughts began to flood his mind; this ancient-looking statue had some kind of power. Jon Paul's thoughts were indeed strange; he had thoughts of a past life of some general in a war long forgotten, in some old place now lost to the mists of time. These were not his thoughts, but those of a person who could access the history records of anyone, at any place or at any time. The Akashic Hall of Records was what Jon Paul was now hearing. The statue seemed to have a life of its own; why had Liz not mentioned it before? Where did she get it, and why, when he touched it, could he hear strange thoughts of the past? As Jon Paul listened to the voices in his head, he was lost in another world. He could hear something, but it was very far away.

"Jon Paul, Jon Paul, where are you?" Liz was standing right next to him when she asked this. Jon Paul had been standing there, transfixed by her statue, and he didn't even hear her calling him until several seconds later. "Liz, yes, what is it?"

"Jon Paul, I was calling you. Are you okay?"

"Yes, I am fine. Where did you get this?"

"What, that little statue?"

"Yes, where did you get it?"

"I don't remember. It was a long time ago, I—"

"Liz, I need to know exactly where you got it, and from whom!"

"Jon Paul—"

"*Please, Liz!* Just tell me."

"Um, I think I found it; no, wait, I remember. This kindly old man gave it to me when I was twenty years old. I was at the coffee shop in between my college classes, and he walked in. He looked rather strange to me, but then, I was young. Anyway, he looked around and when he saw me, he walked over to me and then he just stood there, staring at me. Then he said, 'Hello, miss, would you be so kind as to indulge an old man a silly whim?'

"I was a little scared, but then he smiled at me, and that smile seemed to calm me like everything would be fine, so I said to him, 'Sure, mister. How can I help you?'

"He said, 'I would like to give you this very old and very ancient statue. It has magic properties.'

"Well, I almost laughed, thinking this old man was senile. I felt sorry for him and I said, 'Okay, sure, I will be happy to take this statue from you.' He smiled and handed it to me. I looked at him and he had a kind of sad look to him, and then he smiled at me and said, 'Thank you, my child. One day, you will find what this small piece can do for you, and for me.'

"I found his response strange, but then, he was a little strange; anyway, he turned and walked away, out the door and down the street, and I never saw him again. I guess I just like the way it looks, and it gives me a calm feeling when I hold it; that is why I kept it."

"Liz, what did this old man look like?"

"He was tall, I don't know how tall, but taller than the normal man, and he wore bright clothes, not flashy and not even color-coordinated."

"Did he have anything strange about his appearance, other than his clothes?"

"Yeah, he had a shaggy beard and long, white hair—he needed a haircut—and he had these old glasses on the end of his nose. I remember thinking, *how can he see with those glasses?*"

"Liz, I know who you are talking about; this same old man visited me when I was young. He told me I would find something shiny and that it would make me wonder where it comes from!"

Liz was surprised that Jon Paul knew who she was talking about, and she began to wonder, how could the same person have known her *and* Jon Paul? Something was not right about that. She wondered if somehow Jon Paul had heard her tell the story before. It was crazy; how could he have known him? It was so many years ago; it must be fate or something, she thought. Liz was right; it was the same old man that had talked with Jon Paul when he was young. But what did he want, and why had he given her the statue?

"So he told you it was magical?"

"Yes, but he never did anything else; he just walked away. What do you think it means, Jon Paul?"

"I don't know, but I think we need to hide it away somewhere safe. It has a power I have never felt before." Suddenly, Liz began to feel nervous. "Jon Paul, I think we should go home now."

"Yeah, I think so too. Let's go, Liz." Jon Paul and Liz closed the door to her old apartment and left. They walked down to the street where they had parked the car and got in. Jon Paul started the engine and pulled away from the building and out in to the street to find their way back home.

***

Paul and Michelle had been working all afternoon; as the sun began to set and the night began to draw in, Paul was closing his work for the day and looking forward to a night out with his girl Michelle. Paul walked in to where Michelle was sitting in the living room, relaxing after her day's work. He saw her on the couch and said, "Hey, Michelle, I am going to go get ready for our dinner."

"Okay, Paul. I am going to get ready too. So where are we going?" Michelle looked at him seductively.

"Oh no, missy, you wanted a surprise, and that is what it will be." Paul smiled at Michelle and winked.

"Well, all right then, I guess I will just have to be surprised, since you won't tell me."

Paul looked at Michelle and said, "It will be a good surprise, I promise." Michelle smiled, looked away, and said, "I guess I better get myself ready." She got up from the couch and walked with Paul to the bedroom, where she had some of her things, like her makeup and a few nice clothes.

They both got dressed in some nice evening attire, and Paul, who finished dressing before Michelle, went back downstairs to wait for her. Michelle didn't take long; she was almost done when he had finished earlier, so Paul wasn't sitting too long. Michelle walked down the stairs to the living room. Paul, seeing her, looked stunned. Michelle had on a nice, mid-length, black skirt with a white top that showed her bare arms. She had on blue high heels that finished her outfit and made her look very beautiful; she wore her hair slightly curled, down past her mid-back, and Paul thought he would fall over from her beauty.

"Michelle, you look absolutely beautiful!"

"Why, thank you."

"How Jon Paul could ever leave you, I will never know; he must be a fool."

"Yes, he is a fool!" Paul and Michelle smiled at each other and knew they were in true love.

"Well, should we go?"

"Yes, I am ready. Let's go, Paul." Michelle and Paul walked out of his apartment and down to the parking garage, got in his car, and headed off to the restaurant.

***

"Liz, about this running for office thing, where do we start? I mean, I have no political background."

"Me neither, Jon Paul, but I think if you ask the coin to help, it can."

"So are you saying I should ask the coin to help me win office, or maybe educate me first?"

"Yes, why don't you ask it how to proceed? I mean, where do we start first; who do we hire or call or whatever?"

"Okay. How about when we get home, I will do exactly that. I will ask the coin how we should begin."

"Yes, Jon Paul, that sounds good to me." Liz and Jon Paul would ask the coin to help them with his wish of running for political office. It would help them find a starting point. They drove through the city and after awhile, they began to find themselves entering the country; the green pastures and wine fields began to make their appearance. The beauty of the tended fields always amazed Jon Paul.

"You know, Liz, I don't think I will ever get used to the beauty of these fields. It takes my breath away." Liz smiled at Jon Paul and nodded in agreement with him.

They were almost home when Liz suddenly had a thought. "Jon Paul, what if we have to move back into the city?"

"What do you mean, Liz? Why would we have to move back into the city?"

"Well, when you get elected, the city might want you to be close to the town hall. Or maybe the courts, I don't know exactly, but I know I don't want to leave our home."

"Yeah, that might be a problem. Why don't we just take it one step at a time for now; when we get home, I will ask the coin how to begin and we will go from there, okay?"

"Okay, Jon Paul. I just don't want to have to move."

"I know, sweetie, and hopefully we won't; I should be able to conduct any business from our house." Jon Paul was right, but he would soon learn that having two homes was better than one.

***

Paul and Michelle were driving to the restaurant to have a special dinner. Paul wanted to treat Michelle like a queen, and he was going to do just that. Buying her dinner in a very nice, five-star restaurant was just the start. La Patouille was known for having great service and great food. They would surely enjoy their time at this restaurant. "You know, Michelle, I think you are going to enjoy the place a lot. I have been there a few times and the food is beyond great, and with all your chef skills, I am sure you will enjoy how they prepare the meal."

"You have me very curious, Paul; just where are you taking me that is worthy of such high praise?"

"Ha, you will see, it is only another few miles further."

"So you still aren't going to tell me?" Paul only smiled; he knew Michelle would be surprised and impressed with his choice of restaurant.

***

Liz and Jon Paul were nearing their home and as they did, they both were thinking the same thing: *How do we start this political machine?* Jon Paul knew it was going to be difficult; any politician who ran for office and was elected had a very busy life. Oftentimes, they had little time for families or even themselves. This could very well be what fate had in store for Jon Paul and Liz, to be chosen for power and office, to be in the public eye; only time would tell.

"Hey, Liz, do you think we should maybe eat first before we get started with this whole political thing?"

"Are you saying you are hungry, my dear?"

"Yeah, I am, actually."

"Why don't you just have Mr. Falid prepare us something when we get home?"

"That is exactly what I was thinking, but knowing him, he already has something ready for us."

Jon Paul was right. Mr. Falid was preparing a meal for them; he had begun to cook fresh salmon with lemon, baked potatoes with fresh vegetables, and fresh garlic bread. He also had a bottle of a 1982 merlot chilling in the butler's fridge. It would be a most amazing meal for the two of them. Jon Paul turned into his long driveway and slowly made his way to the garage, where his manservant, Mr. Bestion, was waiting. He heard the car and he opened the garage door for Jon Paul and Liz. Jon Paul stopped the car just outside the big door and turned off the engine.

"Hello, Mr. Bestion, how was your day?"

"Very good, sir. I checked the alarm and the sprinklers, and they are in perfect working order. How was your trip into the city?"

"It was good. We have loaded the car with Miss Bourg's things; after you park it, can you bring it all to the house, please?"

"Of course, sir. Hello, Miss Bourg, how are you?"

"I am doing well, thank you. Mr. Bestion, could you just put my things in the hallway when you bring them in?"

"Yes, ma'am, I will set them by your room in the hallway, if that is okay."

"Thank you, that will be fine." Mr. Bestion smiled as Jon Paul and Liz walked up to their house to find Mr. Falid and something to eat.

"Jon Paul, do you think we should talk with Mr. Falid and ask him for advice?"

"Probably not a bad idea, I am sure he could offer us good advice."

As they entered the front door and walked in, Mr. Falid came walking out from the kitchen, saw them, and said, "Hello, sir, glad you are back. I took the liberty of preparing you a small meal, if you are hungry."

"Thank you, Mr. Falid; yes, we are hungry."

"Would you like to eat in the dining room tonight or perhaps in the breakfast nook instead?"

"Liz, what do you want to do?"

"How about we eat in the dining room? I want to stretch out after our long drive from the city."

"Yes, ma'am, I will set up the dining room for you."

"Thank you, Mr. Falid." Mr. Falid smiled, nodded, and went back to work in the kitchen. Liz and Jon Paul were happy to be home. The stress of the day's move and the little statue Jon Paul had found were weighing heavily on his mind. He had to figure out what to do with the statue, maybe talk with his manservant, and even ask the coin for help. This was a lot for even one man. Liz would be there to help, though.

***

As Paul and Michelle pulled up to the restaurant to park, a valet came out and stood by their car. Paul looked at Michelle as if to say, *are you ready?* And then stopped the car and opened his door. The valet smiled at him and as Paul walked around and opened the door for Michelle, he held her hand to help her. He was a perfect gentleman for her. The valet drove off and the two of them entered the restaurant. Paul noticed the head maître d' and walked up to him.

"Hello. Dubois, party of two."

The waiter found their reservation, smiled, and said, "Follow me, sir." He led them down a large hall to an even bigger room. Many tables were full, as couples both young and old enjoyed their dinners. Paul and Michelle followed the man until he finally led them to a nice table, not in the middle but off to the side by another young couple. They sat down and began to look at the menu.

***

Jon Paul and Liz had gone upstairs to their room to unpack some of Liz's small things. Mr. Bestion had not brought all of her things to the house yet, so they sat down in her dressing room and began to talk. "You know, Liz, I think we need to plan when we can get my things from my old apartment, and probably soon."

"Okay, sweetie, whenever you want."

"Well, how about in the next day or two, we go back in to town and get my things?"

"Jon Paul, do you have any idea what our next move is?"

"Not yet, my dear, but I am working on it."

"Can you call Mr. Bestion, Jon Paul, and see if he can bring up my black suitcase, the one with the tag on it from Paris?"

199

"Sure thing, honey. I will get him on the intercom." Jon Paul walked over to the wall by the counter and pushed the button for the intercom. "Mr. Bestion, are you there?"

"Yes, sir, I am here."

"Oh, good. Miss Bourg was asking if you could bring her black suitcase with the Paris tag on it up here right away."

"Of course, sir, I will be there shortly."

"Thank you, Mr. Bestion." Jon Paul looked at Liz, who was sitting at her table filing her nails, and said, "He will bring it up here right away."

"Thanks, Jon Paul." Liz smiled at him. Several minutes passed as they made small talk with each other, and then the buzzer on the intercom rang.

"Sir, your dinner is ready."

Jon Paul pushed the button and said, "Thanks, Mr. Falid, be right there." Jon Paul and Liz walked down to the dining room, where their manservant had set out a very nice dinner for them. Jon Paul helped Liz with her chair and then sat down himself.

"Wow, it all looks so wonderful."

"Isn't he the best, Liz?"

Mr. Falid smiled as they said this; he was pleased to hear such high praise for all his hard work. He then looked at Jon Paul and said, "Can I get you anything else, sir?"

"No, I think this will do nicely. Liz, do you need anything else?"

"No, thank you, Mr. Falid." Jon Paul motioned for Mr. Falid to leave. As he waved him off, he looked at Liz and said, "I hope you will love his salmon as much as I do."

"I am sure it will be great!" Liz and Jon Paul ate their dinner, and it was wonderful.

After some time had passed, Liz and Jon Paul began to talk, and this talk led them to his soon-to-be political career. "Jon Paul, I have been thinking. We need to hire a political campaign manager. I think that should be our first move."

"Hmm, a campaign manager. Yeah, that does sound right. How about as soon as we finish here, let's go downstairs to the game room and use the coin to get some more answers."

"Why the game room, Jon Paul?"

"The game room is where all political things should be held. I mean, it is all just a game anyway, right?"

"Oh, I don't know about that; it can be very serious, Jon Paul."

"I know. I was just trying to keep things light. It can be very serious and maybe even dangerous; I mean, assassinations happen all the time. At least most of those are unlucky and fail."

"See, now you made me nervous. I don't want someone to hurt you; I can't lose you."

"Don't worry, my dear Liz, I won't be hurt. I have the coin!" Liz was worried, though; she knew that with one mistake, Jon Paul could lose. He took a few chances every now and then, so he wasn't afraid of taking a gamble if he thought it would pay off. This made Liz a bit uncomfortable. As they finished eating and were just about to go downstairs, Mr. Falid walked in and began clearing the table. Jon Paul looked at him and said, "Mr. Falid, we are going down to the game room for a while. When you are finished with your work, can you please come down there as well? I would like to talk with you for a short time."

"I will, sir, as soon as I finish here." Jon Paul smiled and took Liz by the hand and led her down the hall to the stairs that led to the game room in the bottom floor of their house. He sat down at the bar and poured Liz a drink and then one for himself. He had walked past their game room and straight to their bar, which was adjacent to the game room.

"Okay, my dear, shall we use the coin?"

"Yes, Jon Paul, this is very exciting!"

"It is. I begin to feel the coin heat up each time I do this!"

Jon Paul reached for the coin in his pocket; it was indeed heating up as he began to concentrate.

"I wish to have knowledge of political office and how to get elected." As Jon Paul said this, the coin began to spin in his hand. It had never done that before. He was a bit startled and thought maybe something was happening that shouldn't be. The coin spun faster and faster till it was only a blur. Jon Paul had to blink as he finally saw it slowing down, and then he began to hear that familiar voice in his head. *"You must hire a manager first, and then you can have him hire others to do your bidding!"* Jon Paul listened as the voice told him what to do. *"Look for a law firm to do this for you. Find them in your book."* Jon understood the book reference to be his local white pages. He would need to hire a law firm to represent him, and they could find other people to finish the job.

"Liz, we need to look in the book for a law firm to represent me." The coin slowed down and stopped spinning. Liz had been transfixed by the coin and its power.

"What, Jon Paul?"

"Liz, we need to look for a law firm to help us; that is where we start."

"Okay, Jon Paul, let's look in the phone book." After Liz and Jon Paul had regained their composure, Jon Paul put the coin back in his pocket and they began to talk.

"Liz, can you find the phone book so we can begin looking for a law firm?"

"Sure thing, Jon Paul. Is there one in your office?"

"Um, yeah, in the second drawer, on the left side of my desk." Liz went upstairs to his office to get the phone book. She knew exactly where he was talking about. Just then Mr. Falid had walked downstairs to find Jon Paul. He saw him and walked over to where he was sitting at his bar and said, "I finished my work in the kitchen. How can I help you, sir?"

"Well, Mr. Falid, I am thinking about running for political office, and I wanted your opinion on the matter."

"Oh, very good, sir! I believe I can help you. What is it you need to know?"

"I have asked the coin what I need to do and it has given me much information; however, I want to know if you ever held office or know something on the matter."

"I do, sir. I never held office, per se, but I was a general, so I was also acquainted with many others who did."

"I see; so what can you tell me about this?"

"When I was in the war, I was surrounded by many men of what you would call 'political power.' These men made laws and regulations for the people. Sometimes the people did not like or even understand many of these laws, but they were bound to follow them under penalty of death. Not all would result in death, but a lot did. Some penalties were whippings with a leather strap; others were salt in open wounds. Usually, for something like stealing, it resulted in your hand being cut off! Maybe a little harsh, but not many people stole things; anyway, these men sat at high places in the council seats. They were almost untouchable, and most thought themselves above the laws that they themselves had written. I was at one time told by one of these officials that I must attack a certain village; he said the elders had ordered it. I asked who and which elders, and he replied that it was not for me to know and that I should just give the orders or I might be the next one executed for treason! Well, I gave the orders and it was carried out. I never knew who this man was, but I did know he was very high up in the political party, so I had better do as I was told. I had heard that soon after that, he was killed in some battle over some difference of opinion on a matter."

"That is very interesting, Mr. Falid, but what I was wondering was if you know anything about the process itself, of getting elected and holding a high place in the council."

"Forgive me, sir, I did get on about my past a little too much."

"It is okay, Mr. Falid. I truly enjoy your stories."

"Thank you, sir. I really don't know much about how one gets elected to office; I suppose it is by some kind of vote by the people."

"Yes, well, thank you for your great story, Mr. Falid. If you have anything more to add, I would be willing to listen later."

"Thank you, sir; may I retire to my room? I have some personal things I would like to attend to."

"Of course, Mr. Falid. We can talk later." Jon Paul returned to his drink at the bar; Mr. Falid walked back upstairs and to his room. Jon Paul was contemplating his next move as he waited for Liz to return with the phone book.

Liz had been looking in the drawer for the phone book. She had found a small black book, some pencils and some pens, a few pieces of paper, and a stapler. Then, as she moved the paper, she saw the phone book lying there. She grabbed it, closed the drawer, and headed back downstairs to Jon Paul.

"I found it, Jon Paul. What do you want to look up?"

"Thanks, Liz. Let's start by finding law firms that will represent political candidates."

Liz smiled at Jon Paul. She was happy to help her man further his life's amazing adventure. She thought Jon Paul would be a great politician. After all, he was logical and smart, and he was charming in his own way. Oftentimes, she would just stare at him in wonderment. Jon Paul was never aware of this, she thought; if he was, he didn't show it. As they searched for a law firm, a few that they saw looked interesting, but one in particular had a full-page ad and stood out above the rest. Jon Paul thought, *that is the one; we must contact them.* Dewey, Johnson, and Kline is the firm he chose; they specialized in politics. Jon Paul smiled at Liz, who nodded in agreement with him.

"That is the one, Jon Paul; we should call them, set up a meeting, and go see them."

"Great idea, Liz. You read my mind!" As Jon Paul said this, he had a strange thought occur to him—the statue. What should they do with it? It was obviously something very odd, and it had some kind of power that was attached to it. Liz had been looking away at the moment he had thought this, but she noticed him in deep thought and said, "Jon Paul, what is it?"

"The statue, Liz. I had forgotten about it, till now."

"What should we do with it?"

"I don't know, Liz; maybe I should ask Mr. Falid about it."

"Yes, that seems like a good idea. I will go find him."

"Wait! No, use the intercom; he will hear that." Liz stood up, walked over to the intercom on the far wall, and pushed the button. "Mr. Falid, sorry to disturb you, but could you come back down here immediately?"

"Yes, ma'am, I am here. I will be right there."

Liz walked back over to where Jon Paul was sitting and smiled at him. "He will be right here, Jon Paul."

"I think I better go and get the statue."

"Where is it, Jon Paul?"

"I put it in your bag with some of the things from your old apartment. It is wrapped in a white kitchen towel."

Liz looked at Jon Paul and said, "No, you just sit here. I will go get it."

Liz got up and walked up the stairs to her room; she was hopeful that Mr. Bestion had put all of her things close by the door so she could find the statue right away. As she walked up the stairs to the first floor, she passed by Mr. Falid and smiled; he was going to see what his master wanted. Liz continued her walk to the second floor at the other staircase, and as she approached her room, there on the wall by the door were her suitcases and some bags with her things. She scanned the bags for the one with the kitchen stuff and the little statue. She didn't want to touch it anymore after what Jon Paul had said; she was glad it was wrapped in a kitchen towel. She searched the first bag and didn't find it. She grabbed a second bag that was lighter and began searching it. After a moment of looking around, there it was, nearly at the bottom but wrapped securely in a protective towel. She grabbed hold of it, stood up, and started to walk back downstairs to the game room. As Liz walked with the small statue, she suddenly thought she could feel it pulsating. It seemed to be alive!

Mr. Falid had joined Jon Paul at the bar and had just begun to pour himself a drink when Liz came walking in. "Here it is, Jon Paul."

Jon Paul smiled at Liz and said, "Thanks, honey, can you bring it here?" Liz sat down next to Jon Paul and handed him the statue to unwrap. She was a little anxious, as she could feel some kind of power attached to it.

"Jon Paul, that statue makes me nervous; I never felt it was anything special before. Why is it now something I fear?"

"That remains to be seen, my dear, but perhaps the coin of mine is bringing out its power."

Jon Paul was right; the golden coin of his was somehow attached to Liz's statue.

"Mr. Falid, have you ever seen anything like this before?"

"Yes, sir, I have. It is from my time in the desert during the war. I saw it a few times and felt its power before it disappeared. I haven't seen it in years."

"You felt its power? What do you mean?"

"That statue is cursed. It was made by a man who claimed to be a prophet for the ages. He came into my camp and was trying to sell it to some soldiers."

"How is it cursed, Mr. Falid?

"The statue is tied to the coin through magic means. The Jinn have placed a curse on it so that whenever it comes into contact with the coin, it comes alive with power."

"Then we need to rid ourselves of it as soon as possible!"

"Yes, sir, but I believe you can place it in a secure storage and it will not be able to do any harm."

"What kind of secure storage, like a safe box?"

"Yes, sir, a safe box lined with silver or gold should keep its power in check."

"Mr. Falid, why silver or gold?"

"Silver and gold vibrate at a higher frequency than other lesser metals, and they can contain the power of the statue."

"I see, thank you, Mr. Falid. Anything else you can add?"

"Not at this time, sir, but if I remember anything else, shall I tell you?"

"Yes, that will be fine. You can retire to your room now, if you want."

"Thank you, sir, I will. Good night." Mr. Falid smiled at them and walked to the stairs and up to his room. Jon Paul and Liz sat there at the bar, thinking about what they had just heard. It was a fascinating tale to say the least, a gold- or silver-lined box. Jon Paul would have to hire someone to make this for him.

***

Paul and Michelle were enjoying their dinner when the waiter approached them and said, "Will there be anything else, sir?"

"Michelle, would you care for anything else?"

"No, Paul, I am good. Thank you."

"No, thanks for now. Can you just bring the bill?"

"Of course, sir, be right back." The waiter smiled and walked away. Paul and Michelle had had a great dinner. They had eaten fresh lobster and had fresh-baked rolls. Their dinner was perfect.

"Paul, thank you for such a wonderful meal; this is just what I needed." Michelle smiled at Paul.

"You are quite welcome, my dear, anything for you." Paul winked at Michelle, who then smiled back at him. The waiter returned at that moment with the bill, handed it to Paul, smiled, and said, "Is there anything else you require, sir?"

"No, we are good. Thank you for such a great meal and service."

"You are welcome, sir." Paul handed the waiter the money. He then stood up to help Michelle, smiled at her, and said, "I am so very happy you are with me here tonight!"

Michelle seeing his smile nodded and said, "Me too, Paul. Me too."

Michelle and Paul drove back to their place and settled in for the evening; their night would be spent in close companionship, enjoying each other's company.

***

Liz and Jon Paul were still sitting at their bar when Jon Paul suddenly looked up from his drink and said, "Liz, I have an idea!"

"What is it, Jon Paul?"

"Why don't I use the coin to wish for a safe box to put the statue in? Then I can put it in the wall safe."

"Jon Paul, do you still think it will be dangerous?"

"No, it should be okay. At least, I hope so." Jon Paul grabbed the coin from his pocket. As he held it, the familiar feeling came over him as it heated up, and he said, "I wish for a golden protective box to store this statue in." *Poof!* In his hands was a golden box. It had a lid with a lock and a small key to lock it with. He placed the statue in the box, closed the lid, and locked it. He took the key and held it in his fingers. "Liz, I am going to hide the key in a safe place too, somewhere no one will ever find it."

"Okay, Jon Paul. I don't want to know; just do it." Jon Paul got up and took the box and the key back upstairs to his office, where he had a hidden wall safe. He opened the safe and placed the box in the back. It was a rather large safe, big enough to put several large encyclopedias and even some handguns in. He taped the key to the top of the safe, closed the door, and locked it. He looked around as if someone might be watching him and walked back downstairs to see Liz.

"Okay, Liz, it is safe and locked away. No need to worry about it anymore."

"Thanks, Jon Paul. I never really liked the statue anyway. It was mostly for decoration."

"Not much decoration, Liz."

"Ha ha, Jon Paul; are you saying I have no decorating style?"

"Um, no, I think you have great decorating skills!" Jon Paul smiled at Liz and kissed her on the mouth. He got up to reach for the phone; he was going to call the law firm to represent him in his political career. He dialed the phone and got an answer. As Jon Paul explained to the receptionist who he was and what he was looking for, she agreed to set up an appointment for him to meet with their law firm. He would meet with the top three individuals who owned and ran the firm. Jon Paul and his political career would soon be taking off. Liz would be by his side to help guide him and provide him strength when he needed it.

When Jon Paul had finished talking with the men at the law firm, he had made an appointment to meet with them in a few days. It would be at this time that Jon Paul would learn of his political aspirations and could fulfill these to the greatest of his abilities. Jon Paul and Liz spent the rest of their day in the game room talking about their plan and what they could each expect to see happen in the coming months. They discussed the kind of protection he would need from the general public, and just what would be provided by the French government, as he would be elected an official. Liz talked about her concerns of Jon Paul being in the public eye and whether he felt his life might be on the line from hostile enemies. They also talked about how their lives would change and the traveling he would have to do as an elected official. Jon Paul and Liz's lives were just about to get very interesting.

***

Paul and Michelle were enjoying their simple life together; they had formed a loving bond that neither had experienced before. They were so compatible that many were amazed at how often the two of them would say the same thing. Oftentimes, when they were out at work or going to a restaurant, people would stare and ask, "Are you brother and sister?" Paul would only smile and nod. Michelle, on the other hand, was not so forgiving. She would always correct them and say they were a married couple. This made Paul smile, and Michelle would comment he was crazy. Paul and Michelle were happy; they had a simple life and, most of the time, very few problems.

However, one day as they sat eating lunch, Michelle said to Paul, "Paul, do you ever regret not seeing Jon Paul anymore?"

"What kind of question is that, Michelle? Of course I regret not seeing him or talking to him. It makes me sad to think of how he has changed. I might never talk with him again."

"I am sorry, Paul. I don't mean to be insensitive."

"It is okay, Michelle; we will have to deal with him soon enough. Who knows, maybe Seraphiel is waiting just around the corner and we are going to have to fight Jon Paul tomorrow!"

"Oh, Paul, now I am nervous. What if you are right?"

"Not to worry, Michelle. We will be all right; I promise."

Chapter 12

— •●• —

KNOWLEDGE

Many months have passed, and Jon Paul has been elected to office. He is a very powerful political man now. Liz occasionally accompanies him on his visits to other nations and countries. Liz and Jon Paul work out of their home a few days a week; most of the time, though, Jon Paul is at his office in the headquarters of the French government buildings. Safe and secure from the public, he and other elected officials vote on new laws to pass and old laws that need to be revised. Jon Paul has risen to the top of the French government very quickly. Many that he works with are in fear of Jon Paul and his power. He has a reputation for dark qualities. Many won't even look him in the eye for fear of some kind of political retribution.

***

One day, as Paul and Michelle were sitting in their apartment, Paul looked at Michelle and said, "Hey, Michelle, I feel like having a drink somewhere."

"Really, Paul, where?"

"Um, how about The Goat's Head Bar?

"That place? I haven't been there in almost a year. Why there, Paul?"

"I don't know, maybe I am just feeling a bit nostalgic."

"Okay, Paul, whatever you say. When do you want to go?"

"How about later today?"

"Sure, we can do that. I have some work to finish up, and that will give me time to do that!"

Paul smiled at Michelle, knowing she would finish her work and he could take her out to a place neither had been in a very long time. It would be a nice change of pace for them. They didn't go out much anymore; in fact, they had both become homebodies. For some reason, they were very content to spend most of their time alone in Paul's apartment. Michelle often wondered about her angel, Seraphiel; when would she return? Paul had gotten used to his daily routine of waking up next to his love Michelle, eating breakfast, and then beginning his work for the day.

They both needed time out to get fresh air and see other people, though. As the day passed slowly for Paul, Michelle's work kept her busy planning and putting together menus for clients. Paul wondered if Michelle was as anxious as he was to get out of their apartment.

"Hey, Michelle, how is it going? Are you almost done?"

"Yes, Paul. I am almost done. Why don't you get ready, and I will join you in a few moments."

"Okay, Michelle. I am really looking forward to going out." Paul smiled at Michelle, who smiled in return.

"Me too, Paul, me too." Paul walked upstairs to their room and decided to take a shower. He would clean up and get himself ready before Michelle did. *Michelle will not have to do much to get ready,* thought Paul, *she always looks great.* Michelle took her notebook and her favorite organizer with her to their room. She heard the shower running and knew Paul was in there. Michelle sat on the bed and found her favorite pair of black high heels. She slipped them on.

As Paul finished in the shower, he heard Michelle in their room closing the closet door.

"Michelle, can you grab me a nice shirt to wear? Please?"

"Sure thing, honey." Michelle reached for his black silk shirt. It matched her black heels perfectly. Paul dried himself off, walked out of the bathroom, and got dressed. He had his favorite black shirt to wear, and he was taking the love of his life out. Paul was feeling good.

"Hey, Michelle, I think we should maybe grab dinner after we leave The Goat's Head Bar. What do you think?"

"Yeah, that sounds great, any idea where?"

"No, not yet, maybe we can figure that out later."

Michelle nodded; they would figure that out later at the bar. They walked downstairs to their living room and grabbed their coats. Paul opened the door for Michelle, looked at her, and said, "You look really beautiful today, Michelle."

"Thanks, Paul, and you look really handsome." She smiled at him in a most alluring way. They walked out to his car and got in. Paul started it up and pulled out into traffic. Paul and Michelle were excited to be having a date.

"Paul, do you think we will see anyone we know at the bar?"

"I don't know, Michelle, it has been such a long time. We might."

"Do you think Jon Paul ever goes in there?"

"No, he is probably too busy to be seen in a place like that now."

"What do you mean 'a place like that'?"

"You know; now that he is in office; I am sure he wouldn't be caught dead in a bar. Besides, he is not stupid enough to put his life in danger by going to one."

"Oh, I see. Because Jon Paul is in office, he is too good for a bar."

"Well, yeah, Michelle, he won't ruin his reputation by going there; besides, he could run into people that don't like him." Michelle looked at Paul and knew he was right. Even though Jon Paul had been elected to the UMP, there were those who did not like him. There were enemies who thought Jon Paul had weaseled his way in somehow. Not many in office had risen to the top of the French government so fast. It was as if Jon Paul had gotten there by unnatural means. Jon Paul had enemies; some of these were in office and others were not. It was a risky time for Jon Paul; he had few friends. People would head-bow to Jon Paul, mostly out of fear; after all, he had an intimidating aura about him now. This made many people uncomfortable.

As Paul drove to the bar, he noticed the people on the street as he passed them by. *Not all bad,* he thought, *could use some new streetlights, and the roads were not too bad.* If Jon Paul could get some of these things done, maybe his being in office would not be that bad. As soon as Paul thought this, he caught himself and sighed. Jon Paul was once his friend—his best friend—and now he was his enemy. Paul felt sad as he remembered so many good times and so many memories of times now past; some, he had even forgotten. Paul missed his old friend.

"Are you okay, Paul? You look like you have something on your mind."

"Yeah, something on my mind—just remembering days past with Jon Paul. I miss him, Michelle."

"I know, Paul, I miss the old Jon Paul too, but we cannot live in the past. We must keep on with our lives and wait for the final battle with him."

"I … you are right, he is no longer someone we know; the Jon Paul we knew is long gone."

Michelle reached over and gently held Paul's hand. He smiled briefly at her and continued their drive to the bar. As Paul pulled into the parking lot, there were a few places left open. The Goat's Head Bar was a busy place in the late afternoon, filled with lots of local patrons and some visitors. Sometimes there were people who were on vacation who just wanted to stop in an authentic French bar for a drink. Paul and Michelle walked into the bar and looked for a place to sit down.

Paul saw a spot close to the bar, a little booth that they could sit in that was semi-private. Michelle was the first to sit. Paul followed her and sat on the opposite side, across from her.

"How is this, Michelle?"

"It is fine, Paul. I haven't been here in so long; I'd forgotten how nostalgic this place looks."

Michelle was right; The Goat's Head Bar was nostalgic. It had been around since at least a hundred years ago, and the décor was old and distinguished. On the ceiling were evenly placed large, old, oak beams, and there were old pictures of many different ports in France. The walls were made of some old kind of wood paneling. At the tables, including the booths, were old seats that were screwed into the wooden floor, which was covered in oak planks. The entire look of the bar was very inviting, to say the least. The only new things in the bar were the pool table, the video games, and the new jukebox. Michelle had fond memories of this bar; she and Jon Paul had been there a few times and she was comfortable there, despite it having the reputation of being a rough place. Soon, the waitress came over to them; she walked with a style that was familiar to Michelle.

"Hi, folks, what can I get you?"

"I will have a house lager."

"Can I get a glass of wine?" asked Michelle.

"Sure thing. We also have food items, if you get hungry." As the waitress said this, she suddenly realized who she was talking to.

"Michelle! It is me, Maggie Martin."

"Maggie! Hi, how are you? When did you start working here?"

"Almost a year ago. How are you?"

"I am fine. This is my love and best friend, Paul."

"Hi, Paul, nice to meet you."

"Hi, Maggie, nice to meet you too. How do you know each other?"

"We were in school together a long time ago," Maggie replied.

"Maggie was my roommate in college, Paul."

"Michelle, I don't want to bring up bad news, but have you seen the newspaper today?"

"No, not today."

"Okay, hold on. I will go get your drinks and then bring the paper back to you." Michelle smiled as Maggie walked back to the bar and gave their order to the bartender.

"She seems nice, Michelle. I wonder what she wants you to see in the paper?"

"Yes, she is a nice girl and a friend I have neglected over the years."

"Why is that, Michelle?"

"Well, she moved away after college, and I never really stayed close to her. We would talk once a month or so. She was the one who told me about Jon Paul and his affair."

"Oh, I see. But you trust her?"

"Yes, she is okay; we just are not too close." Michelle looked at Paul with sad eyes; he knew she regretted not being a better friend to her college roommate.

"You know, Michelle, it is never too late to be a good friend."

"I know, Paul, and I should, but right now is not the best time for this."

"Okay, Michelle, I will let it go for now." Paul smiled at Michelle, who smiled back.

Maggie Martin had grabbed the daily newspaper and their drinks and was walking back to their table when she noticed another man, who was scowling at her. As she got closer to him, she stared him in the eye and said, "Is there a problem here, sir?"

"No problem, just noticed that piece of crap Jon Paul Chavalier on the front of the paper. I don't trust him. And I don't like him. I didn't vote for him, and I wonder how he got elected."

"I don't know, sir, but if you need anything, I will be right back." Maggie Martin walked over to Paul and Michelle's booth and set their drinks down on the table, and then she handed Michelle the newspaper. Michelle looked at it in surprise; on the front page was a big picture of Jon Paul. Michelle read through the article, which stated that Jon Paul was the best thing to ever happen to France's economy and the tourism industry. He had brought France back from an uncertain euro and a failing economy.

The article went further to say how Jon Paul's foreign policy had brought several neighboring states together in mutual friendship with France. Jon Paul was doing an amazing job.

Michelle wondered, *who is this man Jon Paul?* Certainly, he was not the same man she had envisioned herself spending the rest of her life with. Had the coin really changed him and even his personality so much that she didn't even know him? It must be true, she thought; the coin had turned her once-lover into a completely different person. Paul watched her read the article, as did Maggie, who stood by their table until she was finished reading.

"Sorry, Michelle, if that brings up bad memories for you. I just thought you would like to see this."

"Thanks, Maggie. It is not a problem. The man who is in this picture and the article is not someone I know. The Jon Paul I was with is gone."

Maggie smiled at Michelle, and then she walked away and back to the man at the other table.

"Are you okay, honey?"

"Yes, I am fine, Paul. It was just a little disturbing seeing him on the front page, and obviously he is doing a good job."

The man who was sitting close to Paul and Michelle overheard her speaking and said, "A good job? Are you serious? I knew him a long time ago, and what he is doing, I didn't think he could ever do. Jon Paul is just a puppet, a good for nothing, and a waste of humanity. I would say that if he ever comes in here, I would kill him. Jon Paul Chavalier is a backstabber and a liar and a cheat. Never trust a politician."

Michelle stared at the man, who was now irate and upset, as he slammed down his drink and stormed out of the bar. Paul and Michelle looked at each other, and then Maggie walked over to them and said, "Sorry about that. He gets upset when he drinks and talks about politics."

"Nothing to worry about, Maggie, he was just saying what was on his mind."

"Yeah, but Paul, I have to keep this bar under control as best as I can."

Paul smiled at Maggie, who smiled back and then said, "Well, I better get back to work. If you need anything else, just holler!" Maggie smiled at Michelle and Paul and then walked back to the waitress station behind the bar so she could clean some glasses and do some other work.

"Wow, Paul, I didn't know that Jon Paul was doing so well; he is making a difference."

"It would seem, Michelle, but remember: we will have to work with your guardian angel one day, and that is not going to be an easy thing. I mean, working with her will be easy, but the great battle with Jon Paul will not!"

Michelle and Paul continued to enjoy their drinks and small talk as they spent time together. And as the evening began to draw in, they both began to get hungry; it was not late, and there were many fine restaurants that Paul was thinking about taking his love to. He said, "Do you want to go get something to eat now?"

"Yeah, Paul, that would be good; where do you want to go?"

"Well, how about we take a drive and see where we end up?"

"Paul, that sounds wonderful; we can find someplace that looks fun."

"Anything you want, my dear." Paul smiled at Michelle, who smiled back. They finished their drinks and got up to leave. Maggie saw them and walked over to say good-bye.

"You guys leaving?"

"Yeah, we are going to get some dinner."

"Sounds fun, Michelle, call me?"

"Okay, Maggie, I will." They both hugged and smiled. Michelle was happy to have found an old friend, and Maggie—well, Maggie was always a happy person, especially when she was given the opportunity to get to be closer to her old college roommate.

***

Jon Paul and Liz had been enjoying the good life for some time now, as their lives had changed dramatically from what they were several months before. Jon Paul had become very comfortable in his new lifestyle, and Liz was happy being with the man she loved with all of her heart.

"Hey, Lizzy, I think I will take a walk out in the gardens today."

"Really, Jon Paul? Do you want me to come with you?"

"Not today, okay? I need to inspect the grounds as well, and this might take awhile, and besides, I need some alone time."

"Okay, sweetie, but if you need me or anything, I am here."

"I know, my dear. I just need some time to myself, you understand?"

"I do, Jon Paul. Be careful, okay?"

Jon Paul smiled at Liz and walked out of the kitchen to the back greenhouse, which led to his backyard; it was a quicker route than to go through the rest of the house and around it to the back. Jon Paul walked out of the greenhouse, with all its beautiful flowers and plants. He had become a very good gardener in his spare time. As he approached the back garden, he couldn't help but notice how lovely the roses were; they were almost in full bloom, and he was amazed at the pure beauty of them. He walked past his garden and out into his open lands. The forest that surrounded his property was vast and heavily wooded. It was only a short walk, about two hundred feet to the edge of his yard and then into the forest. Jon Paul loved to walk in his forest. He didn't have this luxury when he was young, or even just a few years ago. He had lived in a small apartment with a woman whom he loved, and he would walk the streets to relax. Now, with all his land, he could walk for hours and just enjoy the trees of his forest; it was by far more preferable to the streets of Toulon.

Jon Paul walked deep into the woods; the farther he walked, the more relaxed he became. Soon, he found himself feeling a bit different than usual. The golden coin in his pocket felt like it was heating up; this usually meant that it was time for him to make another wish. He grabbed the coin, and when he opened his hands, the coin began to spin, just like it had before. He watched it spin and rise several inches above his open hand, and then, suddenly, it stopped abruptly. It never had done that before; usually, it slowed down and then stopped.

This time, however, he noticed a dark cloud of mist begin to form just a few feet in front of where he was standing. It grew and changed to white as he watched it rise to almost his height. Then it began to dissipate, leaving a dark figure standing there, as the mist vanished back into the ground from where it came. There, standing in front of him, not more than three feet away was a familiar figure. Jon Paul was dumbfounded; he froze as the figure became clear.

"*Well, Jon Paul, we meet again.*" He said in a loud booming voice like thunder.

Jon Paul stared at the figure, unable to speak.

"I see the little boy has grown into a man. Tell me, Jon Paul, what have you been doing with my coin?"

"Your ... I mean, *your* coin? What do you mean *your* coin?"

"*My coin, little man!*"

"I don't know what you mean—what coin?"

"*Don't play with me! I told you that you would find something shiny and you would wonder at its beauty!*"

"You mean the coin I have now?"

"*Yes!*"

"But ... I found it; it is my coin!"

"*Liar! I gave you that coin.*"

"Why would you do that?"

"*You dare question me? I am not to be questioned!*"

"Sorry, but how else am I supposed to know?"

"You have no need to know."

"If you gave me this coin, then why?"

"There are many things you don't understand. How can a mere mortal understand the workings of a god? You, Jon Paul Chavalier, are my messenger here on this earth, and you will carry out all that I instruct you to do."

"Okay, but if I am to do this, I need something from you." Jon Paul was pushing his luck with the tall man. He wanted to see if he could get something valuable from this being before he left him.

"*You want something from me? I gave you a coin that can grant your every wish, and now you ask for more! Ha! You, Jon Paul, are an interesting man. What is it you would have from me?*"

Jon Paul was going to take advantage of this being; of that, he was sure. "Well, as I see it, you can give me something this coin cannot."

"What would that be?"

"You can tell me how to destroy it." The tall man looked surprisingly at Jon Paul; he had not expected this. Jon Paul knew he had asked something that was probably impossible, but he had to know.

"The coin can only be destroyed by me or another Jinn. We created it from fire and magic, and only we can destroy it."

Jon Paul smiled; he knew now that the coin was immune to the workings of mortal man. Only the Jinn could destroy it; he had absolute power with it. "Well, now, if only you can destroy it, are its powers limited in any way?"

"The coin has no limits, as you would understand. *Now, if you are finished, give it to me!*"

"Give it to you? Why would I give you my future?"

"I want my coin!"

"It seems to me that you are unable to take it from me."

"You mortal, weak, insignificant worm; I will take it from you!"

"Okay, wait, wait. I have another question before you do." Jon Paul was playing all his cards right. "If you made this coin and it is all-powerful, can you please tell me about its past? I mean, more specifically, about *my* past, and how and why I was given this coin. Was I chosen for this?"

"You were chosen, Jon Paul Chavalier, to carry out my wishes as a mortal man here, in this time. I have a message that you are to give to mortal man now."

Jon Paul looked at the Jinn with curious eyes. He knew he was getting exactly what he wanted.

"You are a curious human being. As I told you many lifetimes before, you were chosen by me. Remember, Jon Paul Chavalier, in a past life of yours, you were the general in a vast army. Thousands of men were under your command, and as I told you then, you have a mission. You have been my messenger from the start. All the people you know now, you have known before. All of your friends and acquaintances are under your control, as they were in the war of the holy lands. You have been my messenger since time began. You were my first, and you shall be my last. The gift of my coin is for you to influence men and do what I command for *my* benefit, not yours. My message, you do not know. I choose to give it in a way that mortal men receive it and obey it without question," the Jinn stated menacingly.

"Am I doing exactly as you want me to?"

"Indeed, you are. I have chosen you for the way in which you can do my bidding. You have a certain charm about you that I find curious; it benefits my will. The coin is from another time—a time without time. I created the coin from fire, water, air, and earth. It contains all the elements of this world. It was cast in the furnace of hell, so there, it can be destroyed by me."

"So I have the coin because I am your servant, and I am to do your will here on this earth, even though I know it can't be understood by a mortal man."

"Yes."

"Then what am I to do now that you are here, and why are you here now?"

"I am finished with you, mortal. I wish for my coin back."

"So you want the coin back because you are done with me?"

"Yes."

"I see. Well, if that is your wish, then I have no other recourse but to comply."

"Yes."

"I wish for you to be gone from my sight forever!" Suddenly, as Jon Paul said this, the Jinn began to scream. He seemed to be going up in a puff of white smoke as he screamed. Jon Paul had taken a risk, but after what the Jinn had told him, he knew he could probably do this; the coin is all-powerful and could not be destroyed—except by the Jinn.

Jon Paul watched the Jinn slowly evaporate back into the mist from which it came. He was surprised that it happened that way, but then, he had the coin, and it was his. The story the Jinn had told him about his past had caused a forgotten memory to resurface for him, and he knew what he could do with the coin if given the chance. Jon Paul walked back to his home from his forest. The talk with the Jinn had excited him and given him a new reason to live. Now that he had Liz at his side, he could rule the world, if he so chose. He could be another Napoleon or perhaps Hitler, but killing people was not his thing. Power was where Jon Paul wanted to excel, and so he would.

"Hi, Jon Paul. How was your walk?"

"My dear Liz, it was invigorating. I feel like a new man."

"Wow, you do seem different; did something happen to you?"

"No. Everything is fine; I think the fresh air of the trees helped me to recharge and get ready for this next voting session. There are some sticky matters that need to be cleared up before we can vote on them."

"What issues, Jon Paul?"

"Now, Liz, you know I am not supposed to reveal those things till after they have passed." She smiled at him, and then she saw that he was serious and let the matter drop.

"Well, just tell me if it is anything serious that I need to know, okay?"

"I will, my love; just don't worry. We are always fine."

Jon Paul had some issues that involved other politicians, but these were minor men. They had no power except through family connections and in knowing other men of power. They needed to be handled properly, and that was something Jon Paul could do very well.

***

As Paul and Michelle drove the city looking for a place to eat, something occurred to Paul that he had not thought of before. What would they do after the battle with his old friend? Would they still be alive; would they even survive this battle? He wondered, *what will happen to Michelle? Maybe I should do something before this all happens.* Paul decided right then and there that he wanted to spend the rest of his life with Michelle. He loved her with all of his heart, and he wanted to marry her.

Michelle sat next to Paul and began to wonder what he was thinking; he had not said a word since they left the bar. "Paul, is something on your mind?"

"What? Um, yeah … I mean, no, well … I just was thinking about what is going to happen soon. I mean, will we survive this battle with Jon Paul, and what will we do after that? Are we going to have to do something else for Seraphiel?"

"Wow, Paul! Try to lighten up a little, okay? We are not even there yet and you are already thinking about our future."

"I know, Michelle, but it just occurred to me as we were driving."

"Paul, when that time comes, we will do what is right; you must believe in what Seraphiel said, and we will be okay."

"You are right. I must believe that we will be shown what the right thing to do is. I still can't help worrying about it, and you." Paul smiled at Michelle and reached for her hand; she let him hold her hand and smiled back lovingly.

"Paul, I am so happy you are here with me now. I don't know what I would do without you. I really need you to be strong and confident for me."

"Okay, Michelle. I will, and I am." He smiled at her and squeezed her hand tight. Michelle breathed a sigh of relief; she felt his strength and was comforted.

***

Liz had been reading a book in the library when Jon Paul entered. "Hi, sweetie, what are you doing?"

"Hey, you. I am reading this book on cane toads in Australia; glad we don't have them here!"

"Cane toads, wow, I didn't know we had that book. Where was it located?"

"Right there, on that shelf by the other books on reptiles." Liz pointed to the third shelf from the bottom of the bookcase.

"Oh, I see. Yeah, I haven't had the time to get to that shelf yet, what with all the work I have to do these days." Liz smiled at Jon Paul. He was a busy man, and he spent a lot of the week at his office in the city, but when he was at home, it was a little more relaxed for him. The pressures of the city were gone and Jon Paul could unwind a little; at least, he tried to.

"Hey, Jon Paul, what do you have planned tonight?"

"I have to look over some new proposals from the UMP, but it shouldn't take too long. What have you got in mind, my dear?"

"Well, I was thinking maybe we could have a nice, romantic dinner tonight."

"Hmm, a romantic dinner. What are you up to, Lizzy?" Jon Paul smiled at her and winked.

"Jon Paul, you are too much. I just want some time with you."

"Yes, I think we can do that, but it will cost you."

"Jon Paul, what are you talking about?"

"There is a price for my company tonight. Are you willing to pay?"

"Of course, silly man, what is your price?"

"I want a nice, hot bath; then I would love a massage!"

"Oh, Jon Paul, you know I would do anything for you, and if that is the going price, then let's do it!" Liz put the book down and grabbed Jon Paul in a passionate embrace. She kissed him fully on the lips as she held him tight.

"Wow; oh, wow! If you kissed me like that all the time, I would never get any work done!"

Liz smiled at Jon Paul and let him go. She was always willing to do anything to keep her man.

"I will go talk with Mr. Falid and have him prepare a special romantic dinner for us tonight. Any special requests for food?"

"No, nothing in particular; just have him make something nice and romantic for us."

"You got it, my dear. Be back in a little bit." Jon Paul walked out of the library and to his kitchen, where he hoped to find Mr. Falid working. As it turns out, he was working in the kitchen, doing his usual chef duties, cleaning and arranging utensils. The kitchen was his domain, and Jon Paul let him have it that way.

"Mr. Falid, how are you tonight? Miss Bourg asks if you would prepare us a fine and romantic dinner tonight."

"Of course, sir. Does Miss Bourg want something in particular for her dinner?"

"No, nothing in particular. She just asks that you make it special and romantic."

"Will do, sir. Is eight o'clock fine for your dinner?"

"It is; let me know when all is ready. Thank you, Mr. Falid."

"Thank you, sir. I will reach you on the intercom." Jon Paul walked out of the kitchen and upstairs to his office; he wanted to go over some papers that would need to be reviewed in order to be put to a vote at the next legislative meeting.

***

Paul and Michelle had been driving for a little while when Michelle saw the old restaurant, La Rotonde. It was an upscale place with fine seafood, and she thought that would be a good place to get something to eat.

"Look, Paul, let's go eat there. It looks like a fun place."

"You sure? La Rotonde is a bit expensive."

"Yes, I want to eat there." Paul pulled into the parking lot and parked his car. They walked up to the front door and went in. The place was very beautiful, with crystal chandeliers hung from the ceiling; most men were dressed in suits and ties, and the women wore dresses.

"Hello, sir, welcome to La Rotonde. How can I help you?"

"We need a table for two, something semi-private, if you have it."

"Yes, sir, we do; follow me, please." Paul and Michelle followed the waiter to their table; they sat down and he handed them the menus and told them about the evening's special, which was roasted shark with steamed rice and snow peas.

"Yes, that sounds good; I will have that. What about you, Michelle?"

"Um, yeah, that does sound good. I will have the same, please."

The waiter smiled and walked back to the kitchen to give their order, and Paul and Michelle would have their food in just few minutes.

***

Maggie Martin had still been keeping busy with her work at the bar. She was still a bit uneasy about what had been said earlier by the drunken man. He had said he would kill Jon Paul Chavalier if he ever set foot in the bar. Maggie was not sure, but she thought he might really be serious; after all, Jon Paul was once a familiar patron of this particular bar and was known to quite a few people there. Could this man be serious, this man who was known by the name Henri Muller? She sat and wondered—what did she really know about him? Well, he was in his late thirties, he only worked on occasion, and he was usually alone. He seemed to fit the profile of a serial killer, but whether he could really commit such a crime was unknown to Maggie.

Maggie finished up her work and decided to close the bar early; there were no customers in and she was alone, so she counted up the money from the evening's shift and put it in the deposit bag. She grabbed a broom and began to sweep the floor. This didn't take her very long, as only a few customers had been in and it had not gotten very dirty. She finished sweeping, put the broom away, and grabbed her coat and purse; she still thought about the man, Henri Muller, and wondered if he was serious.

***

Henri Muller was an angry man. He lived in a small one-bedroom apartment just this side of downtown Toulon. He owned very little, and all that he did own fit inside this tiny apartment. Life had not treated Henri fairly. He was always broke and never happy. He felt life had walked all over him; he could not understand why some had so much and others had so little. He hated most of the government—including the men and women who worked for the government—and now that someone he knew was in office, someone who just a year ago was like him, a common man, he wondered how things could have changed so fast. He thought about how he would love to confront this man and tell him to his face how he hated him; he wished he could actually trade places with this man. *Why him,* he wondered. Henri picked up the newspaper to read the daily news, and he saw the article about how Jon Paul Chavalier had changed France, especially Toulon, for the better; he was creating jobs.

People had money and things were looking up, or so it seemed. Henri Muller was not going to be left out this time. He would try to get an appointment with Mr. Chavalier and explain his situation and ask for help; after all, this was a man of the people. They had elected him, and he was doing their work. After finishing the article, he grabbed his phone book to look for the number to his local politician's office; he would ask for his appointment.

Henri Muller found the number and dialed it.

"Hello, Mr. Chavalier's office, how may I help you?"

"Yes, hello, I would like to speak with Mr. Chavalier."

"Mr. Chavalier is not able to speak right now. He is in a meeting and away from the office."

"I need to see him about an urgent matter."

"What is this concerning, sir?"

"It is personal. I will only say what it is about to Mr. Chavalier."

"I can set up an appointment if you wish to see him."

"Yes, that would be fine, the sooner the better."

"Let me see; we have an opening at three p.m. tomorrow."

"Three p.m. it is. I will see you then."

"What is your name, sir?"

"You can call me Mr. Muller."

"Very good, Mr. Muller, we will see you tomorrow at three."

Henri Muller hung up the phone and sat back in his chair. He picked up his pipe cleaner and began to clean his gun.

***

Almost two days had passed since Paul and Michelle had their dinner at La Rotonde. Paul had been very romantic, and Michelle loved each and every moment that they spent together. Michelle was working at her small desk by the kitchen when Paul suddenly got up from his couch and asked her, "Hey, Michelle, you got a moment?"

"Yeah, honey, just a minute, though; these latest orders have got me very busy." Michelle was busy; her business was improving each and every day, and soon she would have to hire a helper.

"Um, Michelle, I was thinking—do we have a free Friday this month?"

"I don't know, I will have to check the calendar. What do you have in mind?"

"Oh, nothing special, just was wondering."

"Paul, what are you up to? You are being very mysterious."

"What, me? Mysterious? C'mon, I am just asking a question."

"I know you, Paul, but if you say nothing, then I will check later on the calendar and see."

"Okay, yeah, me too, Michelle." Paul smiled a crafty smile at Michelle, who looked curiously at him.

Paul was planning something special for sure and Michelle would find out soon enough.

***

Jon Paul opened his eyes to see a familiar face staring down at him, smiling; however, the other face he didn't recognize. Why was he in bed, and why was this stranger looking at him?

"Who are you? Why am I in bed? Liz, who is this person?"

"Easy, Mr. Chavalier. You need to take it easy; you were bitten by a black widow spider. I am Dr. Brian Lombard."

Jon Paul looked at him in disbelief; he didn't remember being bitten by some spider. The last thing he remembered was eating his special romantic dinner with his love Liz. "Liz, is this true? Was I bitten by a spider?"

"Yes, Jon Paul, the bite is on your leg. Apparently it happened while you were on your walk in the forest the other day."

Jon Paul looked at his leg, and there on his right calf muscle was a large, swollen, bright-red wound.

"I don't remember it happening. I do remember feeling a pinch there on my way back."

"Mr. Chavalier, that would be it. The European black widow is a small spider, and its bite might feel like a pinch if you have tough skin; for others, it might feel worse. You are lucky, though. Your wife called and I was able to give you anti-venom, so you won't lose your leg—or your life. How are you feeling?"

"I guess I am okay, just a little weak."

"That will pass in a few days; you should be back on your feet in no time. Just be careful from now on, okay?"

"Yes, Dr. Lombard; do you think I can go to work soon? I have many important things to do."

"I don't see why not, just take it easy and you will be fine; don't push yourself too hard. You are young and should be back to perfect health in a few days." Jon Paul nodded and smiled quickly at the doctor, who acknowledged him with a smile in return.

"I will send a bill from my office in Toulon. Mrs. Chavalier, if he needs water or anything else, bring it to him. He is strong and will be fine. Now, if you will excuse me, I must be getting back."

"Thank you, Dr. Lombard. I don't know what we would do without you."

Liz hugged the doctor and walked him to the front door; he waved good-bye, and she closed the door behind him. Jon Paul had had a close call. Sometimes people who were bitten suffered much more serious effects from the spider bite. Liz went back upstairs to their room, smiled at Jon Paul, and thought to herself, *I think I like being called Mrs. Chavalier!*

Liz spent the rest of the day tending to Jon Paul, whose strength was returning fast; being a young man helped.

"Hey, Liz, I think I can go into the office tomorrow. I am feeling much better, and my strength is returning."

"Are you sure, Jon Paul? Don't push yourself too hard. I am worried that you might be."

"No, honey, I am fine, I promise."

226

"Jon Paul, did you hear the doctor call me 'Mrs. Chavalier'? I think I like the sound of that."

"Really, Liz? I didn't hear him say that, but it does sound good to me too!" Jon Paul smiled at Liz, who smiled back.

"You know something, Liz? Maybe we should do something like that."

"Like what, Jon Paul?"

"Like get married; I mean, I am ready if you are."

"Jon Paul, are you serious? Are you asking me to marry you?"

"I am, my love; will you marry me?" Jon Paul got down on one knee, held her hand, and looked deeply into her eyes. Liz began to shed tears of joy. She felt she was the happiest woman in the world right then.

"Of course, Jon Paul, I will!" She helped him up, and they hugged each other tightly in such a loving embrace, they were as one.

***

Paul and Michelle were both working when Paul stood up and said to Michelle, "Hey, Michelle, I need to go to the store to pick up a few things."

Michelle looked at him curiously and said, "Okay, Paul, what are you going to pick up?"

"Nothing much; don't you worry about it, I will be back shortly." Paul was indeed acting strange to Michelle, but he had a plan. He was going to find a diamond engagement ring to give to his love, Michelle. Driving to specific jewelers was what he had planned, so he couldn't tell Michelle where he was going.

"Paul, can you pick me up a few things too, please?"

"Sure, honey, what do you need?"

"I need you to pick up a new pack of printing paper and some new hanging files. I am running low, and my desk is filling up fast."

"Do you want any specific kind or will just any do?"

"Just any will be fine, thank you." She smiled at Paul, who was putting on his coat. He kissed her quickly and headed out the door. Paul was going to buy Michelle a ring.

***

Jon Paul spent the day recuperating. Liz would help him as he needed it, but his strength was returning quickly. The spider bite had been serious, but not serious enough to put his life in danger; some people had actually been worse off than Jon Paul after that kind of bite.

Liz was so excited; she was going to marry the man of her dreams! Jon Paul had become so much a part of her that she could not live without him. She wanted to tell the world about her happiness, but she knew the world would find out soon enough; after all, Jon Paul was a public figure now that he was in office. The press seemed to follow him wherever he went; sometimes, it was very annoying. As Liz was thinking about who she could call and tell first, a thought occurred to her. *What would happen if Jon Paul didn't have the magic coin? Would he still be the same man he is now?* She wondered.

***

Henri Muller finished cleaning his gun and put the pipe cleaner in the trash. He had a few more, so he didn't reuse the old ones; a clean gun barrel was very important when hunting.

He turned on the news to see what the stories of the day were; saddened, he thought, *It is always the same.* Violence in the Mideast, a shooting here, some other car crashes in the city where someone was hurt or killed.

Henri Muller was losing his grip on sanity. He had grown up in the southern part of France with only his mother; he never knew his father. His mother worked two jobs just to try and stay ahead of the bills, but she never could seem to catch up. As Henri grew into a young man, he was always jealous of other people who had money and always wished he could be in their shoes; why must he be so poor? He didn't do well in school, and when he was sixteen, he left school and joined the French Royal Navy. He was kicked out of there after only two years. It seemed life was looking down on Henri Muller, and he didn't like it.

A lot of times, as Henri got older, he would get into fights at his local bar after drinking himself into a stupor. Some he would win; some he would lose. Henri worked at the docks as a deck hand on occasion. The work was hard and didn't pay well, so he wasn't always willing to work. He would go to The Goat's Head Bar after working and drink and complain about whatever was on his small mind. The night he saw Maggie Martin and the couple talking about the politician Jon Paul Chavalier was the straw that broke his back, so to speak. He was going to do something with his sad life, no matter what it took.

***

Liz was sitting in her dressing room when she picked up the phone to call her mother. As she dialed the number, she noticed that she needed to have her room cleaned up; clothes were all over the place, and shoes too. She was never this messy when she lived in her old apartment, but now, with so much space, she had become a bit spoiled.

"Hello."

"Hello, Mom? This is Liz."

"Lizzy, hi. How are you?"

"Good, Mom. How are you doing?"

"I am doing well; things are good. How is life in Toulon?"

"Well, everything is fine. Jon Paul is busy with work, and I just try to keep him happy. You know, being in politics is not easy; oftentimes, we are gone for days at a time in some other country."

"Yeah, it certainly isn't easy, but he is doing a good job, from what I read in the papers."

"Thanks, Mom, he really is; sometimes I think he works too hard. Listen, Mom, I want to tell you some exciting news!"

"Yes, what is it?"

"Jon Paul asked me to marry him!"

"Are you serious? That is wonderful news, my dear. I can't wait to see you walk down the aisle!"

"Thanks, Mom. He just asked, so we don't have any plans yet, but I am going to start working on that soon. I will let you know when for sure as soon as I get it all worked out."

"Now, Lizzy, you know I am going to want to help you with everything; you can't leave me out."

"I know, Mom, but it is a little overwhelming right now. I will hire someone, or rather, some company, to help with all the planning, but I want you to be there with me also."

"I will, my dear. Just tell me when, okay?"

"Okay, Mom. I better go for now. I will call you in a couple days."

"Don't forget; bye now."

"Bye, Mom." Liz hung up the phone and walked into her bedroom. Jon Paul was sitting up watching the TV.

"Hi Jon Paul, I just talked with my mom. She is so very excited for our wedding."

"Yeah, it is going to be great! We can hire whoever you want and cater everything, I will have Mr. Falid watching and supervising it all."

"Do you think we can do this soon, I mean, like, let's make a date for it?"

"Okay, when do you want to do this?"

"I don't know; let's go find a calendar and pick a day." Liz and Jon Paul got up and walked to his office. He had a nice, full-size calendar there on his custom walnut desk.

***

Paul got in his car and drove to the jewelers; he was looking for a specific engagement ring for his love Michelle. Driving through Toulon was not easy, since many of the cab drivers were very bad drivers and traffic was never good. Paul drove until he saw Gauthier Jewelers.

They were a very nice and upscale dealer, mostly in fine gems, some loose and others set, and prices were always reasonable for the quality, which they claimed was their trademark. Paul had heard of this place before and knew they sold quality gems, and as he parked and got out of his car, he noticed the lot had many fine automobiles in it. Paul walked up to the door and went in; his first impression was he had made the right choice. The store was very nice, with wall-to-wall carpet. Nice, bright chandeliers hung in the right places above the glass displays. Some of the furniture was leather for the customers to sit on; others were just fabric chairs. Coffee and tea was offered to all customers, and the higher clientele were offered wine or champagne.

Paul looked around and found a case with some engagement rings in it. A few other people were looking at the same case. One of the people Paul overheard talking was a young lady who was remarking how beautiful a certain ring was. Paul immediately looked at the ring she was looking at; it was beautiful, a one-and-a-half-carat diamond engagement ring set in a gold circular band entwined like ivy. Paul thought it was perfect, but he moved closer to get a better look. The young lady backed off and gave Paul room to look, and as he got closer, the saleswoman asked him if he wanted to see one in particular. "Yes," was Paul's response. Upon careful examination of the ring, he decided it was perfect, and he bought it and walked out to his car. Paul drove back to his apartment without picking up Michelle's supplies; he wanted to give her the ring.

Michelle was busy working when Paul came in through the door; he saw her sitting there and said, "Hi, Michelle, how's it going?"

"Fine, Paul; if this keeps up, I am going to have to hire an assistant."

"Um, Michelle, I didn't pick up your things. I do, however, have something I think you might like instead."

"Paul, what is it that you have for me?" Michelle was very curious as to what he could have brought her.

He reached in his pocket and pulled out the black velvet case. Michelle was surprised and began to shake.

"Michelle, I want to give you this and ask you if you will marry me."

"Oh, Paul, I never imagined you would do this. I, I … of course I will!" Michelle began to shed tears of joy. She had found the man she would spend her life with.

***

Jon Paul and Liz walked to Jon Paul's office and looked at his desk calendar; they were looking for a date to plan their wedding, a wedding that would be one for the record books. After looking at the calendar for several moments, Liz suggested a June wedding, and Jon Paul was okay with that. Now Jon Paul and Liz were planning a marriage and Paul and Michelle were getting engaged, each having shared love with each other for a limited amount of time. However, it seemed that both couples had found their true loves.

Jon Paul was preparing to go into the city to get his workday started when Liz said, "Jon Paul, I think I will go into the city with you today, if that is okay."

"Sure thing, honey. I am still a little weak, and I could use your help in any way you can."

"I will help you, Jon Paul; whatever you need, just ask."

"I am almost ready to leave, are you?"

"Yeah, give me a couple of minutes, okay, Jon Paul?"

"Sure thing, honey. I will be in the kitchen waiting." Liz smiled at Jon Paul, who walked downstairs to his kitchen, where Mr. Falid was preparing the evening's meal.

"Hello, Mr. Falid, how are you this fine day?"

"Hello, sir, I am well. You seem in a special, happy mood today."

"I am very happy, Mr. Falid. I asked Miss Bourg to marry me, and we have set a wedding date for June!"

"Congratulations, sir, I am so very happy for you!"

"Thanks, Mr. Falid. We are going to hire a catering company for the wedding, but I want you to oversee all the preparations."

"Thank you, sir. I will, to the best of my abilities." Jon Paul smiled at his manservant; he was very happy to know it would be perfect.

Chapter 13

— •●• —

THE BETRAYED

Liz had finished getting herself ready and was walking down the stairs when she saw Jon Paul walking out to greet her.

"Are you ready, sweetie?"

"Yes, I am. Did you tell Mr. Falid our plans, Jon Paul?"

"I did, and he is very excited; it's going to be perfect!" Liz took Jon Paul by the hand, and together, they walked out the front door and down to their garage. Jon Paul decided to drive his Range Rover; it was a bit more comfortable than his Ferrari, but not as comfortable as his Rolls Royce. He only used that car on special occasions. As they drove down his long driveway to the street, neither could help but smile at the other—what with the wedding and all, things in their life were going so perfectly right now.

***

Henri Muller got in his old, rundown car and started the drive to Mr. Chavalier's office. It was located at the French headquarters in downtown Toulon. It was not a particularly long drive, but with traffic, it was always hectic. He drove in a very non-aggressive manner, compared to the other drivers at this time of the day.

***

Jon Paul and Liz pulled into the office building and into the covered garage parking reserved for the bigwigs who were in office. Jon Paul had a special parking place close to the elevators, since he was one of the most powerful politicians in the building. They took the elevator up to the fourteenth floor, which was the top floor, and then walked to his office. They stepped off the elevator and into the hallway and then walked down the hallway to his secretary's desk.

"Good day, Mrs. Roux, anything I need to know about?"

"Good day, Mr. Chavalier; good day, Miss Bourg. Yes, sir, there is one thing. You have an appointment with a Mr. Muller at three today."

"Oh? Who is he, and what does he want?"

"He wouldn't say; he only said it was private and he would only discuss it with you."

"I see. A Mr. Muller, at three, you said?"

"Yes, sir."

"Thank you, Mrs. Roux." Jon Paul and Liz walked through the double doors and into his office.

"I wonder who he is, Jon Paul."

"Yeah, me too, most likely a concerned citizen who is going to ask for some kind of favor."

Jon Paul was right, in a way. Henri Muller was going to ask for a favor, but not the kind Jon Paul was thinking. Jon Paul and Liz spent hours going over his work, mostly because Liz wanted to learn more about what he did. She accompanied Jon Paul quite often, and she did enjoy coming to work with him, but it was a long drive, and most of the time, it was boring for her. There was so much paperwork and there were so many meetings where nothing got done, and Liz wondered how anything ever gotten done before Jon Paul.

***

Henri Muller parked his car outside the office building and walked up the steps to the lobby; he was looking for the elevators that would take him to Jon Paul's office. He talked with the reception person at the front desk, who pointed him to the right elevators and told him which floor Jon Paul's office was on. Henri Muller got off the elevator and walked to Jon Paul's office; he saw the secretary, Mrs. Roux, and walked over to her desk.

"Hi, I am Henri Muller. I have an appointment with Mr. Chavalier at three."

"Hi, Mr. Muller. Please sign here, and then take a seat over there. I will let him know you are here." He signed his name and then sat down near the doors. Jon Paul's office was very nice and plush; it had leather furniture and a coffee machine. It also had wall-to-wall beige carpet that seemed to flow with the colors of the wall perfectly. It was a delight and a pleasure to be there, Henri thought. He could work there. Henri didn't have to wait long; Jon Paul prided himself on being fairly punctual, especially with his meetings.

"Mr. Muller, Mr. Chavalier will see you now." She smiled at him and got up to open the doors. Henri noticed that the doors were metal and looked heavy; stainless-steel handles accented the doors perfectly. She opened the doors, and Jon Paul got up to shake his hand as he approached closer.

"Hello, Mr. Muller, please sit down. This is my fiancé, Miss Bourg. How can we help you?"

"I came here looking for help, Mr. Chavalier."

"What kind of help are you looking for?"

"I need money, and I need someone to pay for my bills."

"Pay for your bills? Why don't you work and pay them yourself?"

"I do work on occasion, but it is not enough."

Jon Paul studied the man's face and said, "If you are working, then I think there are some government programs you might qualify for."

"Do you not recognize me, Jon Paul?"

"Recognize you? No, but you seem familiar."

"You and I are a lot alike, Jon Paul, but somehow, you have risen to the top very fast. I want to know how you did this."

"So we are on a first-name basis now?" Jon Paul stared at Henri Muller in a disrespectful way.

"You still don't remember me, Jon Paul? We used to drink at The Goat's Head Bar a year or more ago."

"The Goat's Head Bar—now I remember you." Jon Paul did remember him. He remembered he didn't really like Henri Muller; he was always complaining about some political person or how he was getting screwed by the city officials. Jon Paul never said much to him; he knew he was just another barfly.

"So, Jon Paul, are you going to help me?"

"How can I help you? Do you want money from me personally?"

"Yeah, that would be good, for starters. See, I figure you owe me."

"How do I owe you, Henri?"

"I don't know how you have gotten this far, but you owe me!"

"I owe you nothing! I got here with hard work. The people elected me because I said what they want to hear."

"You lie!"

"I lie? No, Henri, I am creating jobs and putting money back into the peoples' pockets. That is what they want."

"Liar! You are only doing what *you* think is right. I don't know how you got here, but I want my share!"

"I have nothing for you, Henri. Leave my office."

"You lie!" Henri Muller then pulled his forty-five-caliber gun from his belt and pointed it straight at Jon Paul's head.

"Easy now, Henri. Just take it easy." Jon Paul was scared. He had a gun pointing directly at his head, and if he was not careful, he could be shot. He could possibly even die from that shot, too.

"I want my share—*now*!"

"Okay, okay, Henri, take it easy; maybe I can come up with something for you." Jon Paul was stalling for time. He had this madman pointing a gun at him, and he needed time to figure something out. Liz had moved behind Jon Paul and was relatively safe.

"I am waiting, Jon Paul."

"What if I told you I have something that can do anything you want?" Jon Paul felt the coin heating up in his pocket.

"What are you talking about?"

"I have a magic coin that can do anything you ask it to."

"C'mon, Jon Paul, do you think I am stupid?"

"No, seriously, Henri, this coin can make your every wish come true." Jon Paul smiled an evil grin at Henri.

"Jon Paul, don't give him the coin!" said Liz.

"Shut up, lady!" Henri yelled.

"It is okay, Liz; we don't need it anymore."

"Jon Paul, no, please." Liz was begging Jon Paul not to give Henri the coin, but it looked to her like he had made up his mind to give it to him.

"I have it right here in my pocket, Henri."

"Easy, Jon Paul, no sudden movements or I'll shoot you dead."

"Okay, no sudden movements." Slowly, Jon Paul reached in his pocket and pulled out his closed hand with the coin inside. He slowly opened his hand, revealing the glowing, golden coin. Henri stared at it in disbelief and became mesmerized by its beauty.

"See, Henri, I didn't lie to you. It really is magical."

"How does it work?"

"That is simple; you just ask it for what you want."

"Give it to me now, Jon Paul."

"Hold on, now, Henri, let me first show you how it works. If you will please lower your gun, I will show you." Henri Muller stared at Jon Paul, not knowing whether to trust him. Slowly, he lowered his gun, but he kept a watchful eye on Jon Paul.

"You better not be lying to me, Jon Paul."

"I am not lying. Now, if you will just give me a minute—and this important; listen to me closely." Jon Paul began to remember his first encounter with the thugs from the store where he had wished for his painting.

"You must listen close, Henri Muller. I … I wish you dead and gone from me forever!" Jon Paul spoke the words fast, and as he said them, he laughed a very wicked laugh. His eyes became dark, and he looked evil to Liz.

Henri Muller screamed and vanished instantly into thin air. Jon Paul calmly put the coin back into his pocket and sat back down in his leather chair. Liz stared at him in disbelief. She had never seen this side of Jon Paul, and it frightened her. He was wicked and evil, ruthless and unforgiving. Liz did not like this Jon Paul; he was a stranger to her.

"Jon Paul, I … I can't believe you did that! You just killed that man, and you didn't even blink. How could you do this?" Liz began to cry. Mrs. Roux had heard the scream and knocked on the door to his office.

"Mr. Chavalier! Is everything all right?"

"Yes, yes, everything is all right; we just had a bit of a disagreement."

"Okay, then, if you need anything, I will be at my desk."

"Thank you, Mrs. Roux."

"Liz, just calm down. He was pointing a gun at me and might have even killed me; then where would we be? I did what was necessary for our survival."

"No, Jon Paul, you did what was necessary for *your* survival."

"What would you have me do?" he asked her.

"I need to leave for a while, Jon Paul; I think I need some fresh air."

"Liz!" But she had gotten up and was walking out of his doors to the hallway. She walked down to the elevators and from there out into the street, where she could get some fresh air.

"Mrs. Roux, Mr. Muller left by my private entrance in the office, and he won't be coming back."

"Oh, okay, Mr. Chavalier, I was wondering where he went. Is Miss Bourg okay?"

"Yes, she will be fine. As I told you a few minutes ago, we had a little misunderstanding, but everything is fine now."

"If you don't mind me asking, sir, what was the scream I heard earlier?"

"The scream? Oh, that, yes, I was showing Miss Bourg how the guy in the movie we watched earlier did it."

"Oh, it was from a movie?"

"Yes, I just turned it up really loud for the effect. Now, when Miss Bourg returns, let me know what she looks like. You know what I mean, like, has she been crying, or is she mad, you know?"

"Yes, Mr. Chavalier. I will call you as soon as she returns." Jon Paul smiled at his secretary and went back into his office to continue his work.

Liz walked out of the building and out into the street; she was visibly upset, and tears streamed down her cheeks. She wondered if this was the same man she fell in love with, or if this was a side of him she didn't want to know—a side that was wicked and evil, a side that had been corrupted by the coin. Liz walked down the sidewalk, and the thoughts that were in her head were like demons plaguing her. She was hysterical and many people looked at her strangely as she walked past them, but she didn't care what they thought. She only wanted to get away from this man whom she had thought she knew.

***

Paul and Michelle spent the day celebrating their new engagement. Although they had not yet set a date, they were still planning on a wedding soon. "You know, Paul, I never thought it could be like this."

"Like what, Michelle?"

"You know, to have someone so close to you that you can't even see yourself living without. That is how I feel about you, Paul." Michelle had tears of joy streaming down her face.

"I know, Michelle. Its like, how did I live without you before? I wasn't living at all!"

Paul and Michelle were happy. They had lived their lives separately for so long that neither realized how much they were missing. As Paul and Michelle were celebrating their love, a sudden flash occurred, and Michelle began to speak to Paul in a voice that was not her own.

"Paul Dubois, the time is almost near. You must be prepared for the battle to come. Take this woman and be her husband. Marry her, for your love is being blessed by the powers of heaven."

Paul stared at Michelle; she had a blank look in her eyes, and she didn't seem to be aware of what was happening to her.

"What shall I tell Michelle, and how should I prepare for this battle?"

"Tell her what you wish; for it is I, Seraphiel. I have chosen to speak to you directly like this. You will know when I come again to teach you how to prepare for the final outcome. It is not preordained. It can only be finished by you destroying the coin. I will speak to you in a similar fashion when the time has come. Until then, continue your lives in love. I shall return soon, Paul Dubois! Be ready!"

"I shall, Seraphiel. We shall be as ready as we can." As soon as Paul said this, the flash was gone, and Michelle returned to her normal self. She looked at Paul strangely, as if she had missed something.

"Paul, what just happened? I feel strange."

"Your angel, Seraphiel, just spoke through you. She told me to prepare as best we can and that we are to be ready for the final battle. It is to be soon."

"Seraphiel! I didn't even realize ... you mean, she spoke through me?"

"Yes, you became distant and your eyes glazed over, and then you were speaking with a different voice—Seraphiel's voice."

"Really? What did she say? I mean, what are we to do?"

"Just to be prepared and live our lives in love, as we are blessed by heaven."

"We are blessed by heaven?"

"Yep, we are!"

Paul and Michelle sat there in their living room after the encounter for some time. Neither of them spoke much, but they were feeling happy and content, to say the least.

***

Liz had been walking for a while when she realized that it was getting late and she had better get back to Jon Paul; he would be getting worried by now, and who knew, he might use the coin on her. She was still afraid of what she had seen Jon Paul do, and her mind was heavy with thoughts of doubt about her upcoming marriage to him. She climbed the stairs to the front door, went in, walked to the elevators, and pushed the button for his floor. As the elevator took her to the fourteenth floor, she wondered what she would tell Jon Paul as to where she had been. The doors opened and she walked down the corridor to his office; she walked in and Mrs. Roux saw her, smiled, and said, "Hello, Miss Bourg, are you okay?"

"Yes, thank you, I am fine. Can you tell Jon Paul I am here?"

"Yes, ma'am, I will." She buzzed Jon Paul on the phone and told him Liz was back. Jon Paul smiled at Liz, who didn't smile back. She sat down in a chair away from his desk, looked at him, and said, "Jon Paul, I don't know how I feel about what happened earlier. It is something I can never forget. I just don't know anything right now."

"My dear Liz, it was nothing; *he* was nothing. Let's just focus on what we are doing right now; we have a wedding to plan, and I, for one, am ready to get that started. I am almost finished here, and then we can go home and relax."

Liz looked at Jon Paul and nodded. She was ready to go home and get away from this place of bad memories. Jon Paul did finish his work and as he finished, he looked up at Liz and said, "Well, I think we can go. I am done for today, you ready?"

"Yes, Jon Paul, let's go, please."

They got up and walked out to the secretary's desk, and Jon Paul said to her, "Thanks for your work today, Mrs. Roux, it was very good. We are heading home now, so we will see you tomorrow."

"Thank you, sir, I will see you tomorrow." Jon Paul and Liz walked to the elevators and found their way to the parking garage to get in their car to drive home and relax, away from the city.

***

"Paul, do you think we will survive the great battle with Jon Paul?"

"I really don't know, Michelle. We are immune to the effects of the coin, but I don't know if Jon Paul could hurt us some other way."

"What do you mean, 'some other way'?"

"What if he shot one of us? I don't know if that is part of the plan or what. Will Seraphiel protect us from a bullet? What if one of us drowns, or maybe is hit by a bus? I just don't know."

"Paul, I see what you mean. Maybe next time, you can ask her if we are protected. If we are blessed, then I would assume that would be so, but like you, I don't know." Paul looked at Michelle and nodded. The next time the angel appeared, he would have to try and ask her if they were protected.

***

Jon Paul and Liz arrived back at their home in silence. As Jon Paul pulled up to his garage, he stopped, looked at Liz, and said, "You know, Liz, everything will be all right. Try to just forget what happened today."

Liz looked back at him and said, "Just try to forget? How can I forget, Jon Paul? You just killed a man in cold blood."

"Ah, Liz, it was not like that; you saw, he was going to shoot me or you! I had to do something!"

Liz got out of the car and slammed the door. Jon Paul followed her up to the house, and as they entered the front doors, they saw Mr. Falid waiting.

"Good evening, sir and ma'am, how was your day at work?"

"It was fine, Mr. Falid. We had a bit of trouble, but nothing to concern yourself over."

"Very good, sir, would you and Miss Bourg like to eat something?"

"Yes, we would, thank you."

"I will set up the table for you. Shall I call you when all is ready?"

"Yes. I would like to change my clothes and relax for a few minutes before we eat. How about you, my dear?"

"Yes, that is fine." They walked upstairs to their room and began to unwind. Liz went into her changing room and Jon Paul into his. There they remained, until Mr. Falid buzzed them on the intercom. Jon Paul walked into Liz's room and said, "Are you ready to eat dinner?"

"Let's just go downstairs and eat. Okay, Jon Paul?" Liz replied, very sarcastically, to Jon Paul; she didn't want to eat with him, and she didn't want to be around him. She was still very upset at what he did earlier; it was as if she never really knew him at all.

Jon Paul and Liz sat down at the table to eat the evening meal prepared by Mr. Falid, and as usual, he had outdone himself. He had prepared a trout amandine with scalloped potatoes and fresh corn. A salad on the side with avocado and spinach finished the meal. Jon Paul loved the way Mr. Falid always made the perfect meals for him and Liz. Liz was still upset about the day's earlier events. She sat in almost complete silence and said very few words to Jon Paul.

Jon Paul saw that she was still upset and said to her, "Liz, are you okay? Is the dinner not what you wanted?"

"The dinner is fine, Jon Paul. I am just not very hungry tonight. Jon Paul, how can you be so cold?"

"What do you mean, 'so cold'?"

"How can you just kill a man in cold blood?"

"He would have killed me if I hadn't."

"Was it really necessary to do that?"

"Yes, Liz, it was."

"I don't know, Jon Paul. I think you are becoming possessed by that coin."

"I am not possessed by anything! The coin is mine, and I am in control! I will not give my coin up for anybody or anything."

Liz was feeling very distant from Jon Paul now. "I can't eat any more, Jon Paul. I am going upstairs to my room."

"Okay, Liz, I will be there shortly." Jon Paul finished eating alone, and he eventually walked downstairs to his game room to shoot a game of pool by himself. He thought about his actions of the day, and the more he thought about it, the more he was sure he had done the right thing. After all, that man,

Henri Muller, was threatening to shoot him if he didn't help him. That was a form of extortion, and Jon Paul bowed to nobody—nobody in his office or in his work area.

He finished his game of pool and walked back upstairs to the main floor and then up the stairs to his room. Liz was already in bed; she was feigning sleep, but she lay there quietly, thinking.

"Liz ... are you awake?"

"Yes."

"I want to ask you something."

"What, Jon Paul?"

"Liz, when you saw what I did today, what would you have done differently if you were in my shoes?"

"I don't know, maybe nothing. Maybe we should have given him money. We have more than enough for our lives. We could spare some for that poor man."

"Okay, Liz, but I didn't get here by bowing to every piece of trash that says I owe him or threatens me with some type of extortion."

"I know, Jon Paul, but ... never mind. I am going to sleep. Good night, Jon Paul." Liz turned her back on him and went to sleep.

For Jon Paul, the dreams were just about to return.

***

Paul and Michelle slept like babies; they had the blessings of heaven on them, and it showed. The following morning, they both awoke feeling refreshed and new. "Hey, Michelle, what do you want for breakfast? I am cooking!"

"Really, Paul? If you are offering, then how about something fresh, like eggs and coffee cake and maybe juice?"

"You got it, honey. I will cook up the best breakfast you ever have eaten!"

"Okay, Paul, let's do this!" Paul and Michelle got up, dressed in their robes, and went downstairs to his kitchen to cook breakfast. Paul was not a bad cook; of course, he was not as good as Michelle—in fact, not even close—but in time, he would learn some valuable lessons from her. They sat at the table in his kitchen and ate their wonderful breakfast. Both Paul and Michelle ate their fill.

"Hey, Michelle, do you want to do something today?"

"Like what, Paul?"

"I don't know; let's think of something to do." They cleaned up the kitchen and walked into the living room to discuss the day's plans.

"Hey, Paul, have you been to the Toulon Museum lately?"

"Well, no, Michelle, you know I never go out. I spend all my time here with you."

"I know, but I was wondering if maybe you stop in there from time to time when you are out."

"Well, no, actually, I don't; I haven't been there in months, or longer."

"Then why don't we go today? My work is light, and I can spend a few hours looking around at some works of art."

"Okay, Michelle, we will go to the museum today." Paul and Michelle had a plan to go to the museum and see the works of art that the world cherished. They would spend several hours there admiring the different pieces of art—some were sculptures, some were paintings, and all were a sight to see.

***

Jon Paul tossed and turned all night and barely slept. The dreams of his wicked past came back to haunt him, a past where, as a general in the war, he gave orders to kill many men. The dreams helped him to remember his former life as a powerful, but evil, general. The tall man who had given the coin to Jon Paul had not told him of its curse and that as soon as he used the coin to fulfill all of his desires, the dreams faded for only a short while. It seemed that the curse gained a hold after awhile, and the person holding the coin was doomed to relive his past. Jon Paul was that man.

When morning broke, Liz had already gotten out of bed before Jon Paul and was downstairs in the kitchen drinking coffee with Mr. Falid. She talked with him about the coin and learned some of its history and the evil influence it had on men. All of the men who had held it in the past, including Jon Paul, had fallen to the evil of the coin. There was no other way; that is the way of the coin, thanks to the Jinn who created it. The Jinn could not control its power any more than a mortal man; the coin had power unto itself.

Jon Paul came into the kitchen looking for breakfast. He saw his manservant talking with Liz, and he smiled and asked, "Mr. Falid, have you prepared a breakfast this morning? I sure could use some coffee."

"Yes, sir, I have. We were just talking about the morning."

"The morning, Mr. Falid?"

"Yes, just how beautiful it is this morning." Mr. Falid had not told Jon Paul the whole truth; he neglected to reveal just how much he had told Liz. Liz had heard Jon Paul coming in to the kitchen and asked Mr. Falid not to say anything about what they were talking about.

"Good morning, Jon Paul; how was your sleep?"

"Well, you should know, I barely slept. Those damn dreams about my past just kept waking me up. I never really did get to sleep very well."

"Yes, I know, Jon Paul. You were tossing and turning a lot last night. You almost kept me up too."

"Liz, are you feeling better this morning?"

Liz looked at Jon Paul and said, "A little. I am going to take some time to make sure I am okay with this. I won't be going into the city to work with you for a while; I can't right now, Jon Paul. You understand. I need a break." But Jon Paul didn't understand. He was lost on her words; he thought she meant a break from him, but he was wrong.

"Okay, Liz. I am going to go upstairs and get ready for work. I think the rest of the week, I will work at home."

"You are going to work at home this week?"

"Yeah, but only the last few days of the week; the rest of the time, I am going to be at my office."

"That sounds good, Jon Paul. Maybe the break from the city will be good for you; you know, to be able to unwind and just take it easy."

"Yeah, maybe; we will see." Jon Paul walked upstairs and into his bedroom. He walked into the closet and sat down, and then he looked in the mirror and thought to himself, *Maybe Liz is right. Maybe I should have given him some money; after all, I have enough to live like a king forever. Yeah, but he did point a gun at me, so maybe it is all for the best.* Jon Paul got dressed and headed back downstairs to the front foyer. "Mr. Falid, I am leaving, so please tell Miss Bourg I will return later this evening."

"Very good, sir, I will inform her of your plans to return later."

"Thanks, Mr. Falid, you really are the best." Jon Paul walked out to his garage and got in his Ferrari; he drove down the driveway and out into the street.

As Jon Paul was driving to work in the city, Liz was talking with Mr. Falid again; she was asking more questions about the power of the coin. She wanted to know more about its limits and what could it do. Mr. Falid told a tall tale about some of the history of the coin's last owner, Jon Paul.

He recalled the tale of the general in the war who had sent hundreds, maybe even thousands of men to their deaths. Liz was stunned; she never knew the coin had such a colorful past, not to mention its present day.

"Mr. Falid, I have a question. If Jon Paul was the last owner of the coin, why did it take so long for him to remember his past?"

"First, Jon Paul was not the last owner of this coin; it was a Korean general. Jon Paul was before that, in the years of the Byzantine War in the Middle East. I mistakenly said that. I thought you knew its past."

"No, not so much. Jon Paul doesn't talk about the coin too much; it is like a secret part of him."

"Yes, the coin does become like a part of its owner, in a certain way."

"Is there any way to take the coin from its owner? I only ask as a curiosity; please don't tell Jon Paul I asked."

"I won't tell him, Miss Bourg, if you remember this: take the coin from him in any way you can—steal it, trick him, drug him—whatever way. I will then serve you, as I serve him. That is my only request for my silence."

"Why would you ask such a thing? Aren't you loyal to the owner?"

"I am, indeed! However, there are some who are better suited for the ownership of this coin; you are one of those rare people. The coin was not meant for women; it really can only corrupt a man. My preference would be for you, a woman, to have the coin. Mr. Chavalier is already corrupted by the power of the coin; for him, there is no turning back. It is only a matter of time before he gets rid of me or loses all he has gained by destroying himself."

Mr. Falid's frightening revelation had Liz worried. She knew Jon Paul was corrupted by the coin; she just didn't know how much. Funny thing how love can put blinders to the truth on one's eyes. But Liz's eyes were opening; maybe, for the first time in her life, she was really able to see just how evil Jon Paul had become and how different he had become after finding the coin.

Liz remembered how Jon Paul used to be years ago—a sweet, young, happy man. Now she only saw a power-hungry beast of a politician. "So why didn't you tell me this before? If the coin is not meant for women, why would you wish me to have it?"

"Ah, that is easy to answer; the coin was meant to influence men. At the time of its making, the world was ruled by men; women were subservient to men. The Jinn, in their infinite wisdom, made the coin to use against men, not women. It is easier to influence men than women; for some reason unknown to us, women are better able to handle the power of the coin. You could say men are weak, and women are strong. Throughout the years, there have been a few women who have held the coin, but through their own weakness for men, they lost it, and so it stayed in the hands of a man, for the most part."

"Mr. Falid, that is an amazing tale. I had no idea about the coin." Liz was beginning to get some insight into the coin, and she wondered what she would do if she had it.

***

Paul and Michelle were preparing to go to the Toulon Museum when all of a sudden, a bright flash of light blinded them both and filled the whole room with a pure, holy air. It was Seraphiel, Michelle's angel; she had appeared again to further instruct Paul and Michelle about the coin and the coming battle with Jon Paul.

"Paul Dubois, I have come again to tell you what you must do. The time is upon us now, and you are to take the coin from Jon Paul Chavalier."

"But how am I to get the coin from him? He lives far away and is protected by the coin."

"Do not concern yourselves with that now; the time is ripe for you to talk with Liz Bourg. She is the one who will give you the coin. Then you will call me, and I will come to take the coin and destroy it."

"How am I to talk with her?"

"You must call her and ask for help; she will give you the help you need."

"Is there anything else we should know, Seraphiel? Oh, I almost forgot to ask you, are we safe from Jon Paul if he were to try and kill us in some way with the coin?"

"I cannot say, but you must be careful. Your destiny is to have this great battle. The outcome is unclear, but do what you must to retrieve the coin!"

Paul stared at the great angel and was filled with a courage he had never known before; he felt as if he could conquer the world. As the angel lifted up and seemed to fade into the ceiling in a bright mist, their eyes were suddenly blinded as before with such a bright light that neither could see for several seconds.

As the light slowly faded away, their eyesight returned, and Paul looked at Michelle and said, "Are you okay?"

"Yes, thank you, Paul. Is it always like that? You know, when Seraphiel appears?"

"Um, no. This time, she didn't allow us to see her appear or disappear. Maybe there is some sort of rule about that; did you hear all she said?"

"I did this time! I am feeling very confident, Paul. I feel like I can conquer the world!"

"Yeah, me too, Michelle! It must be from the angel blessing us."

Michelle smiled at Paul, who automatically smiled back and then held her hand gently. He led her into the kitchen and sat her down. "I am thirsty, Michelle. Do you want something to drink too?"

"Ah, yeah, whatever, Paul." Paul grabbed a couple of bottles of soda, opened them, and poured the contents into two glasses. He handed one to Michelle and set the other one in front of himself.

***

Jon Paul drove to his office; he had been thinking about what Liz had said, and he was happy to be alone on this day. He drove the same route as before, but with Jon Paul thinking about what had happened, his mind and attention were not on the road, and the drive passed quickly. Soon, he was in the city and approaching the parking garage at his office. He pulled into his parking place, grabbed his briefcase, and headed over to the elevators to go up to his office on the fourteenth floor.

Liz had been talking with Mr. Falid and had learned a great deal about the coin; she knew it was indestructible by mortal man. She knew it had been created millennia ago by evil Jinn who wanted to destroy mankind, and she knew once it was in someone's possession, that person was basically

news; ever since his meteoric rise through the French government, he had become somewhat of a celebrity. A lot of articles were written about him, and he was recognized by many. In fact, Jon Paul had been pulled over just a few days before his spider bite at home. Jon Paul wondered if maybe he was having some bad luck all of a sudden, what with Liz and the bite and now this article; was something up?

***

Michelle picked up the phone to dial the office of Jon Paul, and as she did, she began to feel a little nervous.

"Hello, Mr. Chavalier's office, how can I help you?"

"Ahem, this is Ms. Durand from the police, and I was wondering if I might ask you a few questions."

"The police? Is something wrong?"

"No, no, Miss ... What is your name?"

"I am Mrs. Roux."

"Mrs. Roux. I have a few questions that I need to ask you."

"How can I help, Officer Durand?"

"I, of course, can't go into specifics, but it does involve some people that Mr. Chavalier might know."

"Is he in trouble?"

"Well, as I said, Mrs. Roux, I can't reveal everything to you; I just need you to verify some things for me, and we will contact him as soon as we need to."

"Yes, how can I help?"

"Okay, first: Was Mr. Chavalier born on the twenty-fifth of October, 1980?"

"Yes, he was."

"Has he ever been married?"

"No, not that I know of."

"Has Mr. Chavalier had a recent change of address?"

"No, he has not."

"Is his home number: 33 4 9436 3000?"

"Um, no, it isn't."

"What is his home number, Mrs. Roux?"

"It is 33 4 94 1833 08. Are you sure all these questions won't get me in trouble?" Mrs. Roux asked nervously.

"No, ma'am. I am just verifying my info; you are not in any trouble."

"Is Mr. Chavalier in trouble? Please tell me."

"I can't reveal that information to you; what I can say is that there is an ongoing investigation and I am checking all my sources. Mr. Chavalier is one of those."

"I need to get back to work; can I help in any other way?"

"Well, no, for now, that is all I have, but remember, I will call you if I need anything else. Have a nice day, Mrs. Roux."

"Thank you. Good-bye." Michelle hung up the phone, smiled at Paul, and said, "It worked! She gave me his home number!"

"Michelle, I can't believe you did that! It was incredible; remind me to never get on your bad side." Michelle laughed, as did Paul; they now had Jon Paul's home number, and they could call to ask Liz to help them get the coin from Jon Paul.

***

Mrs. Roux now began to worry about Jon Paul; she got up and knocked on his door and said, "Mr. Chavalier, can I speak with you for a moment?"

"Yeah, sure, come on in, Mrs. Roux." She walked into his office, and Jon Paul motioned for her to sit in a chair by his desk.

"So how can I help you, Mrs. Roux?"

"Well, I was just talking with a policewoman on the phone, and she told me there is an investigation going on right now that might involve you. I am worried about you; is everything okay?"

"An investigation about me? What did she say, exactly?"

"She wouldn't give details but said it involved someone you might know and that you were a possible source for her to follow up with."

"That is a bit strange. I don't know of any investigation going on that might involve me. What was her name?"

"She said it was Officer Durand."

"Hmm, Durand. I've never heard of her. Maybe she just transferred from another branch."

"I don't know, but if I could go back to my desk, I have a lot of work to do."

"Of course, Mrs. Roux. If this officer calls again, please let me know. I wish to speak with her."

"I will, right away, Mr. Chavalier."

Jon Paul sat at his desk and wondered if this was just a strange day or if there was something in the air that was not quite normal. There *was* something strange in the air. Jon Paul didn't know it, but his life was about to change, dramatically.

***

Michelle and Paul now had the number to Jon Paul's home; they were going to call Liz to ask for her help, something that might not be so easy. After all, Jon Paul is her life; she would give all she had for him. As they sat and thought about what to say, the words came easily for them. The task of retrieving the coin would not be so easy, but Paul and Michelle had something special about them: they were blessed by heaven.

"Paul, I was thinking about what we might say to Liz."

"What did you come up with, Michelle?"

"*Me*? What did *you* come up with?"

"Well, Michelle, I was thinking we should just be honest with her. That is probably the best way."

"That is what I was thinking, too, Paul!"

"Okay, then, we will call her and just explain to her that the coin is cursed, although I am sure she knows this. Then we will just tell her about how the coin corrupts every man that holds it. Maybe her love for Jon Paul will be enough for her to give it to us."

"Maybe, Paul. That is a big gamble, but with Seraphiel on our side, I am sure it will all work out like it is supposed to. We just need to have faith." Paul smiled at Michelle, who was right; they needed to have faith. Everything would work itself out the way it was supposed to.

Paul looked at Michelle and said, "Well, are you ready?"

"Ready? I don't know. Give me a minute, please."

"Okay, honey, take your time; we will call when you are ready."

Michelle took a deep breath and slowly let it out; she was about to call Liz, and this would not be easy. Paul dialed the phone number for her, handed her the phone, and smiled, hopefully instilling a little confidence in her. It worked.

"Hello."

"Hello, can I speak with Liz Bourg, please?"

"Who is calling, please?"

"This is Michelle Dubois; is she available?"

"I shall check. Hold the line, please." Mr. Falid contacted Liz on the intercom. She had been in her room reading some new book that had her spellbound.

"Yes, Mr. Falid, what is it?"

"A phone call for you, ma'am, a Ms. DuBois."

"Okay, thank you, Mr. Falid, be right there." Liz walked over to her dressing room and sat down on the chair. "Hello, this is Liz."

"Hello, Liz, it's Michelle."

"Michelle? Oh—Michelle from Jon Paul's past?"

"Yes, the very same."

"How did you get this number? It shouldn't be available to the public."

"Oh, never mind that, I need to talk to you about Jon Paul. I think he is in danger, and so are you."

"Danger? What danger? What is this about?"

"Liz, it is about that evil coin of his. We have found out that no matter the man, it will eventually corrupt him and turn him evil."

"How do you know this?"

"We have had contact with a source that is indisputable!"

"And what would be this source that is so exact?" asked Liz.

"You wouldn't believe me if I told you."

"Well, it is your time. Try me."

"Do you believe in angels, Liz?"

"Angels—what does that have to do with anything?"

"That is my source; an angel named Seraphiel has said it is so. She explained that Jon Paul was in danger and we needed to do something."

"I think you are crazy! An angel named Seraphiel, really."

"Yes, that is the God's honest truth."

"I don't believe you. Prove it to me."

"I can't right now. Will you give me some time to prove it?" Michelle pleaded with her.

Chapter 14

— •●• —

DESTRUCTION

"Time to prove it? If you can prove it to me, I will listen to your story."

"Thank you, Liz, thank you! Jon Paul really is in trouble; can you promise me you won't tell him I called?"

"I will give you two days. If you can't prove it to me in that time, I never want to hear from you again, is that clear?"

"Perfectly. I will call you in two days' time to give you my proof; remember, this is about Jon Paul and his life. If you really love him, do the right thing and keep an open mind."

"You have two days. Good-bye." Liz hung up the phone.

Michelle looked at Paul and said, "How are we going to prove it to her?"

Paul looked just as perplexed as Michelle as he said, "I don't know right now, but at least we have two days to figure it out!"

***

Liz wondered just how and why this woman from the past was going to prove to her that an angel had told her Jon Paul was in trouble. She never was very religious, and throughout her life, she had never really had any proof that there were such things as angels. As Liz sat there, she started to feel like something had been truthful about Michelle's statement. After all, she had just been a witness to the awesome power of the coin as Jon Paul killed a man who was standing right in front of her. She thought maybe Michelle was telling the truth; maybe Jon Paul was really in trouble. What could she do if this was true? Maybe she could help him with it, somehow, someway.

***

"That was good, Michelle; what did she say?"

"Well, she gave us two days, as you heard, to prove that Seraphiel really did talk with us and warn us that Jon Paul is in danger."

"Okay, I think for now, let's just take everything slow. We need to contact Seraphiel and ask her what to do about this. Do you think if we just call out to her, she will appear?"

"I don't know, Paul. I don't think angels are at our beck and call."

"You may be right. How about this: we will go to the church and pray for her return to answer our questions. Does that sound good?"

"Yeah, Paul, that does. I think that would be a good way to prove our faith."

Paul and Michelle were going to go to church to pray for the return of Seraphiel. This guardian angel would hopefully provide them a way or an answer as to how to prove to Liz that what she had been told was true.

***

Jon Paul sat at his desk and looked over some documents that he needed to sign. Most were simple things, like where to send this amount of money to whatever fund or to help this organization with some financial means; his workday was not always about political matters. As the day drew to a close, Jon Paul shut down his PC and grabbed his coat and briefcase. He walked out to his secretary's desk and stopped. He looked at her for a second and said, "Mrs. Roux, I don't think I will be in the rest of the week. I am going to just work from home; it has been a long week so far, and I am tired. If you need anything, just call me at home."

"Yes, Mr. Chavalier. Say hi to Miss Bourg, please."

Jon Paul smiled, nodded, and walked out the doors to the elevators; he was ready to go home and see Liz.

***

256

Liz had walked out to the greenhouse; oftentimes, when she was upset, she would go and look at the flowers and smell the beautiful fragrance of so many prize-winning roses. Jon Paul had a special touch with gardening; perhaps it was a gift he never knew he had until he planted some flowers and found out. The greenhouse was set at the back of their house; it opened up to the backyard, which faced the forest and the open land of Jon Paul's estate. It was a rather large greenhouse compared to others; the windows rose up to the height of the second-story balcony that looked out over the yard. The glass doors let in sunlight, as there were no trees to block it, and the flowers and other plants that Jon Paul had planted did extremely well. It always had lots of oxygen to breathe and it always made Liz feel better and relaxed. She sat down on a wicker bench and began to think about what Michelle had told her.

***

Jon Paul got in his car and started the engine; it fired to life as he pushed the pedal, and he sped out of the garage and into the street. He turned into traffic and headed for the freeway that would lead to his house in the country. As he drove, he thought about how his life had been before Liz, how he had thought he was happy with Michelle, but sometimes it was like they were two strangers sharing similar space. He didn't understand why it was that way, but maybe it had something to do with his past.

***

Liz sat in the wicker chair enjoying the sounds of nature; suddenly, she was aware that it had become very quiet. She listened, and as she sat there, all the birds that had just been singing and other sounds of the insects had gone; there were no sounds at all. *What is happening?* Thought Liz. *This is very strange; why am I not able to hear anything?* Just as suddenly as the sounds had disappeared, she was keenly aware that someone was watching her. The small hairs on the back of her neck stood up, and she thought, *who could be here, if anyone?* Mr. Falid was somewhere else in the house, so it couldn't be him, and she could see the door to the backyard and there was no one there. Still, Liz could not shake the feeling that she was being watched.

***

Paul and Michelle drove to the church, where they were going to ask the angel Seraphiel to appear to them so they could ask her what they should do about Liz and her demands. Although Michelle and Paul were not regular attendees of the church, they were firm believers in God. They arrived at the church, parked the car, and entered the big double doors. They walked up to the front of the church, and as they knelt before the altar, they reached out and held each other's hands.

"Michelle, I love you so much, and I want you to know that this means more to me than anything we could ever do."

Michelle teared up and said, "Thanks, Paul, you know I feel the same; ever since we found each other, I have been happier then I could have ever imagined. I love you with all my heart."

They smiled at each other and then bowed their heads and began a silent prayer to the angel Seraphiel.

***

Liz was cautiously looking around for what could have caused her to have this strange feeling, and just as she was turning her head to the right, she noticed something approaching her. She turned, fully aware, and saw something she could not believe—a white-colored figure was walking toward her. It seemed to be coming downstairs, and as it took the last step, it fully materialized and walked toward her. She sat there, totally transfixed; she stared at the angel.

"Hello, Liz Bourg. I am Seraphiel the angel. I come to you to tell you that what Michelle Duvalier has told you is true. The man you love is corrupted by the coin of the Jinn. He is in danger of losing his immortal soul forever to the dark. You must find a way to retrieve the coin from him."

"How … how can I do such a thing? I am not strong enough to take it from him." Liz found it hard to speak to the angel.

"You have been given a choice; you can take the coin, or you can perish with him and lose yourself forever."

"But … but … how? I mean, can you tell me how?"

"There will come a time when you will be given an opportunity; do not let it pass!" the angel replied sternly.

"Okay, I will be given this opportunity, but when will I know it is time?"

"You will know. It is written. The time approaches fast, and the final battle is not yet written, but you must get the coin and save humanity."

"Save humanity? No pressure, Seraphiel—I have to save humanity? Wow, are you sure I am the right person for that?"

"Indeed, Liz Bourg. Your destiny was written long ago, and you shall do this. It is commanded!"

"Okay, sorry. I will do my best to get the coin from Jon Paul, but what do I do with it then?"

"It is written; it shall be given to the ones."

"What do you mean 'the ones'? Are you talking about Jon Paul's ex, Michelle?" Liz asked.

"Yes, you shall give them the coin, and they, in turn, shall give it to me."

Liz stared at the angel, who was beginning to fade to a mist. As she watched it fade and eventually disappear, she thought, *this is great; how am I going to take his coin?* The thought of going up against Jon Paul was frightening for her, she had watched him kill a man without even blinking, and she was sure Jon Paul would do the same to anyone in a heartbeat; he was ruthless and evil, just like the angel had said. Liz still loved Jon Paul with all of her heart, but now she had doubts as to their future; an angel appearing and telling you that you need to take something from your love is not an easy thing to deal with. She felt shock and fear, as the idea of battling against him was scary. She turned around to go back into the house to get a drink, and she walked in an almost dream-like state of disbelief. She continued her walk all the way to the lower level, where there was a bar and a place to sit down and think about what she had just witnessed.

***

Paul and Michelle continued their prayer for several moments; no one disturbed them, as it was quiet and the priest that saw them only smiled and waved at them as if to say, *"It is okay for you to be here."* When they had finished their prayer, they stood up and looked around; there were several other people milling about, and they drew little to no attention to themselves. They walked out of the church and to the car.

"Michelle that was a very good thing we did. I think Seraphiel heard us, and I hope she will be showing up soon."

"What do you mean 'showing up soon'? Didn't you hear what she said?"

"Hear what she said? I didn't hear anything."

"Oh, Paul, it was the most beautiful thing; she appeared right there, above the front of the altar. Didn't you see her?"

"Really, Michelle? I didn't see or hear anything; maybe it was only for you."

"Maybe it was, if you didn't see her or hear her, but I did." Michelle was right; the angel had only appeared for her benefit. It was as if the message intended for only Michelle had been something special, and it was.

Paul and Michelle were both feeling rather elated about what had just happened in the church, even though Paul did not see the angel Seraphiel and Michelle did. It gave her a special message that no one else was aware of, a message that might spell the downfall of one Jon Paul Chavalier.

As Paul started the car and began the drive back to his apartment, Michelle was noticing that some things had changed for her. She felt stronger than usual, her mind was as sharp as a tack, and her awareness of her surroundings had been enhanced, or so it seemed to her. Paul, noticing the change in Michelle, looked at her and said, "Hey, Michelle, are you okay? I mean, are you feeling strange or something after your talk with Seraphiel?"

"No, I am fine, actually, Paul; in fact, better than fine. I feel great! I am ready to take on the world!"

Michelle was indeed fine. She was energized by the angel Seraphiel, and it showed; the angel was prepping Michelle for the final battle.

***

Jon Paul pulled into his long driveway, feeling a bit of relief from the city traffic, which was always murder with its long, congested lines and bad drivers, but that was city life. He saw his groundskeeper, waved at him, and said, "Hello, Mr. Bestion. How are you this evening?"

"Fine, sir. How was your day?"

"Oh, you know, I am glad to be out of the city; in fact, I am working from home the rest of the week."

"That will be nice, sir. Do you have any plans to use the cars this week?"

"As of right now, I have no plans, but things can always change!"

"How true, sir, how true." Jon Paul smiled at his groundskeeper and walked up to his house to find Liz. He walked quickly to the house, and as he entered through the huge front door, Mr. Falid greeted him with an open smile and said, "Hello, sir, how was your day?"

"My day was fine, Mr. Falid, but I am tired and wondering if you have something to eat that is not too much trouble for you to prepare."

"Indeed I do, sir; I prepared lasagna with spicy Italian sausage and a salad on the side. I also have fresh garlic bread I just baked earlier today."

"Not too much trouble? Mr. Falid, that sounds like a lot of work to me."

"Not at all, sir; it is already prepared. If you will give me a few moments, I can have it ready for you on the dining room table."

"Thanks, Mr. Falid. I am going upstairs to find Miss Bourg and see her first; then we will both be down to eat dinner."

"Very good, sir. I can have it ready in about fifteen minutes, is that acceptable?"

"It is. We will see you in about fifteen minutes." Jon Paul turned from his servant and walked up the grand staircase that led to his room. He wanted to find his love, Liz, and talk with her.

Jon Paul entered his room and was surprised to find that Liz was not there; he checked her dressing room, and then he checked her bathroom, but to his amazement, there was no Liz. He wondered where she was. He decided to call her on the house intercom.

"Liz, where are you?"

After a few seconds had passed, her voice came on the intercom. "I am here, downstairs at the bar, Jon Paul."

"Okay, I am coming down. Be right there." Jon Paul cleaned up a little bit and headed downstairs to his bar. As he descended the giant staircase, he saw Liz sitting at their bar, sipping a drink; she seemed sad to him.

"Hello, Liz, how are you?"

"I am fine, can't you see?"

"Yes, I can see; are you feeling all right, Lizzy?"

"Fine, Jon Paul," she said sarcastically.

"Liz, Mr. Falid is preparing a meal for us right now; are you hungry?"

"Not really, but I will go up with you and sit there."

"Okay, what did I do now?"

"Nothing, Jon Paul. I am feeling a little down and thought I would have a drink. Is that okay with you?"

"Sure thing, honey, I think I will join you!" Jon Paul walked around to the back of the bar, grabbed a glass, and poured himself a scotch.

"Mmm, now that is good." He said, smacking his lips. "Nothing like a stiff drink to wake you up!"

Liz stared at him, surprised at his juvenile behavior; she wondered why she never noticed this before.

***

Paul and Michelle drove back to his apartment. They didn't stop to eat or drink; Paul felt they needed to be home in case the angel Seraphiel showed up. Upon arriving at Paul's apartment, he parked the car and helped Michelle out, and they walked up to the building.

"Paul, I don't know why exactly, but Seraphiel has given me an inner courage that I never had before; I feel great!"

"I can tell, my dear, you are glowing!"

Michelle smiled at Paul and said, "Paul, I am thirsty, do you want anything to drink with me?"

"Yeah, sure, what are you thinking about?"

"Umm, how about a soda?"

"Sounds good to me, Michelle." Michelle walked into the kitchen, opened the fridge, grabbed two cans of Coke, and brought them to the living room, where Paul was sitting there waiting for her.

***

Jon Paul and Liz walked upstairs to the dining room, which was adjacent to the kitchen and just down the hall from the formal living room. Mr. Falid had set their table with the very nice china and had the meal ready for them to eat; as they sat down, Jon Paul looked at Liz and said, "You know something, Liz? You have never looked better!"

Liz had been feeling down and had her doubts about the two of them, but she loved Jon Paul with all of her heart, and she was willing to do anything to make their relationship work.

"Thanks, Jon Paul, I am starting to feel better." Mr. Falid served them dinner and then retreated back to the kitchen. Liz said, "Jon Paul, let me ask you a question. Do you think you have changed because of the coin?"

"What do you mean, Liz? Have I changed in spite of the coin or because of the coin?"

"Yes."

"Um, I think, because of the power of the coin, it has simply helped me to bring all my inner desires to the surface—some good, some maybe bad. The coin has brought us many things that we never had before, and that is a blessing. So to answer your question, yes; because of the coin, I have changed."

"I see. So, is it for the better?"

"Of course, my dear, what do you think?"

"I don't know, Jon Paul, that is why I am asking."

"Well, rest assured, everything is fine, and we will be fine too." Liz sat back and nibbled on some of her food; she was not too hungry, and Jon Paul noticed. For the rest of their meal, they sat in silence; the only sounds were those of them eating.

"Liz, I was thinking about watching a movie downstairs in the rec room. Will you accompany me?"

"Sure, Jon Paul. I will watch a movie with you; do you really have to even ask?"

Jon Paul smiled at Liz, and when they finished eating, they got up and went downstairs to their rec room. Jon Paul searched his vast library for a movie to watch.

After several moments of searching, he settled on *Beverly Hills Cop*, an early Eddie Murphy movie. He opened the DVD player and put it in.

***

Paul and Michelle were sipping their drinks when Paul said, "Hey, Michelle, you know what we should do?"

Michelle, intrigued, said, "No, what, Paul?"

"Have you ever played chess?"

"Um, no, I never have learned how to."

"Well, then, this is your lucky day; you and I are going to play a game of chess." Paul was excited; he was a very good chess player. Oftentimes, when Jon Paul was still his best friend, they had enjoyed a cup of tea while they played chess. Paul was very confident in his abilities, but Jon Paul had always been a little bit better than he was. For some reason not known to Paul, his old friend could always find a way to win; however, it was not the same when they used to play darts or even pool, which usually was an even match. He set up the board and chose his side of the table. Michelle was already sitting down where Paul had set up the game.

***

Jon Paul and Liz sat in their recreation room and watched the movie, and although they were only a foot apart in different chairs, Liz felt miles away from Jon Paul; her mind wandered as to how she would get his coin.

***

Paul and Michelle were playing chess when suddenly, Paul jumped up and said, "Michelle, I think I know what happened!"

Michelle jumped at his sudden movement, stared at him, and said, "What are you talking about?"

"Do you remember me telling you about the dream I had the other day? You know, the one where I was a soldier in some camp in some war long forgotten?"

"Yeah, sort of."

"Well, that is where I first met Jon Paul. I mean, not the Jon Paul that we know now, but in his former life as my general in that war."

"Paul, I am lost. What do you mean?"

"Years ago, in a past life, I was a soldier in a war, and Jon Paul was the general. He had the coin then too, but not at first! He was like any other soldier; we struggled with our battles and we lost sometimes, but then, after some time in the desert at the front lines of a battle with the Ottoman Empire, we got to be victorious. Jon Paul began to have success at each and every battle.

He had changed from a mediocre general to one that was a brilliant genius! That was the power of the coin influencing him. I remember one day, I was in his tent talking strategies with him and he had this flash of light in his eyes; it was like he was illuminated with some sort of inner divine genius. It was scary. I saw him change but I didn't know how or why. He had become powerful and dangerous. Most of the men in the camp saw it too."

"How do you know this, Paul?"

"I don't know, Michelle. It was like a door was just opened in my head, revealing my past; it is all so clear. I know what we must do with the coin." Paul had been granted a vision and memory of his past life with Jon Paul—a life that was spent fighting in a war in which he was only a soldier, but one that he knew was important.

"Paul, do you think it will be safe to get the coin?"

"Yes, it should be; your angel Seraphiel has said it so. We just need to trust her and it will all be fine."

"I know, Paul, and you are right, but I am still a little worried. I don't want to lose you." Michelle looked at Paul and smiled a gentle smile, a smile that told him she loved him with all her heart.

***

As the movie Jon Paul and Liz had been watching came to an end, Jon Paul stood up and opened the DVD player. He put the movie away, looked at Liz, and said, "What do you want to do now?"

"Um, I don't know; what do you want to do?"

"How about a game of pool? You know, you still haven't evened the score."

"Well, Mr. Jon Paul, you set 'em up, and I will finally win this time!" Liz was doing better; she felt that the pressures of the angel commanding her to get the coin from Jon Paul had lessened from earlier. She had enjoyed the movie and the laughter had set her mind at ease; she now was thinking more clearly and more rationally.

"You know, Jon Paul, I am going to win this time!"

"Are you now? Well, we will just see about that!"

Liz smiled at Jon Paul confidently, letting him know she was serious about her game. She had been practicing recently and was getting good.

Liz broke the rack and watched several different pool balls drop into different pockets. She smiled. Jon Paul was not ready for that, and he looked a bit surprised as Liz began to make several shots that he didn't think she should make. He thought she must have been practicing. *Damn her, I am going to have to really play now,* he thought. And he was right, Liz had been practicing and she was getting a good eye for pool; Jon Paul was in trouble.

Jon Paul and Liz played their game of pool almost as well as professionals; both made amazing shots till just about at the end of the game, when Liz smilingly said, "Well, Jon Paul, I think that will be eight ball in the corner pocket."

"Okay, if you really think you can make that shot, although I would probably go long with it instead." Jon Paul was playing Liz, trying to make her take a more difficult shot instead of the one she was planning. As she shot, the cue ball rolled perfectly toward the eight ball, and it hit and went in. Liz had finally won a game against Jon Paul.

"Wow, that was amazing! I have never seen you shoot so well; have you been practicing?"

"To tell you the truth, Jon Paul, I have been; I didn't think it would be so easy. Aren't you proud of me?"

"You know, I am, Lizzy; you have become a really good pool player." Jon Paul smiled at Liz and placed his pool cue in the holder on the wall. He looked at her and said, "I am going upstairs, Liz, you coming?"

"Of course, after I put my cue away." Liz and Jon Paul went back upstairs to their room. They would enjoy the night together as the pressures of the day melted away.

***

The memory of Paul's past had been given him by the angel Seraphiel; she had opened the door to his mind to help him see a time that was now long gone. Paul and Michelle continued playing their game of chess. With Paul teaching Michelle the beginnings of the game, she was a quick learner and took to the game fast, memorizing certain pieces and their powers like a pro.

"Paul, do you think you were given this look at your past for a certain reason?"

"Yeah, I do; like I was saying, I know what we have to do with the coin once we get it. It has been a long time in coming, but I am confident with my knowledge of what to do."

"What do we do, Paul?"

"Once we have the coin securely in hand, we go to the church and contact Seraphiel; she then will take the coin from us and do whatever it is that they will do with it."

"But don't we need to do something else with it?"

"No, our job is simple: get the coin to Seraphiel any way possible. I remember from my past that when Jon Paul was the general, there were some other men who decided to go against him; there were a few who thought the coin was evil, and they wanted to destroy it. I was one of those men; however, I didn't survive the battle. Jon Paul found out our plans, and I was caught and killed."

"You were killed?"

"Yes, I remember it clearly now. The problem we had back then was that we were not educated like we are now, so we couldn't grasp much in the way of subtlety or espionage. Sure, there were some bright individuals, but they were loyal to Jon Paul. He had them under his control and command; they were firm in their worship, so we planned to take it any way we could, and if that meant we would have to kill him, we would. That was the problem, though; he had so many followers that were loyal, which made it nearly impossible to take the coin.

"After I was killed, though, the other men planned to take the coin by distracting Jon Paul; he loved women and always had his fill. There was one, however, that he never seemed to be able to get, the wife of our commander and king, who was Jon Paul's superior. He had always been enamored with her, but he never crossed the line, as far as I know, until he saw her bathing one day; that was the proverbial straw that broke the camel's back. He would say in private company that he was going to get her any way he could. I think that he respected his superior, though, which is why he never crossed that line until one day, when word came that his superior, the king, had been ambushed, and his life hung in the balance.

"I believe right then and there that Jon Paul decided to take his coin and try to have her for himself; one of our men suggested that he could help with this and summoned for the woman to be brought to Jon Paul's tent. She arrived, accompanied by one guard, and as he brought her in, Jon Paul motioned for her to sit and for the guard to leave. 'So, my lady, you are here by my request. I summoned you to ask you to do me a favor.'

'I have come, but not willingly; as you know, my husband is not long for this world. What would you have with me?'

Jon Paul stared at the woman; there were not many to rival her beauty. 'My request is a simple one; you are to give yourself to me and your husband will live.'

The queen laughed out loud at the insane request. 'Ha! Are you serious? Why would I agree to something so outrageous?'

'It is simple. Like I said, you agree to be with me and your husband lives.'

'How can you help my husband?'

'My lady, I have my ways. So what do you say? Precious minutes are slipping away in your husband's life.' The queen sat there and thought for a moment. *What if he can really help my husband? What if he is serious?*

'So tell me, my general, how can you help me, if I agree to this?'

'I have in my possession a certain object that allows me to do whatever I wish, and that includes helping your husband, my king.'

'A certain object—what is this object?'

Jon Paul looked at his queen and said, 'A magic coin.'

Again, she laughed in his face. 'A magic coin? You must be joking, General; who ever heard of a magic coin granting wishes?'

'I am serious; it is from the Jinn.' At this, the queen suddenly became very still and very quiet; she sat there in disbelief at what she had just heard. She knew of certain legends that told of a coin created by the Jinn that granted wishes but also had a curse attached to it.

'So you have this coin, General?'

'I do, my queen; it is in my possession right now.'

'May I see it?' Jon Paul reached in his robe and pulled out the golden coin; it shone in the lamp light like a yellow sun. The queen stared at the coin, mesmerized by it.

'So, my queen, you see, I do possess the coin of legend. Now, as to my request, what is your answer?'

The queen heard his voice, looked at him, and said, 'If what the legends say are true, I will stay with you tonight, providing your every wish, if you agree to help my husband, your king.'

'I will, my queen, and so, we are in agreement.' Jon Paul smiled a wicked smile. He had no plans on helping his king, and he wanted the throne for himself and the king's wife as his own. As time slipped away for the two of them, the queen, knowing that time was passing and each and every moment might prove fatal for the king, looked at Jon Paul and said, 'Will you help your king now? Time grows short for him, and I fear he might be losing this battle.'

'I will help, my queen.' Jon Paul, holding the coin in his hand and making sure the queen could see him doing it, said, 'I wish for the king to be dead and his throne to be mine!' The queen screamed in anger. She had been tricked by Jon Paul, and now there was nothing she could do.

The king died at that very moment, and Jon Paul was now the new king. Jon Paul's laughter rung out in the night; he had tricked the queen, taken the throne, and placed himself in the most powerful position in all the land. He was unstoppable—or so he thought.

The other guards, hearing the queen scream, came running into Jon Paul's tent; fearing the worst. They saw the queen crying and their general smiling; the soldiers were then waved off. As Jon Paul sent the soldiers away, he looked at the queen with contempt; she was nothing but a whore for Jon Paul now. He would place himself on the king's throne, marry the queen, and become king himself.

A few of the soldiers that were not loyal to Jon Paul had heard about what he did and vowed to kill him in any way possible. Three soldiers came up with a plan to cause a distraction in or near Jon Paul's tent, rush him, and kill him, ending his reign of terror; they knew he was evil, and they would not stand for it. The three men gathered at the back of Jon Paul's tent. One agreed to walk in and cause the distraction as the other two rushed in, stabbed Jon Paul, and then freed the queen. They would all then run back out of the tent. As the lone man approached the entrance to the tent, he heard no noise; it was quiet.

He boldly walked in and, seeing his general, said, 'My general, excuse the interruption. I have urgent news.' The other two men heard this, ran in the tent, and rushed Jon Paul. They caught him by surprise and killed him with knives; they stabbed him repeatedly till he was lifeless. The queen watched this with widened eyes, and then she thanked the three men and promised them a special place in her kingdom. This is the story as I remember it now. It is history and one can find it in the dusty old pages of books."

"That is an amazing story, Paul. I have never heard of such a tale. You lived this life and you remember it all?"

"I do remember; it is so very clear for me, Michelle."

"Wow, I wonder why you were given access to such past knowledge?"

"I don't know, maybe to help with the coin somehow." Paul was right; he was shown his past life with the coin and Jon Paul to give him some sort of experience to learn from. He had made a mistake last time and it cost him his life; this time, hopefully, would be different.

***

Many months had passed since Jon Paul had talked with anyone from his family; after his election to office and his incredible rise to the top of the UMP, he had become very hard to get a hold of. Neither his mother nor his father had spoken with him, and even his young sister Sara had not been in communication with him.

Sara, concerned about her brother, said, "Dad, I am going to try to call Jon Paul again today. Is there anything you want me to say to him?"

"Just ask him if he is okay. God knows we worry about him now more than ever, especially being where he is in office."

"Okay, Dad, I will." Sara went into the kitchen of her mother's house to get a quick snack before calling Jon Paul's office.

"You know something, honey, we should maybe take a drive in to town to see Jon Paul. I mean, we haven't spoken to him in months," said Sara's father.

"If you think it best. I think a nice drive to see Jon Paul would be wonderful!" her mother replied.

"Okay, then, after Sara finishes with the phone, I will tell her to leave a message at his office that we are coming to visit." Jon Paul's father had a plan to visit him in the city; they would drive there to Toulon, spend the night at a hotel, and visit their son Jon Paul. Sara had just finished eating a sandwich when her father came in.

"Hi, sweetie, have you called Jon Paul's office yet?"

"Not yet, Daddy, I was just about to."

"Good. I want you to leave a message for him that your mother and I are going to drive to Toulon tomorrow to see him at his office."

"Sure thing, Daddy. I think I am ready to try and call him." Sara smiled at her father, who smiled back; they would indeed speak with Jon Paul this day. As Sara dialed Jon Paul's office, she reflected back on how many fun times they had as young children; she missed him.

"Hello, Mr. Chavalier's office, how can I help you?"

"Hi, this is Sara, Jon Paul's sister; is he in today?"

"He is working at home today."

"Oh, okay, I will try him there, thanks."

Sara hung up the phone and dialed Jon Paul's house.

Jon Paul picked up the phone and said, "Hi."

"Hi, Jon Paul, it is me. How are you?"

"I am good, Sara, just so damn busy with everything, you know."

"Yeah, you need to call more often. We haven't spoken to you in so long. Mom and Dad are worried you are working too hard."

"Sorry, sis, but this job requires so much from me, and most of my time is very busy. I will try to call more often. How are Mom and Dad?"

"Mom is fine; you know, she stays busy around the house trying to keep it clean. Dad just keeps on doing what he does best, lots of household chores and making a mess for Mom." She chuckled.

"That is funny, Sara. Dad does like to make a mess. Glad to hear they are okay."

"Um, by the way, they are driving out tomorrow to see you at your office; they are going to spend the night in Toulon and then drive back here."

"*Tomorrow*? Damn, I am working at home the rest of the week."

"Are you sure, Jon Paul?"

"Yeah, it is fine; do you know what time they will be here?"

"No, Dad didn't say what time, but if I have to guess, I would think early afternoon."

"Okay, that is good. I can get most of my work done by noon, so that would maybe free up my afternoon to spend with Mom and Dad."

"I am so happy to hear your voice, Jon Paul; everyone has missed you so much."

"I know, sis. I missed you too. Tell Mom and Dad I will see them tomorrow, and make sure they know to come here instead of my office."

"Okay, Jon Paul, take care. Call me."

"You got it, sis, bye."

Sara hung up the phone with a happy feeling and then walked out to the living room where her mom and dad were sitting and said, "Okay, Mom and Dad, Jon Paul will be expecting you early tomorrow afternoon at his house, not his office."

"Early tomorrow afternoon, okay; why, then, at his home, and not his office?"

"He is working at home the rest of the week, Daddy. I figured by the time you got ready and left, it would be after lunch, so early afternoon, is that okay?"

"That is perfect, sweetheart." Sara smiled at her father, who smiled in return; it would be a good day for Sara till she had to go home.

***

As Jon Paul sat back in his big executive chair, he reflected back on a much simpler time in his short life, a time when he was not known globally, a time when he was just Jon Paul.

***

Liz had seen an archangel, which was something she had never thought she would see in her life, let alone talk with one. As she sat thinking about what Seraphiel had told her about her love, Jon Paul, she began to think about just how much danger she could be in if she was to do something wrong or upset him in some way. God knew, it had been great for a long time now, but if she slipped up and Jon Paul was to use the coin … she shuddered to think what might happen next. Right then and there, Liz decided she would do what the angel asked. Hopefully, Jon Paul would not get hurt and they could continue their lives just as they were, except without the dreaded coin.

***

Sara got in her car and began the drive back home to her husband, Claude; the drive was not too far for her, though for some, it might've seemed long. Sara used the time to unwind behind the wheel as she drove back home. Her husband, Claude, was a good man. He worked at a law office and made a good living for them; she never had a want or need for anything. As she drove down the highway, she noticed a car had pulled over and had the hazard lights flashing a little way in front of her. She decided to slow down and see if she might be able to help. Sara was a trusting woman, and this was a good part of the outskirts of the city. She slowed her car and stopped behind the other car, where two people were waving at her; she got out and calmly walked over to the man and woman. She was a good judge of character and thought these two were just having a bit of bad luck.

"Hi, do you need some help?" she asked.

"Yeah, the car seems to have died right here on the highway. We could use a hand."

"Sure, what can I do?" asked Sara.

The man walked slowly and calmly toward Sara, and he smiled at her. Suddenly, he grabbed her by her arms, and his woman friend opened the door of their car and then helped him wrestle Sara into the backseat, where they handcuffed her and put a rag soaked with sodium chloride over her mouth till she passed out. Sara was in trouble.

"Did you secure her hands?"

"Yeah, I got 'em cuffed. How long will she be out?"

"Long enough for us to get her to the warehouse." He smiled the evil grin of a man with a plan.

***

Jon Paul sat and remembered his game from the previous night with his beloved Liz; she had been practicing and was getting quite good. *No wonder,* he thought, *she doesn't do much anymore, so she must be playing all day now.*

He vowed in his mind that he would make sure he was on top of his game so that he could win the next time they played. This had the strange effect of easing his wandering mind; his work was overloading him, and he needed a vacation, or so he thought.

***

Paul and Michelle had finished their game of chess, and Michelle had come very close to winning. Paul was so happy she was a quick learner; he wondered why he had waited so long to teach her.

"Paul, the next time we play, I want to make a bet with you."

"A bet? Do you think it wise, Michelle?" he said, grinning.

"Are you making fun? I am serious, Paul."

"Okay, okay, what do you want to bet?"

"I don't know, let me figure it out first, and then I will tell you." Michelle smiled at Paul, who winked at her. He knew she might just win, and this little game of chess was a good way to keep her occupied, keep her mind off of trying to get the coin from Jon Paul and waiting for Liz to call her back. Michelle had made her case to Liz and Liz had seen the archangel Seraphiel; Michelle didn't know it yet, but that would be a turning point in their lives. Seraphiel would her hear prayers and influence them through her dreams; sometimes, Michelle would do something in her waking life and she didn't understand why, but she knew it to be right.

***

"How much longer to the warehouse? I am getting a bit nervous."

"Don't worry your pretty little head. We are almost there."

These two kidnappers had done something very bad. Although they weren't sure who exactly they had kidnapped, they both knew there was a lot of money to be made from this. Selling women into the sex trade or even the Russian mafia was big business; one could get rich if the girl was just right. As they drove down the back roads of the city, they soon saw an abandoned warehouse, just out of sight of the road, unless you knew where it was.

"So what is the plan, Remy?"

"What is the plan? The plan is that we are going to contact some people I know and make some money. Is that enough of a plan for you, Margo?"

"You know it isn't, Remy. I never wanted to do this."

"You are doing this!"

Margo lowered her eyes and sat back in her seat; she didn't like the thug life she and Remy had gotten into, and she was afraid of him and what he might do.

Remy was a small-time criminal; he had a rap sheet—most of it filled with petty crimes—so when he came up with the idea of kidnapping someone and selling her for money to some crime syndicate, it seemed perfect to him, and fairly easy. Sara had just been in the wrong place at the wrong time, and now her life was in very grave danger. Remy and Margo pulled up to the warehouse and stopped.

"Go open the gate, Margo!"

Margo got out and opened the gate, and Remy pulled in; he stopped a few feet after that to let her back in. They pulled forward to a huge metal door, and as they stopped and parked next to it, Remy looked around with cautious eyes. He noticed all was clear, so he opened the side door to the warehouse, went in, and then opened the big door.

"Margo, pull the car in so I can close the door!" he shouted.

"Okay, I will."

Margo got in the car, pulled it into the warehouse, and parked it. She looked back at Sara still passed out in the backseat.

"Hey, Remy, what do we do now?"

"Let's move her to the office and check out who she is."

They opened the door and lifted Sara out, carried her to the office, and strapped her to a chair. The whole place smelled bad. It was a mess, with papers on the floor, broken furniture, and broken windows. Remy began searching Sara's things; she had a driver's license and a few euros too, and a credit card and some makeup. As he looked at her license, he noticed something odd: her last name Chavalier, hyphenated and then her last name Pouisant. He knew that name, but where had he seen it? Remy searched his limited mind for the answer. Margo looked at the license too and, seeing the name, she immediately jumped up and said, "Do you know who this is?"

"Um, no, who?"

"This is Jon Paul Chavalier's sister!"

"His sister? How do you know?"

"I remember I was reading the news the other day about how well he is doing in the UMP. At least, I think this is his sister."

"If this is really his sister, baby, we have it made! He will pay a million to get her back, and then we are rich!" Margo smiled at Remy and gave him a big hug. Margo had never known true love; she grew up with an alcoholic mother, a father who was never there, and a life just a short drop away from poverty. They struggled to have food on the table and some nice clothes to wear. Oftentimes, when her mother wasn't around, she prostituted herself on the city streets. She never knew her father, at least in the strictest sense of the word; he was only there every few weeks, and then he would disappear for months at a time. When he was there, her mother and father would fight constantly.

At fifteen years of age, Margo ran away from the troubled mess and found herself selling her body for money to men. One day, while she was in a convenience store, a man came in with his face covered in a mask; it was Remy. Immediately, she found his forward commands and confident nature attractive; maybe he reminded her of her father. He proceeded to rob the store of the little cash it had and ran out of the store to safety. Margo followed him; compelled by his presence, she called to him, and he stopped.

From that moment on, they had found each other and been committed to one another. Remy had been in and out of foster homes since he was a child; he had anger issues and never was quite at home with any one of his foster homes. He had found petty crime exciting and had a large rap sheet, being busted many times for theft, robbery, assault, and several other misdemeanor offenses. Because he was a minor at the time of most of these offenses, he never did spend much time in jail; he had served a few months in a juvenile facility, but never a prison. Remy had also found a crime family and some members that would talk with him on occasion, even giving him harmless jobs to do. He was well on his way to a life of crime—or worse. Remy and Margo floated around Toulon and oftentimes would spend the nights in old, abandoned warehouses; since the one they were in now was found by Remy a while ago, he knew it was a safe place to hide out.

"So what do we do now, Remy?"

"I need to call someone, maybe find out if we can set up a deal."

"What do you mean, Remy?"

"*Never mind*, I will handle everything. You just watch her!"

"Okay, Remy." Margo sat down next to Sara in an old office chair, she watched her until Sara began to stir.

"*Remy*, come quick; she is beginning to wake!"

"Blindfold her. I don't want her seeing our faces!"

Margo wrapped a handkerchief around Sara's eyes, blinding her from their faces.

As Sara came to, she struggled to comprehend what had happened to her. She knew something really bad was happening, and she was scared; she didn't know what to do.

"Hello, is anybody there?"

Margo sat in silence watching her.

"Hello, please, can anyone hear me?"

"Sit still and be quiet!"

"I ... I ... why am I here? Who are you?"

"I told you, be quiet!" Margo was looking at Remy, who seemed a bit confused as to what to do. He motioned for her to join him in the hall away from the office where Sara was being held.

"Listen, we need to figure out what we can do with her; I made a call to a friend, and he is going to help us with this."

"How is he going to help us?"

"I don't know, Margo, we just need to sit tight till he gets here; then we will find out what to do."

Margo smiled at her man and gave him complete trust. She loved it when he told her what to do. The man that Remy had called was a low figure in the mafia; he was driving out to the warehouse to help them figure out how to make some easy money with this woman. Kidnapping was not so serious an offense to him, but it could be very lucrative if carried out to completion.

***

Liz walked the halls of her estate; she found that this had a way of easing her spirit for a short period of time. She was still confused and a bit in shock at having actually spoken with an angel. Although Jon Paul was home, she was avoiding him, as she needed this time to think and arrange her thoughts. She found herself in the kitchen and she sat down at the counter on her favorite barstool. She heard Mr. Falid walking into the kitchen from the adjacent butler's pantry.

"Good evening, Miss Bourg. Is there anything I can do for you?"

"Um, no … well, maybe just some advice."

"Of course, anything you need, Miss Bourg."

As Liz began to talk with Mr. Falid about her experience, she left out the part about seeing the archangel; she felt that would be a bit too much, so she talked to him without being very specific. "So that is what I am thinking; what should I do, Mr. Falid?"

"You must do what is right in your heart. Trust that you will know what is right and that you will do what is right."

"Thank you, Mr. Falid, I do know. I am just a little scared."

"All will be as it is supposed to be, for it was written long ago." Mr. Falid smiled at Liz and walked away, leaving her to her thoughts. She would have a very restless night.

***

Paul got up and walked into his kitchen. He had had a relaxing evening with his love, Michelle, teaching her to play chess and even agreeing to make a small bet with her for fun. Michelle was serious about it; she would bet something that meant so very much to her that a price could not be set.

***

The morning broke with beautiful rays of golden sunshine; the sky was clear and the temperature warm. This fine day would change the lives of so many. As Jon Paul's mother and father woke and began their day, his mother had a strange feeling that something was not quite right with the world. Something was wrong.

"Frederick, tell me something. Why does it feel like something is wrong?"

"What are you saying, Elysse? Something is wrong—what on earth do you mean?"

"I don't know; I feel like something is wrong. Maybe someone is in trouble."

"Who could be in trouble?"

Jon Paul's mother was right; someone was in trouble. Her daughter, Sara, was in grave danger.

"Listen, honey, just get some breakfast ready, and we will go see Jon Paul. Everything will be all right."

"Okay, Frederick, I will, but maybe you could just call and see if he's all right."

"Sure, dear, I will do that while you cook breakfast." He smiled at his loving wife and walked out of the kitchen, but Frederick would not call anyone.

***

"Morning, you, how did you sleep?" asked Paul.

"I slept perfect, sweetie." Smiling at Paul, Michelle got up and put on her robe, walked down to the kitchen, and started cooking the morning meal. Soon, Paul was walking into his kitchen, and as Michelle cooked them breakfast, he opened the fridge and got out some juice for them. Oftentimes, he would help Michelle cook, even though she was such a fine chef.

"I wonder if we will hear from Liz today?" asked Michelle.

"I don't know. We should, I hope."

"Do you think the angel heard us pray?"

"I am sure, Michelle; just be patient. They have an agenda that we cannot know, and when the time is right, she will contact us." Michelle nodded in agreement with Paul; he was right, but she felt that she needed to say what was on her mind.

***

Remy and Margo sat in silence. They stared at Sara, not knowing what to do with her. As soon as Remy's contact arrived, he would help them; after all, he was a thug for the Russian mafia.

"Did you hear that? Sounds like someone is here," asked Margo.

Remy got up and slowly and silently crept to the side door, opening it just a little to peek out to see who or what the noise was. He saw an old friend, Louis Moreau. Louis was a hardened criminal who had spent years in and out of prison. He had made many contacts in the Toulon prison, known as one of the worst in all of southern France. Louis Moreau had met Remy years ago in the back alleys and streets of Toulon; he was just a punk then, and he had not changed much. He had grown into a man, but his dangerous and drifting way of life was still with him.

Remy opened the door for Louis to enter; he waved at Remy to open the big door so he could park his car inside. Remy did as he was told.

"Hurry up and close that door!" shouted Louis. "You never know if someone's looking."

Remy closed the big door, and as soon as Louis was in, he parked the car next to Remy's and got out. "So, you have something for me to see?"

"Yes, and she is something of value, if I say so myself."

"I will be the judge of that, Remy." Louis followed Remy to the old, dirty office where they were keeping Sara; he walked up to her, staring at her as he sat down in the chair next to her.

"Have you searched her, Remy?"

"Yes, she had some money, a credit card, and other ID."

Remy handed the personal belongings to Louis so he could examine them. Upon seeing her driver's license, an evil smile crossed Louis's face as he looked at Remy. "You know something, kid, you might have just made it to the big time!" Remy smiled and glanced at Margo, and she smiled in return.

***

Liz and Jon Paul walked downstairs to the kitchen to eat some breakfast. The night before had been nothing special for either of them. Liz had not slept well and was looking forward to a perfectly made breakfast by Mr. Falid.

"God, I am so hungry this morning, Jon Paul." Jon Paul nodded in agreement with Liz.

"Yeah, I am hungry too, Liz." As the two sat down at the kitchen table, appearing as if on cue was Mr. Falid; he was carrying a tray with two sizzling plates of eggs benedict, with two small glasses of orange juice and some freshly brewed vanilla-flavored coffee. He set the tray down and put the two plates on the table in front of Liz and Jon Paul.

"Will there be anything else, sir?"

"Mr. Falid, you are the best. I don't know what we would do without you, thank you."

Jon Paul smiled at him, and Mr. Falid walked back to the butlers' pantry to do some more inventory work.

"Jon Paul, what are your plans today?"

"I don't know, but I need to work in the office for a few hours this morning, and my parents are coming here to visit later too."

"Your parents are coming? You are always so busy; I never get to see you. What time will they be here?"

"You know, Lizzy, I don't know exactly, but I have to keep up with work. The economy is picking up, jobs are being created, and the people are doing better than before. I can't just stop."

"I know. I just need to spend some time with you, Jon Paul."

"I know, honey, I know. How about this: after lunch, if I can get a few hours free, we will saddle up the horses and take a ride out to the forest and maybe have a picnic before my parents get here?"

"Really, Jon Paul? That would wonderful!" Liz smiled and touched Jon Paul's hand.

***

Frederick and Elysse were getting ready to go visit Jon Paul at his estate in the country, and as they packed for the short trip, Elysse looked at Frederick and said, "Did you get a hold of Jon Paul?"

"Um, no, no answer, but I am sure everything is fine." Elysse looked at her husband and smiled, but she couldn't shake the feeling that something was still wrong.

***

"So, Louis, what do we do with her?"

"I can think of a few things right now!" With an evil grin, Louis looked at Sara and pawed her blouse.

"Now listen, you two, we are probably sitting on a lot of money right now; keep her in here while I make a call." Louis looked at Remy with a commanding eye and left the dirty office. He walked out to the cars, pulled out his cell phone, and made a call.

***

Paul and Michelle sat in the kitchen finishing their breakfast. They would have a good day as it moved forward for them.

"Paul, I have been thinking about our bet."

"Yeah, what have you come up with?"

"No, you are going to think it silly."

"What do you mean? I promise I won't laugh."

"Well, okay. I want to bet you my heart."

"What? I already have that, Michelle."

"Yes, you do, but this is the only thing that I could come up with."

Michelle smiled shyly at Paul, who took her hand in his and said, "Michelle, I will promise you this: as soon as this is all over, this battle with Jon Paul, we will get married." Michelle began to tear up; she loved Paul with all her heart, and he had just proved it to her that he felt the same.

Michelle was overjoyed and she smiled at Paul, who smiled in return.

***

Jon Paul and Liz were eating their breakfast when Liz suddenly stood up and said, "Excuse me, Jon Paul, I need to get something." Jon Paul was a bit confused at her sudden abruptness, but he smiled and nodded. Liz got up and walked up the grand staircase to her room. She walked into her closet, sat down in front of her very large makeup table, and picked up the phone and dialed it.

***

Louis stood out in the abandoned warehouse alone as he talked with another from his gang; he would be heard briefly by Remy and Margo, arguing with the other person at the other end of the phone.

"What do you think that was all about, Remy?"

"I don't know, but it didn't sound good." It was not good. Louis had been arguing with a superior and did not like what he was being told to do. But in the end, he had no choice; it was a superior, and if you wanted to make it in the mafia, you did as you were told or you had your life ended. Louis had been involved with the Russian mafia for many years now, and he knew that if was told to do something, he better damn well do it—there was no other way. As he hung up the phone, he knew what he must do. He walked to the car, opened the trunk, and pulled out an AK-47. He checked that it was loaded and went into the office, where three people were sitting.

**

Liz sat in her chair, and as the phone connected on the other end, she heard a woman say, "Hello."

"Hello, this is Liz."

"Hi, Liz."

"Hi, Michelle. I wanted to call you to tell you that I will do it; whatever you need me to do, I will. I love Jon Paul so much, and I don't want him to be hurt in any way."

"Oh, Liz, that is such good news. I was a little worried that you might not want to help us; we were just wondering if you would call."

"So, what do I do now, Michelle? I mean, how do I get the coin?"

"If you can find a way, maybe when Jon Paul is in the shower or something?"

"That might work. I better go now; he might be getting suspicious. I will call you later."

"Okay, Liz, please be careful, bye." They both hung up the phone and Liz grabbed a book and walked back downstairs to the kitchen, where Jon Paul was sitting and enjoying his morning coffee.

"I felt I needed to bring this book to talk about. I need your opinion, Jon Paul." Jon Paul looked at Liz strangely. She had never asked for something like that before. He pursed his lips and said, "Okay, Liz, what do you need my opinion on?"

"Well, there is this part where the character sacrifices someone for his own good, and I want to know your thoughts."

"Hmm, tell me exactly what happens." Liz talked with Jon Paul for an hour about her book, till at that time, Jon Paul said, "Lizzy, I would love to debate this with you more, but I need to get some work done this morning; how about while we are at our picnic this afternoon, we talk about it further?"

"That sounds good, Jon Paul. I will have more questions by then. Go and finish your work before your parents get here so we can have a nice visit with them today." Jon Paul smiled at Liz and got up and walked to his office, and Liz breathed a sigh of relief.

***

"Well, we got our answer; that was Liz, and she said she will help us!"

"Thank God, Michelle. I thought that might be her calling; we will need her help if we are to get the coin from Jon Paul."

"What now, Paul?"

"Let's just see what happens with Liz. Let her call us when she has the coin, and then we can go from there." Michelle smiled at Paul. Finally, after so many months, there was hope.

***

Remy fell back and landed on Sara, and as he sank down to the floor, he caught a final glimpse of Margo lying on the floor. Louis stood still for a moment and surveyed the damage the AK-47 had done to his victims. He had never wanted to do this. He liked Remy, and he thought he had a future in the mafia. This had been done against his wishes, but if he was to stay alive himself, he had to do as he was told. It was too risky for him to help kidnap someone like Jon Paul Chavalier's sister, for this was a respected and feared man, and the mafia wanted nothing to do with him.

As he turned and walked out of the dirty office, he walked over to the big metal door, opened it, got in his car, drove through and stopped just clear of it. He closed it quickly and never looked back as he drove away; the guns he planted on Remy and Margo would make it look like a deal gone bad—at least, he hoped it would.

Sara held her breath as the gunshots rang out; she felt a hot, burning sensation in her shoulder and her lower calf muscle. She had been hit by two bullets. She listened intently to make sure there were no other voices; she heard nothing. Struggling to free herself from the bulk of a dead body on her, she finally was able to sit up and pull the blindfold from her eyes. The weight of Remy falling on her as she sat in the chair had broken the armrest of the chair, and she only had the handcuffs hanging to her wrists.

As she heard the sound of gunshots playing over and over in her head, she surveyed the area around her; blood had been splattered everywhere, pieces of what appeared to be flesh stuck to old, dirty walls, and she was sickened by the sight of Remy and Margo lying in pools of their own blood. Sara was barely able to recognize her two captors, so much damage had been done. She wondered where, exactly, she was. Suddenly, her shoulder and leg were in incredible pain; the sight of two murdered people had caused her to block the pain, at least temporarily. She sat there for a moment, contemplating her next move. She must find a key to the handcuffs, so she gathered her courage and began to search the dead body of Remy.

Slowly, she searched each pocket. She found nothing unusual, a few euros and his ID, and then, just as she was almost finished, she found a key. Holding the key in her blood-covered fingers, she put it in the lock of the handcuffs and turned it. She was free; she unlocked her other wrist and then looked around for some kind of tourniquet she could use to stop the bleeding. Eventually, she just decided to tear a piece of clothing from Margo, wrap it around her throbbing calf muscle, and somehow attach one around her shoulder; the pain was excruciating for her. As she completed her bandages, she found a piece of wood that she could use to help her walk; she didn't know where she was, but she knew she must get out of there before someone returned.

She looked around, saw the doorway, and hobbled over to it. About a dozen feet down the hallway, she thought she could see the front end of a car; as she got closer, she saw she was right. Sara, being cautious, took her time before seeing the car up close. She wanted to make sure she was safe, so she hobbled around to the side door and peeked through. She saw no one, so she opened the big, metal door and drove out, and then stopped just outside the entrance to close the big door before driving off.

Remy and Margo had lived short lives; they had both struggled to keep up with the norms of society and to be law-abiding citizens. However, Remy never did follow rules very well, and Margo, well, she just did whatever Remy did. It was certain that they would not make it in such a dangerous world.

Louis had planted drugs and guns on the bodies of Remy and Margo to make it look like a deal of some kind gone bad; hopefully, this would satisfy the police. He drove down the highway back to Toulon, but never would he forget what he had done this day.

Chapter 15

• • •

THE JINN

The great army prepared for battle. Many had been lost in this millennial-old war. The armies of both sides had suffered casualties with numbers so high, many could not even count. Both sides were evenly matched at different times, but there would be some times when one had an advantage over the other. Men could no longer remember when this great, old war had begun; even the soldiers who fought this continuing battle had long forgotten its beginning. With soldiers uncounted, each side waged war with the other; sometimes, yes, sometimes, one side had a faithful belief that they were on the edge of winning, but this was not ever happening. Some soldiers felt that this was just a part of their chosen jobs, to serve and never question; some felt the honor, and some were just made for it. As the dark-side army gathered its troops and prepared for battle with the light-, small skirmishes would erupt between certain groups, which were renegade soldiers who didn't like taking orders but felt their lives would be in danger if they didn't. They obeyed out of fear, not respect.

"Blast you! Didn't I tell you to get in line?"

"You did, Lord Shax."

"Then what are you waiting for? *Step up!*"

"Yes, my lord." Dealing with subordinates was never easy for the Great Lord Shax, commander of hundreds of legions of dark ones. He had seen a thousand battles and commanded even more; he was one of the best generals the dark army had, trained by the commander and chief of all, King Amon.

As the great army of light gathered, their high commander drew attention to himself as he rallied his troops.

"Gather, my brothers; the dark army is preparing for battle as I speak. Now, open your sheaths and reveal your swords. We go to war quickly!"

General Acar was good at preparing his soldiers; they were good fighters, but as with any war, they were evenly matched with soldiers of the dark army. These two sides had been battling each other for thousands of years, with neither side having an advantage over the other.

"My brothers, as we go to fight the great serpent, know this: we shall be victorious! I have said it is so. Now, mount your steeds and strengthen yourselves; we go to fight!"

Lord and General Acar mounted his steed, held his sword high, and waved it at his following soldiers as they began their ascent into the air to do battle with the dark army of King Amon. As winged horses and winged beings of light clashed with beings of the dark, a loud noise was to be heard above the earth. Most who heard this only thought of thunder. But it was so much more, a battle for humanity had been staged so long ago, and a continuing war for the souls of mankind had been fought without end. Each warring faction had desires for the human soul, for it is power, pure and simple. Men fail to know this through a blockage and ignorance of the third eye, which exists on each and every human being alive. But the soul contains the power, and whoever has the most would obviously be the stronger and be able to finally win this war and put an end to it.

It seems that both the light and the dark don't really want an end to this war, however, for neither can get a firm hold on the control of more souls, which would, of course, allow them to be dominant.

The fighting between these two armies was intense. Each time they fought, soldiers of light would die and soldiers of the dark would fall; when they die, they are not reborn like a human—no, they are gone from existence forever. Only the human soul is immortal, and that is why both sides desire more human souls: more souls equals more power. The beings of light care not for human souls; they are only a means to an end. They see no reason for humans to be alive, for we are only monkeys to them. The beings of the dark, however, are different; they see human souls as freedom and a way of rebellion from the creator of the all. They rebel in any way they can, establishing themselves as independent from light. They create their own world, a world where humans are free.

Battling continuously has taken its toll on both sides; it is no wonder they have little sympathy for the human being.

"My brothers, we must fall back now. Fall back!"

Lord Amon spoke, and the beings of light began to fall back and retreat into their region of safety.

Lord Shax saw that the great army of light had pursued them as far as they could, and the dark army could only ascend so high. The vibrations of their countenances were of a level that they were only able to rise to a certain point, and then they must descend or be burned up alive, and no being wants that. They turned back and began a great descent back to their region of safety, and a celebration for their victory would ensue shortly after that. Lord Shax would indeed be a great general this day.

"Lord Shax, shall we bring the slaves?"

"Indeed, bring them now!" The slaves were a group of humans that had died in their sins and were weak and unable to fight with the Great Army of Darkness.

The soldiers sat around the massive hall where they had gathered for the victory celebration; many dark beings had come from far away to attend the event. It would be a celebration of an almost epic proportion; the dark army had beaten the great army of light and made them turn and run. This was indeed a great victory, one that would be remembered for thousands of years. Although many had fallen, there was always another one standing in line waiting to take his place. The humans brought food and drink for the dark ones, who sat around a stone table with the top generals sitting at a special table away from the rest.

"So how many do you think fell, Lord Shax?" asked his sergeant.

"Many fell, my brother, many. But we have yet to fulfill our destiny; we have so much more to do. It is only just beginning."

"But, my Lord, if so many fell, can we not say we have won?"

"No, we cannot, for as long as there are those who would oppose us, we must battle on." Lord Shax stood up and spoke. "My brothers, we had a great victory today, but our fight continues on. We must be strong and keep our heads high; we have so much more to do. We will continue to fight and battle until every last one of those dogs is dead and gone. *This is my vow to you: we will fight, and we will win!"* Lord Shax raised his glass, made a salute to the others, gave an inspiring wave, and drank.

For the beings of light, it was different; they came home to lick their wounds and to prepare for the next battle, which would not be far off, knowing the dark army's predictability in these matters.

***

Jon Paul and Liz would enjoy their time at a picnic while waiting for his parents to arrive. Liz had been unable to get the coin from Jon Paul while he was in the shower; he had nearly caught her reaching for it. He never let it out of his sight for very long, so she would have to find another way or time to try and get the coin from him.

***

Sara drove as fast as she could; she needed to get to the hospital quickly. The bullet wounds were still bleeding, and she was getting a little dizzy from the blood loss. She hoped she would make it and be able to heal back to normal. She had so much to live for. She loved her family and didn't want to leave her parents like this; it would break their hearts. She pushed on and was soon close to the hospital. Sara drove up to the emergency entrance; she stumbled out and into the door, and a nurse saw her and rushed over to help her.

"Are you okay, ma'am?" she asked.

"No, I have been shot." Sara fell down, and the nurse waved at the orderly standing close by.

They helped Sara onto a gurney and rushed her into emergency surgery. She had lost a lot of blood but was young and strong; this would be in her favor. The thug, Louis, that had shot Sara thought her dead with the other two, Remy and Margo. He had no idea Sara was still alive, and this could spell trouble for the man.

***

Jon Paul and Liz sat in the quiet of their forest and enjoyed their picnic. Mr. Falid had put together a small collection of fruit and some sandwiches for them to eat, and he had also put in a couple of bottles of soda for them to drink. They were connecting on a very deep level when Jon Paul asked Liz, "Liz, why were you reaching for my coin this morning?"

"What do you mean, Jon Paul? I can't even touch it?"

"Sure, Lizzy, but you must remember, it is mine; it can destroy me if it ends up in the wrong hands."

"So you don't trust me with it?"

"Of course I do; if you want to hold it, just ask me first." Liz stared at Jon Paul. He had given her an answer that might be a way for her to get the coin from him. She smiled.

"So, do you want to hold it?"

"Hold what, Jon Paul?"

Jon Paul smiled and winked at Liz. "You know … *it!*"

"What *it*?"

"My coin, of course!"

"Jon Paul, you silly man; yes, I do, but not right now, we are eating." Liz was very smart in putting Jon Paul off to take any suspicion away from her about the coin. Jon Paul looked at his watch, saw the time, and said, "We need to get back. My parents will be here soon."

They packed up their picnic basket and their blanket and began the walk back to their house from the forest. It wasn't a long walk, only a few minutes, but it would be one done in silence. Liz was lost in thought as they approached the back lawn, which grew right up to the edge of the forest where the ever-so-tall trees grew with lushness and plenty of ground cover and green foliage.

***

At the hospital, Sara would get the best care in all of southern France; she spent hours in surgery and many more recovering. As evening approached, a policeman from the local precinct had arrived at the hospital. He been called by the head doctor, which was normal procedure for the hospital. His job was to uncover what happened and to catch whoever had committed the crime. Stuart Rolland had risen through the ranks of the fifth precinct of Toulon quickly; he had a certain knack for catching criminals. He had learned from a very young age that he was good at solving mysteries. After his college years, he had enrolled in the police academy of Toulon and found his calling, and he learned to use his own methods of deduction to solve crimes. Others in the academy began to say that he had a nose like a bloodhound—he could just smell crime. This stuck with him as he rose through the ranks and began a very successful career as a policeman. He spent many years investigating different crimes, and after some time, he had become the local expert on murders and shootings of the mob, or crimes that appeared to be mafia-driven.

The pain in Sara's calf muscle and her shoulder was excruciating. Even though the bullets were now gone, having been successfully removed by Dr. Brian Lombard, she still could feel the burning sensation from the hot lead that had penetrated her flesh. The sounds of gunshots being fired in quick succession still echoed in her head, but she lay in the hospital bed and thought, *I am alive.*

"Well, how are we feeling, Mrs. Pouisant?" asked Dr. Lombard.

"I feel like I've been shot."

"Ha ha, that is funny, but you were! I have removed the bullets, and except for some minor scarring, you should make a full recovery."

"Really, doc, that is good news," she said sarcastically. Sara was happy to be alive, though.

"There is a detective here to see you, but only if you are up for it."

"Yeah, sure, doc. I can answer a few questions, but will you stay close just in case?"

"Sure, I will be right outside the door." Dr. Lombard smiled an easy smile and walked out of the room, closing the door behind him; it clicked with a familiar sound.

In walked Detective Rolland. Standing six feet three, he was an imposing figure, and Sara looked at him with curious eyes. His grey-and-black peppered hair was cut short, and he gave the impression of a military man. Sara was impressed.

"Hello, Mrs. Pouisant. Can you answer a few questions for me? I will be brief and try not to upset you." He smiled at her. Sara nodded her head yes.

"What is your full name?"

"Sara Pouisant."

"How old are you?"

"Twenty-nine years old."

"Is there family we can contact to let them know you are okay?"

"Yes, my husband is Claude and my parents' names are Frederick and Elysse Chavalier."

"*Chavalier*! Are you related to Jon Paul Chavalier, our UMP leader?"

"Yes, he is my brother."

"Well, now, that is interesting. Do you know who did this to you, and why?"

"Actually, no, I was driving home and saw a couple with their hazard lights flashing, so I pulled over to ask if they needed help."

"Did you help them?"

"No, they put a wet cloth over my mouth, and I passed out; it must have been some kind of drug."

"Yes, obviously, a drug. Then what happened?"

"I don't know exactly, I woke up sitting in a chair somewhere, blindfolded with my hands cuffed behind me."

"I see. Can you describe these two people?"

"I think the man was about six feet tall with short brown hair, and the woman was maybe five foot three."

"Did either one of them have a certain mark or scar or maybe a tattoo, something out of the ordinary?"

"Um, no, but the woman did have a streak of dyed-blonde hair on the side of her head."

"What side was the streak on?"

"I think it was her left; yeah, definitely her left, and she had a small tattoo on the inner side of her left wrist!"

"A tattoo? What was it of?"

"I think it was a name. I am not sure. Maybe Romy or Rome."

"Okay, thank you, Mrs. Pouisant. I hope that wasn't too bad for you."

"No, it was okay."

Detective Rolland smiled at Sara; as he opened the door to her room to walk out, he paused, turned to face her, and said, "Thank you again. I will be in touch."

He closed the door and was gone. Detective Rolland had some fine clues to go on. Now was the hard part—looking through old mug shots to see if he could find a woman with a small tattoo on her left wrist.

***

Jon Paul and Liz had enjoyed their picnic, but as they entered the house, they were greeted by Mr. Falid. "Sir, a phone call for you from Detective Rolland; he has news about your sister."

Jon Paul grabbed the phone from his manservant, put the receiver to his ear, and said, "Hello, this is Jon Paul Chavalier. What has happened to my sister?"

"Mr. Chavalier, I am Detective Rolland. I am investigating the attempted kidnapping and possible attempted murder of your sister."

"*What! Murder and kidnapping?* Is she all right? Where is she now?"

"Slow down, sir; she is fine. She is at the hospital recovering; she was shot in the leg and the shoulder. The doctor removed the bullets, and she will be fine. Now, do you know who might have wanted to hurt your sister?"

"No, what hospital?"

"She is at Toulon emergency; she was treated by Dr. Lombard."

"Ah, I don't know, detective. I have a lot of enemies. But I need to go see her!"

"Okay, sir, but I am going to need you to come down to the station and make a statement for me. I will need anything you can tell me about your enemies."

Jon Paul hung up the phone; he was in shock. His sister had been shot and almost killed, and he didn't know who might have done this. He looked at Liz and told her what the detective told him; she stared in disbelief as he recalled what the man said. They agreed that they would wait for his parents to arrive and then they would all take a drive into town to see her at the hospital.

It wasn't a long wait for Jon Paul and Liz. As they sat in the kitchen sipping tea, Mr. Falid answered the door and showed his parents in. They sat in the kitchen, and they sensed something was wrong. His father said, "Jon Paul, what is it? What is wrong, son?"

"It is Sara. She is at the hospital right now recovering from gunshots to the leg and shoulder."

"Are you serious? What has happened, Jon Paul?"

"I am serious, Dad; she was apparently on her way home and was kidnapped and held against her will, and then somehow she got away and survived."

"Can we see her now?"

"Of course, Dad, we can leave as soon as you are ready." They drove back in to the city to see Jon Paul's sister at the hospital.

***

Paul and Michelle had been having a slow day; nothing much exciting happened to them anymore; they had become homebodies and both enjoyed it that way. Michelle was sitting in the kitchen when suddenly she noticed a circle of bright-white light beginning to form in front of her, and she called to Paul, "Paul, come quick! Something is happening!"

Paul was in their living room when he heard Michelle call, and he jumped to his feet and ran to the kitchen. It wasn't far, so he was there rather quickly; he stood next to Michelle as the light began to fade, and they could see a figure standing there. The figure standing there in such white brilliance was none other than Seraphiel, Michelle's guardian angel and protector.

"My children, the time is come for us to talk again. The coin is drawing close, and you must be strong. When you have the coin, you will call to me, and I will come. Do not be bothered by what noises you hear; it is deception."

"Will we have the coin soon, Seraphiel?" asked Michelle.

"Indeed, you will. The time approaches fast. Stand ready!" The angel then began to dissipate and vanish from their sight; in an instant, she was gone, and Paul and Michelle were left standing there, feeling enlightened.

***

As they drove into town to the hospital, Jon Paul searched his mind for information as to who could have done such a thing to his sister. Was it someone from his past, he wondered, or maybe a new enemy? Jon Paul had few friends and many enemies.

***

Detective Rolland searched many files for these two people he had been told about. A woman with a blonde streak in her hair, that might be easy, but the man, well, that would be something entirely different. He would have to find the female first, and then hope she would lead him to her accomplice. Detective Rolland dialed Toulon emergency and asked for Sara Pouisant. He had a few more questions to ask her.

"Hello, this is Sara."

"Mrs. Pouisant, this is Detective Rolland. We spoke a few hours ago. I have a couple of questions I need to ask you."

"Sure, Detective, anything I can do to help."

"How did you get to the hospital, with your wounds?"

"I drove myself."

"And where were you driving from?"

"I was on the outskirts of town, in an abandoned warehouse."

"Where exactly, Mrs. Pouisant?"

"Um, just off of highway seven, near the Toulon River."

"I see, how far from the road?"

"Not very far, but you won't like what you will find there."

"Oh, and why is that?"

"They … they are dead."

"*Dead?* You killed them??"

"No, there was someone else."

"Who else, Mrs. Pouisant?"

"I don't know, I didn't see him; I was blindfolded."

"What does this warehouse look like? Are there any distinguishing marks on the building?"

"Ah, no, just old and broken down, you know, just abandoned, but close to the river, no other warehouses in the area."

"Thank you, Mrs. Pouisant, for your time. I think that will be all for now; you get some rest. I will be in touch with you soon." Detective Rolland hung up the phone. He had a solid lead and was not wasting any time, so he grabbed his coat and headed for the door.

***

Paul and Michelle sat there, amazed that the angel had told them that they were ready. In fact, they both had never felt such a strong connection to each other and to the angel Seraphiel.

"Michelle, I think my head is about to explode. I need some fresh air. Wanna go for a walk?"

"A walk? Sure, that would do me good too; where do you want to walk to?"

"Anywhere, I just need some fresh air."

"Okay, Paul, let's go!" So Paul and Michelle took a walk together. This was a rare thing for them, for they never walked anywhere; it reminded Michelle of her days with a man named Jon Paul Chavalier.

***

Jon Paul, Liz, and his parents arrived at the hospital; they immediately went to his sister's room after having stopped at the nurses' station to find out exactly which one she was in. As they walked to her room, no one said a word; they were still in a state of disbelief as to how and why this happened. Jon Paul was the first one to enter Sara's room.

Upon seeing him, she smiled a big smile and said, "Hey, Jon Paul, took you long enough."

"Thanks, Sara. Are you okay? How are you feeling? I mean, what the hell happened?" Jon Paul stared at her intently.

"Well, I was driving home after visiting Mom and Dad, and there was this car stopped on the side of the highway, so I pulled up behind them and stopped. They looked harmless, just a young man and his girl, so I got out and asked if they needed help. The next thing I know, I am handcuffed and blindfolded, sitting in a chair."

"So how did you escape? How did you get here?" Their parents looked on intently as Sara continued.

"When I came to, I heard another man's voice; he was arguing with the young man. They were not very loud and I didn't hear very much, but it was as if the one man was his boss. Then all I heard after a few minutes of silence was the sound … the sound of gunshots." Sara began to cry. The memory was so new, and she couldn't control her sadness; it poured forth on her face for all to see.

***

Paul and Michelle were having a peaceful walk around their neighborhood; the traffic was light and the sun not too bright. It was a perfect time for them to recharge and enjoy their young lives before the final battle with one Jon Paul Chavalier.

***

"Sara, listen to me now. I am going to find out who did this, and they are going to pay; this will not go unpunished, I promise you." Sara looked at Jon Paul and knew he was serious; with his connections in the political realm and his very real power, he could do this.

"Thank you, Jon Paul. I know you will catch this criminal." Sara smiled meekly at Jon Paul.

"Jon Paul, are you sure you will be able to do this?" asked Frederick.

"Yeah, Dad. I will handle it properly, nothing to worry about."

Jon Paul got up, looked at his family, and said, "Will everyone please excuse me for just a moment? I need to call the headquarters of the police." As they looked at him, his father nodded in agreement with Jon Paul; he knew he would handle this as only he could.

***

The army of dark sat motionless for what seemed an eternity; they had regrouped their forces and were on the brink of a surprise attack on the army of light. They sat, poised, and they knew they had the advantage this time. The army of light had not been expecting an attack so soon after the last one; usually, the army of dark waited for days before launching their attack for so long now, it had become predictable. As the dark began to move and surround the unaware army of light, the thundering sound of many loud hooves and wings flapping, the cries of great power and conquest filling the air.

The army of dark had taken the army of light by surprise, and it was a devastating move; many hundreds and thousands of angels fell to their deaths at the hands and swords of the dark army. It was a purely evil attack. As the army of dark continued their slaughter, the army of light was heard to be crying in fear and retreating as fast as they could; it would take many months for the army of light to recover from this last attack.

***

"This is Jon Paul Chavalier. I wish to speak with the investigating officer; his name is Detective Rolland."

"One moment, sir. I will connect you to his phone."

Detective Roland was not at his desk, though; he was driving to the abandoned warehouse where Sara had been held captive. He didn't know exactly where it was, but he had a good idea. As he got to the edge of town, he knew instinctively where he should go; after all, throughout the years, he had investigated a lot of crimes in this area, and he was familiar with some of the warehouses here. Detective Rolland drove around to the place he thought Sara had told him about, and as he drove down an old, dirt road, he saw what he was sure was the old warehouse where she had been kept. He drove slowly as he got nearer; it seemed to be quiet, so he stopped his car a few hundred feet away from the warehouse and got out of his car to check on foot. This way, he could sneak up and maybe check it out before anyone saw him, if anyone was still there.

Quietly and stealthily, like a cat, he hunched down and stepped closer to the building. He approached from the side and peered in a broken window just enough to see if there was any activity; all seemed quiet. He moved over to the metal door, which was ajar, and he peered in. He could see that the place was dirty and smelled bad—not a good combination. He steadied his hand on his gun, which was now drawn and pointing at the doorway in front of him, and he slowly pushed the door open. The whole place was a mess, with broken chairs and windows and even some dirty needles on the floor; obviously, this was a drug hangout.

Detective Rolland had seen worse in his days as a rookie officer, but as he focused his search for the office where Sara had been held, he remembered that he had been here many years before, but the memory of this warehouse resurfaced in his mind. He had been here investigating a crime of theft when it was a fully functioning and productive warehouse with many workers. He had solved the case, as it was just an angry ex-employee trying to get back at his boss. Now, though, he was surprised at how dirty it had become, nothing like when it was new all those years ago.

He found what he thought to be the office, and he walked into the mess on the floor. There, lying in stains of blood and urine, were two people, what appeared to be a man and a woman—young, maybe in their late twenties or early thirties. As he radioed back to headquarters, something caught his eye, something shiny over by the dead woman.

***

Jon Paul left a message for Detective Rolland to call him, since he wasn't answering his phone, and then he walked back to his sister's room. His mother and father were happily talking with Sara and trying to comfort her.

"Hi, sis. I want you to know we are going to catch this criminal no matter what; you have my word."

"Thanks, Jon Paul. I know you will."

He smiled at her and sat down in the empty chair. Eventually, as time passed slowly for Jon Paul and his family, Jon Paul noticed his sister seemed to be getting tired. "Hey, sis, I think we better get going now; you need to get your rest so you can heal."

"Yes, we should get going, Jon Paul; your sister does need her rest." Frederick smiled at his daughter and then looked at his son and nodded in agreement.

Sara smiled at her family and gave them big, gentle hugs, as her shoulder was still hurting, and said good-bye. Jon Paul, Liz, Frederick, and Elysse would drive back to Jon Paul's house in the country. Frederick and Elysse would stay a few days with Jon Paul to make sure they could see their daughter again before returning to Le Beausset.

***

Detective Rolland picked up the key and examined it. He had not seen one quite like this before. This key had three separate marks on it, each looking similar to a runic language of old; he was not familiar with the inscriptions but knew of a man that might be able to help. This key could possibly lead to the real murderer.

***

"Jon Paul, do you think you might know who did this?"

"No, Dad. I have no idea, but I am going to find out who, and they will pay for this crime!"

Frederick looked at his son, who was obviously upset. "It is okay, Jon Paul. I know you will find him and bring him to justice."

"I will, Dad. I will." Jon Paul looked at his father in a most determined way and pulled onto the highway.

***

Paul and Michelle were walking in their neighborhood when Paul said, "I am getting hungry; you want to stop somewhere and get a bite to eat?"

"Sure, I am a little hungry, maybe some coffee too!"

"Anything you want, my love." Paul smiled at Michelle, who smiled back. He gave her a quick kiss and then looked ahead and said, "How about we go in to that little place right there?"

"Right there? You mean Pepe's Pastries and Coffee?"

"Yes, they always serve us well."

"Okay, Paul, sounds good to me; you know I can never say no to one of their cinnamon rolls!"

Paul smiled at Michelle, who knew exactly what he was thinking.

***

Louis Moreau was still kicking himself as he walked back to his apartment. He never should have lost that damn key. Where it could be, he had no clue. He did know one thing: if he didn't find it, and quick, he might be in some serious trouble with his employer, who had little patience for sloppiness.

***

As Detective Rolland and other police officers who had now arrived to help him investigate this grisly murder scene searched for clues as to who had done this, he kept the key in his pocket; he wasn't ready to present this piece of evidence just yet. Detective Rolland wanted to have his friend look at it first, rather than to have it just locked up in the evidence room where he might never be able to tie it to this case.

***

Jon Paul pulled his car into his long driveway toward his house, and as he got to the garage, he stopped to let everyone out so they could go to the house. Jon Paul got out too; he would leave his car out for his servant to park it in the garage later. They walked the short distance to his house and opening the big front door. Mr. Falid was standing there to greet them and said, "Hello, sir, how is your sister?"

"She will be fine, Mr. Falid, thank you for asking; is anyone hungry?"

"I could stand to eat something if it is no trouble, Jon Paul."

"No trouble, Dad. Mr. Falid, could you prepare something for us to eat?"

"Right away, sir; will you be eating in the grand dining room?"

"No, I think we can just sit in the kitchen, if that is okay with you."

"Of course, sir. I will have the table set and dinner ready in just a few short minutes." Mr. Falid smiled at them and excused himself to prepare the meal. Jon Paul motioned for everyone to follow him downstairs to the game room to sit and relax.

***

Louis Moreau sat down at his kitchen table and sighed. He had lost his key somewhere, and without it, he was just another flunky, for that special key gave him a pass to all the best things crime money could buy, like backstage concerts, access to certain famous entertainers who were in town, and the best restaurants in all of France. He was certain he must do one thing, and that was to find it.

***

Detective Rolland drove back to the station to gather his thoughts and to decide his next move. Should he go to his friend first, the one who could tell him about this strange key, or maybe just try and solve this case? He didn't know for sure, but he would soon.

***

Jon Paul and his family sat down in his family room close to the game room. They had just been through a horrible family incident; the attempted murder and kidnapping of his sister had them all on edge.

"Dad, do you want a drink?"

"Yeah, Jon Paul, whiskey sour, please." His father had always been a whiskey drinker.

"Mom, you want anything, and how about you, Liz?"

"No thanks, Jon Paul," his mother replied.

"I would like a glass of wine, please," stated Liz.

"Okay, coming right up." Jon Paul mixed his father's drink, then poured Liz a glass of wine and grabbed himself a beer.

"Someday, huh, Dad?"

"You said it, Jon Paul, one hell of a day." His father sighed and sat back in his chair to sip his drink.

Jon Paul's parents stayed at his house for another night, after which they decided to visit his sister once more and then drive back to their home.

"Be safe driving, Dad, and say hello to Sara, okay?"

"Sure thing, son, are you going to visit her soon?"

"Yeah, Dad, as soon as I wrap up some work, then we will."

"I will tell her you will be by soon, then."

"Yes, Dad, soon." As Jon Paul gave his dad a hug and shook his hand, his mother smiled a loving smile, as only a mother can; they got in their car and drove down Jon Paul's long driveway to the highway and headed to the hospital. Jon Paul and Liz had had a good visit with his parents; they didn't visit often, and it was always a welcome break from work.

***

Paul and Michelle sat eating their cinnamon rolls and drinking their coffee; they were having a great day. For them, time passed slowly; they had enjoyed the morning walk and were now ready to walk home. "Are you ready to head home, Michelle?"

"Yeah, as soon as you are."

They paid their small bill and began the walk home.

"You know, Michelle, I've had a wonderful day so far with you."

Michelle smiled at Paul and squeezed his hand tighter. "I have too, Paul." The two of them walked a little faster now, and as they walked, they would turn briefly and smile at one another. It was a good day for them.

***

Liz sat down in the kitchen and held her head steady for a moment; the thought of somehow getting Jon Paul's coin had returned to her and had taken her by surprise. The distraction of his sister being kidnapped and almost killed had removed this thought from her mind, but now that it had returned, she was a bit surprised. Why had this thought occurred now, just when they were beginning to settle back into their routine? Was there something she was missing? Had she not tried to take the coin once and failed? A thought occurred to her that had not occurred before: Why not just ask Jon Paul if she could hold it, and then wish it away from him? *It is brilliant,* she thought. *I will do just what Jon Paul has done to so many others and just wish it away.* It could work.

Liz was excited; this new plan could not fail. Jon Paul trusted her, and he would respect her just asking straightforwardly. He would hand her the coin, and she would wish it away from him. Liz knew this would work; she decided to busy herself with some distractions around the house. Jon Paul was working in his office, so she would wait till later this evening to ask, and then hopefully it would all work out just as she planned.

***

Detective Rolland sat at his desk holding the key; he had not been able to visit his friend, who was an expert on antique things. He would again try to call him and set a time to visit; he hoped that this would provide him the clue he needed to solve this case and tell him who these two young people were. Of course, forensics would do that too, but he wanted to get a jump on them and help if they needed it.

***

Paul and Michelle entered their tiny apartment and sat down on the couch in the living room. "Paul, do you think Liz is really going to help us?"

"Well, I have no reason to doubt her at this point. I mean, she could change her mind, but I think if that was the case, we would have been told by your angel Seraphiel that it was so." Paul gave a confident look to Michelle, who caught his eye with hers and smiled in agreement.

"I guess so, Paul. Maybe I am just a bit anxious."

Paul smiled at Michelle and said, "Well, I know a way to take care of that!"

Michelle smiled coyly at Paul and reached out to take his hand and lead him to their bedroom.

***

The evening was slow to approach for Liz; she had busied herself with personal things all day and now was sitting in her room thinking about how she should ask Jon Paul to hold the golden coin. *Maybe*, she thought, *I could ask him for a wish; that would be clever.*

***

Louis Moreau searched his mind for clues as to where he might have lost his special key. He remembered eating at some little coffeehouse earlier; he had it then, but after that, he had driven out to the old, abandoned warehouse to meet up with two of his new recruits who had promise. Problem was, they had taken the next step without his supervision, and he had to go see who it was they had kidnapped. Wait! He remembered that he had had the key as he had driven to meet this young couple, but on his way back, he never checked his pocket to see if it was still there. Maybe all the activity of taking out those two idiots had jarred it loose and it fell out. *Yes, that must be it,* he thought, *it must have come loose when I was taking care of those two.* Well, now then, he was just going to have to go back to the warehouse and see if it was there. Of course, by now, there might be come activity, so he would have to be careful; other lowlifes could be there committing some sort of illegal crime. He decided he would drive back there in the morning and search for his lost key; after all, he was nothing without it.

***

The army of light had been beaten badly; as they continued to try and regroup, it was obvious to all that they might just be defeated. The surprise attack of the army of dark had taken a mighty toll, and the loss was devastating. The light army might not ever recover, which was bad news for them; if the army of dark was to attack again and right now before they could regroup, it would be over. The army of dark would be stronger, and they would control mankind. This could never happen.

***

Jon Paul sat at his office desk and wrapped up some work he had needed to finish all day; it had been a grueling few days, what with his sister ending up in the hospital and then having his mother and father visit on not the best of days. At least his sister was better and recovering; although her recovery would be long, she would survive. He put his head in his hands and sighed. What a day. At this time of the night, he wondered where Liz was and what she was doing. Liz walked into Jon Paul's office and saw him sitting at his desk. She cleared her throat gently. "You okay, Jon Paul?"

"Hmm, yeah, I am okay; what are you doing?"

"Nothing. I wanted to come in here to ask you a question."

"A question, what kind of question?"

"Jon Paul, you know I am serious; will you please let me ask you?"

Jon Paul smiled a sly grin at Liz, who wrinkled her nose in response to him. "Okay, baby, ask away."

"Well, you know how I have been wanting to see your gold coin? Well ... um ... I was wondering if I might make a wish too?"

Jon Paul stared at Liz, and after a moment of silence, he finally said, "You want to make a wish, and just what exactly would you wish for?"

Liz moved uncomfortably in her chair. "I want to wish for something special for me; is that okay?"

"Something special, hmm, well, I suppose; when do you want to do this?"

"How about now?" Liz smiled slyly at Jon Paul.

"Right now? Seriously? Well, I guess. Hold on, I will get it for you." Jon Paul stood up and reached in his pocket; he pulled out the golden coin and held it in his hands. It glowed with an unearthly light. Liz began shaking from nervousness. She was about to betray the man she loved with all of her heart, a powerful man who had killed before and was not above doing it again, if it suited his needs. Liz steadied herself, took a deep breath, and held out her hand. Jon Paul looked at her in complete trust; he placed the coin in her hand and closed it. She felt a warm, pulsating feeling in the palm of her hand as the coin began to heat up.

"Wow, it is hot, Jon Paul!"

"Yes, and it will get even hotter as you make your wish. Now, concentrate and slowly speak your wish." Jon Paul smiled at Liz.

Liz, feeling the time was right, opened her hand and said quickly, "I wish this coin mine!"

Jon Paul screamed, "*My coin!*" but the power of the coin was no longer his. It was Liz's now. He reached out to grab the magic coin, but it was not moving. It was a part of Liz now, and she was its master. Liz turned and ran for the door. Jon Paul, quickly on her heels, stumbled and tripped on the Persian rug by his desk. Liz was out the door before he could recover; she ran downstairs and out to the garage. She found one of his many luxury cars, started it, and drove down the driveway to the street that connected to the highway. Liz would drive all the way to Paul and Michelle's house before she would stop.

***

307

As Louis Moreau drove to the old, abandoned warehouse, he was reminded of all the things that key had done for him: he had gotten into special nightclubs, met famous people, and even met some men from politics, but now, without it, he wondered if his connections would still be there. He drove till he reached the end of town, and then turned off the highway and down a dirt road. He continued to drive for a while, and after several moments, he finally spotted the old warehouse. As he got closer, he could see it seemed to be quiet at the old warehouse; things still looked the same since last he was here.

He parked his car out of sight by some trees, and, keeping his hand on his gun, slowly walked toward the door; he noticed it was still ajar. Things seemed different, though, to Louis; it appeared as though someone had been there since he was last there taking care of that couple. There was no smell of dead bodies, and the place looked like someone had gone through it with a fine-toothed comb. He approached the office where he had disposed of the couple; their bodies were nowhere to be found!

In fact, the office was fairly clean; it had the appearance of a modern office now, with just a few broken windows. "Wait!" he shouted. It wasn't one person that had cleaned it out; it was the cops! Suddenly, Louis Moreau knew what had happened. It had been searched by the cops, and all the evidence was gone. He looked around for his key, but the place was empty; the cops had been through the whole thing. There was nothing left, so he sighed and walked back to his car, got in, and drove home. Life would never be the same for Louis Moreau again.

***

Liz drove as fast and as safely as she could to Paul and Michelle's apartment, and while she drove, she dialed Michelle's cell phone. "Hello."

"Hello, Michelle, it is Liz."

"Liz, are you okay?"

"Yes, I have the coin."

"Really! You got it? Are you all right?"

"Yes, but Jon Paul is following me, I think; he … he almost had me." Liz began to sob. She had just betrayed the man of her dreams and broken his heart and hers.

"Listen, Liz, it is okay, honey; you have saved his life and ours, for who knows what he might have done. Are you almost here?"

"Yes, I am almost there," she said between sobs.

"Good, you have done what we could not; be safe, okay, and we will see you soon."

"Okay, I will be there soon, Michelle. Michelle?"

"Yeah."

"Thanks." Liz hung up the phone, wiped her eyes, and continued to drive into the city to Paul and Michelle's apartment.

***

"Nooooo! I must have my coin back!"

Jon Paul raced out of his house to his garage. He got into one of his cars, started it, and tore out and down his long driveway to the street and onto the highway; he was going to get his coin back if it was the last thing he would do.

***

"Paul, that was Liz. She is on her way here with the coin!"

"Are you serious? She has the coin? Did she say what happened?"

"No, not much, just that she thought Jon Paul was following her and he almost caught her."

"Really? I wonder how she got it from him."

"I don't know, but if he is following her, we need to do something, Paul."

"You're right, we do! As soon as she gets here, we better go to the church and call Seraphiel. I think that is the one place we can be safe and most probably give the coin back to her."

"I think you are right, Paul; let's just hope she gets here fast, before Jon Paul." Michelle breathed a heavy sigh and looked at Paul, who saw her worried look and gave her a glance of confidence she had come to love. She knew he would be there, no matter what.

Paul and Michelle readied themselves for Liz's arrival. They both knew it would be close and most likely dangerous, especially with Jon Paul right on her heels.

"Paul, I'm scared."

"I know, sweetie, me too, but we must be strong; we can't let fear control us."

"I will do my best, Paul, but if I waver, will you please keep me safe?"

"You know I will. I will never let anything harm you." Paul smiled at Michelle, who knew she would be safe.

***

Jon Paul drove like a madman; he had an idea where Liz might be going, but he was so angry that he just drove to Paul and Michelle's without really thinking about it. He didn't know what he would do, only that he must get his coin back.

***

Liz knocked on Paul's door and he opened it immediately.

"Liz, I am Paul. Please come in. We only have a few moments, and then we must leave for the church."

"Hi, Paul. Why the church, if you don't mind me asking?"

"It is the only place where we can be sure to be able to contact the angel Seraphiel."

"The who?" Liz was not a very religious woman, and the name Seraphiel was unusual to her.

"Seraphiel, she is Michelle's angel." Liz looked at Paul like he was mad, but Paul didn't blink even once; his gaze was strong and steady.

"We should get going; we need to leave now." Paul looked at both Liz and Michelle with a commanding glance; both women fell in line and followed him. They walked out to his car and got in, Liz in the back and Michelle in the front. Paul started his car, and, pushing the pedal to the floor and screeching the tires, he drove out into the street and to the church. This is where he knew they could call Seraphiel, and they would also be safe; Jon Paul would never look for them there.

***

Jon Paul was still driving like a madman. He was swerving in-between cars and honking his horn to warn other drivers to get out of the way; he was a man possessed. He drove in such a reckless manner that soon his actions caught the eye of a local authority; a policeman was now following him with his lights flashing and siren blaring. Jon Paul tried to outrun the cop car, but even with his favorite Ferrari, he was no match for a police radio. Somewhere down the street, a few other cop cars had been called and had now set up a roadblock; no car, no matter what it was or how fast, could make it through. Jon Paul was speeding into what would be his last point of freedom. The roadblock was complete. He approached the roadblock fast, hit the brakes, and skidded to a stop. The officers got out of their cars with their guns ready and rushed Jon Paul's car. They pointed their guns directly at him; slowly, he put his hands on the wheel. One of the officers opened the door and pulled him onto the ground, roughing him up.

"*Don't you know who I am?*" he screamed; the cops only handcuffed him, stood him up, and walked him to one of their cars, and then they placed him in the backseat and buckled him in.

"Isn't that the head of the UMP?" asked the arresting officer.

"Yeah, I think it is," said another as he got in his car and drove Jon Paul to the police station.

***

Paul, Liz, and Michelle got to the church and pulled into the parking lot. They got out and ran into the church, finding a safe haven and a sure place to call the angel Seraphiel. They walked up to the front of the church, knelt down, and called to the angel.

"Seraphiel, we are here with the coin. Can you hear us?" said both Michelle and Paul. Liz felt a bit confused and just watched as the two continued to call to Seraphiel.

A priest soon approached and asked what they were doing. "What is going on here?"

"Hello, Father. Please, if you can, give us just a few moments alone; we will be most grateful. We won't damage anything, we promise." The priest, looking rather curiously at these three people kneeling on the floor by the altar, conceded.

"Very well, you may have a few moments, my children."

"Thank you, Father," said Paul.

Chapter 16

— • • • —

A New Beginning

Jon Paul sat in the police station being questioned by the arresting officers. He insisted on his innocence, as the leader of the UMP, and that he should be allowed to walk free. As soon as the head of the French police heard that he had been arrested and was possibly the leader of the UMP, he immediately walked to the interrogation room and excused the other officers.

"Sir, I am Philip Neveu. I run this station, so first let me say we are very sorry for having arrested you, but you were driving recklessly and you endangered the lives of many people."

"I don't care! I must be allowed to leave of my own free will!"

"Sir, we cannot let you leave. There are rules that we must follow, as you know; everything must follow the proper protocol."

"Damn protocol! Set me free!"

"Sir, I cannot, but if you will please be patient with me, I will see what can be done. Meanwhile, we will place you in a private holding cell till I can get back to you."

"A private holding cell! Are you crazy?"

"Please, sir, give me a little time." The chief of police then waved for an officer to come and take Jon Paul to a private cell. They led him to a special part of the station reserved for visiting dignitaries who committed crimes, whether accidently or on purpose. In other words, special people who are or can be above the law because of their wealth and power; Jon Paul was at the top of these.

"Lieutenant, give me the whole story on Jon Paul Chavalier, UMP president."

"Sir, I can." They sat down in the chief's office, and the lieutenant then proceeded to give the details of the chase and subsequent capture of Jon Paul Chavalier.

***

A bright and brilliant white light began to form just over the heads of Paul, Michelle, and Liz as they knelt at the altar in the church; each one looked up simultaneously as it formed into a figure standing there that they recognized as Seraphiel, the angel.

"My children, you have come with the coin."

"Yes, we have brought it," said Michelle, trembling.

Liz glanced up, after having averted her eyes from the light of the angel, and said, "I have the coin; what should I do now, angel?"

"You may call me Seraphiel, child."

"Seraphiel, what do I do now?"

"You may give me the coin, and I shall destroy it."

"Is there no other way, Seraphiel; couldn't we use it to help the people of the world?" Liz pleaded.

"It is evil; there is no other way. The coin would corrupt you, as well."

Liz reached in her pocket and slowly pulled out the coin; it glowed with power, and for a moment, Liz thought of keeping it. She could just wish the angel away, away into oblivion, and then it would be hers.

"*Child, you cannot wish me away. I am forever.*" Liz handed the coin to the angel, but as soon as she did, she immediately felt something was not right. This angel seemed to have a dark countenance about her, and Liz watched as the angel began to transform into a hideous, flying Jinn.

"*Ha! You actually thought you could win. I am forever and can never be undone; the coin of the ages is mine, insignificant worm—ha!*"

The Jinn laughed and disappeared into the thin air; Paul, Michelle, and Liz had been tricked by the powerful Jinn, and now there was nothing they could do.

***

Jon Paul sat in his cell, and after several hours, he was approached by the chief of police, who knocked on his cell door and said, "Mr. Chavalier, I have spoken with the other members of the UMP, and we have agreed that you may post bail if you can; a court date has been set. At that time, you will answer to the charges of reckless endangerment of citizens, driving in a manner not consistent with the law, and possible injury to public safety. You may make your case at that time; now, are you able to make bail?"

"Of course I am. I just need a phone to call the bank." Jon Paul was allowed to make his call to the bank to transfer funds for his temporary freedom. Although this worked for him, little did he know that his life was about to change—and not for the better.

The three young people, Paul, Michelle, and Liz, stared in disbelief at the now-empty altar; all the smoke and the bright light was gone, and the coin was gone too. They had been tricked by the very powerful Jinn, who now controlled the last coin of the ages. When the seven coins had been formed by heavenly fire, all the Jinn had been considered angels, but after a time, the power of the coins corrupted them, and they fled. The host of heaven had tried to keep them imprisoned there, but, because the coins were made with holy fire, they were all-powerful, even against the brothers of light.

As the Jinn flew back to the astral realm with his golden coin, he laughed and thought to himself, *I can now defeat the army of heaven and take control myself.* He landed on a high rock made of crystal and perched himself, waiting for others to arrive; he steadied himself and prepared for a fight.

***

Paul stood up and held Michelle's hand. He looked at her with sad eyes and said, "I am so sorry, Michelle, I don't know what to do now."

"It is okay, Paul. We have been tricked, and there is nothing we can do; maybe we should just go home."

Liz watched the two of them. She felt closer to them and said, "If you are going home, how do we know we will be safe from Jon Paul?"

"How could we not? He no longer has the coin. It is gone, so what can he do now?"

Paul was right in so many ways, but he didn't realize just what losing the coin would do to Jon Paul's psyche. The three of them walked out of the church and out to Paul's car, got in, and drove back to his apartment.

***

Having posted bail, Jon Paul walked out of the police station a free man; at least for now, he was free. He walked to his car and paid for the tow and impound. He got in and sat there; he was unsure of what to do exactly now that he no longer had the coin. He wondered what, and even more, *how* he could ever get his coin back. The answers did not come easily for him; he started his car and pulled out of the impound lot and into the street. Driving came easily for Jon Paul, who could actually get some thinking done behind the wheel. He finally came to the conclusion that Liz would not be at Paul and Michelle's.

There was no way they would still be there after all these hours. They would have found somewhere to hide; maybe they were planning on using the coin on him. This thought made him nervous, and he cringed.

***

"Paul, what should I do? Should I go back home, or what? I mean, Jon Paul could be there, and he might … he might try to hurt me."

"He might, Liz. Maybe you should try to call him and see where he is."

"I don't know, Paul, calling him might be too much too soon. I don't think I can." Liz began to cry; she had broken her own heart with her betrayal of Jon Paul.

"It is okay, Liz. You are right, it is too soon; how about we just find someplace nice to go where we can talk and relax."

"Okay, Paul, that would be nice." The three of them left the church, got in Paul's car, and drove to a park that was close by, where they sat and talked for hours before finally leaving for home.

***

Jon Paul continued to drive home; he had decided to just go back home. He thought maybe Liz had come back and brought the coin with her, and maybe she would return it.

***

The coin, however, was now gone; the mighty Jinn had the coin and was planning his attack on the army of light one last time, this time for total control.

The power of the coin was complete, and it could not be denied. As the army of light was in repose and recouping its losses, which were exceedingly great, the army of dark had begun to gather at the rock crystal; they planned their final and total destruction of the army of light using the power of the coin, and with it in the hands of a mighty Jinn, they could not, they *would* not, be denied.

"Gather around, brothers, and listen," shouted the Jinn with the coin. "We are about to have complete victory; as you see, I have the coin, and the power is ours for the taking. Finally, after a millennium, we have what is rightfully ours. For so long now, we have been victims of the army of light, dogs that they are; we were suppressed by them and made to lick their feet! But now, brothers, we shall *be victorious!*"

All the soldiers of the army of dark shouted in hateful joy; they had the coin, and soon the battle would begin. With the power of the coin, they had just upped the odds of their securing heaven for all eternity.

***

Jon Paul pulled into his garage, wondering if he was right about Liz, but seeing his car was still missing, he knew she had not returned. In not returning, she still had the coin, or so he thought. He walked into his house and, feeling sad, he called for his manservant, who had served him so faithfully and obediently for so long now.

"Mr. Falid! Mr. Falid, are you here?"

Mr. Falid was not there, though; he was free from his master and the curse. It had been broken when the Jinn had recovered the golden coin. He still felt a certain attachment to Jon Paul, though, so after several moments, he finally appeared and said, "Hello, sir, I am here."

"Where were you, Mr. Falid? I called for you, but you didn't come."

"Sir, I am no longer bound to you or any other master. I am free of my curse."

"What do you mean?"

"Simply put, sir, the coin is no longer in mortal hands, and the curse that was placed on me all these many years ago is broken; I am free."

Jon Paul stared at his former servant in disbelief. He had not expected this.

"It is true. I am free."

"But how? I mean, what exactly has happened?"

"The coin is in the hands of the Jinn once again, so my curse and my freedom are complete. I can never again be cursed to serve another. It was written long ago that the Jinn would once again control the coin and power would be theirs for the taking. That has finally happened; now you shall see the power of the coin in reverse. It will take rather than give."

Jon Paul could not believe what he was hearing; as his eyes began to tear and his heart began to break, Mr. Falid saw this and said to him, "Why cry, mortal? You have not lost anything yet; yours is yet to be told, but you have a certain amount of time before the power of the coin begins to take effect. Beware: it is complete, and nothing on earth or in heaven can stop it; you shall see."

Jon Paul then watched as his former manservant began to disappear in a cloud of white smoke; his would be a tale told a thousand times over. Jon Paul walked up to his room to sit and think. Although thinking would mostly escape him, he was comforted in the solace of his solitude.

***

Detective Rolland had time to solve this case; he had been placed in charge completely, and that gave him the freedom to devote all his time to figuring out who and what had been the reason for the deaths of these two young people. He had placed a call earlier to his friend, who was a scientist and would be able to help him with this key.

The information that he was given by his friend had led him to believe that this key was a sort of password, a kind of "open all locked doors" type of key. He knew it would be the one clue that would help him solve this case.

"What's the matter, Rolly, case got you confused?"

"Nah, just a bit on edge. You know I always get my man."

"That I do, that I do." Rolland watched as a fellow member of his precinct walked away chuckling.

***

"You know, Paul, I think I better get myself a motel tonight. I don't want to go home where Jon Paul is, if he is there."

"I think that is a great idea, Liz. Are you sure you will be all right tonight?"

"I hope so, Paul. I mean, the coin is gone, right? So we are safe."

"Yeah, right. I don't know how safe, but at least it is a start for you."

"Paul, she will be fine; she has our number, and we can find her a motel close to our place so that if she has any problems, she can call." Paul smiled at Michelle and Liz; they all knew it would be all right now. Fate had stepped in and removed the evil from their lives, and now they could move forward to continue to live their lives the best they could.

***

The army of dark began to move; they now had uncontrollable power, and this would be the final battle against the army of light. The timing was perfect. The army of light would not expect an attack so soon after the last one; for years now, the army of dark had kept a certain schedule of their attacks and had become predictable, but now, things were different. They gathered all the horses they could find. Of course, these were no ordinary horses; they had wings of enormous proportions, they were able to shoot fire from their nostrils, and their coats and manes were black and red in color. The army of dark wore heavy chainmail made by human slaves; such was their particular punishment for their sins. Some of the helmets that certain members wore had horns that pointed to the sky, and others had no horns but rather two feather-like images on the sides, which made them look rather fierce. Some of the battle gear had what appeared to be knives on their sleeves; others had sharp points made of metal spikes. The army of dark readied itself for the coming surprise attack.

"Gather round, brothers. We have one more thing to accomplish. Our powers are not complete yet; we have one final battle to fight, and we will take our home back from the dogs who stole it. We will reign supreme!" The general spoke very well to his troops. He rallied them with a fire that could only be described as being from hell—it would be a perfect battle cry.

***

Paul and Michelle left Liz at her motel and drove back to their apartment. They had helped Liz escape from Jon Paul, and the coin was now gone. There was no way of getting it back, so they did not concern themselves with it.

"Paul, I was thinking, now that the evil coin is gone, maybe we can plan on starting our own family?"

"Our own family? Are you saying you want to start a family?"

"Well … *yes*! I do, Paul. We have made it this far, and I want to try." Michelle began to tear up; she had never considered a family with her ex, but she was ready now, and the time was right. The coin was gone, and she could finally settle down with the man she loved.

Paul smiled at Michelle and said, "Okay, baby, you want to start a family? Let's do it!" Michelle smiled and soft tears of joy began to run down her face.

***

Liz settled into her motel room and decided to run a hot bath; she was hoping it might help her relax after all the commotion of the day. As the tub filled, she undressed and sat down gently in it; the water was warm and relaxing, and she immediately felt the pains of her betrayal melt away from her spirit. She had finally begun to relax and almost fall asleep when suddenly the phone rang, jarring her from deep relaxation. She sat up and listened to the phone ring … ring … ring … ring … ring … she counted five times that it rang before it stopped, and she began to wonder who could have called her. Who would know she was here? The curiosity of the phone had disturbed Liz's bath, so she pulled the plug on the tub, got up and dried herself, put on a robe, and went into the room, where the phone sat innocently on the table.

"Hello, front desk, this is Liz Chavalier in room 102; can you tell me who just tried to call, or did they leave a message for me?"

"Hold on, please, I will check," replied the worker at the front desk.

"Hello, Mrs. Chavalier? There is no message, but we have the number as belonging to a Mr. Dubois." Liz sat there wondering why Paul would have called her. She decided she had better just call him back. "Miss, are you still there?"

"Yes, thank you. Can you do me a favor and hold all my calls from now on?"

"Yes, Mrs. Chavalier, is there anything else?"

"No, thank you, bye." Liz hung up the phone and sat there for a moment; she thought she would call Paul and ask if everything was all right. As she dialed his number, she was reminded of her earlier transgression against her true love Jon Paul. She waited as the phone rang.

"Hello, this is Paul."

"Paul, this is Liz. Did you call?"

"Oh, yes, just a few minutes ago. We just wanted to check if you were okay."

"Yes, I am, thank you. Are you okay there?"

"Yeah, we are fine. Better call it a night, since it is getting late."

"You are right, Paul. Call me tomorrow if you can."

"Okay, I will, Liz, bye." Liz hung up the phone, as did Paul; they had been smart to check if the other was okay, and they were.

***

Jon Paul sat in his chair and began to sink into a deep depression; his face changed as he sank lower and lower. He grew tired and irritable; he had lost his coin and was losing his humanity as well. The evil of the coin was gone, but its effects on Jon Paul were just beginning; he was slowly losing his battle with humanity. He would continue to spiral out of control, emotionally and physically.

As the morning approached, Jon Paul stirred and found himself awake; although he didn't sleep very much, he had drifted off when the light began to stream into his window, and now, with the breaking of dawn, he would not sleep any more this day.

"I wonder what this day has in store for me?" he mused out loud, not talking to anybody in particular; his house was empty, nothing could be more plain to Jon Paul. With Liz gone somewhere and his coin gone, things were soon to take a turn for the worse. As Jon Paul got up from the chair he had sat in all night, he felt hungry; after all, he had not eaten since yesterday, and his stomach was now beginning to grumble. He got up and walked downstairs to his kitchen and remembered his manservant was gone now that he no longer had the coin, so he would have to find something to eat by himself. He walked to the refrigerator and opened it; looking inside, he found some eggs and bacon to cook, and with a glass of orange juice, he would be set for the day, or so he thought.

***

Liz awoke to find herself alone in a motel room, and she suddenly realized she was now without her love, Jon Paul. Could she ever go back to him? Probably not. Being alone for the first time in a long time had her feeling rather depressed. She called down to the front desk to ask for some food.

"Front desk, how may I help you?"

"Oh, hi. I was wondering if I might get some food delivered to my room."

"What room are you in?"

"102. Now, could I get a croissant with butter, some coffee, black, and a small glass of juice?"

"Will there be anything else?"

"No, thank you, that will be fine." Liz hung up the phone and sat back down on the bed; her depression was not bad, but it didn't help being alone either. She decided to call Paul and see if he could help her feel better.

"Hello, Paul?"

"Um, yeah, who is it?" he said, searching for the words, awakening from a deep sleep.

"It's Liz. Did I wake you?"

"Yeah, but it is fine. How are you doing?"

"I am a little sad and maybe even depressed; I am alone. You know Jon Paul will never forgive me for what I have done." Liz began to cry soft tears.

"Well, no, I don't think he will, but at least the cursed coin is gone."

"That doesn't really help me, though, Paul. I mean, I deceived him, and now I am paying for it emotionally." Liz sobbed but held her composure.

"How about we come over and get you in a few hours and then go someplace nice?"

"Really, Paul? That would be wonderful." Liz smiled on the phone, and Paul could hear it in her voice.

"No trouble at all, Liz. We will see you in a few hours." Paul hung up the phone and saw that Michelle was awake, and he told her the entire conversation he just had with Liz.

"Paul, that is a very nice thing we are doing for Liz. I am happy you are okay with her."

"Yeah, she is great. I am just sorry she had to get involved with someone like Jon Paul, and now she is going to need our help and support." Michelle nodded at Paul in agreement; Liz would definitely need their help, especially now that she was alone.

***

Jon Paul ate his breakfast slowly; he had no idea that things were about to change. The phone rang.

"Hello, this is Jon Paul."

"Mr. Chavalier, this is Detective Rolland. I am going to need to see you as soon as possible; it is a matter I am not willing to discuss over the phone. Can you come to the station right away?"

"Right away? I need a few hours, and then I can be there."

"Very good, sir. I will see you soon."

Jon Paul walked out of his house and to his garage, but as he approached it, he noticed that it seemed to be smaller. He called out for his servant, who did not answer; he was gone. As Jon Paul made his way into the garage, he decided it was definitely smaller, and he began to wonder what had happened. He looked around, but nothing gave him a clue as to what was going on, so he got into his car—one of the few that was still there—and started the engine. He pushed the accelerator down and inched his way out of the big door and down to the street. When he arrived at the street, Jon Paul had a funny feeling that something was not right. He looked back to see his house disappear, including the garage and all the buildings around it. He was now staring at an empty field.

***

After eating her breakfast, Liz got up and readied herself for the day; she had decided to go to the bank to separate her account from Jon Paul's. She didn't know what was going to happen, but she might need money, so she grabbed her coat and went to the front lobby to call for a taxi. She didn't have to wait long when she noticed an old, white, and kind of rugged-looking taxi pull up and stop. Liz walked out to the car and knocked on the window.

"Hello, miss. Did you call for a taxi?"

"Yes, I did, thank you." Liz got in the backseat and said clearly, "Please take me to the First Banc of Toulon."

"Yes, ma'am." The driver sped away and headed for the bank. Liz sat back and reflected on her past few days. It had been more than a difficult experience; she had betrayed the man she loved with all of her heart, she had seen an angel, she had stolen a magic coin and then lost it to an evil Jinn—she wondered, *what next?*

What could life throw at her that could compare with what she had just experienced? Maybe she should take vacation, maybe visit the States; after all, she had distant family there, and a visit might be just what she needed.

"We're here, ma'am. That will be twelve euros." Liz grabbed her purse, found her wallet, pulled out fifteen euros, and gave it to the man.

"Thanks for the ride."

"Anytime. Do you need me to wait?"

"No, thanks, bye." Liz walked briskly into the Banc of Toulon.

***

Jon Paul sped down the highway; he was on his way to see one Detective Rolland, about what, he could only guess. He was still feeling a bit confused about his house and exactly where it had gone, and he was reminded of the words his manservant Mr. Falid had said: "The coin will take rather than give." He thought, *that must be what he meant when he said that. The coin will take all I have, and I will be back to where I was. I must figure out a way to prevent that!*

***

Liz walked into the bank and made her way to the private section, where wealthy people and those with very large accounts were served. She was recognized for who she was, Jon Paul's wife—even though they never married officially—and was told by the head clerk to please take a seat at his desk. She only had to wait a minute when he reappeared, sat down in his chair, and said, "How may I help you today, Mrs. Chavalier?"

"I will need to separate my account from Jon Paul's."

"Is there a reason you wish to do this?"

"Well, yes, we have decided to keep separate accounts, and I would like to have my own account."

"I see, and how much will you be transferring?" Liz hadn't thought about that. *How much?* She wondered. She stirred nervously in her seat and then found her words and said, "Half of the combined accounts."

"Half? Are you sure, Mrs. Chavalier?"

"Yes, please, and then I will need to withdraw some."

The head clerk looked at her and then said, "I will have to clear this with the bank manager."

Liz smiled and nodded her head. This was becoming a real effort. She had to keep herself together; she couldn't break, or it might not work. She steadied herself as the clerk walked away.

***

Jon Paul pulled into the police station; he was going to see one Detective Rolland, who had some questions that apparently only Jon Paul could answer. As he parked his car and walked up to the door, he glanced back to see his car slowly disappearing; like a mirage, it just seemed to fade and then it was gone. Jon Paul stopped abruptly in his tracks; had he just really witnessed his car vanishing? He was not sure if what he saw was real, but he blinked several times to clear his vision, and his car was no longer there in the parking space he had parked it in. He stumbled through the door and said to the clerk, "I am here to see Detective Rolland. Can you please inform him Jon Paul Chavalier is here?"

The clerk was surprised that the head of the UMP was standing right in front of him; he smiled meekly, picked up the receiver, and dialed Detective Rolland's desk.

"Yes."

"Sir, a Mr. Chavalier is here to see you."

"Good. I will be right there." Detective Rolland got up from his desk and headed out to the entryway and thought, *I will get some answers finally, even if he doesn't know anything.*

"Sir, he will be right here." The clerk smiled, and Jon Paul sat down in a chair to wait.

He began to wonder if what was happening would be his complete downfall. Would he still have money, even though the coin was now gone? If he just knew where Liz was, maybe he could talk with her and ask; maybe they could still be together. Jon Paul was disrupted by the loud and commanding voice of the detective.

"Hello, sir, I am Detective Rolland; if you will please follow me, we can talk privately." Jon Paul got up, shook the man's hand, and followed him to a room where they could talk. They passed through several security doors and then to a back office where they would be able to have some privacy; at least the detective was showing Jon Paul respect. He wondered if this would be a short interview or just how long it might take. The detective motioned for him to sit on the opposite side of a table.

"First, let me say thank you for coming in to see me, sir. I won't take too much of your time, just a few questions." The detective smiled easily at Jon Paul.

"Sure, however I can help."

"Mr. Chavalier, have you ever been to the ends of this city, maybe out where there are some abandoned warehouses?" He got right to the point. Jon Paul stiffened at the abruptness of the detective.

"Abandoned warehouses? Um, no, to where exactly are you referring?"

"Have you ever seen this key before?" He produced the key from his pocket and held it so Jon Paul could see it. He moved it around in his hands and showed him both sides of it, from front to back.

"No, can't say as I ever have seen it before; it is old, though, I would have to say."

"Old? How do you mean, sir?"

Jon Paul reached out his hand for the key, and the detective handed it to him.

"Well, look at the writing on it; seems to be some kind of runes."

"Runes? What else do you think it might be? Could it perhaps open a door somewhere?"

"Maybe, but not likely. It is more like a calling card of sorts."

"Really, a calling card, for whom might that be?" The detective's eyes widened.

"A man I knew of several years ago, not the best of citizens. In fact, he was a lowlife thug. He even tried to threaten me once, long ago."

"Who is this thug you speak of? What is his name?"

"His name is Louis Moreau."

The detective wrote the name down, looked at Jon Paul, and said, "Are you sure?"

"Yes, he wasn't much of a man, but then, how many thugs are?" Jon Paul smiled warily and then moved uncomfortably in his seat. "If you are going after him, Detective, I suggest you try the bar off of Fifth and Downing Street; it has been known to me that a lot of these mafia types hang out there."

"Well, now, Mr. Chavalier, I believe that will conclude my questions for now, but I will ask that you not leave the country and just go about your daily routine. I will be in touch with you if I have any further questions." Detective Rolland smiled at Jon Paul, stood and offered him his hand, then motioned for him to exit his office.

"Thank you, Detective Rolland, for making this as brief as possible." Jon Paul smiled and shook the man's hand. Then he turned and walked abruptly out of his office and through the security checkpoints and out into the street. Jon Paul was stranded; his car was gone, as was most of his house and his garage.

He wondered if those things were gone, what else was the coin going to take from him? He checked his pocket. He had just enough for a cab ride or two, somewhere, but where? Maybe back to his house to see if anything was left. He found a pay phone by the parking garage, closed the door, and put some coins in it to call for a cab.

***

As the clerk approached, Liz cleared her throat as gently as possible and watched him sit down at his desk in front of her. "Well, Mrs. Chavalier, all is okay. We have opened up another account with your name and half of the amount in the other account that you share with your husband; do you wish it to be in your married or your maiden name?"

"Let's make it my maiden name; that would be Lizzette Bourg." The clerk wrote down her name, and after punching some keys on the keyboard of his computer, he soon had Liz all set up with her account. Liz would soon be on her way. She had secured money for her future and was now set to live her life separate from Jon Paul.

***

As the cab pulled up to the station, Jon Paul waved him down. As soon as the cab was at a stop, he opened the door and got in. The driver sat back, looked at him, and asked, "Where to, sir?"

"93732 Clemens drive."

The driver smiled and pulled away from the station. He began the long drive back to Jon Paul's house in the country.

***

Liz signed the papers to finalize her new account separate from Jon Paul's. She smiled at the clerk, stood, and walked out of the back and to a waiting taxi. She looked in the rearview mirror and took a slow, deep breath; she held it for a brief second before letting it out, and she began to cry.

Liz didn't know how long she sat there, only that she had blacked out and time had moved forward; she glanced at her wristwatch and saw that the time was 2:47 p.m. She still had time in the day to find a new motel and then maybe call Paul and Michelle to see how they were. She was sure they were probably wondering how she was at this point. She had opened her own account, had received several hundred euros in cash from the clerk, and was now going to try and start her life over.

***

The cab pulled into what looked like it once might have been a driveway of some kind; now, though, it was just a narrow path to an empty field. Nothing was there except for rolling hills and in the way background, a forest that stretched as far as one could see. Jon Paul sat, motionless, his jaw open, as he stared at the scene in awe; he could not believe his eyes.

For a moment, he thought he was dreaming. Just as the cab driver stopped, he turned and parked the car, looked at Jon Paul, and said, "That will be fifty-three euros, sir."

Jon Paul, being startled from his delirium, cleared his throat and reached in his pocket to take out some money and hand it to the driver, who smiled and said, "Is there anything else, sir?"

"Ah, no, can you just give me a moment?"

"Sure." Jon Paul sat there, not believing his eyes; then, after several moments, he finally said, "Take me back to town. I need to find a place to spend the night."

"Oh, sir, I know of a few places. Are you looking for a girl, or—"

Jon Paul stopped him right there and said, "*No*, no girl, just take me to a motel."

"Anything you want, sir." The driver then sped off back to the highway and began to take him back into town to find a motel.

Jon Paul no longer had a house to live in. He was just beginning to realize what else the coin might have taken from him.

"Driver, can you take me to the bank first?"

"Of course, what bank, sir?"

"The Bank of Toulon."

The driver shook his head yes and turned down a front street that would lead him to the main bank of Toulon.

"Yes, that's it!" Jon Paul pointed to the entrance. "Drop me here, please." The driver pulled to the front of the bank and stopped. "That will be thirty-five euros, sir."

Jon Paul reached in his pocket and handed the driver the exact change.

"Thanks."

"Will you need me anymore, sir?" called the driver to Jon Paul.

"No, thanks." Jon Paul walked into the bank. He saw the head clerk, told him who he was, and asked to see his bank statements. The clerk recognized him and went immediately to his computer and found the statements to show them to Jon Paul.

"What the hell happened to my money?" screamed Jon Paul.

"Sir, please calm yourself; this is the exact amount you have available right now. I can double check, if you like, but there is no mistake." Jon Paul nodded, and the clerk double-checked his account. "Sir, this is the amount you have."

Jon Paul was puzzled; most of his money was gone and had been transferred to Liz's new account.

"Sir, your wife was in earlier and she opened her own account; do you wish me to check that?"

"Yes, most definitely! Do I have access to her account as well?"

"Um, no, sir, she opened her own private account this morning, and only she has access to the money." Jon Paul was incensed; his money was gone and stolen by Liz. He wondered how he could get it back, but there was no getting it back; it was gone.

Jon Paul stood up, and the clerk, seeing he was upset, asked, "Sir, will there be anything else I can do for you?"

Jon Paul, eyes burning with hate, simply stated, "No."

He walked out of the bank and down the street. He had no idea where he was going; after all, he had no home, barely any money, and what little he had was in his pocket. His bank account was almost empty and he had to find some place to stay. Suddenly, it hit him. *I will go to my office and get things together there*! This would provide him with a place to stay and some form of communication, or at least a way to have it. He quickened his walk, as the thought was making him eager. The walk was not so far. He had planned it that way, so that his office was within walking distance of his bank. Even after he had become such a high and powerful politician, he had never really outgrown the need to walk; he had done this since he was a child, and it always made him feel better.

He walked briskly and soon found himself at his office; as he opened the doors and went to the elevator, he crossed the expansive and marble-covered floor. He noticed the strange looks he was getting from other men and women walking around; some were even pointing at him. He got in the elevator and pushed the button for his floor. He was alone, so there was nothing awkward about the elevator being empty, but as the doors opened to his floor, he felt rather strange, like he didn't belong there. It must have just been his imagination; or was it?

***

Liz relaxed in her motel room; she had found one close to Paul and Michelle's house, so she felt rather safe. She picked up the phone and dialed Paul's number.

"Hello, this is Paul."

"Hello, Paul, this is Liz."

"Oh, hi! How are you today? We were wondering if you are okay."

"Yes, thank you, I am fine; I have been at the bank, and now I am at the motel."

"The bank? What motel?" asked Paul.

"The one by your place; um, I opened my own account at the bank."

"Really? That was very smart."

"Thanks, Paul. I am going to be okay, except for missing Jon Paul so much." Liz began to cry, her tears staining her white blouse.

"Liz, it is okay. You are going to be fine, and we are here for you. If you need anything, just ask."

Liz's crying slowed and she felt better after talking. She said, "I know, and thanks, Paul; you really are my best friends now." Paul smiled, and, knowing in his heart that Liz would be fine, he said his good-byes and hung up the phone. He smiled at his new bride-to-be and soon mother of his first child, reached over, and held her in his arms.

***

"May I help you, sir?"

"What do you mean, 'may I help you'? It is me!"

"Sir, I don't know you. Do you have an appointment? What is your name?"

"What is my name? Are you crazy? It's me, your boss, Jon Paul Chavalier!"

"I am sorry, sir, there is no one here by that name." Jon Paul stood there staring at his former secretary, his mouth open in disbelief; she really didn't know him, and he was at a loss as to what to do next. He turned and walked out of his office and to the elevators. He thought, *this must be a joke; how can she not know me?* Then, like a bolt of lightning, he knew—the coin. The coin had taken his power, his wealth, and his love from him; he had nothing. As he looked up, he noticed something strange: his suit, he no longer had on a three-piece Armani suit; he was wearing old jeans and a ragged T-shirt. No wonder those people were staring at him. Not only had his appearance changed, but also his demeanor. He no longer carried himself with pride and success, and he was no longer the most powerful man in all of France. He was no one.

The power of the coin had left Jon Paul homeless, destitute, and poor; he had nothing anymore. He was just another vagrant on the street; he wasn't recognized, and nobody cared about him. His life had changed so much for the worse that he sometimes felt like he was dreaming, but this was no dream. Jon Paul was finished; his life would continue to spiral out of control, with no end in sight. The power of the coin had destroyed another, but then, having the coin many lifetimes before, he was not really a casualty—he was just a human being.

***

Detective Rolland had worked very hard on this case; however, it still has not been closed. His work led him to a dark underground where he investigated many different things like prostitution, illegal drugs, murder, and even money embezzlement. His life and his work would gain him national recognition, but still, the case of the two murdered young people had not been solved. In time, he would travel to the States, where he was offered a job and a very lucrative salary. He would again find himself involved with some very dark people and the mob.

***

It has been several years now that have passed, and Paul and Michelle are living a very happy married life. They go to church on Sunday and have a quiet life, no excitement except for the occasional run-in with a street person. Paul works out of their home, and Michelle is a practicing chef at the local restaurant.

***

Liz has had a calm life since all the excitement with her former lover Jon Paul Chavalier; she doesn't need to work, and most of her time is spent with their son, Jon Paul Junior. He is a very active boy, high energy. In many ways, he reminds her of his father, who doesn't even know of his existence. Jon Paul Junior loves to run and play. He started walking very early in his life, and it was like he didn't need to crawl; he just stood up and started walking one day.

Liz has purchased a home for them in the city. It is modest with a small backyard, at least compared to her former home with Jon Paul that was in the country. On this day, Jon Paul is having his sixth birthday. His mother has invited a few close friends and set up a nice party for her son; there are red and yellow balloons, stringers are hung everywhere, and there is a bag of goodies for the kids to play with.

Jon Paul Junior walked out to the table to sit with friends, but he suddenly had a funny feeling that he should not do that. As he stopped and stared out in the backyard, he saw a man standing by the tree in the shade. He walked over to him and said, "Hello, I am Jon Paul, and today is my birthday."

"I know. I am here to give you something very special, but you have to promise me something."

"Okay, anything," the boy replied.

"I want you to hide this somewhere in your closet or another safe place till you hear it call you."

"What do you mean, 'call me'?"

"Never mind, just promise me you will do this."

"Okay, I will promise you." Jon Paul's eyes opened wide; he had never seen such a gift. It shined with the light of the sun. It reflected bright, burning gold in its color.

"This is a magic coin, my son. It will grant you wishes when you are older."

"Really? Should I hide it now?"

"Yes, go hide it now, and remember: it is our secret." The tall man smiled at Jon Paul and disappeared behind the tree. Jon Paul took the golden coin and ran up to his bedroom and hid it in his shoebox. That was the safest place he could think of.

About the Author

Nicklaus Lee grew up in Denver, Colorado, where he wrote his first short story at the tender age of seven. He currently resides in Seattle, Washington, where he enjoys spending time with his son, Lane. This is his debut novel.